BLACK PRINCE

BLACK PRINCE

Elizabeth Gill

Hodder & Stoughton

Copyright © 2000 by Elizabeth Gill

First published in Great Britain in 2000
by Hodder and Stoughton
A division of Hodder Headline

The right of Elizabeth Gill to be identified as the Author of
the Work has been asserted by her in accordance with the
Copyright, Designs and Patents Act 1988.

10 9 8 7 6 5 4 3 2 1

A CIP catalogue record for this title
is available from the British Library.

ISBN 0 340 75091 X

Typeset by Hewer Text Ltd, Edinburgh
Printed and bound in Great Britain by
Clays Ltd, St Ives plc

Hodder and Stoughton
A division of Hodder Headline
338 Euston Road
London NW1 3BH

For Jean and Edmund with love

PROLOGUE

County Durham, 1877

———————◆———————

Mary Cameron stood by the window. The snow was falling faster now, almost horizontal, in those big square flakes that usually meant a hap-up. It was always at its worst in March, just like the dark before dawn. Past the snow she could see the workings of the Black Prince Pit, and beyond that, where the snow blotted it out, was the fell and the road which eventually led to Durham. When she had been little she had thought that road opened up the world. These days it seemed only to heighten her isolation.

The child stirred in her arms and she pressed him more tightly to her so that he opened his black eyes and his tiny fists clenched and unclenched and he made a little gurgling sound in his throat, waving his arms about and smiling. There could be no mistake, no confusion. He was not her husband's child, and though she had prayed long and hard over it, the moment the boy was born she knew that he was the evidence of violence, of a mindless deed. If there had been no consequences she would have tried to draw a curtain in her mind over what had happened more than a year ago, but it seemed to her that she saw more and more clearly the candles lit upon the altar, the gleaming cross shining gold, the ruby that the man wore in his right ear. It was strange and terrible, the detail she remembered. If there had been no child she could have surrounded herself with the rest of her life, her husband, Alf, and her small boy, Tommy, but the talk in the village was that no woman who had tried harder to get away would have had to suffer such things. Born guilty. In the cold quiet, with only the graves of the dead around her, the dark man had turned what should have been pleasure into the kind of sick horror that held her in its grip. She had not since then been able to turn to her husband and not remember, and when she had known that she was pregnant her heart had told her that it was not over.

It never would be over.

'Mary!' Alf called to her from below. 'The Harmers are here. Hurry up!'

He wanted it over and done with. Since the boy had been born Alf had barely spoken to her, not touched her in affection, not looked at the child, which was to everybody's eyes an Egyptian's son, unmistakable, with thick black hair, eyes which turned as dark as the very coal that was their life, and a skin that was toffee-coloured. For all that she loved him, but there was no choice. Alf had said that she must give up the child and end the disgrace.

She held him so close that he began to cry a little in protest. The Harmers were good, God-fearing people. They had no child. They had a house in Oaks Row with a view across to Weardale, they had money because Mr Harmer had a good job as a clerk at the brickworks, but this was the end for her, she must give up the child completely, Alf had insisted, and she could not do it.

'Mary!' His voice was urgent; it held a harsh note. She wrapped a thick blanket around the boy. It would be a cold walk back past the Catholic church and down the Store bank and left into Oaks Row. Such a short way and so far. The snow was a blizzard; it even obliterated the pithead where the wheel went round and round and the men worked night and day and the coal came out. It went on and on, nothing stopped it; even though she could no longer see it she knew. It went on and on like the fell went on and on, and the days and the nights.

She turned away, into the shadowed gloom, and holding him very close she walked out of the bedroom and down the stairs to where she could see Mrs Harmer well wrapped up against the cold, wearing a close-fitting hat, and Mr Harmer looking up. Her instincts told her to run down the stairs and out the door but she couldn't. There was no escape. When she reached the bottom of the stairs Mrs Harmer came and took the child and with sure instincts he began to cry. Mary thought her heart would burst. Alf went and held open the back door and the Harmers left without a word.

Tommy, who had been standing there all the while, wondering what was going on, ran across to her and hid his face against her skirt and then Alf closed the door and she watched them through the kitchen window, going up the back yard and out of the gate and down the lane, and then they were gone from sight and there was nothing but the whiteness of the snow and everything was lost.

The snow was thick on the pavements and the road and it was some time before the Harmers reached the sanctuary of their house. They stamped the snow off their boots before entering. It was cold in the hall. Mrs Harmer took the child up the stairs and put him into the wooden cradle in the tiny freezing back room. He was crying hard by then; she had not realised that a child could make so much noise. She left him there and went out and closed the door, but he could be heard clearly through the ceiling.

A tiny fire burned in the sitting room. She faltered as she went in.

'I think he may be hungry,' she said.

Mr Harmer looked at her.

'Feed the body and destroy the soul,' he said.

✳   ✳   ✳

Rebecca Forster looked doubtfully at the weather. She had planned to leave that day. She had gathered together as much money as she could find, though it was a pitiful amount; her husband paid all the bills himself and gave her nothing. She had spent the last five years of her life here at Stanley Hall and she could bear no more. It was a Palladian house built in the 1740s, and a more plain, stark building she had yet to come across. It was big and square and stood alone upon the edge of the moors beyond the village as though it had lost its way. When her husband Randolph had brought her there she had thought to be happy, but he cared nothing except for the pit which had been his father's; it was his entire life. The pit had made the family prosperous but was making less and less money since the demand for coal had dropped. They could no longer afford fine clothes, trips away or any of the things that would have made life here bearable.

Urgency gripped her. She must leave now while Randolph was at work. The child was six months old, spring was almost here. It was the right time to go. She wrapped him up carefully and looked at him. He was beautiful. He looked like her, with fine fair hair and calm eyes. Since the moment of his birth he had not troubled her and she loved him. She put on her coat, picked up her bag and her child and began to make her way along the hall towards the dog-leg stairs and the front door. She tried not to hurry, she was afraid to drop him, but to her dismay as she reached the bottom the front door opened and there stood her husband, covered in snow, dripping wet.

'Going somewhere?' he said.

Rebecca tried to face him, look him in the eyes.

'I would like the carriage.'

He laughed. It was a most unpleasant sound.

'I'm not going to order the carriage in this weather. If you want to go, get out.'

'I can't walk in this with a child. It's too cold.'

'You're not taking him anywhere.'

4

She let the bag fall and clutched the child to her.

'I can't go without him.'

'Oh yes you can.' Forcibly he took the child from her while it cried and she resisted and then he put him into the pram which stood by the wall near the door and he gripped her arms cruelly and threw her out into the snow. Not content with having deprived her of child, money and possessions, he kicked her where she lay several times. She would have cried out for help though there was nobody about, but the breath was knocked from her.

'Go on,' he said, 'get away! Start walking.' He picked her up and pushed her. It was all she could do to keep her feet. He pushed her several yards and then again towards the huge gates at the end of the short drive, and then he gave her a final push until she was outside and he locked the gates. 'I hope you go to hell,' he said.

There was no way back through the high walls and locked gates. Rebecca leaned against the gates pleading for her child as he walked away without a backward glance. The snow had increased until it was a blizzard, until very soon she could not see the house. There was nothing to do but begin to walk. The village was only half a mile away but she could not see more than a few yards. She was hurt, too, not aching but in a great deal of pain where he had kicked her. The snow increased until she could see nothing, and although she looked hard for the lights of the village they did not appear. Could she have taken a wrong turning? She had walked this way hundreds of times, since he would rarely allow her the carriage or any freedom. She had no friends, he said; what did she need money or transport for? She was going nowhere. At night he shut himself into his study and drank hard, and sometimes he came to her bed and used her similarly, though of late it had not been often. Alone there day after day with the servants and her new baby she had thought she would go mad. He said the child was like her, weak and sickly. It was not true. The baby had ailed little in the past six months since his birth.

She could not bear to think of him left behind without his mother. Randolph had no care for him and servants did what they were paid for. She walked on blindly, but still there were no village lights. She was almost numb with cold, could not feel her fingers or her feet, and the snow was heavy where it had settled upon her clothing. It weighed her down. It was several inches deep by this time and walking was a problem. It was, she thought, smiling a little, like her childhood holidays, wading through water at the seaside, the push and force of it against her legs. It had been cold too, the North Sea, bitter even in September. She imagined what it would be like at this time of the year, the waves breaking hard, crashing against the solid wet depth of the sand.

Her steps grew slower and slower and the wind threw the snow about, round and round her like a ring game. Suddenly she thought she could see the lights of the village in the distance. She was certain she could reach it. There it was again. But the more she tried to go forward to meet it the farther it seemed to move away, like someone beckoning with a lantern and moving back as she moved towards him. It was so frustrating it made her want to cry, except that she was too tired for that. She kept on going, hoping to catch a glimpse of it again, straining her eyes through the white curtain that the snow had become. The light did not come back, as though it had gone out for good, or as though she had taken another wrong turning; it was easy enough in such weather. And then the snow was suddenly higher than a mountain in front of her, and as she moved to the side to go around it she stumbled and fell and then the ground which had seemed so solid beneath her feet cracked and gave like a rotten stair and she was soon enveloped in icy water, which crashed and swirled around her and held her in its deep grip. It was a shock, and she was not certain whether the water was cold or whether in fact it was hot. How odd. She could not get out and to her relief it didn't really matter, it was not at all important. She could see the light again, and unlike before it was getting nearer. It would soon reach her and whoever it was would pull her out of the water and away from the enormous snowdrift and in the meanwhile she must close her eyes because it had been such a long way and she was so tired and she could see her child's face, his beautiful peachy skin and his wide eyes. She could see him, touch him, hold him in her arms. It was going to be all right, all she had to do was wait. She would sleep until help arrived.

CHAPTER ONE

1895

When Joe Forster went to church on Sundays he had to walk past his mother's grave. His father had had her buried as near to the church door as he could, as if he needed to keep an eye on her even though she was dead. Joe didn't remember her. His father never spoke her name, and where he had heard that she had run off with another man and then died and been brought back he was not sure; it was just that he had always known it. Joe did not blame her for running away; he did not understand why anybody would stay here who could leave.

He went to church every Sunday, partly because it was one of the places he was allowed to go without his father and partly to admire Esther Margaret Hunter, who was the prettiest girl in the village. It was Palm Sunday, a fine cold spring day, and the church was packed. People nodded and murmured respectfully at Joe because his father owned the Black Prince Pit where many of them worked, but he also felt, he hoped, that they liked him. They didn't like his father, and Joe could understand that.

He didn't hear much of what went on. He sat two rows behind Esther Margaret and watched her as often as he thought no one noticed, but it was difficult and he didn't want to be obvious. He sang the hymns readily enough, because having always gone to church he knew them, but he didn't listen much to the rest of the service, just followed other people, kneeling and getting up and standing and so on, but all the time he looked at Esther Margaret. She was sixteen.

After the service Joe shook hands with the vicar and then, while people stood around in groups, he made his way across to where she stood with her parents and said hello. Both Mr and Mrs Hunter spoke to him and Esther Margaret blushed beetroot because she was shy, but she smiled too and her eyes lit up for him and all the happiness that Joe was capable of made its way into his head until he was almost dizzy. He didn't need to touch her, he didn't need her to say anything, all he needed was for her to stand there blushing and smiling and being herself.

'Well, now, Mr Forster, and how is your father?' Mrs Hunter could put a great deal of venom into her words, Joe decided. He had talked to Esther Margaret every Sunday for three weeks, just a few words, nothing special, but it was the highlight of his week. For two weeks her parents had tolerated it without saying much, but he could see by the closed expression on Mr Hunter's face and the way that Mrs Hunter spoke that they did not favour him.

'He's very well, thank you.'

'I'm very glad to hear it. We mustn't stand here in the cold. Our dinner will be ready. Come along, Esther Margaret.'

Her mother bore her away. All Joe had said was how was she and had she done anything exciting that week and she had just smiled idiotically at him and said she was fine and no, nothing exciting had happened. He could believe that, with parents like hers. He felt silly standing around, watching as they walked off, so he went home, down the church lane to the main road and up Dans Castle bank and around the corner by the Catholic church and on to the fell beyond the Black Prince Pit with its own row of houses. Up here the air was so clean it made him feel even more dizzy. Esther Margaret liked him, he could feel that she did, and all the way home he devised ways of rescuing them both from this dull little pit town and running away to some glorious place where pit wheels didn't turn and he was out of reach of his father, somewhere he could make a living for them and they

could have their own house and children. Their children would
have two parents and a cosy home and all the things he had not
had, and he would love Esther Margaret all his life. He thought it
would be somewhere like Durham. He would be a professor at
the university and they would live in one of those houses that
surrounded Palace Green, old houses with stone-mullioned
windows and wooden ceilings and oak-panelled rooms, and
there would be fires and books and big dinners and nobody
would get drunk and shout and there would be no silences.

He slowed his steps as he reached his home. It stood upon
the fell where the keen spring wind was enough to cut your ears.
He looked across at the house. Up here was nothing but the
heather and a narrow road and the fell which stretched as far as
you could see. There were no trees. The only life was the thick-
fleeced sheep and the odd grouse and the stone walls that
separated the farms which rose up from the Deerness valley.

The house was as unloved as any person. Its windows were
splintered, the panes were cracked, the front door was shabby and
there was no garden, just great stretches of grass which reached to
the front door. The inside was not much better. As he went in,
his father's servant, Jacob Smith, scowled at him. Jacob was the
only servant in the house. He had always been there, saw to
everything, which meant, as far as Joe could see, that he saw to
nothing. The house was thick with dust, the furniture was old
and scarred, the meals . . . His father didn't eat, he drank so he
considered food unimportant, but Joe understood from the few
times he had eaten in other people's houses, unbeknown to his
father, who wouldn't go out, that things could be better. There
could be comfortable chairs and interesting food, instead of
which the house, with the exception of the study, was always cold,
and bitterly so in this weather, the covers on the bed were grey
with dirt, and there was no such thing as new clothes. In the
kitchen a fire burned for cooking and hot water. The only other
fire was in the study, where his father spent all his time when he
was not at work. Sometimes he slept in there by the dying embers.

'Your dinner's in the kitchen,' Jacob said shortly as he disappeared into the dark depths of the house. Joe went through and discovered on the table something he didn't recognise, brown meat and brown gravy and a sludge of potatoes. He ate it because he was hungry and because there was nothing else and because he was used to it, but it didn't stop him from thinking that it could have been much better. Afterwards he escaped to his room and lay there on the bed with a book and the covers around him. After a short while he could hear his father shouting his name from below, so he left the small warmth that he had made on the bed and put down his book and went downstairs.

His father was always dressed as though he was going outside, which, since he didn't go out unless he was going to the pit, seemed odd. He wore boots and a coat although the room was warm. Joe looked at the huge fire in the grate and thought that as pit-owners they could have had blazing fires in every room. It was just that his father didn't think about other people. He didn't look round from where he had one booted foot on the hearth.

'So, how was church?'

He managed to make it sound as though Joe had spent a morning in debauchery. His voice was low and mocking and perhaps even admiring that Joe could be interested in such a stupid thing. His father hadn't brought him down here to listen to a short recital of the sermon or a list of who had been there so Joe didn't answer him. He waited.

'I hear you've taken an interest in some village lass.'

Joe still said nothing, but this was a surprise. His father turned and Joe looked into his dark face and was reminded for the millionth time that his fair looks and his clear pale skin must have come from his mother. He was aware also when his father looked on him that he was reminded of betrayal, unfaithfulness, the woman who had run away with some common man; he thought it had been a soldier.

'I spoke to her,' Joe said.

'Oh, you spoke to her.'

He hated the heavy sarcasm in his father's voice. 'Yes, I did.'

'And is she bonny?'

'She's very pretty, yes.'

'You think maybe that you'll marry her?'

'I don't think I'll marry anybody yet. I want to go to university and—'

His father laughed. 'But you like her. You like the shop-keeper's daughter?'

'Yes, I like her.'

Joe went on looking into his eyes. He had practised until he could do so for a long time without faltering.

'Shopkeepers' daughters are not for you. Don't speak to her again. And as for university . . . we're pitmen. The world is our university, the pit office is your classroom.' He went on and on. He was drunk, of course; he always went on and on in mocking tones when he got drunk at Sunday dinner-time. Joe was used to that too. 'Don't worry, I'll find somebody for you to marry and she won't be any village lass neither.'

Joe wanted to say that he had to go to university, that he had to go somewhere new, he needed to leave here, he wanted to meet men with interesting minds and talk about books, he wanted to see some other parts of the world. He lay in bed at night and wondered what it was like. He wanted to run and run, to go so far away that he could not find his way back, so that the house would fall out of sight and the village would be lost and Durham would be nothing but a memory.

'Where were you?'

'What?'

'When I called you. Were you upstairs? Reading a book, no doubt. An improving book, was it? You can get back to it now.'

Dismissed, Joe went.

*   *   *

Esther Margaret lived on the corner of Ironworks Road and Oaks Row in the centre of the pit village. She was very fond of her house; it had a little garden along the side, wrought-iron railings with a gate and two steps down. To the side there was a small lawn and a few flowers and in the corner was a lilac tree. At the other side of the gate was another patch of ground, which became a yard outside the kitchen window, and at the bottom was a wash house and inside you turned left into the kitchen or right up two steps into the rest of the house. The kitchen was big with a pantry on the end, and if you went farther into the house the hall ended with a stained-glass inner door and a big solid outer door, and there was the dining room where a bright fire always burned except in the warmest weather and the sitting room where a fire also burned and there were lots of books and two big squashy settees and the windows looked out over both roads, and she loved it. She had a big bedroom to herself and there was also her parents' room and another room. Her parents had lots of friends, mostly from the church but also other shopkeepers and small businesspeople within the village. Her mother ran a sewing circle at the house and helped with various things at the church and her father took her for walks on summer nights and they sat by the fire in the winter and read stories and chatted to their friends.

She liked Sundays. Peggy, who helped her mother in the house, was busy while they were at church, making the Sunday dinner, and the smell hit you when you walked in by the back door. There was nothing in the world as wonderful as the smell of Yorkshire puddings and beef and vegetables. Peggy's Yorkshire puddings were like gold and brown clouds. They did not sink in the middle as Esther Margaret's mother claimed hers did. The vegetables were just right and the gravy was neither too thick nor too thin.

Today when she got home Esther Margaret felt as though she were on some kind of cloud. Joe Forster had spoken to her, and although she had felt awkward and could not look at him she was pleased. Joe was two years older than she, and she thought he was every girl's idea of what a young man should be. He was tall and slender and he had yellow hair and eyes like emeralds, eyes which had been gentle on her that day. The dinner would not be ready for half an hour and in that half-hour, while her parents sat by the fire with a small sherry each, she wanted to go to her room and dream about Joe.

'Esther Margaret, I want to talk to you.' Her mother's voice interrupted her thoughts. Her mother was brown-haired, blue-eyed, neat and always did the right thing. Her father said so. When he was cross once he told her mother that it was very difficult living with somebody who was always right, and her mother laughed and he wasn't cross any more.

'To me?' She blushed, banishing her thoughts, and followed her mother into the sitting room, where the fire licked around the coals. Her father wasn't there. Her mother closed the door. She didn't say anything for a few moments, as though she wasn't quite sure what to say.

'I know that you're very young and . . .' Her mother's eyes flew to her face. 'Joseph Forster is the pit-owner's son.'

That conveyed all it was meant to convey, Esther Margaret knew, even though it was not new information. She blushed harder and looked down.

'Does that mean there's something wrong with him?' she managed.

'There is nothing wrong with him that I have ever heard. I'm sure that he is a very fine young man but . . .'

Esther Margaret knew exactly what she meant. His father was a drunkard who neglected his pit and his workers, and his mother had run off with someone else because she could not control her desires.

'What people come from, their background, their parents and their upbringing, is an important part of them. Loving someone carries a great deal of responsibility, which is why we must choose our partners very carefully. A mistake like that is for life.'

'He does seem to like me.'

That's why I had to say something.'

'You think he does like me?'

'You're very pretty.'

Her mother had always told her that being pretty was a gift from God, and that how you acted towards other people was very much more important.

'And he is a very attractive young man, but he must be flawed, I think, having been brought up as he has been—'

'It isn't fair that you should judge him! You don't know him.'

It made her feel closer to Joe, defending him like this, though her common sense told her that her mother was probably quite right, just as she always was.

'No, I don't, but I know of his family, and he has nothing to recommend him beyond his looks, which he gets from his mother, and she was a very weak, depraved person. His father . . .' She shuddered. 'They don't live a godly life, anything but. How can a young man like that have any values? You must not think of him any more.'

Her mother kissed her and then went into the kitchen, even though Peggy could manage and did so every Sunday without her mother's help. Esther Margaret ran upstairs to her bedroom. It was a big room and held all her most precious possessions, and it had the best view in the house. It looked out across the valley into Weardale and from it you could see the tiny grey stone farms and the moors before they fell away and became fields. It faced west, and in the evenings the sun shone red and blinding gold before it sank spectacularly into the earth. When she had been a little girl the round orange ball of fire had fascinated her. It hadn't changed and she hadn't changed; she still loved it. The problem was that she didn't know whether she had sufficient regard for Joe Forster to defy the parents she loved so much. She didn't want to upset them and her mother was right; Joe had nothing to recommend him but looks and a pit that was doing badly. He was probably not what he seemed; she didn't know. It was difficult to accept that older people knew better just because they were older and had more experience. She cried a few tears and then dried them with the corner of her handkerchief and went downstairs for the meal, smiling bravely as she walked into the dining room. Her father looked up and smiled at her and so did her mother. She could not help but think about Joe, in spite of what her mother said, but she knew that it must go no farther than that.

CHAPTER TWO

The morning was breaking with an orange sun suddenly spilling in at the window where nobody had bothered to draw the curtains. Dryden Cameron opened his eyes. The bed was a puddle of light. Somebody shouted across the street outside beyond the open window and he could feel the breeze in the room which had made its way over the top of the heather. From down below in the kitchen came the clatter of pots and pans, dulled by space and floorboards, but the room was safe, the door shut, the bedclothes a landscape of heaps and troughs, the pillows soft like clouds.

The girl was still asleep, the landlord's niece, Betsy, up from Darlington for the weekend. It had taken him two days to get her here, and that was a record. Dryden yawned. It was Sunday morning and there was no rush. She opened her eyes almost the moment he willed her to and smiled in response to his smile, and Dryden moved nearer and kissed her.

'What are we going to do today?' she said.

The trouble with women, Dryden thought, was that they always wanted to make plans, instead of just enjoying the moment. He kissed her harder to shut her up and leaned over her and in a little while she had stopped talking and was concentrating on what they were doing. It was mid-morning before Dryden got out of bed and poured water into a bowl and began washing his body. She watched. He didn't mind that. Most of the women he knew had never seen a man naked. Strange. Then he began to dress and she sat up.

'You're not going?'

This was the tricky bit. Sometimes he left before they woke up, which was easier. The trouble was that having a woman in the morning was very different to having her in the night, and he enjoyed it. But you had to leave, and doing it neatly was a problem.

'I have to,' he said, and made it sound regretful. She let the bedclothes fall away from her body. It was a good idea, Dryden thought, one of the best. That and crying. He smiled politely as her eyes filled with tears. Dryden watched them cascade down her cheeks, then he edged the window open farther and left without a backward glance, dropping into the back lane. She was at the window, he heard her speak his name, but she wouldn't dare shout or make any fuss.

He walked quickly out on to the main street. People were going to church, all done up in their Sunday best. Drunks from last night were lying in doorways, one or two still asleep. Children were playing in the road. He walked into Mrs Clancy's boarding house at the bottom of the street. It always smelled like the aftermath of a party, with cigarettes, beer, grease and just now the overwhelming smoke of frying. Mrs Clancy herself came out of the kitchen, eyes red and watering, a spoon in her hand. Dryden followed her back in. The kitchen was dark and contained a big table. There was evidence of other people's breakfast; the table was littered with empty plates, crumbs and mugs that had contained tea. Somebody had used one mug as an ashtray. Mrs Clancy thrust a plate of food under Dryden's nose. It was all cooked hard but he was hungry. The tea came out of the pot almost black. Dryden put three spoonfuls of sugar into it and drank it down, and then he left the kitchen and trudged upstairs.

It was almost dinner-time so most people had left their beds and he had the luxury of a couple of hours without anybody snoring beside him before he judged that the pubs would be open. The bed was lumpy and smelled of other people's feet, but he was used to it. He slept. He woke up at exactly the right time and put on his clothes and his shoes and walked slowly down the street, savouring the idea of beer.

The pub was only just open. The fire was on and several men were already inside. Dryden took his beer without a word. Nobody spoke to him. He was used to that. The men here were people he worked with. They didn't talk to him at work and they didn't talk to him here. There had been a time when he had cared, but that was long gone. He had thought that he might leave, though it occurred to him that if you could not be accepted in the place where you had been born then it was very unlikely that you would be accepted any place else. As he drank his beer he could see his reflection in the mirror behind the bar and he knew – he had been told many times – that it was the reflection of evil. Parents in the village drummed into their daughters that they were never under any circumstances to go anywhere near him, but Dryden knew as well as anybody that the Devil always cast himself in irresistible forms and several of the girls in the village had proved that to be true. It was as though they were drawn by the silence, the very wickedness.

That morning Dryden was well aware that his half-brother Tom Cameron had come into the pub just after him. Tom had lots of friends and they came in with him, talking and laughing and shouting at the landlord, who was shouting back at them. Tom was about to get married. Dryden knew this because he worked alongside Tom and was often in the same pub and he heard the talk and the jokes. Tom was to be married to Vinia Brown on Easter Saturday. That was only a week away.

Vinia Brown lived in a little house by herself in Irish Back Street. Dryden could not understand why Tom was marrying her. He could have her as often as he wanted, so why bother? She worked in Miss Applegate's shop at the top of the Store bank, just up from the Store's drapery department, and she was one of the few girls in the village who really, really disliked him. Dryden didn't understand that; he hadn't done anything to her. He knew when people were deliberately ignoring him. Some of the better-off lasses did that and it was all right, but Vinia looked straight through him, like the nasty cold wind off the fell which wouldn't go around and cut your face. And then he realised why it was. It was because she was going to marry Tom.

Dryden stood by the bar and drank his beer and didn't bother anybody, and Tom and his friends at the far end of the bar became very drunk and the drunker they became the more they took up of the bar until everybody else moved away, because they understood what it was like when you were only a week away from being shackled. The laughter got louder, the beer was drunk and they occupied all the bar except the corner where Dryden was standing. He was just about to move well out of their way when Wesley Mathers backed into him and turned around, glaring.

'Come out the bloody road, you!' he said.

Dryden was bigger than him; he was bigger than most of the young men in the village except Tom. Tom was a giant. Dryden didn't say anything. It wasn't cowardice, it was common sense. There were at least ten of them. They would have no compunction at all in kicking him senseless. He would have moved except that Wes was very drunk and didn't let him, knocking into him again on purpose and waiting for his reaction. Dryden did nothing. Wes called him 'a gypo bastard' and then picked up Dryden's beer and poured it over him. Dryden lost his temper and went for him. And then for the first time ever he was suddenly very close to his brother. Tom got in between them pulling Wes away, and then with his back to Dryden he was saying into Wes's face, 'Nay, nay, lad.'

'He thinks he can drink in here with other people. Black bastard!'

In all of Dryden's eighteen years nobody had ever defended him against anything and he could not believe it was happening.

'I promised her. No fights,' Tom said.

'You shouldn't let him in here, George!' Wes shouted at the landlord.

Dryden was feeling better, in spite of the fact that he was soaked. Tom turned around.

'Do you want another drink?' he asked.

'No thanks,' Dryden said, and he levered himself away from the bar and walked out.

After that he felt worse. It had taken Tom eighteen years to speak to him. They worked together, they lived five minutes' walk away, but neither Tom nor their mother, Mary, had ever acknowledged him in any way, and he did not see why things should be different now. It was not right that Tom should make him feel anything positive. He was glad of the anger. He went out and walked a long way across the moors. The wind dried his clothes and when he had walked away his feelings it was well past dinner-time. He had gone much farther than he intended, so it was the middle of the afternoon by the time he came back to the village. As he did so he could see a small figure standing in the middle of the Cutting Bridge not far away from the houses. He recognised her immediately. Every man in the village knew the figure of Esther Margaret Hunter; she was the bonniest thing that had ever lived. She was one of the better-off lot and ignored him although she went to church and was supposed to be a Christian. Dryden didn't really care; he didn't expect people like the daughter of the Store's manager to speak to him. He would have walked straight past her but for the fact that Esther Margaret was crying.

'Here,' he said, pushing a handkerchief at her. She took it without looking at him. She mopped her face and blew her nose thoroughly three times and then she tried to return the soggy, slimy ball of cotton.

'No,' he said.

She stuffed it into her coat pocket.

'He came to tea,' she said, glaring at the cut below, where the railway lines were. 'With his mam and dad. He's boring and . . . he looks like a pig. After this morning too, for them to plan it and . . .'

In Dryden's opinion she shouldn't cry. Crying did nothing for women's looks, though there had been a great number of times when he had enjoyed their tears, usually when he left them. He wasn't enjoying Esther Margaret's tears at all. They were ruining her looks, had deprived him of his best handkerchief, which he had stolen off the market, and he had no idea what she was talking about. He leaned back against the bridge and put his hands in his pockets and waited. He imagined her stripped and under him with her golden hair free and that was quite nice, except that she sniffed loudly twice and ruined the image. She had an exquisite mouth. She took his handkerchief out of her pocket and assaulted it further. Dryden was of the opinion she would have done better to throw it away rather than return it once again to her coat pocket.

'He tried to kiss me,' she said finally. 'He got me in the hall near the coats and then he . . .'

The lad had done more than kiss her, Dryden thought ruefully, and he had made a mess of it. He had frightened her.

'He'd probably never done it before and it was a mistake,' he offered.

She looked at him properly, realised who he was and stiffened. Dryden leaned back farther against the stone wall and looked away across the fell, giving her time to decide whether to stay or not.

'He was all hands and . . .' She pulled a face.

'Not nice, eh? First time, was it?'

'Yes.'

'You remember.'

'I'll never forget it.'

Neither of them said anything else after that, but she didn't seem to have any inclination to go back and he didn't blame her. Maybe the dreaded whoever-he-was was still at the house, which he would be if he had been invited for tea because it wasn't teatime yet. He had mucked his chances up good and proper, and before they had even sat down to eat. Manners were important in these things. She came closer (not to him especially, and he wasn't surprised – she probably wouldn't want to get near a lad again for months) but she leaned and looked over the bridge and he remembered being a child and doing something similar just as the train went under, waiting for the steam to come up towards him and the heat and the smell and the idea of going somewhere. He had sometimes thought of catching a train and going away. He had sometimes thought of putting himself in front of one.

And then she was looking at him. Had she got bored with the view, nothing but railway sleepers and rails?

'You have got the most amazing eyes,' she said, staring.

Dryden was very uncomfortable. Women were always saying such things. It made him feel like a circus animal. He turned away but then it got worse. She squeezed his arm in acknowledgement of having been rude and apologised.

'Sorry,' she said.

After that Dryden considered it was all fair and square, but he didn't rush it, he gave her the benefit of what had always appeared to him to be two big pieces of coal staring back from the mirror at him. She fell for it. They did it every time. Women were hopeless about things like that. If he could have liked them for it he would have. As it was he just leaned forward and very slowly kissed her. No hands or other contact, it was sweet and light, and after what had happened earlier he knew she would either like it or run. She liked it. She was so innocent. He enjoyed that innocence in women. It was their downfall and they deserved it. Esther Margaret pressed against him. Dryden let her but he didn't try to pull her any closer, he just accepted the sweet fresh taste of her mouth and the soft feel of her body.

CHAPTER THREE

Tom's mother had wanted Vinia and Tom to move in with them, to live in Prince Row, and when they had refused she had tried to talk them into getting a house two doors away where Mr Price was on his last legs. Vinia prayed that Mr Price would live to be a hundred and her prayers were answered; Mr Price made a sudden recovery from what had been his deathbed and was seen out and about in the main street within a week. That Sunday afternoon, the last before the wedding, Tom's mother had invited her to tea to make the final arrangements, though as far as Vinia could see there was nothing to do.

She was annoyed. In the first place Tom had gone out and got drunk at dinner-time, and when she turned up for tea he was still upstairs sleeping it off. Sober, Tom was the man of her dreams. Drunk, he was just like all the others, and she preferred not to see him that way. In a village where miners were ten a penny she thought she had chosen well. Tom was so big that nobody would fight with him. He was good looking and made a pretty amount at the pit because he was strong and able. Lots of young men had tried to court her but Vinia would have none of them until Tom noticed her, and after that she found it difficult to say no. She wouldn't have found it difficult today, she thought it was wrong of him to drink like that when they were about to be married, but it was the usual practice in the village so she could hardly expect any less. He was marrying her and not in haste; they had done nothing wrong. Vinia had a great sense of what was right and wrong and she had allowed Tom Cameron nothing more than a few kisses. When he would have taken more she stopped him, which had not been easy. She had her own small house beside the Variety Theatre and they had been alone there many times. The truth was that Tom liked her house, he liked the peace, he liked being away from his mother. Sometimes she thought that one of Tom's main reasons for marrying her was to get away from his mother.

Mary Cameron had spent the last eighteen years trying to make up for the biggest scandal in the village, that she had let some passing gypsy put her down and force her, resulting in a child. Vinia could not imagine any woman getting herself into such a stupid situation. Having been assaulted in the church, Mary had not been near it since, but that was not a problem in terms of the wedding. Vinia was a Methodist and they would be married in the chapel. That was another reason she didn't like Tom drinking, but since he didn't do it often she could not complain. Most of the young men got drunk a lot more often than Tom did, and although she had tried to look favourably upon the young men who went to chapel the fact was that she found them rather dull.

Alf, Tom's father, didn't drink, but he was no asset to the conversation since he had fallen asleep by the fire and it was left to Mary to go over for perhaps the hundredth time what Saturday would be like. Vinia wasn't listening. She wished Tom was sober enough to come downstairs.

'Our Tommy won't want you to go on working you know, Vinia, after you're wed.'

Tom had in fact said nothing to her about her job, but Vinia was in no doubt that his mother thought it beneath her dignity to work at Miss Applegate's women's clothing shop. In fact she hated it, but she was not about to give in to Tom's mother over anything. She put up with the work because what she wanted more than anything in the world after Tom was her own shop, and she had learned through being there what to do and what not to do. She had no money and you could not start up a shop without it, but she dreamed of her name above the door. On bad days she dreamed of Miss Applegate dying and leaving her the shop.

'Looking after a pitman is a full-time job,' his mother was saying, sitting back in her chair. Vinia wished she could get up and walk out. She didn't argue; she had no intention of doing so, she had won every battle so far and she was not going to give in. They would keep on living in her little house with all her possessions and she would go on working at least until they had a child. She could not imagine what that would be like, and lately had taken to watching women with small children and feeling that it was something she would very much like. She could see herself and Tom and a baby; it would be perfect.

She heard his heavy footsteps on the stairs and soon Tom came down looking very much as she imagined he would look in the early mornings. It did things to her inside, his hair all over and his eyes narrowed from sleep, and then she remembered that she was not pleased with him.

'I was telling Vinia, Tommy, that you'll not want her to go on working at that shop after next week.'

'Vinny knows that.' When he called her Vinny — he was the only person in the world who did — Vinia usually felt all soft and squashy inside, but today she didn't. They had not discussed her work at the shop, he had no right to take for granted what she would do, but Vinia did not want to argue with him in front of his mother. He sat down and his mother ran about after him. That was something else which would change. Tom did nothing at home other than tip up his money. To give Mary Cameron her due she had not mentioned that she was losing his wage.

'I'll be able to provide everything we need.'

Vinia smiled at him where he sat at the tea table and Tom looked back at her, making her think of what was to come. Tom's kisses could drive her out of her mind. When he had eaten he walked her back to her house, along Dan's Castle and down the bank and up the main street until they came to the Variety, and in through the small dark passage and then out into her yard.

'Will you come in?' she said.

'I'd better not.' He looked at her for a few seconds and then he got hold of her and kissed her hard. Vinia broke off.

'Tom . . .'

'What?'

'Do you really mind about the shop?'

'What?' Tom's mind was not on the shop, it was on her completely; she could tell.

'The shop.'

'Who cares about the bloody shop?' Tom kissed her again. Swearing was another thing she wished he didn't do, but at least he controlled himself in front of his precious mother.

'Don't you care?'

'No, I don't.' He kissed her harder and then made himself draw away. It was one of the things she liked best about him; Tom had restraint, he would not touch her until they were married. 'I'm going,' he said, and she watched him turn and walk away down the passage back to the main street. She went into her house, and it was then that it occurred to her it would be the last time she ever did so alone. This time next week she would be Mrs Tom Cameron. What a fine sound it had. She would no longer be alone by her fire or at her table or in her bed. In her bed. The thought made her face go warm and she took off her coat and began to attend to the fire.

When Esther Margaret got home in the dim light of early evening her mother came into the hall with a concerned look on her face, whispering, 'Wherever have you been?'

'Just outside.'

'You've been gone ages. I had to give them their tea without you.'

Esther Margaret tried not to look too hard at the place where Billy Robson had got her into the dark corner and put his hands on her breasts. She thought about Dryden instead, the soft sweet taste of his lips. It seemed a very long time since that morning when she and Joe had talked outside the church. She had come a long way since then, and nothing that had happened, except those few minutes when Dryden had repaired what Billy had done, was pleasant to her mind.

'I felt sick. I had to go outside.'

'You could have said.'

Esther Margaret, for the first time ever, found herself wishing that her mother was a little less naïve about men. She had learned more about life in the past few hours than in a great many months preceding them, and her mother had been no support at all. After Billy and his parents turned up the minute dinner was over she saw that her mother was trying to manoeuvre her and that her father was in on it too because he carefully avoided looking at her and greeted the Robsons with false joviality. Criticising her parents had not come naturally to Esther Margaret before, but now she even felt like boasting to her mother that she had let the worst young man in the village kiss her. It made her shiver just to think of it. It was undoubtedly the sweetest thing that had ever happened to her. It put her beyond Billy Robson and his nasty wandering hands and his supercilious smile, and as for Joe . . . She could never have Joe, she saw that. That was the hardest thing of all, because the day had taught her that she loved him and she felt bitter about it all, bitter enough to acknowledge that she had in fact encouraged Dryden Cameron to kiss her because her instincts had told her that he was not like Billy. How had she known that, not having been near him or even spoken to him before? Something had told her that Dryden was careful, adept, had learned a good many hard lessons such as those she had learned today. He knew things that other people didn't and she wanted . . . yes, she wanted him to kiss her again. It was not love, but neither was it what Billy Robson had tried to do. Dryden would not have done such a thing in a thousand years.

She went into the sitting room and was polite to Billy and his parents. She watched him, found in his smile a smirk, and she hardened her heart against him and hated him. It was a strange feeling. She had had no need to hate anyone before. He had destroyed something, spoiled her view of the world, and it could not be altered back into anything better. He looked to her so ordinary, so dull with his dark little face and his piggy little eyes and his awful wandering hands. He had not looked like that before. When she had gone to the shop where he was her father's assistant he was always helpful and smiling, she had even liked him, but he had followed her out of the room and taken hold of her without her consent and in those few moments she had ceased to be a girl.

It was strange. It did not seem as though anything else had altered, but it was as though the beat of her own heart had taken on another rhythm unheard by her parents or their company, as if she had stepped outside her life or beyond them and would not feel in accord with them again. She smiled and said the right things and let her parents believe that all was as it had started out but it was not. When they had finally gone she sat by the fire with a book and pretended to read until it was time for bed, and when she could at last excuse herself she was relieved, glad to go upstairs and undress and wash and fall into bed. She was exhausted, and still had a faint hope that she would wake up in the morning and it would be Sunday again, that this had not happened and she had the day to look forward to. She would start it off at the end of the service when she was standing outside the church and Joe had come up to her and her spirits had lifted and she would keep it there, frozen in time like a painting, herself and Joe, making conversation and smiling at one another in an unconscious bond. She could begin again and this time it would be different.

CHAPTER FOUR

Saturday was overcast. It did not rain but the sky was heavy all day and it looked as if it might. The sun failed to shine and Vinia was only glad that the chapel was on the street not far from Tom's house and not all the way down a narrow little lane like the parish church. Esther Margaret was to be her bridesmaid. She was the only young woman Vinia knew well. She had no friends, she didn't understand why; it was just that other women did not seem to be as she was or want the things she wanted, though that didn't make sense because she was marrying Tom and had a home. Esther Margaret sometimes came into the shop and bought things, though Vinia wasn't sure why because the Store had a more than adequate clothing department, better than Miss Applegate's. She thought Esther Margaret came in for the company, and if Miss Applegate had gone upstairs, as she did often, or had gone out, as she didn't often, Esther Margaret would stay and chat.

Vinia privately thought the shop was in the wrong place because the Store was almost next to it and the clothing department had a manageress and two assistants and she could not see what Miss Applegate wanted with help, though naturally she was grateful for the money. Her parents had been dead for years and she had to make her own way. One of the reasons she had wanted to marry Tom was so as not to have to make her own way in the future. There was something subdued about the shop.

Miss Applegate loomed from the shadows inside like a large grey mouse. Beneath the counter, out of sight, were ladies' undergarments, and hanging up, doing their own advertising, were dresses and shawls. Shoes sat solitary in boxes and the shop was all grey and brown and the sunshine was not allowed in in case it damaged everything.

It seemed to her that Miss Applegate never got any older because she had always been that old. The shop had been her father's, and her parents had lived as she did now above the shop. She led the kind of life which would have frightened anybody else into marrying the first lad who bothered to look in their direction. Miss Applegate boasted that no man had ever walked over the threshold of the shop. Vinia could believe it; there was something stagnant about the place. Miss Applegate didn't pay much and the work was not hard but it was boring. Vinia longed for there to be exciting things to sell and to be asked to alter the windows so that they would attract attention but every time she made a suggestion Miss Applegate turned it down. Since she was small Vinia had made drawings of clothes she would have liked to have worn, clothes she began to make. She would go to the market and buy material and second-hand stuff and would fashion smart clothes for herself. She even made hats, and as time went on she designed clothes and hats for other people for special occasions, weddings and parties.

For her own wedding Vinia had made for herself a costume in grey with tiny white stitching and a hat to match. She was pleased when she saw her reflection in the mirror, and even more pleased when Esther Margaret called for her on the way to chapel. Esther Margaret's father was to give Vinia away. She didn't know him well but she had no one else. She was reassured by the sight of Tom waiting for her at the top of the aisle, and the minister, whom she knew quite well since she went there every Sunday, who was smiling. Many people were there whom she did not know; they liked to go to see any girl in the village married. Afterwards there was to be a gathering in the hall behind the chapel. Mary Cameron cried profusely and said that things would never be the same again within Vinia's hearing, which she didn't think tactful, but then his mother couldn't help it. Tom was the only son she had. You couldn't count that dreadful boy everybody ignored. He had had a good home with the Harmers in Oaks Row, the best street in the village, and he had run away when he was twelve. When Mr Harmer had gone after him Dryden had turned and knocked him into the road. He had lived at Mrs Clancy's ever since. Mrs Clancy was not the kind of woman respectable people bothered with. It was rumoured that she drank and was given to telling off-colour jokes to her lodgers when under the influence of gin.

Vinia had a smile and a word with everyone, including Joe Forster, who was automatically invited to everything that went on in the village. She liked him. He was as unlike his father as anybody could be, and the villagers were pleased at that, but he was also the very spit of his mother, and she had been the most useless woman in the area, apparently, so it was surprising that Joe was so nice. He had brought them a wedding gift, a gravy boat, silver, he assured them. He had undoubtedly taken it from some dark cupboard in his house because it could have done with a good polish, but it was nevertheless a handsome gift and Vinia was pleased with it. She couldn't imagine Joe needing such things if gossip was anything to go by, with nobody but that horrible old man to look after them both.

As the afternoon went on the day brightened up a little and Esther Margaret ventured outside. There were so many people in the hall, and she had had a very confusing week. She hadn't been able to think clearly about anything, even after almost six days. She stood outside in the cold wind and was not aware of Joe behind her until he said her name. She turned around, remembering Billy and backing off slightly and then conscious of doing so, colouring, wishing she could run away, almost in tears.

Joe stood well back, watching her.

'It's a . . . it's a very pretty dress,' he said, and she thought happily that he was not like Billy and neither was he like Dryden, and she was glad of that, she was glad of it all. It was almost last Sunday, it was almost normality if anything could be. She smiled at him.

'Vinia made it for me. She's very clever, she makes all kinds of things.'

'Have you ever thought of running away?'

It was so unexpected she stared into Joe's green eyes.

'You can't run from things,' she said.

Joe looked down at the path and the daffodils that had somehow made their way through the mess that was not quite a garden, and then away at the vast expanse of fell.

'I want to.'

She didn't blame him. People talked of his father being rich because he had the pit and that great barn of a house up on the fell, but it wasn't true. They weren't rich at all, they could hardly keep the pit going. They had no carriage any more, no servants except that awful Jacob Smith, and the house looked as though it was falling down. They didn't go anywhere that she knew of and Joe had never gone to school. He had never done anything that lads might do or wanted to do, she thought. No wonder he was ready to run.

'You can't. If you do everything follows you.'

'How can it?'

'That's what people say, that your problems follow you because they're inside you, things you have to deal with, and that you take them with you.'

'I don't believe it.'

'God helps.'

'God doesn't do anything for people,' Joe said.

Esther Margaret was horrified. Nobody said things like that.

'It isn't true, Joe. God is inside you. "Greater is He that is in you than he that is in the world". He gives people strength.'

Joe's green eyes were like the stained glass in the church, all deep and keen.

'Come with me,' he said.

Esther Margaret stared. The wind coming off the fell was bitter, and from inside the hall she could hear the sound of other people's voices. She thought that because of what had happened this week she would always feel as if they were in there and she was out here and they could not be mixed. For a moment she considered how wonderful it would be to leave, and then she remembered Joe's mother. She had run away from whatever problems were haunting her, she had run off and left her husband and child for some no-good man, and she had died and for ever and ever she would lie in the churchyard, held fast, the punishment for those who ran away – death and spiritual abandonment. It was not to be thought of. Joe's mother had gone to hell for what she had done and burned for ever, looking down and seeing her child unloved and neglected and not being able to do anything about it. That was not for Esther Margaret. She would stay here and try to get things right.

'You can't leave,' she said. 'What about your father?'

Joe laughed. It was not a nice sound. He didn't say anything and they stood for quite a long time while the wind blew cold upon Esther Margaret's dress, which was meant for ceremonies but had not been made for gardens in early spring.

'It's Easter Sunday tomorrow,' she said. 'Good things always happen then. It's joyful.'

'Nothing good ever happens,' Joe said bitterly.

Esther Margaret could see her mother hovering in the doorway and wondered why she had to time everything so badly.

'Esther Margaret, what on earth are you doing out there? You'll catch your death of cold. Get back in here.'

It seemed to her that her mother had been harsher with her that week than ever before. The whole world was turned upside down. She stared at Joe. Irritatingly she was reminded of all those things her mother had said the previous Sunday, that Joe came from weak people who ran from their fears and gave up their children, who did not honour respectability, who put themselves first. He was just like his mother, she thought; he was going to run. She lifted her chin, ignoring her mother's call. 'I have a life here and a family and I could never run away. My future is here. You must go if you can do no better.'

She marched back into the hall feeling smug and self-right-eous and better than she had felt all week. Her mother had been right – he was not the man for her, he was not worthy of her. He was no more to her than Billy Robson. She went up to the minister and asked him how his mother was and saw him smile approvingly upon her.

Joe watched her as she went back inside. He had not expected her to say yes but then he had not thought she would say no. He didn't know what he had thought, just that there was no future in this place, but he could see that if he did leave she would despise him. There was little point in going if she would not go too, but she had so much, he could see that – her family and whatever life brought her – and it would be good, there was no reason why it should not be. People like Esther Margaret deserved rich and rewarding lives and he felt sure that hers would be. She was strong and capable and she believed in God. He didn't believe in anything any more. He had felt as if he couldn't stand another day in that house with his father and in the pit office being told what to do because his father didn't trust him to get anything right. He had had dreams, had thought he might go to university and get away, that his father could not continue to begrudge him an education and some freedom. The truth was that his father saw nothing and cared for nothing. That morning, as Jacob had ladled what he called porridge from a black pan on to plates, thick and sticky, he had said, 'There's to be short time from now on.'

His father never told him anything; he relayed information through Jacob, even though he worked at the office. His father gave him no responsibility, treated him like a clerk. He hadn't cared, had thought he was leaving. It was funny really, when he

thought back to breakfast. He had believed that it was Esther
Margaret who was stopping him but it wasn't, it was himself and
his mother. She had run from everything and because of it he
couldn't go. He had to prove to his father that no matter what
was thrown at him he could endure it.

He knew what short time meant; it was lower wages, but the
pitmen were so badly paid already that they could ill afford any
cuts. His father didn't care and Jacob seemed to take pure delight
in relaying the message. He would not give his father the
satisfaction of asking questions so he had gone off to the wedding,
relying on Esther Margaret to make the decision for him, and so
she had, but in his heart it was already made. The pitmen had
nobody on their side, and if he left nobody would help.

He came back from the wedding ready to tackle him but his
father had consumed a bottle of brandy and was deeply asleep by
a dying fire. The lines were etched deep in his red face and made
Joe wonder what he had been like when he was young. He had
the feeling that every man started off with excitement, enthusiasm, energy, ready to take on the world. His father had long
since given up, and Joe had a sneaking feeling that his mother
was at least partly to blame for that. He went into the kitchen
where Jacob was in his usual seat by the blaze.

'The fire's almost out in there. See to it or my father will
waken to a black grate,' Joe said, and he took a lamp and went
upstairs.

The room was dark. From the windows there was no light of
any kind, neither moon nor stars. It was so dark it was frightening.
It was like being down the pit, a thick darkness that you could
almost touch. Joe imagined that being dead was like that, nothing
around you, no waking. He could hear his father downstairs
shouting at Jacob so the fire must have gone out or the brandy had
run out or some other catastrophe had occurred. It was nothing to
do with him – the door was closed, everybody was shut out, on the
other side, away. Even Esther Margaret. The reality of her was not
what he had dreamed it would be. There was something he

disliked about the way she had spoken and the way she had tripped indoors and left him. If she had intended to make him change his mind then she had succeeded. Joe banished farther from his thoughts any idea of leaving.

'I'm on night shift this fortnight,' Tom said.

Vinia opened her eyes.

'Night shift?'

'Aye.' Tom kissed her, snuggled in against her body. She liked having him there, as she had known she would. Tom's body was bliss — big and smooth and firm.

'What does that mean in particular?'

'It means, my petal, that at some time after midnight you will get up off your sweet backside and have hot water and a meal ready.'

Her eyes flew open.

'Of course I will,' she said.

'Of course you will,' Tom said. 'It's the only difficult shift that way, otherwise I finish at eight in the morning or at teatime.'

'I know that, Tom.'

'I know you do, but there's a difference between knowing it and doing it.'

'Your mother's done it for years. I'm sure I can manage.'

Tom had gone back to sleep. For the first time she began to see what Mary Cameron had meant about being at home. At eight o'clock in the morning she was going to work and at four in the afternoon, when Tom finished, she was at work so to her way of thinking it was only the night shift that would be easy because she would be in. Never mind; Miss Applegate might appreciate her difficulty and adjust her hours. Early morning was rarely busy and neither was late afternoon or early evening; it was the middle of the day that mattered, though you could say they never had a rush on. Vinia wished they would. Most of the time she was sure that Miss Applegate could manage well enough without her. She didn't have to worry about it to begin with anyway, since Tom was on night shift. She closed her eyes and went back to sleep. It had been a busy night in their new home. Tom had wanted her very badly indeed and had not been satisfied until he had plundered her body thoroughly. She had made no objection; it was just that now she was so very tired.

That Sunday Esther Margaret did all she could to keep her thoughts away from the Cutting Bridge, but she couldn't. It was a bright day. It was typical that it should be a much better day after the wedding, but she was glad because it was Easter Sunday, the most important day of the church calendar. And in other respects too it was a better day than last Sunday had been. In the first place Joe Forster didn't turn up at church. She couldn't remember that having happened before but she was glad in a way, though she was also rather anxious because she had felt guilty at what she had said to him – she thought it had been shock and all that had happened that week. She could not help feeling that morning that she was better off without Joe, though she did worry that he might have carried out his plan and left. She didn't want him to go, not for any noble reason, just because she didn't want him to. The good thing was that her mother didn't lecture her. They ate their dinner in peace and Billy Robson and his parents were not invited for tea so the day was a huge improvement all round, only after they had eaten and her mother had taken up her sewing and her father had fallen asleep by the fire she kept thinking about Dryden and glancing towards the window until her mother said, 'Why don't you go out and get some fresh air? You've had a very pasty look this week. Go for a walk until teatime. It'll do you good.'

'I don't think I will. I've got a headache.'

'Walking on a nice sunny day is the best cure for headaches. Off you go.'

'I could help you with your sewing or read to you.'

Her mother practically shooed her out of the door. After that came the decision as to where to go; anywhere other than the Cutting Bridge would have done. Her resolution lasted five minutes, and then she turned around and was walking quickly up the main street and around the corner into Bridge Street and out of the village. When she got to the bridge nobody was there. She was glad and then she was sorry and then she didn't know what to think, but since her mother had told her not to come back for a couple of hours she walked on for almost an hour right away from the village until it fell out of sight and seemed to take her problems with it. She felt much more clear-headed when she turned around. Her mother, as usual, had been right. But when she got back to the bridge she could see him, leaning just as he had been last week, with his hands in his pockets. He didn't look up even when she reached him. She could have gone past and she didn't think he would have said anything but she stopped, and when he looked up she realised that she had been waiting for him to do so, that she had been thinking all that week about how beautiful his eyes were, and it seemed to her now that they were much more so than she had thought – unfathomable, mysterious, like black stars. His skin was like fudge and his hair was black pennies and he was tall and lean and had long legs and . . . She was ashamed of herself, especially when he did nothing. He was not like Billy, putting himself forward, nor like Joe, making impossible decisions. He was uncomplicated, more exquisite than anything she had ever seen. Other men didn't look like that, exotic, foreign, dangerous. He suffered her gaze and then his lashes came down like leaves on a tree, thick and sweeping and shutting everything out, and Esther Margaret took a step backwards.

'I shouldn't be here,' she said.

'Go, then.'

'I don't want to.' All she could think about was his mouth. She had never wanted anything in her life as much as she wanted his mouth. Suddenly she understood fully for the first time the meaning of 'lead us not into temptation'. Temptation had never been something to try to resist before. Giving in to it was the most delicious thing Esther Margaret had ever done and he understood her completely. He kissed her and this time he did it in the way that she had once hoped Joe Forster would, or some man she had never met who would become the whole world to her, and she did not deceive herself that she liked it less because it was wicked, because everybody said he was the Devil incarnate. She needed to embrace sin, she gave herself up to it, and the very trembling reluctance and guilt were the most heady thing that had ever happened. She had never tasted alcohol but she had seen the pitmen when they were intoxicated and it was the right name for it. She almost swooned with pleasure when he drew her close with gentle hands and lingered over her mouth, and it was not just the physical thing, it was much more than that. It was a oneness, an agreement, a meeting of souls, a togetherness such as never before, and he did not for one second try to press her. He was not stupid Billy Robson. He was not damaged Joe Forster. She felt as though he belonged to her as he had not and would not belong to anyone else, yet it had been nothing beyond a kiss. When she moved he released her, but she went to him, unable to bear the distance between them. She felt as though they could no longer be separated. She thought she loved him. There was no mistake. He smiled at her, held her face as though it were something precious.

'You should go home,' he said. 'It's getting dark.'

'I am going.'

He nodded and let go of her again and they walked in the failing light back towards the village as the evening drew in around them. He stopped before they reached the houses.

'You shouldn't be seen with me,' he said.

'I've behaved very badly this week.'

'With me.'

'No, not with you. With just about everybody else. I've been horrible. I've lost where I was, as if I've gone past it and now I can't get back.' It was strange, talking to him; it was as though there were a new person inside her who could say such things.

'Maybe you shouldn't try to, maybe it's too difficult.'

'I want to see you.'

'You shouldn't. Go home. Your mother will wonder where you are.'

'I want the night.'

'No.'

He gave her a little shove in the direction of her home and she walked as somebody in a dream back to the house where her mother, for the second Sunday running, came anxiously into the hall.

'I was worried. It's almost dark.'

'What is there to hurt me here?'

'Come and have some tea.'

She went in by the fire and it was all familiar but it was not the same. She had been a child and was a child no longer. The air was stale and the rooms were too used and she did not want to be there as she had done. Home was suddenly something to be despised, to be rid of. It was hated. She wanted to push back the walls, to tear off the roof, to see the stars, to be outside and dancing, whirling around the streets, laughing and shouting and free like never before. She no longer liked her mother or father, she wanted nothing of their ideas. She wanted Dryden Cameron, she wanted the feel of him, the taste of his lips and the touch of his hands and the special way that he looked at her as though nothing else on earth was important. She wanted to run and run with him, to go somewhere new, to see places she had not seen before, to know things she had not known, to walk with him in the light. She couldn't eat her tea, she couldn't talk. She went to bed early, worn out, and dreamed dreams of darkness.

The first night Tom came back and said there was short time so it was only four nights that week that Vinia had to wait up for him, but it was difficult right from the beginning. It was almost one o'clock by the time he got back to the house and then he had to wash and eat his meal and she had to clear up and make everything right. When she got to bed Tom wanted her, he would not let her sleep, and then she had to get up early and go to work. She sneaked about the room, dressing, but Tom awoke in spite of his tiredness, sitting up and enquiring, 'Where are you going?'

'To work, of course.'

Tom looked puzzled.

'What are you talking about?'

'The shop opens at half past eight. I'm going to be late.'

'Get your clothes off and get back in here.'

'I can't do that, Tom.'

He reached out of bed and got hold of her and brought her back to him and began to pull at her clothes. It might have been funny but it wasn't, and when she objected he stopped and said slowly, 'Pitmen's wives don't work, there isn't time for it. I'll want a big meal in the middle of the day because I want it digested before I go to work, and I need my bait putting up and there's the housework and the shopping and whatever else you're going to do to make me comfortable.'

'But . . . what will I do all day? Stay here?'

'That's what housewives do, yes.'

'But Miss Applegate is expecting me.'

'I doubt she has a shopful,' Tom said, and he pulled her clothes off her and had her before he went back to sleep.

Mary Cameron came to see her that first day and wandered about the room — the house had only one room and a pantry downstairs — taking note of any dust or disorder.

'Those brasses could do with a good clean,' she observed. 'The brasses in my house are done every week. You'd have been better off in Prince Row with me to keep an eye on things. That isn't bought bread, is it? My Tommy isn't used to bought bread.'

'I made it,' Vinia said.

'You'll have to do better than this, my girl, my Tommy's used to the best. The house is to be turned out every day and his meal should be on the table when you hear him coming through that passage. You'll have to get your ideas brightened up. I wish you could have had Mr Price's house.'

'I wouldn't want Mr Price's house. This is my home,' Vinia said. Mary glared at her.

'Don't you back-answer me or I'll tell our Tommy. You stole him from me. The least you could do is keep a decent house.'

Tom was late in from work that evening; he had gone straight to the pub, so his dinner was overcooked. He looked hard at it and then at her.

'My mother caught me outside the pit. Don't argue with her, Vinny, she's had enough problems in her life. What is this meant to be?'

'It got a bit well done. You're late.'

'Well done?' Tom sat back in his chair. 'You'd better make me summat else and quick.'

'There isn't anything else.'

Tom took the plate and threw it across the room. Vinia watched, fascinated, as it hit the wall and the pieces went everywhere, and then Tom got up and smacked her across the face. Nobody had ever touched her before in anger. Tom was big and his hands were big and it hurt. She stood staring at him for a second. Then the world caved in. She ran up the stairs, the rods clinking back into place under her feet, and there she sought the sanctuary of her bed. Her face throbbed and stung. She cried until she couldn't cry any more, and then she heard Tom's more ponderous steps. He pushed open the door. It creaked.

'Look, Vinny, I'm sorry.' He sat down on the bed. 'I wouldn't hurt you for the world, you know I wouldn't. I shouldn't have had the last couple of pints. I didn't mean to yell at you.' Vinia turned farther away and wouldn't speak to him, so in the end Tom gave in and went back downstairs. She couldn't forgive him.

The next day Tom clattered about getting ready for work and when he wanted to kiss her before leaving the house, as usual, she turned her face away. Tom hovered.

'You have to forgive me before I go.'

'No, I don't.'

'It would be better if you did.'

'Why would it?'

And then she realised, looking into his serious, repentant face. Miners always made up with their wives before they left for the shift in case they didn't come back and all that was left was the guilt.

'Oh, Tom,' she said, and cuddled him.

'We'll do better,' Tom said.

She did not understand why she cried after he had gone. When she looked in the mirror there was a livid bruise on one side of her face. It was then that she realised she could not go out. Everybody would see that Tom had hit her. She stayed in and made do with what food they had, but it wasn't much. She cleaned and polished but all Tom said when he came home was, 'Where's my tea?'

'It won't be a minute, Tom. I've been busy.'

'Doing what?' He looked about him at the shiny house.

Vinia found herself running between pantry, oven and table while Tom sat and waited, watching her. When the meal was ready, minutes later, he ate in silence. Afterwards she washed up and then Tom washed and changed and she realised that it had already become a routine. He would go to the pub every night unless he was on shift, and then he would go at dinner-time.

He hadn't been long gone when Esther Margaret arrived. There was something bright and shiny about her which Vinia didn't recognise, though the look didn't last beyond her coming inside. She stared.

'Have you hurt yourself?'

'Oh, it's nothing.'

Esther Margaret was not deceived, Vinia could tell. In a place like this plenty of men knocked their wives about.

'I'm sorry,' she said.

Vinia wanted to cry but pride prevented her. She was so glad to have a visitor – anybody but Tom's mother would have done – but to have Esther Margaret there was a pleasure.

'I came to ask whether you would mind if I went after your job. I called in and Miss Applegate said you wouldn't be there any more and I want to do something.'

'Will you parents like that?'

'My father works in a shop.'

'Yes, but––'

'I have to!' Vinia was surprised at her vehemence. Esther Margaret looked ashamed but she went on, 'I can't go on being just their daughter. I'm suffocating.'

Vinia didn't say anything.

'Would you mind if I did?'

'Of course I wouldn't mind. I'd be glad for you.'

Esther Margaret hugged her. Vinia didn't know what to say to that either. People weren't given to hugging each other.

Thaddeus Morgan owned a steel foundry and a big house in Wolsingham, the first village at the beginning of Weardale. He sometimes came to the office at the pit to see Joe's father, though of late his father had been there less and less. Joe could hear his father's voice when Morgan invited him to a party.

'You haven't met my lass, have you, not since you were little ones? She's the bonniest lass in the county. Next Saturday, Joe.'

When Joe went home that evening his father was waiting and was all questions about Thaddeus Morgan.

'She's the one for you,' his father said. 'Looks and money.'

Joe could not imagine Thaddeus wanting to ally himself with penniless pit-owners but then he remembered Thaddeus Morgan shaking his head over his father's ways and saying, 'There's plenty of coal to be got out, if only your father would bring things up to date.'

Modernising meant borrowing money, Joe thought, and his father could not be brought to do that, but he could see that

Thaddeus wanted the connection. Foundries and pits went hand in hand in a sense, since it was good coking coal they produced. Thaddeus had no son and was inclined to look favourably on him. This idea was reinforced that Saturday when Joe walked the three miles down the hills and followed the river up to Wolsingham. There were lush green fields down here in the valley and pretty farmhouses, some of them hundreds of years old, in grey stone. The fields were full of sheep and there were horses and cows and all along the road were trees on either side. The house itself had a long drive with a gatehouse and there were big gardens with lots of trees. It was an extensive stone building with ornamented turrets and a kind of walkway outside on the upper storey.

When Joe arrived he could hear music and the sound of many people. The only people he was used to in crowds were work-men, which he didn't think would be very helpful. Inside, Thaddeus spotted him straight away in the huge hall and came across smiling in welcome, introducing him to various young people, pointing out his daughter, who was on the other side of the ballroom. She was surrounded by young men. Thaddeus laughed in appreciation and said Joe would meet her later. Joe was uncomfortable. She looked beautiful to him and was laughing and chatting and he could not forget how Esther Margaret had treated him, and although Luisa Morgan was undoubtedly charming and wonderful, as her father had said, it worried him. She even looked like Esther Margaret, with fair hair and blue eyes. She wore a simple white dress and a string of pearls. She came across to him.

'My father told me to introduce myself. Are you going to ask me to dance?'

Taken aback by her directness, Joe said he couldn't and she insisted on teaching him, to general groans from other young men. Joe just wanted to get away. He trod on her several times and it was such a humiliating experience, his face burning, everybody watching. The less clumsy he tried to be the worse it became. She talked at him all the time. Joe tried to concentrate.

'They say you're very like your mother. Did she really run off with another man? How delicious. I wish my mother would run off. I can't abide her.' She nodded her head in the direction of a frail-looking woman who was standing to the side of the ballroom, talking and smiling.

'You don't like your mother?' Joe couldn't believe that anyone, given the luxury of a mother, could possibly dislike her, however bad her faults.

Luisa laughed.

'She's boring, and so is my father. They don't go anywhere or do anything and the people they know . . .' She raised her eyes.

When the dance was over he found himself beside Mrs Morgan.

'I knew your mother,' she said. She had gentle eyes and fine hands. 'We went to school together here, to the convent.' She looked around as though someone might overhear their conversation, and then she said to him, 'I have long wanted to meet you but your father, you know, would never agree to it. I was good friends with your mother. I'm sure your father does his best but . . . You look exactly like her. I always wondered and I'm so pleased. You see, however . . . however difficult her life was she would never have done the things people believe she did. Your mother was a fine, upstanding person, loyal and true, and she loved you.'

'She ran off and left me.'

Her eyes hardened slightly but he could see that it was only resolution. She shook her head.

'I have always found that very hard to believe. You were the greatest delight of her life. Try to think well of her, Joe, whatever people say.' She clutched his hand for a moment and then Thaddeus bore down on them, bringing Luisa with him.

'Find the boy something to eat,' he directed her, and she obediently took Joe away to the supper table, but all the time she was looking past him.

'Who are you watching?' Joe asked.

'Do you see that man with my father?'

Joe glanced in the direction in which she was nodding and saw Thaddeus Morgan with another man of about the same age.

'That's George McAndrew. He's very, very rich and has never been married though women have set their caps at him for years. He would never have any of them. He owns shipyards on the Clyde and pits too and a good many other things.'

Joe could see nothing remarkable about the man. She offered to introduce them. When they went across, Thaddeus put his hand on Joe's shoulder, much to his surprise, and introduced him as the son of a dear friend. Mr McAndrew was polite but his hot little eyes, which lingered on Luisa, made Joe feel uncomfortable. She was all smiles in encouragement and it seemed to please him; his thin mouth began to turn up at the corners.

'We mustn't keep the young people,' Thaddeus said.

'I hoped to have the pleasure of asking Miss Morgan to dance,' Mr McAndrew said.

'I would be delighted.'

They went off. Her father was anything but delighted, Joe thought. After a short while he said softly, 'Do me a favour, Joe. Go and cut in.'

'I'm a terrible dancer.'

'Aye, but you're a good lad. Go and do it.'

Joe did. McAndrew was obviously displeased but couldn't say so and Luisa didn't seem happy about her change of partner. Joe trod on her.

'I don't know why you pushed in when you're so clumsy,' she said.

'I thought you might want to be rid of him.'

She looked hard at Joe.

'Why should I?'

'He's old and . . .'

The music ended, which was lucky because Luisa had stopped dancing.

'He's not old,' she said. 'I don't suppose he's much above forty.'

She walked away.

When Joe got home his father was eager for details.

'She's a fine lass. She'll do for you. Danced with her twice, eh? Thaddeus will be pleased. Make a push, there's no point in waiting. When are you seeing her again?'

'I don't know.'

'We'll ask them to tea.'

Joe was horrified at the idea.

'I dare say she'll breed well, not like her wretched mother. She's like Thaddeus's mother was, plenty of spirit. You'll enjoy that, eh?' He dug Joe in the ribs. 'We could do with some decent breeding – and there's money. You could be like a son to Thaddeus, Joe. He likes you, thinks well of you.' He slapped Joe on the back.

Joe wanted to say that he had no intention of marrying Luisa Morgan but he didn't because he doubted anything would come of it. He could not believe it when his father actually asked the Morgans to the house for tea. It was laughable. His father drank nothing but whisky or brandy, and it was this sacrifice which made Joe realise how keen his father was on the idea of a marriage between himself and Luisa. He would have given a great deal not to be there. Jacob found cups and saucers in the cupboard and washed crockery and flicked a duster over the drawing-room furniture. It was a fine day, and once free of dust the furniture did not look too bad, though the paintings on the walls were so dark as to be indecipherable and the rug, which had been thick and red, was faded and patchy. The chairs were threadbare and the occasional tables stood on thin, rickety legs.

Alice Morgan was by nature a gentle person, Joe thought, but even she could not disguise her dismay at the state of the house that had been her friend's home so long ago. Luisa was openly disparaging.

'I didn't realise you were this poor,' she said. 'And you live so far away from everything. Don't you get bored or do you go to university and so aren't here much?'

'I work at the pit,' Joe said. 'I've always worked there.'

'No doubt that accounts for your stimulating conversation.'

Joe's face turned to fire.

'Though I have to say that you are uncommonly good looking. Every girl at the party noticed. You obviously don't take after your father.'

'Would you like to go for a walk?' Joe managed.

Luisa glanced around her.

'There isn't anywhere to walk. You have no garden to speak of and there's nothing to be seen for miles but what you can see from here. How bleak it is. Have you been to Edinburgh?'

Joe shook his head.

'My aunt lives there. I'm to go and visit. George – Mr McAndrew – has promised to show me around. There will be parties and outings and I'm to have new dresses and there'll be the theatre and shopping.'

'It sounds very exciting,' Joe said.

She looked at him for a long time.

'You aren't taken with me at all, are you?' she said bluntly.

'I think you're very beautiful.'

She laughed.

'Haven't you ever wanted to get away?' she said.

'Yes, but I can't.'

Why not?'

'My father, as no doubt you can see, is a drunk. The village depends on the pit and I've always been there. I know all there is to know so I have to be there.' Joe hadn't realised until he said it that it was the truth. She could talk all she liked about shopping and theatres but it wasn't real. Everything that mattered to him was here and, much as he would have loved to cast off the responsibility, he knew in his heart that he couldn't.

Her eyes mocked him.

'How important you are. My father says that if you don't get some help over the next year or so the pit will go under. He has taken a liking to you. Perhaps it's because I'm not a boy. There was a boy but he died in infancy. I don't think my parents have ever forgiven themselves. Let me just tell you this. Nothing in the world would induce me to marry a man as poor as you and with so few prospects.'

'I haven't asked you,' Joe said, stung.

'No, but you were going to, or are you so stupid that you don't realise your father and my father are plotting together? I intend to marry George McAndrew.'

'Why?'

'He can give me the whole world, furs, clothes, jewellery, houses, carriages, travel, and most especially of all I shall get away from this horrible dull place and from all these dull people. George is exciting, he knows everybody and I can win him. Such a prize.'

'I don't think your parents see it like that.'

'The only reason my father won't want me to marry George is because George doesn't need his silly little foundry. George tolerates my father because he wants me. He has no interest in my father's business — it's nothing to him.'

'What does your mother think?'

'I think she wants me to marry better than she did so I don't believe she minds very much, though she considers George much too old. I could hardly do worse than she did, unless of course I married you. Perhaps she's worried that I might want you because you look like an overgrown choirboy.' She laughed.

When they had gone his father retreated to the study and a generous glass of whisky and called Joe to him there.

'Well, what did you think? A beautiful girl, eh, and her father's business into the bargain.'

Joe said nothing. He didn't need to. Thaddeus came often after that to the pit and in time reported that Luisa had gone to stay with Alice's sister in Edinburgh.

CHAPTER FIVE

'Going to work in a shop?'

Her mother made it sound as though she had taken to prostitution, Esther Margaret thought.

'Miss Applegate is very respectable.'

'Miss Applegate is an old maid,' her mother said, 'and you are not going to work for her.'

'My father works in a shop.'

'Your father is the manager of the co-operative society department store and that is different. Young ladies do not work.'

'I want to do something.'

'Then you can come with me and clean the church. It will be good for your soul.'

'I want to do a job, with money.'

'There's plenty to do here. Your father would never permit you to take up work outside the house. It isn't respectable. You wouldn't want to end up like Miss Applegate.'

Her mother told her father when he came home and Esther Margaret was sent to her room supperless — like a child, she thought.

Two Sundays after Easter, Esther Margaret's parents went to visit her Aunt Florrie, who wasn't very well. It would mean, she shyly confided to Dryden, when they met as usual on the Cutting

Bridge, that they would be able to spend a little more time together. He seemed doubtful. It had not occurred to Esther Margaret that she would have to persuade the worst boy in the village that she really did like his kisses. She had not expected him to be open and worried; she had thought he would be devious and sly.

'It isn't a good idea,' he said. Perhaps he was losing interest. 'If anybody saw us . . . What would you say to your dad?'

Esther Margaret was inclined not to care whether or not her father found out. Her parents had no idea that she was unhappy. She could have accused them of lacking imagination. They didn't mind what she did or what her state of mind was; they didn't care that they had seen off Joe and that they had invited into their house a lad she despised. She thought people had got it all wrong about Dryden. It was just that he was lonely. He had not tried to put his hands on her or to do anything he shouldn't have done – nothing but the odd kiss. It seemed to her that what he really wanted was company, but she was entranced by the kisses, lay in bed thinking about them, wanted him to draw her close and . . . but he didn't. She couldn't sleep for thinking about him. She knew it was a sin to think about his body but she couldn't help it, the more she tried to the less it worked. She conjured pictures of him naked and in her arms. It made her blush just to think about it. Her parents not being there for a whole day was too much of an opportunity to miss. Peggy would not notice what she did. They could go for a walk. The days were getting warmer. They could have a picnic by a stream; nobody would see them. They could spend hours together.

Things did not, however, go according to plan. Her parents changed their mind about what time they were leaving and it was a good two hours before they finally went, and after that Peggy was all over the house.

'Are you not off yet, miss?' she said twice as she went past the bedroom door. Esther Margaret had tried to be devious and now was despairing. She had told Dryden she would meet him on the bridge at nine o'clock, and it was now well after eleven. He would have given up and gone home by now. She was meant to be having her Sunday dinner with the Robsons. To her discredit she had lied and told her parents she was going. She would have to think up some excuse for the Robsons later. She was not going to be in the same house with Billy.

Peggy finally went downstairs and did not come back. Esther Margaret stuffed food and drink into a bag and then she heard a noise behind her, and when she turned around Dryden was standing in the doorway. She almost screamed.

'Shh!' he said. 'Sorry. You didn't come.'

Esther Margaret flew to him.

'I was so afraid that you wouldn't have waited.'

'Miss Esther!' Peggy shouted up the stairs. 'I'm away now.'

Peggy had been given the day off since everybody was going out. Esther Margaret went to the head of the stairs and wondered what would have happened if Peggy had left a couple of minutes sooner and had seen Dryden walking into the house or going up the stairs.

'Right,' she said brightly. 'See you tomorrow.'

She listened as the back door slammed and then she went back to Dryden.

'She could've seen you.'

'She didn't,' he said. 'I came in the front and I could hear her singing in the kitchen with the door closed and I knew your parents must have gone by now.'

Esther Margaret realised quite suddenly that it was the first time she had ever been in a bedroom with a man. If you could call him a man – he looked so young and strangely vulnerable, innocent.

'You ready, then?' he said.

'I packed the food.' She went over and opened the basket and Dryden looked hungrily in at the contents.

'Is it apple pie?' he said eagerly.

'We have the whole day.' Suddenly she could hear rain

throwing itself at the window, and when she ran across she could see it was beginning to fall heavily. She couldn't believe it; nothing was going right. He came to her and they stood watching from the bedroom, the whole countryside turning greener as the rain poured down.

'We can't go for a picnic in that,' she said. 'I am so stupid. We don't have to go. We can stay here. They'll be gone all day and Peggy won't be back.'

'What if somebody comes, though?'

'I'll lock the doors.'

She ran downstairs and did so, and then ran back. Dryden was sitting on the bed. They would have to stay upstairs, she thought; people were passing the windows. As she watched he let himself fall back, drop completely into the covers, and it was such an act of abandonment somehow, such a relaxation, that she started to laugh. She went over and sat down beside him and looked at him, and it was as though his eyes drew her. She found herself kissing him with no more encouragement than that, and it was a kiss like never before. She was frustrated because Dryden didn't touch her and didn't make more of it. She broke away and sat up and said, 'This isn't how I thought you were.'

'Oh?'

'I thought you were . . . low and mean and wicked.'

'I am,' Dryden said with a touch of humour. 'Mind you, I did spend twelve years being birched and preached at and starved. You'd think I would be a much better person by now but I don't claim owt. I can recite great pieces of the Bible. Would you like to hear some?'

Esther Margaret said nothing and he laughed and sat up and then he put one arm around her and drew her down on top of him and after that he was everything she had thought he was and she was glad. It made up for what had happened since the first conversation she had held with Joe Forster in the churchyard. Things could have been so civilised, her parents could have reacted differently. Joe cared about her, she knew he did, hadn't she heard it from his own lips? Why could they not have been allowed to see one another? Would it have been so very dreadful? If his father hadn't liked it they could have waited a year or two until Joe was older and could find some sort of business to establish himself in. She would have been proud to be with him, and surely in the end his father would have relented. Did it matter so very much that Joe had a pit and a crumbling country house and she had nothing but respectability? Was it such a difference? They could have found a house, it didn't have to be anything special, and he could have come home to her in the evenings and they might have had a child or two. It hadn't seemed like so much to ask, other people had that and more, but obviously it was, it was as unlikely as that they should gain the moon and the stars.

She no longer cared. Dryden was familiar with women's clothing and his hands were deft and her body went completely out of control as it had been threatening to do since the first time he had kissed her. It seemed so wicked too, that this was happening in her parents' house, in her own bedroom, in a place where nothing but godliness had existed for as long as she could remember. Her parents always did the right thing and they had encouraged her to do likewise, had brought her up to be God-fearing and good. The only good thing about this was how it felt. Dryden's look of innocence was camouflage. It soon became apparent that he had done this before and knew a great deal about it. His body was smooth and brown and to touch it was like a dress her mother had once had – silk. She remembered how when she was a little girl, and her mother could still pick her up, feeling the soft warmth of her mother through the material.

He did to her what Esther Margaret considered extremely disgusting things and she realised why people ought to be married before they did them because it must be very sinful to enjoy anything quite as much as she enjoyed this. Embarrassed, her cheeks burning, wanting to stop him but unable to find the will to do so, Esther Margaret was almost in tears. Nobody had seen her undressed that she ever remembered, and it was daylight. The curtains were open, and the rain lashed itself against the glass, stotted off the pantry roof. She was already regretting every second. She could not understand why nobody had talked to her about this. She didn't know what was happening, just that the feelings in her body outweighed everything else. Nothing mattered. It was a complete downfall. She couldn't help crying.

He kissed her tears and offered to stop but Esther Margaret had forgotten how. She shook her head wordlessly. There were a great many times later when she remembered that he had said did she think that was enough and it was the last chance to say 'no' and she wished, even when she knew it wasn't fair to wish, that he had been as crass as Billy Robson and treated her body like a plaything, but he didn't. He was cautious, careful, asked her if he was hurting her, treated her as if she were glass. It was impossible to blame anybody who behaved so well, and that left her with nobody to blame but herself and her parents, and since they weren't there she belaboured them in her mind for what she did not want to feel responsible about.

It hurt, it was uncomfortable, her body went into shock, her mind couldn't accept what was happening, it was messy and he was more close than anyone had ever been and she was not happy. When it was over he wrapped her up in a blanket and held her near and she listened to the rain beating against the window before she fell asleep.

When she woke up it was the middle of the afternoon and she was hungry. They ate the picnic in bed, giggling, and after that she wanted to be close and this time it was entirely different. She didn't want to get out of bed for the rest of her life, she didn't want to leave him, she didn't ever want her parents to come home, but she knew that they would. Then she was afraid that somebody might see him. It was almost dark when he left. They had to risk it, and even then she clung to him at the outside door. They had agreed to meet at the bridge the following Sunday, and it was an eternity until then.

Her parents came home and she felt like a different person, older, knowledgeable. She had lied and deceived them and sinned and it was very strange to be that new person. They tried talking to her and she tried talking back but it was nothing to do with her and they seemed strange, so much farther away. Her parents had always been everything in the world to her and now Dryden Cameron mattered more. He was the only person who mattered. She loved him. She knew what love was, how it felt. She wanted to run out of the door all the way to Mrs Clancy's boarding house and claim him for her own. Her mother questioned her about dinner with the Robsons, having assumed that she had been, and Esther Margaret could see the shocked look on her face when she confessed that she had not. She lied again, said she didn't feel well, and her mother understood that; sometimes she had pain when she was due to bleed. Thinking no doubt of her father, she did not question her further.

The week went by on slow old legs and it would never be Sunday, Esther Margaret thought. She went dutifully to church though she didn't hear a thing and it lasted for ever and when it was over there was Sunday dinner to get through and she couldn't eat.

'You're not still unwell, are you?' her mother asked her when she was leaving the dining room.

'A little. I think I might go for a walk.'

'I think that's a very good idea,' her mother said. 'Don't be too long.'

Esther Margaret's heart felt like a flag flying in front of her. She tried not to run, she didn't want to draw attention to herself, but her footsteps quickened. He was waiting and she had to force herself not to grab him. They walked, away from the village and into the country, to a certain barn that Dryden seemed to know, and there they spent the afternoon. She realised that she should get back but the more she should the less she wanted to and she was in tears long before she reached her house, so when her mother came into the hall, concerned, she said, 'I'm not a child!' and ran up the stairs.

After a short time her mother followed her, saying softly as she walked in, 'You're not ill, are you?'

'I'm not ill, no.'

'Good, because your father has invited the Robsons around tonight.'

'What?' Esther Margaret glared at her through her tears. 'Doesn't he know that I hate Billy Robson?'

Her mother stared.

'How can you hate him?'

Esther Margaret's throat closed so tightly that she couldn't speak.

'Esther Margaret . . .' Her mother moved closer. 'There is no point in you thinking that you will ever have anything whatsoever to do with Joseph Forster. Your father would not allow it. He has bad blood. You could not be happy with someone like that. Be sensible and the adult you think you are and then you will understand. Billy is one of us. He is very fond of you—'

Esther Margaret began to laugh.

'He's so fond of me he put his hands on me in the hall.'

'How can you say such things?' Her mother faltered. 'You used to be such a truthful girl. I don't understand what happened to you. Billy will do well, he has ambition. He will very likely be manager after your father. Don't you think that would be very nice for all of us?'

Esther Margaret stopped laughing and put her hands to her eyes as the tears fell. And then she faced her mother.

'Do you think nice is all I want? Do you think nice is all I can hope for?'

'I think you must learn not to speak in so intemperate a manner. It's very unbecoming in a young girl.'

Esther Margaret pictured herself in a pile of hay, almost naked, being pleasured by a young man her parents allied with the Devil. It took all her restraint not to laugh again. Her mother was brisk.

'Wash your face and comb your hair and then come downstairs. Billy and his parents will be here soon. I won't have any more of this nonsense,' she said.

Esther Margaret went to the window. She wondered what Dryden was doing. She knew that he went back to Mrs Clancy's for something to eat and then he went to the pub. He didn't have any friends. Was it more lonely for him or was this worse?

Dryden stood in his usual place in the Golden Lion. Nobody bothered him. They were used to seeing him there. Nobody spoke except the landlord; quite often he would talk to Dryden if he was not too busy. It was just general chat but Dryden was glad of it. Otherwise there was nothing else to do but go back to his room and watch the darkness for a long time before going to sleep. He wondered whether Tom would come. They were very often on the same shifts so when he went to the pub Tom was almost always there with his friends, Ed and Wes and others. Wes hadn't knocked him about again since the time Tom had stopped him. In his mind Dryden had created a whole volume of books about Tom, about the childhood they had not had together and all the days since, when Tom was not his friend or his brother. If he thought hard enough he could see them, the world that he had made up, created for himself when Alf and Mary Cameron were his parents and he had lived with them in the house in Prince Row which looked over the pit where they worked. He had a vision in his mind, he knew it wasn't true but it was there, of Tom on his father's shoulders being carried high along the row, and then he imagined himself there and Tom running beside Alf, and Mary waiting at home with a fire and the tea ready and the doors to shut the darkness out.

Most precious of all was the reality of that day in the pub, that one golden magical Sunday dinner-time when Tom had put himself between Dryden and Wes, and even though Dryden had attempted to convince himself a hundred times that Tom must have had some motive other than protection he could not see it. He did not need to protect Wes. Dryden would not have hit Wes in a thousand years, not with all his friends there. He would lie in his bed late at night and remember Tom Cameron's back; it was the most sacred thing in his life. He was there for ever between the pub wall and his brother's back and he was safe. It was the first time that he had felt safe in his life, and it was the warmest feeling that he had ever had. He never felt like that about a woman – he just screwed them and despised them for letting him because they liked the look of him – but the way he felt about Tom was the nearest he had ever got to love. He loved Tom so much that just being in the same room in the pub was enough to create a warm glow of happiness. He listened for Tom's voice constantly, was disappointed when Tom was not there, could sit for hours while Tom and his cronies talked. Tom's voice was the nearest thing to heaven.

Tom came in. Dryden knew it was him even without moving his eyes. Tom's footsteps, his way of walking into the pub, were different from anybody else's. He paused at the door, looking around to see if any of his friends were there, and then he strode across the room with a kind of swaggering confidence that Dryden would have done anything to be able to emulate, and then came up to the bar, sometimes very close. He didn't ever speak and Dryden didn't ever look up but he could feel the space between them, the air, as though it held something extra.

'Wes been in?'

'Nah,' the landlord said. 'Think he's gone down with summat.'

'What, like?'

'Don't know.'

The landlord gave Tom his first drink without being asked, and while Tom downed it he poured another. Dryden watched. Tom took the second and then turned around with his back to the bar and complained mildly as he looked around, 'There's nebody in, Fred, man.'

'Aye, I'm sorry like,' the landlord said with fine sarcasm.

Tom grinned. Then he turned to Dryden.

'What are you looking at?' he said flatly.

Dryden moved back into the corner, into the shadows.

'I'm speaking to you!'

'Nothing.'

'Don't start on him, Tom,' the landlord said tiredly.

'Miserable snivelling little bastard!' Tom jeered.

The landlord looked at Dryden.

'Drink your drink and get out,' he said.

Dryden had almost reached the door when somebody stuck a foot out and he went sprawling across the floor.

'Get up,' Tom said, and Dryden could feel the injustice of it hit his brain. He got carefully to his feet, and when Tom came over Dryden turned around and floored him. He made a good job of it too; it took three punches, Tom was so big, but he managed it, as if all the strength in him had gone into his hands. Tom lay there for a few moments as though he couldn't believe it and then he got slowly to his feet, watching. Dryden couldn't breathe. And then suddenly Tom began to laugh. Dryden couldn't believe it. He would have gone but Tom put a hand on his shoulder and stopped him.

'Howay man,' he said. 'I'll buy you a drink.'

There is a theory that each man has a single perfect moment in his life and that when he dies that moment goes on for all eternity, and when Tom Cameron put his hand on his half-brother's shoulder Dryden's life was changed for ever. Nobody had ever touched him like that. The only time Mr Harmer had touched him was to punish him. The only women Dryden had known were those who wanted something from him. Beyond that there was nothing. This was the first time that anybody had touched him in affection. He was entranced. It got better. Tom put that arm around him and walked him back to the bar and they stayed there, talking and drinking, and it was perfection.

By three o'clock they had drunk so much that Dryden had lost count, and Tom was insisting on Dryden going home with him for dinner. This seemed like a good idea. They hadn't far to go, just up the bank and across the road and through the passage, coming out into Tom's yard at the end of it. A good smell was coming out of Tom's house, the door was open, the fire was burning brightly, and the dinner, like a miracle, was upon the table.

It seemed to Dryden that Vinia was a different person. She was a lot skinnier for one thing, which didn't suit her. She had been a bonny lass and wasn't any longer. Her face was white and pinched and her eyes were guarded. She didn't say anything. It was just as if Dryden came every Sunday for dinner, whereas in fact it was the first time he had been invited anywhere. It was such a contrast to the Sundays he remembered the last time he had been in anybody's house, when he was twelve. Sundays had been filled with church, twice, Sunday school, once, bible-reading in between and food that was only memorable for being scant and badly cooked. In the summer the house was hot and musty and in winter it was freezing. He had never seen a house like Tom's with a huge fire and platefuls of good food, and in spite of the fact that he was there it made him feel more left out than ever for all those years of nothing better than Mrs Clancy's boarding house. Surely he deserved better than that.

Dryden had not experienced a woman like Vinia, who ran about after them, refilling plates and topping up beer. After he had been there for an hour, and Tom had finished his meal and lain down upon the settee and gone to sleep, Dryden's greatest fear in life was that he would not be asked back. Vinia went in and out of the pantry, clearing up and washing up. She didn't look at him or speak to him and Dryden felt that he ought to go. He didn't know what to say to her. The only woman in a house he had had anything to do with was Mrs Harmer, who quoted the Bible a lot and made him eat burned porridge. Vinia was another world to him. He made himself go to the pantry door. It was fairly dark in there, nothing but a tiny window and a flagged floor and the sink and her. She wore a neat black dress. There was something about her. Dryden didn't know what it was, something he almost remembered, and then she turned around, frowning, and he didn't know what to say. She was not pretty like Esther Margaret nor horrible in a birdlike, beaky way as Mrs Harmer had been. She was neat, the opposite of Mrs Clancy, no spilled food down her front. The black dress had a little white collar and her hair was pulled back without a single curl, each strand perfectly held.

'Did you want something else?' she said.

'No, I . . . thank you very much.'

She looked surprised.

'It was only a dinner,' she said.

'It was wonderful. It was very kind of you. Thank you.'

He thought she might have given him a smile but she didn't and there was nothing else to be said, so Dryden left Tom snoring on the settee and went out into the afternoon.

He could not bring to mind anything about the evening that followed other than Tom's presence. It was frustrating in a way, because all he ended up with was a rosy glow in his mind. He couldn't remember what the conversation had been or what the beer had tasted like or even what Tom's face looked like. The good part was that he didn't have to remember it because Tom talked to him at work the next day and they went drinking together the next evening and the one after that and the one after that.

Other people began to talk to him in the pub and at work. Dryden had never felt happiness before and it was a surprise to him. He didn't take it for granted. Each day he woke up and told himself that it might be the last day that Tom would ever speak to him, but the days went on, they ran one into another. Even Wes talked to him. Ed and Tom played him at dominoes and the world was quite suddenly a wonderful place.

'Eh, lad, I think your face has cracked,' Mrs Clancy teased him.

Sundays were the best. Sundays had once been a day to be dreaded because there was nothing to do but hang about and wait for Monday, but Sundays had turned into the kind of day that made you smile the minute you woke up. He would have a late breakfast and then sleep until the pubs opened and then he would meet Tom and the others on the doorstep. They would drink until halfway through the afternoon and then go back to have some dinner and a sleep and then they would get together in the evenings and drink until late if they were on the late shift.

The following Sunday afternoon he went back to Mrs Clancy's for his lie-down and he had just taken his boots and his jacket off when there was a knocking on the door. When he opened it there stood Esther Margaret.

Dryden didn't know what to say. Had she no more sense than to come to him here? People would see her. Mrs Clancy would make sure it was all over the village by tomorrow. She didn't look pleased.

'You were supposed to meet me.'

'Was I?' Dryden couldn't remember.

'At the Cutting Bridge. I waited. I waited all last Sunday afternoon and I waited all this afternoon.'

Dryden drew her into the landing. He didn't want her there and he didn't want her standing in the landing and neither did he want Ma coming up the stairs telling him how as she didn't like females in her establishment, it only caused trouble. Dryden didn't doubt she was right, if Esther Margaret's sour face was anything to go by.

'I'm sorry. I forgot.'

'Forgot?' She stared on him. 'How could you forget?'

'I just did.'

'You've been drinking.'

'Aye, I've been to the pub with Tom.' How proud he was to say that. 'And then I went to his house for my dinner.' That was another milestone. 'Look, you mustn't come here. Folk will know.'

'Then where?'

'I don't know right now.' Dryden was tired. He wanted to sleep before spending the evening with his friends.

She started to cry. Dryden hated this bit, when they cried. Women were like that, they couldn't accept that you'd had enough, that you were tired of them. She was so serious.

'You're going to have to go.'

She cried harder. She clung. She kissed him.

'Look, it was nice, all right.'

'No. No. Please.'

He rather liked the way she begged but he pushed her gently along the landing and walked her down the stairs. He could still hear her crying even when he had put her outside and closed the door. He took off most of his clothes and lay down on the bed and was very soon fast asleep.

CHAPTER SIX

Esther Margaret went to Vinia's house when she began to feel unwell and to think that something was the matter. She had nobody else to talk to and she felt that Vinia was the one person who would understand. She had cried a great deal in the weeks after Dryden had stopped seeing her. Pride prevented her from going to him again. She was surprised that her parents noticed nothing, that she couldn't eat, that she was tired, that she took no pleasure in anything and finally that she was sick, more tired, stopped bleeding, started worrying. She walked the streets with her head down so that nobody would notice her, and then she dived down the passage and into the yard. The door of the little house was standing open as usual and from there she could see the big fire which burned at the far side of the room even in good weather because it was used for all the hot water and cooking. She knocked and Vinia came to the door. Esther Margaret was shocked. She had not seen Vinia for some time, since she had become absorbed with Dryden and then with her misery. Vinia had lost a lot of weight. The dress she wore was big on her.

The little house was very clean even by village standards. The brasses shone, the fire surround was bright. It occurred to Esther Margaret that Tom Cameron might be at home.

'When the pubs are open?' Vinia said with a tight smile, and she urged Esther Margaret to sit down and to pour out her tale.

She listened with whitening cheeks and a dismayed face. Esther Margaret stumbled on about how she had been prevented from seeing Joe and how they had tried to make her see Billy and . . . The farther she went into the story the more stupid she sounded.

'I'm so unhappy and so ill. There's something wrong with me.'

Vinia didn't respond straight away; she sat for several moments before she said, 'Esther Margaret, you aren't ill, you're having a baby. Did you give yourself to Mr Forster?'

'No. No, of course I didn't. I wouldn't do such a thing.'

'Billy, then?'

'No!'

Fallen women in the Bible and suchlike had illegitimate babies and wicked girls from bad backgrounds and those whose parents did not forgive them. She remembered seeing a picture of a painting where a girl in London had been cast out and was sheltering under a bridge in the winter weather.

It was not possible, it could not happen. She could not have gone from good to evil in a few short months. With her parents and her home and her church to support her she could not have let them or herself down. She sometimes thought that Dryden was a figment of her imagination – he had disappeared as completely from her life as though he did not exist. She did not even see him on the street any more, and she had made herself tired looking for him during the first few weeks after he told her that he did not want her any more. She could not believe that she had behaved so badly, so irresponsibly as to bring something like this down on herself.

'Who did you go with?'

Esther Margaret told her.

'You went with Dryden Cameron?' Vinia said, and Esther Margaret understood why she said it like that.

She got up.

'Why?' Vinia said.

'I can't remember.'

'Did he make you do it?'

That offered an escape route, a solution; people would believe that he had. The trouble was that it had been the very opposite. If she had even for a second been doubtful he would not have done it, not out of any regard for himself or her but just because he was so very handsome and there were plenty of women who would bed with a good-looking boy. He did not have to take on an innocent girl, and she did not in honesty believe that he was so bad that he wanted to deflower a virgin. She had not for a second believed it of him. She knew now that Dryden only did it because he had nothing better to do on Sundays, and when he had found something better to do he had gone and done it, without dishonesty, without consideration. He was thoughtless, careless, but the one thing that he was not was what his father had been.

She shook her head.

'What am I to do?'

'There are only certain things you can do. First you have to tell your parents—'

'I can't!'

'And then you have to tell him.'

'Why do I have to do that?'

Vinia looked at her as if she were an idiot.

'Because the only respectable thing left is for you to be married to him.'

'I don't want to marry him!'

'If you can persuade him to do it you'll be lucky. I doubt he had marriage with anybody in mind.'

'I can't marry him of all people.' In her earnestness she sat down next to Vinia and took her hand.

'There are alternatives,' Vinia said. 'You could be sent away to have the baby and then give it up, but everybody would find out and although you could come back here nobody would have you.'

'Give it up? I couldn't do that.'

'You could blame another lad, somebody you like.'

Esther Margaret gazed into the fire.

'But everybody would know when the child was born that it was his, wouldn't they? I mean he isn't ordinary looking.'

'I think the best thing is to tell your mam and dad.'

Esther Margaret found a certain bitter satisfaction in telling them. They were sitting in the tiny garden which meant so much to them. Her mother was sewing beneath the lilac tree and her father was reading a book on the small square lawn.

She almost didn't tell them. She nearly went inside. Her mother looked up as she came into the garden.

'Where have you been?'

'I went to see Vinia.'

'Esther Margaret, you really must learn to choose your company better. Tom Cameron is a pitman who drinks and they live in a back street. Go and tidy yourself up. You and I are to be at Mrs Robson's sewing circle later, or had you forgotten?'

'I'm having a baby,' Esther Margaret said, and her whole body shuddered with the horror and relief of having told them.

They didn't believe her at first; the shock stopped them from doing so. Her mother got up and tried to go to her and then sat down again and her father tried to get her to tell him more but after Vinia's reaction she felt that she could not announce the name of the worst boy in the village. Her tongue wouldn't make its way around that.

Somehow, before she had told them, it had seemed unreal. Now the nightmare was following her into reality. She cried and stuttered incoherent sentences and her mother insisted on going into the house for fear that the neighbours might notice something.

'I think you must have got this quite wrong,' her mother announced when they were safely in the sitting room. To Esther Margaret the house had not been safe since Dryden Cameron had been there upstairs in her bedroom, doing to her what men did to women. It had been an invasion of the most basic kind. There was no use her mother trying to put up barricades now. The enemy had been and gone and there was nothing to be saved.

'Boys . . . some boy kissing you . . .' Her mother stopped again and glanced across the room at her father, who looked away in embarrassment. 'You know nothing of such things. Has Billy tried to kiss you? Is that it? He is naughty upon occasion, I know, but if it's that then there is nothing for you to worry about. It's natural but it isn't really wrong.'

Esther Margaret wanted to laugh but was afraid that if she did so she might never be able to stop. Was this really how they saw her, as a child so ignorant and dependent? Was this how parents saw their daughters, as some kind of attachment to them, not separate with a mind or body which might want something else? Had they never considered that she might choose to live some other way? Not that she had chosen this. The whole idea of bearing Dryden Cameron's child made her shudder with horror and disbelief.

'I went with a man. Billy Robson is not a man,' she said.

It was early in the evening when Joe saw Esther Margaret's father arrive at their house. It seemed most unusual. If it was business he would come to the pit, surely. What else could it possibly be? It was the kind of summer evening that made you want to go out walking, to admire what the countryside looked like. Even the fell looked good, though he preferred August when the bell-heather was out and it was nothing but a purple sea, but this evening the sky was clear and cloudless and he had come back from work feeling better than usual. It was only a short while before he heard his father's voice bellowing his name from the hall, so he left his room and walked downstairs and as he did so he saw the inside of the house with Mr Hunter's eyes and was ashamed. The evening sun fell on the surfaces, showing up the dust and the shabbiness of the furnishings more than ever.

His father had gone back into the room. Joe followed him. Randolph Forster was very often angry. Joe had learned not to care, but the expression on his father's face made him pause as he walked into the room. Joe was used to being blamed for things. At work his father blamed him for everything that went wrong and the pitmen, afraid of his father, complained to him and he would have to try to approach his father with the problem. Randolph looked carefully at him.

'So,' he said softly, 'not content with denying a lovely girl from your own social level you went and ploughed the shop-keeper's daughter.'

Joe stared first at his father and then at Mr Hunter. He was about to deny it and then changed his mind. His father's gaze was unfocused and drunken as always, but the look Mr Hunter gave him was severe, unforgiving, accusing and shocked. Mr Hunter looked like somebody who had shrunk — old, unhappy and wizened. Joe couldn't remember him having looked like that before. If they were accusing him of having seduced Esther Margaret then she must be pregnant, otherwise there could be no evidence. He thought of her when they had last met, how scornful she had been of his wanting to run away, how good and dutiful. She couldn't have done such a thing in a thousand years.

'Tell us that you didn't,' his father urged him. 'Make us laugh! Don't think about Luisa Morgan and her beauty and her father's money and her social appeal. Don't give a thought to all those miners you say are important to you, not so important of course that you would marry to help them or us. We don't mind the disgrace and the inevitable squalling brat!'

Joe had stopped listening. He tried to imagine Esther Margaret having a child, having encouraged anybody when she was so proud, so pious. What had driven her to do such a thing? Why and who? Joe couldn't think. He was sure that it wasn't true, that something awful had happened, that somebody had forced Esther Margaret. He was angry too that Mr Hunter and his father thought he was the kind of person who would sneak away and seduce the girl he loved. They could not recognise the good qualities of an honest person, they could not tell the difference between good and evil. And he wanted to question Mr Hunter, to find out what awful thing had befallen his daughter. In the meanwhile, if she had said that it was his there would be a good reason, and while he did not want anyone to think he might have done such a thing he tried to think of circumstances that would make him admit to it. It was also one way of getting her to marry him. But with another man's child in her?

'Has she said it was me?' If she had then there was no help for it. All his denials would go unheard and he would be obliged to marry her. If she had said so then it was because something dreadful had happened and she needed him to lie for her, to accept her in deceit, to believe that there was no other way.

'She has said nothing but it could be nobody else. She knows no one, she goes nowhere. The young man we wanted for her she would have nothing to do with. Are you denying it?'

'Talk to her,' Joe said, and he walked out with his father's insults raging in his ears. He could still hear them when he got upstairs to his room, but after he shut the heavy door the noise was almost drowned out. He turned the key in the lock just in case his father was energetic enough to come up the stairs and rage further. The door was stout, it had kept his father out a good many times before. It wouldn't fail him.

Her mother sat doing nothing and crying afresh from time to time. She kept out of the way, as though she knew the sight of her was too much for them. Her father had gone out. When he came home in the late evening he called her into the sitting room and demanded that she should tell him who the boy was.

'It was . . . it was somebody I didn't know, somebody I'd never met before—'

'Esther Margaret, it isn't any use to lie.' She hated the patient note in his voice. 'We know who it was.'

'You know?' She thought back. Maybe somebody had seen her with Dryden, walking in the country, coming in or out of the barn, standing talking on the Cutting Bridge or even when he had left the house the first time they had been together. It had been such a precious memory; now it seemed so tawdry. 'How could you know?'

'I went to see his father.'

Esther Margaret wanted to laugh; at least the part of her that wasn't ready to cry or scream did.

'We did everything we could to keep you away from him because he comes from bad stock. People think just because they have possessions, just because they have power over other people, that they can take what they like, do what they want. We tried to save you from yourself. He has bad blood in him, no good will come of it, but now we must make him marry you. You'll have to go there and live with them, we wish you well of it, we won't be coming to visit. You have made your bed, in spite of all our efforts to guide you, and so you must lie on it.'

And then she realised. They thought Joe had done it, sweet, lovely Joe who was the most honourable person she knew.

'You went to see Mr Forster?'

'I did, yes.'

'And what did he say?'

'Nothing. Not much. He didn't deny it.'

Esther Margaret felt her insides twist. If only she had agreed to go away with Joe. If only she had had more sense then, she could have been free, she could have had for herself the nicest man in the area, perhaps in the whole world, who hadn't even the sense to deny that she was carrying his child, who cared so much for her that he was prepared to do anything to help. She wished she could have said that it was Joe's. She almost thought that despite what she had done Joe would take her, marry her, that she could have her wish come true, she could wind back the days. She saw that he was not weak, that he was strong enough to support the mistakes she had made. If she chose, if she was weak enough to involve him, Joe would save her. And she was only glad that she cared too much about him to do that to him, that her better side would not let her accuse him because all she had to do was say it was him and there would be nobody to stop it. Joe had put that power into her hands, given himself like some awful ancient sacrifice. For people who did not know better he was ready to burn. Joe cared nothing for his existence and she had been stupid enough to turn him down.

'It wasn't Joe.'

Her father shook his head and looked sorrowfully down at the floor.

'You can't shield him. He must answer for what he did and you must marry him. It's your own fault.'

'It wasn't Joe.'

Her mother turned a tear-stained face towards her.

'Who taught you to lie? Who taught you to deceive us and in such a way? We tried to bring you up respectably. We are . . . we are important people in this village. How will we hold up our heads? His mother was a slut who ran off and his father is a drunkard who is ruining the village. Could you choose anybody worse? You did this to spite us when we did everything we could for you. We found a nice young man for you—'

'I went with Dryden Cameron,' Esther Margaret said clearly.

It shut her mother up, that was the first good thing about it, and then their faces showed disbelief.

'He came to the house the day that you went to visit Aunt Florrie. We spent all day upstairs in my bedroom and the Sunday after in an old barn just above Bridge In.'

Her mother sobbed, broke down, would not have it, said over and over that it was not true, that Esther Margaret was just saying such things to hurt her feelings, and her father said that it was no use her trying to protect Joe Forster by making wild accusations, that she was being ridiculous; had she lost her mind?

'It was nothing to do with Joe. You can't make him marry me for something he didn't do. I went with Dryden Cameron and he didn't force me, so don't think it. I wanted to.'

'You couldn't do such a thing,' her mother managed. 'You are a wicked girl to cause us such pain. You couldn't have, not with him.'

There was a look on their faces that she would remember all her life. The best they could contrive was to make the most hated young man in the village their son-in-law. They would have no choice if she continued to deny that the baby was Joe's and insist it was Dryden's. They could not send her away against her will, though the idea of being married to Dryden was enough to make anybody go cold. She had no choice.

CHAPTER SEVEN

Vinia had taken to going to bed before Tom came in drunk at night, but this time he was early and she was not undressed before he came upstairs. She had learned to gauge how drunk he was. She preferred it when he was so drunk that he couldn't manage the steep stairs because then he would have to sleep on the settee, but very often he would make the stairs and be just sober enough to undress before he fell into bed. She had no objection to that either. It was preferable to being pawed before sleep. It was obvious to her, however, that Tom was not drunk, because he asked her who had been there. He didn't tell her how he knew somebody had been there. All he said was, 'Has my mam been round?'

'Esther Margaret called in.'

'What did she want?'

It was no good putting him off.

'She's in bother.'

Tom paused in undoing the buttons on his shirt.

'What, real bother?' He stared for a moment longer and then started to laugh. 'Never in this world!' he said. 'That prissy little cow? What brave lad got inside her knickers, then?'

It was with a certain bitter satisfaction that she told him.

'Dryden.'

Tom didn't react at all as she had thought he would. The laughter died.

'How do you know?' he said flatly.

'She told me.'

'She could be lying.'

'What would be the point of that? What girl would claim Dryden as the father if she could claim anybody else?'

'The bloody stupid little sod!' Tom said, and wrenched his shirt off. He stood for several minutes calling Dryden every name he could think of, and then neither of them said anything more until they got into bed and lay there, thinking about it.

'He'll have to marry her,' Vinia said.

'Aye, I suppose he will. There are worse reasons. We don't seem to be able to do it.' And he blew out the candle and turned his back on her.

Esther Margaret could not imagine what Dryden would say. She was sure that he would refuse to marry her, that he would not have anything to do with her, and she lay in bed at night and shivered thinking of what would happen then. To be an unmarried mother was unthinkable. She had already decided that she would not give the baby up. She would never give it up, not for any reason on earth, and if that was so then she could not stay here. She imagined wildly that she would go to her mother's distant cousin, who was the only relative who lived away, in some remote little fishing village in Northumberland, and she would . . . she would do what? She couldn't think. Her days were filled with being sick and feeling ill and her nights were full of dread and terror.

She wanted to see Dryden before her father got round to it, but he was difficult to catch at home; his shifts varied and she was unused to such things, and on Sundays he was only to be found in the pub, or so Mrs Clancy said. Mrs Clancy thought she was pursuing Dryden for romantic reasons and was inclined to laugh about it. Esther Margaret had to press her to find out when he was at home and Mrs Clancy was either not truthful or was disinclined to answer her questions. She wanted to tell Dryden before her father reached him so that if he was going to be cowardly about it she would know straight away. She finally caught up with him on the street early one Saturday evening.

'I'm going to the pub,' he said, trying to brush her aside.

'This won't take long,' she said, hurrying after him. 'Dryden, please. It's . . . it's important.'

He stopped.

'Look,' he said, and he found her face, glanced away, and then looked more determinedly at her. 'You're a lovely lass, Esther Margaret, but I don't care for nobody that way. I'm sorry if you think I did it wrong. It wasn't meant to hurt you.'

Esther Margaret grabbed his sleeve as he began to set off again. Dryden waited.

'I'm expecting,' she said. She hadn't meant to blurt it out like that, but really there was no good way to tell somebody something like that, especially when he had just confessed to you that he didn't love you or want you. Dryden stared.

'Give over,' he said, and started to walk away. She ran after him.

'Please, Dryden, listen.'

'I don't have to listen. You can't be. We hardly did it. I've been with lasses dozens of times and it's never happened. You're daft, you are. You go to church too much.'

'Please, Dryden.' She clutched at his coat pocket.

'How do you know?' he said.

'I am.'

'You've been with another lad? You went with Billy Robson?'

'No. No.' Her fingers clutched hard at the material of his coat.

'You're just saying it.'

'Why would I?'

Dryden turned away as best he could given that she had both hands fastened in the front of his coat. People were looking, some of them slowing down, watching and listening, two things he was trying not to do. Esther Margaret thought it must be somebody else beseeching Dryden Cameron to believe she was carrying his child. It could not possibly be the so respectable Esther Margaret Hunter, who was too high and mighty to work, who could have run away with the pit-owner's son or married her father's assistant manager, who went to church every Sunday and said her prayers night and morning and embroidered tray cloths with her mother in the sitting room. It could not be her standing in the main street crying over a lad like Dryden Cameron, who got drunk and went with low women and had no home.

'Please, Dryden.'

'Let go of me.' Dryden unlatched her fingers from the material of his coat and walked on. Esther Margaret couldn't move. She stood, watching him move away, and the tears ran down her face.

She went back to her house. Her mother must have been listening for her because when Esther Margaret had gone up to her room she followed her.

'You can't marry a lad like that,' she said. 'We'd never be able to hold up our heads in this village again. You must go to the mother-and-baby home in Newcastle. You could have the baby and we would find a home for it and then you could come back—'

'And you think nobody would know?'

'Nobody would know for certain.'

'My baby.'

'His baby. You have forgotten what he is, Esther Margaret, what his father did. I believe, though you have not said so, that he forced you. You have only to say he did and it will be his shame not ours.'

'They would kill him,' Esther Margaret said softly.

'He's evil.'

'And then I would have to live unmarried, bringing up a child here, and know nothing else ever but the knowledge that I had killed its father.'

'He deserves to die.'

'No. I told you. He didn't force me. I wanted him.'

Her mother blushed beetroot.

'You couldn't,' she said, and put a hand up to her throat.

'Why couldn't I? Just because you wanted me to like another lad, a lad who I think is awful, who molested me. Dryden didn't do any of that and he was second best. You know he was. You knew I cared for Joe but I couldn't have him.'

'You can't marry Dryden Cameron,' her mother said, beginning to cry.

'I can't marry anybody else.'

Tom was waiting for Dryden in the pub. They were both early and Tom seemed keen to leave and go somewhere else, to a pub they didn't normally go to where none of their friends would be, the Station Hotel in the main street. He sat Dryden down at a table well away from everybody else and got the beer in and then looked seriously at him.

'You've got a problem,' he said.

'Who, me?'

'Don't pretend, Dryden. Esther Margaret Hunter.'

Dryden didn't want to look at him, and he didn't want his beer either.

'You're going to have to marry her.'

Dryden glared at him.

'No, I'm not.'

'You're going to go there and offer.'

'What would I want to do that for?'

'Because if she says that you did to her what your father did to my mother you'll end up dead in a back street. Nobody likes you. People will say that you did it — all she has to do is give people the idea that it happened.'

'Do you think I did that?'

'You only have two choices. Either you marry her or you end up dead.'

'I don't want to marry her. I don't even like her. It was just
. . . something to do on Sunday afternoons, that's all. She's
serious and . . . churchy and . . . You don't really think I
would—'

'Other people would be glad to think it. Go over there and
offer before Mr Hunter starts telling people or before he comes
to you.'

'You want me to go there and be nice to Mr Hunter?'

'Aye,' Tom said with a smile. 'Had any practice, have you?
And then you go to the pit and talk to Joe Forster about a house.'

'A house?'

'You'll need somewhere to live.'

In the end Dryden went to Esther Margaret's house, but it
wasn't because of her or the baby; it was because of Tom. He
couldn't bear the idea of losing Tom so soon after finding him,
and if he ran away, which was his only alternative, he would. He
walked slowly up to Oaks Row and banged on the door in the
middle of the evening, and when Mr Hunter himself answered it
Dryden followed him into the sitting room. Dryden hadn't been
in a sitting room since he left the Harmers. His memories of it,
the tiny fire that always burned there, the brown walls, being
made to sit in the musty silence on sunny days while other boys
went building dams in the beck in the valley and ran through the
fields in game, it all came back to Dryden with a vengeance, and
although this room was comfortable there were Bibles and prayer
books and other religious books in the little wooden glass
bookcase against the far wall. Mrs Hunter was there but Esther
Margaret wasn't. Mrs Hunter stared at him with harsh eyes and
Dryden felt, as he always felt with women her age, that deep
sense of hate.

'I came to your lodgings earlier but you weren't there,' Mr
Hunter said.

'Our Tom took me to the pub. I've had Esther Margaret to
see me. She says she's expecting—'

Mrs Hunter fairly flew out of her chair and tried to hit

Dryden. He couldn't hate her any more than he did, and he couldn't possibly hit her back, so he just held her off carefully and waited for Mr Hunter to stop her, and when he did Dryden put up with the things she called him. They were nothing people hadn't said to him before so he didn't take much notice of it when she said he had come from hell to torment people, that he was the Devil's spawn. Esther Margaret came softly into the room and she also was surprised to see him, he could tell, but not as displeased as they had been. It took Dryden everything he had, and the constant nagging in his mind of what Tom had said, in order to ask her to marry him. He didn't want her, he didn't like her, he couldn't imagine how awful being married would be. He blamed her for getting him into such a mess, no other lass had done so, but Tom was right, there was no alternative.

'Esther Margaret, look . . .' He wondered if he could ask to see her on her own and then thought it was unlikely; they were going to make him do it here and now. 'We should get married. I'm willing if you are.'

Mrs Hunter screamed and cried and Mr Hunter didn't look at him.

'I don't know,' Esther Margaret said.

Dryen was not prepared for this; he had assumed she would say yes immediately. He knew as well that Tom was right. If they didn't get married, no matter what the reason might be, he would end up knifed. Being married to her could not be worse than that, he told himself.

'Esther Margaret, you're going to marry him,' her father said, 'for all our sakes.'

'She can't,' her mother wept, 'not him.'

Dryden went to the pit office the next morning and got in to see Joe Forster. They had known one another all their lives but had rarely spoken. Joe had of late spent a lot of time down the pit seeing to things, as he called it. The deputies and the men

resented him there, but Dryden thought that things had improved since Joe had been more involved and his father less so,
though the older men said nothing good would come until some
money was put into things, and Joe had no money. A rumour had
gone round some time since that Joe was to marry a rich lass and
the pit would prosper and they would go back on to full time,
but he wouldn't do it. Joe, Dryden thought, looking carefully at
his employer's son that hot summer morning, was not the sort to
be shoved into anything.

There was nobody else there. It was his dad's office, not the
main one. Joe used to work in the main office with the clerks and
everybody, but now that his dad didn't come much he had moved
into the little office. Dryden was glad of it, considering the
embarrassing subject of his visit. He was glad also that Mr
Forster wasn't there; he was the kind of man who swore at you. If
anybody did anything wrong in the old days Mr Forster used to
knock them down. A lot of people had left and gone to the
brickworks or the ironworks or to other pits, but times were
more difficult now, there was less work about, so you couldn't
afford to leave if you had a family, and he was about to have a
family. It was not a pleasant thought.

Joe closed the office door. Dryden liked that too. He
couldn't think where Joe had got his manners from. He had
no mother and his father had none and it was hardly likely that
Jacob Smith could teach anybody owt. He was a dirty old
bugger.

'So, what can we do for you?' Joe said.

Dryden liked that too. Joe treated everybody alike – it didn't
matter that the rest of the village thought you were muck. All Joe
cared about was how you did your work. You were looked after
fairly even though things weren't going well. Dryden didn't
know how to put it.

'I just wondered, like, Mr Forster, if you had a house free?'

'A house?'

'Aye.'

Joe stared. He stared for such a long time that Dryden was inclined to think Joe's manners had completely left him.

'Are you getting married?' he said, and his voice was sort of hard and flat and his eyes took on a look that would have made Dryden back off if he had been the backing-off kind of person. It wasn't polite to ask questions; it was an unwritten rule between the pit-owner and the men that you didn't ask anybody owt that wasn't to do with work.

'Aye,' Dryden said.

'And who's the lucky lady?'

Dryden wondered whether Joe would sack him if he didn't answer the question. It would look like cheek. He didn't think Joe was like that but he couldn't afford to take the risk.

'Esther Margaret Hunter,' he said softly.

Joe looked at him as if he were filth. Dryden was used to it, expected it, but it didn't make it any easier because Joe wasn't given to judging people. The quiet after that went on and on, but Dryden wasn't going to break it because he had the feeling that if he did Joe would break him somehow or other. He just stood there and waited, making himself not shift around like he was inclined to. He wanted to tell Joe that he didn't want to marry her, hadn't intended getting her into trouble, it had happened like that. It was not as if he had had to persuade her into it, talk to her nice and slow and gentle. Esther Margaret had been easy, that was the truth of it. He didn't know why, just that something had been wrong to begin with and it had carried on from there. He lowered his eyes and stood and waited until the quiet was like a great big river between them.

'What if I don't have a house?' Joe said.

Dryden knew the name of this game, had had it played against him since he was a child. He looked up and Joe's eyes were full of contempt.

'Have you got one?'

'I don't know. Maybe I do and maybe I don't.'

'You could look,' Dryden said.

Joe glanced at the door and then he shouted, 'Riley! Bring me the housing book.'

He could hear rustling outside while the clerk found the appropriate book and then he came into the office and went back out again and Joe spent a long time perusing the book and then he gave a little smile.

'You're lucky,' he said, 'I have got a house. Mr Price's house in Prince Row. He died a couple of weeks ago and his son's moved out.'

Dryden knew the house, it was two doors down from where Alf and Mary Cameron lived.

'I can't go and live there,' he said. 'Have you got another house, Mr Forster? Anywhere else would do.'

Joe closed the book.

'No,' he said.

The bridegroom was drunk at the wedding. Vinia was disgusted but not very surprised. Tom practically had to carry Dryden into the church and let him lean all over him during the short service. There were just the four of them; even Esther Margaret's mother and father weren't there. Vinia was convinced that the last time Dryden had been in a church was before he left the Harmers'. Esther Margaret's face was marked with dried tears, her eyes huge and disbelieving. Tom was inclined to think it funny. Tom's parents didn't think it very funny that Dryden and Esther Margaret would be living two doors away. Mary had complained loudly.

'You could have had that house. It's a much better house than the one you have, it has two rooms downstairs. Do you think I want that lad living near us after what he's done?'

If Dryden had been the kind of lad you felt sorry for Vinia would have felt sorry for him, but he wasn't and she didn't and she hated the way he was so drunk. They had nothing, no furniture and no money to get any, so Tom had gone off to the salerooms in Crook and come back with a bed, a table and chairs and a settee. Vinia wanted nothing to do with any of it but Esther Margaret kept turning up at her house, crying. Vinia assumed it was something more Dryden had done, but Esther Margaret shook her head.

'He hasn't done anything,' she said, sighing and sitting down by the fire. It was early evening and Tom was at the pub. 'He doesn't want me, that's all. He doesn't want me and he doesn't love me. What place is that to start from?'

'You don't love him either,' Vinia pointed out.

'Who could love him?' Esther Margaret looked into the fire as though it might give out extra warmth if she did. 'He frightens me. People hate him. They'll hate me after this.'

'No, they won't.'

'They won't speak to me any more.'

'Tom and I will.'

'I don't think I can bear it.'

'It's too late for that. You don't have any choice.'

She had thought Esther Margaret was going to pass out in the church but she didn't, though she went very white and swayed. When the ceremony was over Tom was still propping Dryden up and had to walk him all the way back down the church lane and up the bank towards Prince Row. Vinia thought that the fresh air might have helped, but when they were inside the house Tom let Dryden slip down on to the settee and he didn't wake up.

'You're not going to leave me with him,' Esther Margaret begged, and clutched at Vinia's sleeve.

'Are you coming, Vinny?' Tom called from the door.

Vinia looked at the length of Dryden stretched out on the settee.

'I doubt he'll wake up until tomorrow,' she said. 'Why don't you make yourself a nice cup of tea?'

'Stay and have one with me.'

'I've got a meal to make for Tom before he goes out to the pub.'

'Vinny, are you coming?' Tom called, louder, from outside.

Vinia left Esther Margaret and went after him, walking fast to keep up with his long-legged strides as he set off down the back lane.

Vinia was wrong about Dryden sleeping until the following morning. Round about eight o'clock he began to wake up. He didn't speak, he lay not moving for about ten minutes, and then he got up, and when Esther Margaret was about to offer him tea because Tom and Vinia had bought them a teapot and crockery from the market as a wedding present he collected his jacket and walked out. He slammed the door after him. The late evening sunshine poured into the house, showing up the bareness of the rooms, the places where the wallpaper was peeling off. Esther Margaret had never felt quite so alone. All she wanted to do was go home. There was nothing to do, nobody to talk to. There wasn't a book in the house, she couldn't go anywhere. The last thing her mother had said before she left was, 'Don't think you're bringing that lad here, and we won't be visiting.' They had let her take her clothes and nothing more. There had been no wedding present; they did not ask about the house or whether she had anything she needed to set up home. They had not and would not forgive her. She could not go to Vinia's, even though Tom would be at the pub by now and Vinia would be alone. Vinia had done enough for one day.

Esther Margaret was very tired and went up the stairs to bed. There was nothing in the room but the bed and a chair which they had brought up from the kitchen. She lay there with the curtains open. Vinia had insisted on having curtains in there. She cried herself to sleep.

She awoke in the darkness when Dryden came home and lay

there, holding her breath. She didn't understand why she was afraid of him. He didn't love her, it was true, but he had shown no violence towards her, he hadn't even shouted. She didn't know what his voice sounded like except when soft and even. Her parents had shouted, her mother had wailed, her father had not even offered to take her to the church to be married, the church she had attended for as long as she could remember. She had imagined being married there, the happiness, the friends, her mother and father proud of her, a home, a husband, the prospect of a future.

Dryden didn't fall over any furniture simply because they hadn't any, but he was obviously drunk for the second time that day. He pulled off his clothes and lay down and passed out. After that Esther Margaret couldn't sleep. Being in bed with a man like this was new and nothing like her only experience of such things, the day that she and Dryden had been together for the first time. He had held her; it had been pleasurable and exciting. She lay there, listening to his steady breathing, aware of his naked body. He was turned away so it could hardly have been threatening, but she couldn't sleep. As the light began to come up again in the very early morning Dryden's smooth brown body was visible above the bedclothes.

She got up and put on the fire and the kettle so that when he finally did open his eyes she could offer him tea. Dryden looked hard at her, as though he had forgotten her existence, and then he said, 'That would be nice,' and rolled over again.

When she brought the tea, however, he sat up and accepted it. Esther Margaret sat down on the edge of the bed. Dryden regarded her intently.

'Do you still fancy me?' he said.

'I don't love you.' Esther Margaret didn't look at him.

'I don't care much about you either but I fancy you.'

'Dryden—'

Esther Margaret backed away. She had imagined him doing a great many evil things. She had not imagined him inviting his wife into bed. She shook her head and then for seconds together she imagined him forcing her, and she backed off even more. Dryden went on looking at her until her actions answered his question and then he drank his tea and lay back down, rolled over and went to sleep.

At midday Dryden went to the pub and came back at three. He didn't eat the food that she had prepared, he went to bed, and at six o'clock he got up and went back to the pub and she didn't see him any more that day.

She ran out of money that first week and said to Dryden, 'Have you got any money?'

'Not until I get paid.'

'There's nothing to eat.'

'We'll have to do without, then, won't we?'

'It doesn't stop you drinking, though, does it? It doesn't stop you going to the pub.'

'I need to do that,' he said slowly.

'And we don't need to eat? And me in my condition?'

He tried to go to her. Esther Margaret drew away.

'I can't be bought,' she said.

'We're married.'

'If you think I will ever let you touch me again you are mistaken. This is entirely your fault. You are sinful. You were conceived in sin and born out of marriage. You came from violence. There's no good in you and I will not have you near me. You can force me, of course, like your father did with your mother.'

'I don't have to force women. They want me,' Dryden said.

'Sluts want you.'

'Then you were a slut.'

'I was an innocent!'

'So is everyone at the beginning.'

'Not you,' she said.

Before the end of the week Esther Margaret put the problem before Vinia. Her solution was simple.

'Go and take it off him when he gets paid.'

'To the pit office?'

'That's what plenty of other people do.'

'Do you do that?'

Vinia laughed shortly.

'Tom would kill me,' she said.

Pay day arrived. Esther Margaret passed out that morning; she wasn't sure whether it was the baby or her nerves. Vinia called in.

'Thought you were going to the pit,' she said. 'You look terrible. Are you all right?'

'I'm fine.'

'Do you want me to ask him? Tom's at home, he had a bad night. I'm going up for his pay.'

Esther Margaret begged her not to.

'I'm frightened of him,' she said.

'He hasn't done anything yet,' Vinia pointed out. 'And he can hardly do much to me, can he?'

Vinia regretted immediately having offered to help. Dryden was that most dangerous sort of man, unknown. He looked the kind who would not tolerate opposition, but so far he had provided not a penny and Esther Margaret couldn't go on like that.

It wasn't far from Prince Row to the pit and she had timed it well. She knew that Dryden went drinking with Tom, but she also knew that without Tom nobody would bother with him, so he was alone when he came away from the pit. It had not once occurred to her that she could like Dryden. Nobody liked him except Tom, and to her that was no recommendation. The times Tom had brought Dryden to the house for dinner the only thing that kept her silent was her fear of her husband. She would not have had him over the threshold. She went jauntily up to him.

'Hello, Dryden.'

'Now.' Dryden stopped.

'I'm going shopping for Esther Margaret. Have you got any money?'

Dryden laughed. It was the last thing she had expected. She had never seen even a glimpse of humour in all the times they had been together recently, and as far as she was concerned there had been too many. Mind you, most of the time Dryden had been drunk and they had not, as far as she could recollect, addressed a word directly to one another.

'Aye, I've got plenty of money,' he said.

'Let's see it.'

He poured it into her hands and it sat there all bright and heavy and shiny. Vinia had never seen so much money. Tom doled out very small amounts and she had learned never to spend a farthing more than was necessary because some weeks he gave her nothing.

'Why don't you have that much,' she said bravely as she counted it into his hand, 'and I'll give this to Esther Margaret.'

'I was actually on my way home,' Dryden pointed out. 'I can give her it.'

'No, it's all right.'

He didn't say anything else, he just stood there while she sorted the money out, but she got a strange feeling about it, and when she looked up there was quiet amusement in Dryden's eyes which she was sure had not been there before. She could not understand why he gave in, and so quickly. If she had done such a thing to Tom he would have slapped her round the ear there and then, and done much worse when he got her home. She did not deceive herself either that Dryden was a better man. There was no pub between the pit and the Row but she knew very well that Dryden would most likely turn the corner and go to the nearest pub before he got home and that very likely Esther Margaret would see little of his pay.

Not that Dryden could have slapped her around the ear but

he could have refused or he could have grudgingly handed her a few pennies. She didn't understand it. He behaved as though it were some kind of game and he was letting her win without any contest. He could of course be the sort of man who tipped his pay up, but she didn't believe that. She knew that they had had little food in the house for the last three days because they had no money, and Esther Margaret was too proud to ask for tick and she wouldn't run up bills like other women did because she hadn't got the hang of housekeeping. She had borrowed what she could from Vinia but Vinia had little enough, especially by the end of the fortnight. She was just lucky Tom wasn't feeling well and had sent her for his pay. She wouldn't dare touch it; she would wait to have it doled out to her in small grudging amounts when she was brave enough to ask. She understood what Esther Margaret meant when she said that she was afraid of him. He was unpredictable.

'I've got nowt more,' he said as she stood there.

'No, I . . . no, I know.'

'Can I go, then?' Flirting, Vinia thought, amazed, standing there in the pit yard, black from work and probably very tired, flirting with her. She didn't remember any man having done that before. His cold black eyes were dancing. Vinia felt her cheeks getting warmer. She had not been able to understand how a girl like Esther Margaret could have succumbed to Dryden's charms, but she did now. Clutching the money in her fists, she muttered something and then walked on towards the pit office, stuffing it into the pockets of her dress before she got there in case Joe Forster thought she was mad.

Vinia was interested in Joe. Esther Margaret often talked about him and Vinia wondered what it would be like to be married to somebody really nice like Joe. He was nothing like his father, and he didn't play the big man. He knew everybody by name, and as she came in he called her through into the little office, though he needn't have done so, and gave her Tom's pay himself. She would have taken it from any of the clerks but Joe wasn't like that. He asked after Tom, even though she had no doubt he knew that Tom had just drunk too much and couldn't get out of bed. No doubt he had seen other women in her predicament. As he chatted, Vinia watched him. He was lovely, gentle and kind and he ran the pit better than his father had ever done, simply because he cared about the men and their families, and because he was well liked the men gave their best, even though Tom complained because Joe spent too much time down the pit and not enough on the surface, he said.

He greeted her with, 'How are you, Mrs Cameron?' as though this was polite society and they met every day.

'I'm very well, thank you, Mr Forster. I've just come to collect Tom's pay. He wasn't feeling too good this morning.'

'I hope he'll soon be a lot better. We're back on full time next week.'

He smiled and gave her the money and Vinia walked down the bank towards the shops, imagining what it would be like to be married to him, without his father of course, but with that great big house and him coming in all polite and nice and maybe even having some money and not wondering how drunk he would be when he came back. Joe didn't get drunk, she was sure he didn't.

Joe watched her as she walked back down the pit yard. There was a defeated look about her. He had seen it many times before. Some people couldn't take the isolation, some people couldn't take the drinking, some women had children and managed. Vinia Cameron was unhappy. He understood that. He was unhappy himself. He had been able to bear the idea of Esther Margaret not marrying him but he couldn't bear her married to Dryden Cameron, who quite obviously didn't care about her and had got her pregnant. It hurt Joe to think that she would rather give herself to a young man like that than go off with him.

He wished that he had an excuse to get rid of Dryden

Cameron. He treated Dryden badly that summer and did not bother to hide the fact that he did not like him. Dryden ended up working in a lot of wet areas, being told that his pay was docked for bad language or for fighting. He was guilty of both, Joe was sure, but as far as he was concerned it was a personal thing. Dryden was pushed around, was told that his tubs had slack in them, got his pay docked for that too and it was unfair, Joe knew it was, because Dryden was a good worker. There were a lot of men in the pit who weren't as good. Joe wished that Dryden would leave instead of going home to his wife at the end of each shift. Esther Margaret was so near each day, in the little house in the pit row beside the office and the Black Prince, and Joe had to make himself not look for her.

Dryden didn't leave, he didn't even seem particularly un-happy, at least no more so than usual. He just went on working regardless. He didn't complain about his treatment or his pay until Joe gave up in disgust, ashamed of himself. Worse was to follow. One day that October, when Joe was below ground, chatting to the deputy, there was a rush of air and a movement above him and then an almighty crash and at the same time he was shoved heavily sideways and the whole world caved in and the noise bounced and echoed against the walls. When the world stopped Joe was flat on the ground with somebody on top of him so that he was away from whatever had happened and protected. It was a weird feeling, the sort of thing that a father might do for a child, or a good mate for his own.

For Joe it was a first, and he was surprised to see Dryden Cameron launch himself up and run back to the scene of destruction. Joe followed him. Under a huge piece of rock a man was trapped. It was the deputy, Carrington. Dryden didn't wait for anybody; he started trying to lift the rock off him and other men soon appeared and helped. Joe didn't think that in normal circumstances men could have moved such a heavy burden but they did it. When they got a closer look at him it was obvious that the man was hurt badly. Dryden got down on his knees and held the man's head and gave him a drink, wiping a dirty handkerchief around his face to clear his eyes. Joe had seen accidents before but it never got any easier and he didn't think it should. There was blood everywhere. Carrington didn't even speak, he lay there and died, and Joe had the unpleasant sensation of being both sorry for the man dying, and down his pit, and glad that it wasn't him. It might have been him if it hadn't been for Dryden Cameron and his quick reactions.

There was a lot to do afterwards — the doctor came, and Joe went to tell Carrington's widow. He could not get over the whole thing, it had been such a shock. He had not been so close to death before and he began then to wish it had been him, though what would have happened to the pit he could not think. When he went to see Mrs Carrington at her house in Ironworks Road there were two small children beside her as she opened the door, and Joe knew it was a bigger death than his would have been. There wasn't a single person who would have mourned his passing. It was a sobering thought. He promised to look after her but it was so little to offer, and in the days that followed he couldn't sleep or eat or find anything normal.

On the Saturday evening, without thinking, he went down Prince Row and knocked on the door of Dryden's house. Esther Margaret answered it. She was huge; the baby must be due, Joe thought. There was another shock. She looked like a different person; her looks had gone. She wore a plain dress which somehow made her look bigger. She moved clumsily, as though she could not get used to the baby inside her, and seeing her Joe felt physical pain and a dislike of Dryden that was like nausea. Her hair was scraped back and dull and her face was pale, her eyes dark and unhappy. She let him in with scarcely a word. Dryden was seated at the kitchen table. They had just finished eating and he had a mug of tea in his hands. Joe was astonished at how bare the house was. They had nothing. He had not seen them together before and to him they looked less like man and wife than anybody he knew. Dryden got up, though Joe urged him not to, and Esther Margaret offered him tea and a seat. Joe wanted to refuse but he didn't like to, so he sat at the table with Dryden while she hovered with the teapot.

'I didn't thank you,' Joe said, trying to concentrate on the reason he was there.

Dryden looked blankly at him.

'The accident. You saved my life.' Dryden didn't answer that either, almost as if Joe hadn't said anything.

'I can't stop thinking about it.'

'Why him and not you?' Dryden said at once.

Joe was astonished at his quickness of mind.

'Yes.'

'Luck.'

'Not this time.' Joe shook his head. 'You were there. Unless you call that luck. You could have pushed Carrington out of the way instead.' Joe thought he detected a glimmer of amusement in the depths of Dryden's dark eyes, but he could have been wrong. 'Let me do something for you—'

'I didn't do owt,' Dryden said.

Joe would have been glad to leave it at that. He had argued with himself over it, tried to tell himself that he had not treated Dryden badly and that Dryden had not saved him. It seemed to him, in spite of what Dryden said, that there had been a conscious choice to make between himself and Carrington and that Dryden had made it. Perhaps he hadn't, perhaps he had thought that Joe was closer or had not cared enough to do anything deliberately, it had just been chance. The hard fact was that Dryden didn't have to attempt to save either of them; he could just have got himself out of the way, as the other men had done.

The trouble was, Joe thought as he left, that Dryden had already taken everything. The golden-haired girl, teapot in hand, was the biggest prize of all, though he doubted Dryden knew it. She was awkward with child and he was sorry for her. She had no comforts, nor would Dryden allow her any by the looks of things, so Joe went back to his own comforts, wishing he was not so much in debt to a man he couldn't like. Dryden hadn't considered his own death, hadn't thought about it; he had just pushed Joe well clear and let his own body follow. It occurred to Joe that Dryden had no fear of death and maybe even no particular reason to live, certainly not the love of the woman he was married to or the regard of the village people. It could have been himself or Dryden underneath that rock and dying, with massive injuries inside and eyes that filled with blood.

CHAPTER EIGHT

There was a vacant shop in the main street. Every day when she went out Vinia saw it. Sometimes she went past it more than once, and one day in the rain, when there was nobody about, she stopped and pressed her face against the wet window and imagined what it would be like to have a shop, to be able to design and make clothes for it. She had no money to buy anything, not even second-hand things from the market to remake as she had done before she was married, and when she sat down one day and made some drawings on paper she was still absorbed when Tom came home. She had not noticed the passing of time; she had been enjoying herself, enthralled with what she was doing.

'No tea ready?' Tom said

Vinia scrambled up, gathering the papers.

'In a minute,' she said.

'What's this?' Tom said, and as she tried to get past him he barred the way. She held the papers from him but Tom took her wrist and forced them from her fingers.

'It's nothing,' she said.

He moved closer to the table and put the papers down, spreading them out so that he could see them, and they looked stupid and trivial as she saw them through his eyes and her face burned.

'You've got time to draw daft pictures, have you? What are they?' Tom shot her the kind of look that made her turn away.

'Nothing.'

'It doesn't look like owt I've ever seen.'

'It's a design, a dress.'

'A dress?' Tom opened his eyes wide. 'Oh, well, in that case we won't worry about it, eh? We'll just sit about all day drawing frocks.'

Even as he spoke she could imagine the shop with her name above the door and people inside, in the back, making up the designs she had thought of, and she in the front in a plain black dress and all the posh folk of the neighbourhood coming to the shop and ordering dresses and hats, wonderful hats made from soft material with exotic birds' feathers and wide brims. She would make things people could not get in Newcastle or even in London, so good were they, so different and so exciting. It was her favourite daydream.

Tom picked up the papers and dragged her over to the fire and there he fed them one by one into the depths of the flames. For some reason she couldn't stand it, began to cry and tried to stop him. Tom went on putting the papers to burn and very soon they were gone. She shouldn't have let him know how much it meant to her but she couldn't help it. The fire died down as though they had never been, and still she stared into the dead embers.

'They were for my shop.'

'What shop?'

'The shop I'm going to have.'

'You're not going to have owt,' Tom said, and hit her so hard that she banged into the kitchen table and fell. He pulled her up off the floor and shoved her in the direction of the pantry. She made a meal in spite of the fact that she was in pain, and while Tom ate she sat at the table with him.

'If you'd wanted summat else you shouldn't have married me,' he said, and then he left and went off to the pub.

She sat down at the kitchen table and cried for the shop and
for herself and for Tom and for the baby she did not seem able
to produce, and then she realised that she was not alone and
when she looked up Dryden was standing in the open doorway,
watching her with dismayed eyes. He didn't say anything and she
turned away and then got up to attend to a fire that didn't need
any attention. She cleared her throat.

'Tom's long gone,' she said.

Dryden's silence perturbed her. She couldn't think why but
she wanted to say something to him that would absolve Tom of
responsibility for her distress, she didn't want him to look bad to
Dryden. She no longer cared about Tom and she had never cared
for Dryden but her honesty compelled her to admit to herself
that Tom was the only person in the whole world whom Dryden
loved. He adored Tom, she could tell when they were together
from the shine in his eyes, and because it was all he had she could
not destroy it.

Dryden moved into the house and stood with his head down
for what seemed to her like a very long time. He had beautiful
hair, thick and black and shiny, not wavy and not curly and not
straight, like black pennies, a sort of black storm, the kind of
thing that women loved to put their fingers into.

'Tom hit you?' he said finally, and to her astonishment she
lied.

'He . . . no, he . . . it was just . . .'

The illusion went from his eyes until they were dulled.

'It was nothing, he didn't mean to. He never did it before and
. . . we want different things.'

'Like what?'

'Well . . .' She smiled at him. 'Tom wants a baby and I want
a shop and we don't seem to be able to agree or have either and
. . . it makes things difficult. He didn't mean to do it.'

'It doesn't matter, though, what you mean, it's what you do,'
Dryden said.

He moved nearer and she would have moved farther back

away from him but he put up one hand. Hands were associated with violence for her and a little noise of fear escaped her lips, but all he did was to close his fingers around her hair at one side of her face in reassurance. Nobody had ever done such a thing. Tom knew nothing of caresses. When he let go she moved away and Dryden left the house and all she could hear were his footsteps hurrying through the passage.

CHAPTER NINE

Esther Margaret went into the front room and cried when Joe had gone. He was like nobody else, so far above them all, and she could not but think that he might have been hers. Joe loved her, she could see that, even though he attempted to disguise his affection. His look had held dismay at her condition. She knew, though she had no mirror, that she was nothing more than a coarse pitman's wife and that she would be tied for the rest of her life to a man everybody despised. No one except Vinia bothered with her any more. The neighbours nodded hello but, having no regard for Dryden, they had none for her either. He opened the door and stood there, not saying anything.

'Is that right? You saved his life?'

Dryden didn't reply and she turned around into the silence to find him not looking at her or at anything else very much.

'Mr Carrington died,' Esther Margaret persisted.

'Forster wasn't quick enough, that's all,' Dryden said. 'I had to get him out of the way to get me out of the way.'

Esther Margaret looked at him and thought how strange it was, that the husband she didn't love should have saved the man she did and that she could have the one and not the other. Dryden moved forward slightly and she moved back.

'Don't touch me!' she said.

Dryden looked at her, right in the eyes.

'This isn't a marriage,' he said.

'Oh, it's a marriage all right. Look at the state of me. Besides, you don't need a marriage, you'll go with anybody.'

'I haven't!' he said.

'Haven't you? Well, you always did.'

'So we're going to go on like this for ever?'

'As far as I'm concerned you can go to hell before you ever touch me again! You have cost me everything.'

'You were keen enough.'

'I was upset. The truth is that I love Joe. I always did and I always will!'

'Joe?' Dryden stared.

'Isn't that amazing? And if you had known it would Mr Carrington be walking about now and Joe be six foot under?'

'You love Mr Forster? When did this happen?'

Esther Margaret followed his train of thought.

'It wasn't like that,' she said. 'He didn't touch me.'

'I hope not because if this bairn has his colouring I'll be out of here so fast you won't have time to catch your breath.'

'Nobody touched me but you,' she said.

'And Billy Robson? What a busy person you were.'

'I didn't let him near me.'

'You let me, though. Why was that? You held off Mr Forster and Billy Robson but not me.'

'You can't think how much I wish I had.'

'You certainly manage it very well these days.'

'The damage is done,' she said, and moved past him and up the stairs out of the way.

Dryden couldn't wait to get out. He thought even if she had asked him to stay he would have found an excuse. Forster had spent weeks needling him, he didn't know why, and now the situation had been made impossible. He hadn't intended saving Joe, it was just instinct. If Carrington had been standing there he probably would have pushed him. He didn't like Joe and he knew that Joe hated him and he knew what it must have cost Joe to come to him and be grateful. Gratitude made Dryden want to throw up.

Esther Margaret was stifling him. She was always there and she was getting bigger and bigger until now she looked like a whale. She was always waiting with meals and with her hand out for money. And he resented it.

It was lovely to get out of the house and take deep lungfuls of air and walk away from the pit and the row and her. Tom would be waiting for him in the Black Horse at the very top of the street. It was a cold starry night and Dryden was pleased with it. He felt much better when he reached the pub. The beer always helped so much, the soft brown cushion of it against the warring of his mind and senses. In the beginning it was the anticipation. The first two pints were bliss to smell and taste, and the feel of it going down was as good as a woman's fingertips soft on your skin. Not that he really remembered. After that it created a nice glow all around. The pub became merry like a Christmas which had yet to exist, and everything anybody said was interesting or funny. Tom and Wes and Ed would play darts or dominoes. It was like home, like home had never been, like it might be for some people, though he hadn't met any yet, a narrow, comfortable, almost suffocating world where you were always welcome and everybody called you by your first name. He knew that without Tom he would not have been accepted, but he could stand inside the space that Tom's shadow cast and be safe there.

The beer went down, the laughter rose and the woman behind the bar, Dora Sims, looked enticing. She smiled at him a lot but then she smiled at everybody a lot, so he did not quite understand why, when the night was dark and old and the pavements were empty, she was there, walking on her own as the landlord shut and locked the doors, and he was there too.

He walked her home, back to Baring Street beyond the main street. There was no conversation, no invitation; he had no idea where her husband, Hart, was, just that he followed her into the cool darkness beyond her front door and once the door had shut with what sounded to his ears like a distant echo he was kissing her and to his surprise she didn't stop him. It had been a long time since Dryden had kissed anybody, and then it had been Esther Margaret. The stupid part about it was that Esther Margaret had not been his wife then. It had been in a barn the last time they had touched. He remembered it more and more clearly because as each day went by his body hungered more. She would not let him near and Dryden had been so angry with himself for getting her pregnant in the first place that he had determined to have nothing more to do with other women. It had not occurred to him at the time that Esther Margaret could hold him off always. He kept telling himself that she would give in, that it would get better, that there would come a day when they would be glad to be married to one another, it would be easier, they could laugh and talk and they would get together.

The landing gave way to the bedroom. Outside, the sky was blue and the street was black shadows. The bed creaked as they met it and Dryden concentrated on her mouth. It was a nice mouth, in fact the same kind of mouth as on most of the women he had bedded in his life, not like Esther Margaret's, which was all cool hesitation. He liked that it was wise, that she knew what he knew, that she knew everything, that he was not asking for anything to which he was not entitled. Dora Sims would not be turning up on his doorstep, pregnant, wanting him to do something about it. He reached for her body, his hands found her breasts. He closed his eyes gratefully at the warmth, the roundness, the soft feel of her skin against his face. He wanted to stay there for ever in the darkness, in the bedroom, in the silence, safe.

After she heard him leave the house Esther Margaret sat upstairs on the bed, etching in her mind exactly how Joe had looked, the way his fair hair would fall forward and his eyes so dark green and full of love, and how well he wore his suit and how gracious he was, whereas Dryden said little. Joe was clever and polite and she would never have him.

The pain caught her by surprise It went away almost immediately and she breathed quickly for a moment or two. Then her body eased. It came back after a few seconds and her breathing stopped against it until it ceased. She sat waiting, clutching at the huge bump that the baby had become, waiting for it to happen again. It didn't. She lay down on the bed, suddenly very tired. The pain didn't come back so she dismissed it. Everybody got twinges. She slept.

When she awoke it was dark. She had been dreaming that she was hurt but it was not a dream. The pain was there. It went again and then it came back. If it was important she must get help. She slid off the bed with no idea of what time it was. For the first time ever she wished that Dryden was at home. She lit a candle and began to walk slowly down the stairs. A draught from under the front door blew the candle out when she was halfway down and somehow she missed her footing and fell the remaining steps. Within seconds she was lying in the darkness at the bottom and the pain had started up again insistently. She concentrated on breathing until it went away and then she got to her feet carefully and then it struck again and this time it was like a dagger inside and Esther Margaret came to her knees and then doubled up over it.

When it stopped she willed herself to crawl as far as the door, and then she pulled herself up and opened the door and when the night air came rushing inside she began to shout. She shouted and shouted. Was it so late that everybody was in bed? If it was that late Dryden would soon be home. He would come back, the pain would go away. Somebody would hear her.

When Dryden awoke the first thing he heard was the rain. He opened his eyes and there beside him was Dora Sims. She looked so old. She was not young and beautiful like Esther Margaret, but she was smiling at him.

'You don't have to stay if you don't want to,' she said. 'I know. You ought to get back before your wife wakes up.'

'I should be . . .'

'Go on, then,' she said. Her eyes were wicked. Dryden leaned over and kissed her and once he had kissed her he wanted to do it again and then he couldn't stop himself. What did it matter? Esther Margaret didn't care about him anyhow. He didn't need to hurry. The rain was running down the window, banging itself off the pavement below, the skies were dark, the curtains on either side created shadows, and as the rain got heavier the room grew bigger shadows and the less he wanted to leave.

Dora was laughing. She had a lovely deep, throaty laugh. Dryden covered her in kisses.

It was not that late when he left, and since it was Sunday Esther Margaret, he thought, was probably still asleep, though she could hardly blame him for stopping out when she wouldn't let him near her. The rain had stopped. It gave the town a clean, washed look which he approved of. He walked down the back lane and into the yard and then into his house by the back door. To his surprise Vinia was in the kitchen attending to an already brightly burning fire. As she saw him she turned around, poker in hand, and fixed him with a look of contempt.

'So,' she said, 'you finally bothered to come home.'

Dryden asked nothing. He recognised disaster when he saw it.

'The doctor is here and the midwife. Esther Margaret went into labour in the middle of the night.'

'The baby isn't due,' Dryden said.

'It may not be due but it's definitely coming.'

'It's weeks away.'

'It doesn't seem to know that.'

'What happened?'

'I don't know. By the time I got here she was unconscious and very cold. That's how we knew she'd been there a long time.' She spoke in clipped tones as though she were making a report.

The doctor was there all afternoon. Vinia stayed. She didn't speak to him any more; she went upstairs twice with various things and came back down again after a long time. There was a bit of noise from upstairs too, Esther Margaret crying, and the creaking of people's feet as they moved around. In the early evening the doctor came downstairs and told them that the baby had been born too soon and was dead.

'And my wife?' Dryden said, getting up.

'She will be better in time, with care. You can go up if you want to.'

They did. The room had been cleared and cleaned. Esther Margaret lay in bed as though there had been no child; there was no evidence. What had they done with it? The bed was so well made, so perfectly straight. Dryden didn't dare go near, but he watched Vinia go to her and sit down on the bed and take her hand. Esther Margaret opened her eyes.

'My baby,' she said softly.

'It was too soon,' Vinia said.

'I know. I knew it was. It went wrong.'

'Dryden's here.'

Esther Margaret closed her eyes and whispered loudly, 'I don't want to see him, not ever again. Make him go away.'

'Esther Margaret—'

'Make him go away.' She turned her face towards the window.

Dryden left the room. He walked slowly down the stairs. After a long while Vinia came down. He was standing by the fire.

'It wasn't completely your fault,' she said. 'The baby probably wouldn't have survived even if Esther Margaret hadn't spent all those hours alone on the floor in pain. It was a boy. At least it's spared having a Cameron for a father.'

'I'm not a Cameron,' was the only defence Dryden could think of.

'It's the only name you've got! You and Tom, you don't make one decent man between you! You couldn't take responsibility if it was going to kill you.'

'I married her, didn't I?'

'Oh yes, you did that, and ever since then I dare say you've laid every bloody loose woman for miles! You useless miserable bastard!' She started to cry. Dryden wished she wouldn't; it was hard crying, as though she didn't really want to let it out. 'Why don't you go back to the pub, it's all you're good for!'

'Aren't you going home?'

'Just for once your brother has gone to his mother's for his dinner. I'll stay here, unless you have some particular objection. She has to be watched carefully for the next few hours. If you want to go to bed you can always use the other room.' She turned away, went into the pantry and banged about, so Dryden left. Tom was waiting in the Golden Lion. He could pretend nothing was wrong there, though he couldn't swallow any beer or the pie Tom had bought him. Dryden had thought Tom would say lots of helpful things like 'She'll be all right, it was only a bairn, she can have lots more', but he didn't. When Dryden told him the baby was dead Tom looked down and then away.

'I thought having bairns was going to be easy,' he said finally.

'The McMortons have ten.'

'Mr McMorton must have summat we haven't,' Tom said in a vain attempt at humour.

Dryden never wanted to go home again but he had to get some sleep before his shift in the early morning so he went in the end. Tom was staying at his mother's. Dryden wished he could have gone somewhere else to stay.

'My mother's pleased,' Tom said. 'She likes having me there.'

Vinia didn't even come out of the bedroom when he got home. Dryden didn't go upstairs. Vinia might not know it but there was no bed in the back room. He slept on the settee, in as much as he did sleep. She came down in the morning and told him that Esther Margaret was feeling better. She gave him his bait.

'Is the doctor coming?'

'Do you really care?'

Dryden didn't say anything to that. He hated the way she was looking at him. It was like being showered with needles.

'She could have died,' Vinia said flatly.

Dryden went to work. Nobody could keep up. He worked until he could have dropped and then he hardly dared go home for fear there would be a termagant waiting for him. The fire was on, the meal was ready, the water was hot. Vinia banged about for a while and then she went upstairs and let Dryden wash in peace. He couldn't eat. The smell made him feel sick. She took it off him and threw it away.

'Aren't you going to the pub?' she said.

'No, I thought I'd stop here and listen to you shouting at me all night. It obviously makes you feel better.'

'It does not make me feel better.'

'Well, it doesn't make me feel any better either, so I don't know what you're doing it for.'

Vinia glared at him. She made him feel worse than anybody had ever made him feel before. When he had been little and the Harmers had punished him and told him regularly that he was evil and who his father was and what he had done to Mary Cameron, Dryden had always thought there was a small part of him that wasn't really all bad and he had maintained that idea all through his life, but it was as if that part of him had given up. When she looked at him like that he felt there was nothing left, and at the same time that a woman like her would never do anything other than despise him.

'Don't you realise what you've done?' she said. 'If it hadn't been for you Esther Margaret could have married a nice lad and had a decent life. She's heartbroken about her baby. The fall brought on the child—'

'But you said—'

'I was trying to spare you. Why was I? You don't care about her. You don't care about anybody.'

The trouble was, Dryden realised suddenly and miserably, that she was wrong. He did care about somebody. It was a very strange realisation and totally alien, and it had crept up on him from nowhere. He denied it to himself half a dozen times while she ranted on about what a dreadful person he was and then he told himself that it would pass and then he realised that he didn't mind her shouting at him, all he cared about was that she was there in the room, not as pretty as lots of women in the village and nowhere near as bonny as Esther Margaret and more precious than the sun and the moon and the stars. Everywhere she wasn't there was total darkness like the pit with nobody to light it. She was horribly right too – he felt guilty about Esther Margaret and sorry about the baby but it was nothing compared to the great mountain of feeling that he had for her. He felt as if there were sunshine all around her and it was stupid and ridiculous.

'Is what I'm saying funny?'

Dryden came back to her voice.

'What?'

'Am I amusing you?' She came nearer, almost threatening, which was either very brave of her or particularly foolhardy considering how small she was, how big he was, and the fact that she was a woman in a pit village. But he could see that she wasn't thinking about that, she was so upset about Esther Margaret and the baby.

'Can I see her?'

'She doesn't want you to. I thought I would sleep down here tonight so that she has some rest. You can sleep in the back bedroom.'

'There's no furniture in the back bedroom,' Dryden said, 'and besides, she's my wife.'

Vinia's eyes wavered.

'You mustn't . . . The doctor said that . . . you mustn't touch her.'

Dryden held her reluctant gaze.

'I haven't been anywhere near her since the day we were married,' he said. 'For my sins I'm not allowed.'

Vinia didn't say anything. Dryden took some satisfaction in having silenced her. 'I have a day's work to do tomorrow,' he said, 'I need to sleep.'

He got himself out of the room and up the stairs. Luckily Esther Margaret was sleeping and turned the other way. All he did was peel off his clothes and fall into bed.

CHAPTER TEN

———————◆———————

Joe came to visit Esther Margaret. It made Vinia's eyebrows lift and Esther Margaret smile for the first time in days. They both knew that pit-owners did not visit the wives of their men after a child had died, and she in bed too. It was most improper. He seemed not to know. His voice wafted up the stairs.

'But I must see her.'

'Mrs Cameron is in bed. Mr Forster, really!'

Though she did not love Dryden, Esther Margaret felt the loss of his child dreadfully. She was desolate, inconsolable. She had not spoken a word to him in three days. They had slept in the same bed and not touched, but that was nothing new. She was finished with him for good. She could not look upon his face.

Joe got his way. He came upstairs, Vinia with him, and his arms were full of roses and apples, pears and plums.

'It was all we had,' he said as if to explain it.

Vinia took the fruit from him and left it by the bed, and the roses she took downstairs with her. She threw him one mildly disapproving look before going down. Without ceremony Joe sat down on the bed and grasped Esther Margaret's hand and kissed it. For a moment she was deceived and saw him as he had been, the impetuous boy who had asked her to run away with him, and then she realised that he had changed. He was running the pit almost single-handed which was, she knew, a great deal of responsibility for one so young.

'I was so sorry to hear about your child. How awful for you.'

Esther Margaret could only nod and wonder that he was there and at his caring enough for her to come when talk of any kind would cause them both problems. He must have been seen. Joe was a conspicuous figure in the village. The impossibility of their situation made her long for her child. Only the idea of the baby had kept her there with Dryden. Her life was cheerless; her mother and father had not spoken to her since she had left their house to be married. The baby was dead and she could see the future without it and she was afraid.

Joe held her hand. She thought that with encouragement he might have kissed her fingers, but she must not encourage him, however longingly he looked at her, because it was unthinkable that he could take one of his workmen's wives, most especially the man who had saved his life. He had the whole of the community to think about; they depended upon him for their livelihood. He could not be seen to make mistakes. It was much too late for him to have anything to do with her.

She asked him how his father was, just for something to say, and he replied suitably and all the while he held her hand. Esther Margaret dreaded his going but she knew also that he could not stay for long, he could not be seen to do so, and even sooner than she had thought he got up, muttering kind words and saying that he must go. When he had gone, when she heard Vinia seeing him to the front door, she began to cry. Vinia came upstairs and Esther Margaret tried to hide the tears but it was no good.

'He asked me to run away with him once. You can't think how much I wish that I had done so.'

Vinia sat down, her eyes wide with surprise.

'Who would have run the pit and looked after the village?'

'Joe shouldn't have to do that!'

'But he does have to,' Vinia pointed out.

'We were younger then.'

It had not been so very long ago but it felt like a long time, it felt like for ever. They were trapped, but then perhaps Vinia was right and even if she had consented to leave with him Joe could not have gone. It had been something she could never think about. She felt that the trap had closed around her and she could barely breathe.

'His father isn't doing it, is he?' Vinia said reasonably. 'And their family should. After all, they made the most money out of it.'

'They don't seem to have much to show.'

'No, well, his father wouldn't, would he?'

Thaddeus Morgan came often to the pit to do business with Joe. He came that week with the information that his daughter was to marry George McAndrew.

'I have to tell you, Joe, that it isn't what I wanted for her,' he said, as Joe closed the office door and they were private together. 'There was a time when I rather hoped you might take to one another, but there's no accounting for tastes. She has a lot of spirit and . . . well, to be honest I think she'd be too much for you. She isn't like her mother. Alice is biddable, Luisa is like me. She's marrying a rich man so I've nothing against it, I'm proud of her, but she's our only child and the Clyde is a long way off. She didn't take to you when she saw you and I don't think you took to her so you won't mind me speaking so plainly. We make plans for our children and they don't work out. I don't know why we bother in the first place but that's parents for you.' He looked straight at Joe. 'I had thought the businesses would go together well and I had thought . . .' He stopped there.

'What?'

Thaddeus hesitated again.

'It doesn't matter what it is, you can say it,' Joe prompted him.

'Your father was never an easy man to deal with and he's not a good businessman but I think you could be given the chance and a bit of help. You've got the men back to full-time work through your own efforts—'

'I don't know how long it's going to last.'

'I could introduce you to people. George wants nowt to do with my business and I'm hurt by it but you and I might deal well together.'

'A partnership?'

'Aye, summat like that. I wouldn't do you down, Joe, don't go thinking it. Heavy is the head that wears the crown, you know, and it's a bloody sight heavier when there's nobody to talk to.'

'I can't say I know much about foundries.'

'You could, though, and I do know summat about pits. I started off as a pitman.'

'I didn't know.'

'It isn't summat I spread about. I started at the bottom. You've started at the top and come down, at least your father did. Your grandfather left a good pit here when he died. He'd got it nicely under way and then your father took over. Mind you, I do think times were easier then but I'm sure we all think that. It'd be a bit of a challenge to try and help it and get my mind off weddings and the like and that bugger McAndrew. I don't like him. I'm disappointed but he's a shrewd businessman for all that and she cares about him so it will have to do. This place needs investment, it needs capital. I have money doing nothing I wouldn't mind sacrificing for it. Why don't we try?'

Joe was inclined to be suspicious, even though his father thought well of Thaddeus and his grandfather had thought well of Thaddeus's father and he could well believe that Thaddeus was quite alone at the top of his little empire. Of late Joe had felt so solitary – nobody to talk to or help, nothing to make the business worthwhile, and having to make the decisions alone, nobody to blame.

'It seems you made an impression on Alice. She knew your mother well. She talks about her even now and you are like her.'

'I know.'

Thaddeus looked uncomfortable for a few moments before saying, 'I asked your mother to marry me but I wasn't good enough for her parents. They knew I'd been a pitman whereas your father had been born to own the pit and that draughty bloody place you call home and it seemed like a better idea to them, I'm sure.'

'Did she care for you?'

'No, I was too rough for her. I married Alice to spite her because they were such good friends and she didn't really like me neither. It was her parents' idea, God rot them, they made her do it. The mistakes we make.' He shook his head. 'But I could do you a good turn, Joe, as your mother's son and because I cared, and you could do me a good turn by learning about my business and we could run things together. I don't see why not. You don't have to answer me, I know your father's name is on everything, but we could have summat drawn up to suit both parties. Think about it.'

Joe did think about it, especially after seeing Esther Margaret and realising once and for all that he could not have her. His brain had known it all along but his stupid heart had hoped somehow until then. Now it didn't. Seeing her lying there and the look in her eyes since she had lost Dryden's child had finished him off. Joe could not go on hating Dryden because Dryden had risked his life to save Joe, and he could not go on coveting Dryden's wife. Dryden had nothing except her and they had lost their child, and it was too much for Joe's honour to bear, loving hopelessly in such a situation.

He went home, and there was nobody to look after his horse, nobody to give him comfort of any kind. His father was snoring by the study fire and Jacob was snoring by the kitchen fire, and that finished him off too. He could not do any worse than to go in with Thaddeus Morgan.

That weekend Thaddeus asked Joe – and his father, but that was only for politeness' sake – to stay overnight at his house in

Wolsingham. His father refused and Joe had had so little experience of any kind of society that he was worried he might do or say the wrong thing. Luckily Luisa was not there, she was in Scotland visiting her future family, and he saw again the goodness and kindness of Alice, who came to him, smiling and clasping his hand.

'Joe,' she said, 'my dear boy, how lovely to see you again.'

They lavished their hospitality upon him. Joe had a bedroom that looked out across the dale and was glad that the weather had turned chilly because a fire was lit and burned brightly there all day and most of the night. They had company, but not the kind to which a young man might object, just half a dozen people to dinner, and such a dinner — beef and roast potatoes and good wine — and Thaddeus introduced him to the other men and they talked about business and Joe began to feel quite at home. On the Saturday he visited the foundries — there were two of them, one at Deerness Law and the other in Wolsingham — and Thaddeus explained the various processes that the iron and steel had to go through and Joe talked to the skilled workmen and the office staff.

On the Saturday night there were only the three of them, and to Joe it was almost like having a family, something he had not experienced, sitting over the fire with Thaddeus, talking, and Alice doing her needlework, and it made him realise how much he had lost and how much more he had never known, and in a way it made him the more lonely, all those evenings with no one to talk to, all the days without people of his own. He could not be comfortable because he knew that the following night he would be back in his room, keeping away from his father, eating the messes that Jacob provided instead of food, no fires, a few paintings on the walls or elegant furniture or servants or a carriage or any of the things that he might have been entitled to as the pit-owner's son.

He could see that he took the hardship and the responsibility without any of the benefits, and the more he listened to

Thaddeus the more he was inclined to take the risk and go in with him. What would become of himself and the pit and the people otherwise? He had no money to improve conditions and he wanted to do so much. Thaddeus and Alice showed him all the wasted years, all the loneliness, all the things his father could have been to him. In some ways it was worse being there because he could no longer comfort himself that other people were worse off than he was. It was true, of course, but you didn't think of that, only that other people were better off, so much better off. Even Dryden and Esther Margaret could turn over in the night's darkness and reach out, and although he knew that Thaddeus and Alice were not always happy they sat by the fire together and lived in relative luxury. Envy, Joe knew, was a bad sin, and he would have to alter his life so that there would be no more of it.

Therefore two weeks later he was able to pass Esther Margaret in the street and merely smile and nod. It didn't hurt any more. He couldn't allow it to.

The days were short and dark and wet as Christmas approached. Vinia tried to cheer Esther Margaret up but nothing seemed to shift her mood, and every time Vinia visited she was sitting by the window staring out at the road that led past the Black Prince Pit and up on the moors. She did little. When she had been unwell after the death of the baby Vinia had kept on going to the house to see to the fire and the cooking and Esther Margaret went on being incapable of doing anything. It was hard. If Vinia left her to do anything she got it wrong because she was not thinking about what she was doing, but when Vinia had to keep going day after day it became very hard. First there was the question of money.

'I'm doing the shopping. I need to be able to afford it,' she told Dryden flatly.

He nodded in the direction of the mantelpiece.

'It's always in there,' he said.

When he had gone to work Vinia took down the little wooden box he had indicated. It was stuffed with money. Esther Margaret could not have spent much in weeks, and he was obviously taking nothing from it other than beer money. Even so she used as little as possible when buying the food.

It was unfortunate that Dryden and Tom were almost always on the same shift; it meant that she had to leave Dryden's dinner in the oven and everything prepared and run home before Tom got there. After a fortnight of this they went on to different shifts, which would make it impossible. Dryden caught her as she was there cleaning the house.

'This has to stop,' he said.

Vinia paused in washing the kitchen floor.

'You've got a better idea, have you?'

'She does nothing all day.'

Vinia got up, leaning wet hands on the bucket.

'And you're going to get her to do something more?'

'I have tried to talk to her,' he said.

Vinia had tried too, but she did it again when he had left for work. She went through into the front room. As ever Esther Margaret was sitting on a kitchen chair by the window. There wasn't much to see. The road disappeared into fog, everything was wet and the day was dark and gloomy. She kept a fire on in there because it was so cheerless. They had no furniture. She thought they could have afforded some by now from somewhere, but neither of them had the heart to care about things like that.

Esther Margaret heard her and stirred.

'The road seems as if it goes into the clouds there, Vinia, look. It goes into nothing, disappears.'

'We should go out and get some holly this afternoon,' Vinia said.

Esther Margaret frowned, though she did not take her gaze from the scene outside.

'Shall we?' Vinia said after waiting for her reply.

'Later.'

'Come and help me. Everything's to do.'

'I will.'

But she didn't and neither did they go out gathering holly. Vinia went by herself one day and it was a relief to get beyond the village down towards the dale and find the holly trees red with berries. It was the sign of a hard winter, she knew, and she didn't like to take too much because she knew that the birds would depend upon it, but Christmas was a time of hope and she wanted to bring a little of it into the houses. She went home after leaving a meal for Dryden and when Tom went to work, she went back again only to find Dryden sitting alone over the kitchen fire.

'Aren't you going out?' she said.

'No.'

Every night that week Dryden sat over the kitchen fire and Esther Margaret in the other room. They didn't speak either to one another or about each other and neither of them was any help. Dryden didn't go out to the pub at all, even when Christmas drew nearer and the men were making an excuse of something they did all year anyhow. He went to work and he came back and slept.

'Maybe you could have some new things,' Vinia suggested brightly one day just before Christmas.

He looked blankly at her.

'Furnish the front room.'

'Do you think Esther Margaret would like that?'

'I'm sure she would.'

But she listened to him suggesting this to Esther Margaret. There was no reply.

'Perhaps we ought to get the doctor,' she said, but when the doctor came he could suggest nothing useful and Vinia listened to him briskly telling Esther Margaret that she would have lots more children, she was young, it was nothing to worry about, she had a husband to look after. Vinia felt like telling him that the way these two were going on her chances of having a baby were slight to say the least.

She wanted to suggest to them that they should come and spend Christmas Day at her house. Tom would have liked that, she knew, but they had to go to his mother's, she wouldn't have dared suggested anything else, but nonetheless she mentioned it to Tom and he sighed and said, 'I'm worried about our Dryden.'

Only in her presence did he call Dryden 'our' in the family sense.

'He never comes to the pub any more since the bairn died and he's got nowt to say at work.'

'He didn't exactly behave very well.'

Tom shot her a keen look.

'No, I know. He made a mess of things from the beginning but he did the right thing, he did marry her. Many a lad would have run away. Since then I don't think she's given him a kind word. It was her fault too, you know. Lasses do take part in these things, though to hear them you'd think they didn't. You'd think they'd held you off with a bloody gun. And anyroad, surely losing your bairn's enough pay-off for owt. Could we have them over to tea on Christmas Day, do you think?'

Vinia looked at him across the fire.

'What about your mother?' she said.

'After that.'

Vinia suggested it to Dryden and Esther Margaret. Dryden was pleased, she could tell, but Esther Margaret didn't lift her eyes from the view out of the window, though it was dark and there was little to see.

Christmas Day arrived and they had a lie-in. Vinia was just cooking breakfast for Tom when there was a banging on the door. She opened it to reveal Dryden, wild-eyed and dishevelled. He burst inside.

'Is she here? Is Esther Margaret here?'

'No. We haven't seen her.'

'She's gone. She's gone. I can't find her.'

Vinia shouted Tom down the stairs. He appeared some moments later, quickly dressed, fastening his shirt.

'What's happened?'

'Esther Margaret's not there. I've been all over. She must have left when it was still dark. Where can she be? She wasn't there when I woke up and I've looked everywhere for her. I thought she might have been here.'

'She could have gone to her mam's,' Vinia said.

'She never sees them. They didn't even come when the baby died.'

'It's Christmas. Maybe she thought it would alter things. I'll go, shall I?'

Vinia was glad of something useful to do. Tom put on his jacket and boots and accompanied Dryden, searching the streets. It occurred to Vinia that Esther Margaret was not in her right mind any more, and that anything could have happened. She hurried up the street and the maid opened the door, speaking stiffly and trying not to allow her entrance. Mr Hunter, hearing the fuss, came up behind her and permitted Vinia inside.

He took her into the sitting room, where his wife was standing by the fire, and there she explained calmly that Esther Margaret could not be found.

'We thought she might be here.'

'I cannot imagine why you thought so.'

'Because she must be somewhere. She hasn't been well since the baby died.'

There was silence at that, as though the baby had not existed for them, as though Esther Margaret had meant nothing, as though what she had done was unforgivable.

'I must get ready for church,' Mrs Hunter said, and left the room.

Mr Hunter looked apologetically at Vinia.

'My wife hasn't been the same since everything went wrong. We thought we had brought her up properly, you see. I have my position in the village to think of and . . .' He smiled, almost against himself, she thought. 'We had plans. We had a nice young man for her and . . .'

'You do know what they say. Make a plan and see God laugh.'

He didn't appreciate that, she could tell. His God obviously didn't do much laughing of any kind that Mr Hunter could see. Esther Margaret had done no worse than many a village lass, but they obviously considered themselves far too fine for such goings-on. Mr Hunter offered no help, and it seemed pointless to stay and expect anything. Vinia could not understand such behaviour, but if this was how they had gone on with Esther Margaret then it was hardly surprising she had done wrong.

The two men were nowhere to be seen. She went back to the house in the vain hope that Esther Margaret would be there, and then she went to the neighbours, including Tom's mother, who had the dinner on the go and said that it was nonsense for them to worry. She was, Vinia thought in disgust, more bothered about Tom coming back in time for his Christmas dinner than by the disappearance of a girl who was not in her right mind as far as she could tell.

Tom did not come back. Vinia went to everybody she could think of who might have seen something, she searched the back streets and the shop doorways and every old building where a person in distress might hide or might think of as a haven, and as the cold dark day wore on she began to lose her grip on the idea that Esther Margaret was all right and would come back. She began to cry from time to time, making herself stop but unable to hang on to any positive thought. She returned home at the end of the day to find Mary Cameron standing outside, saying agitatedly, 'Where's our Tom? This is disgraceful. It's Christmas Day. The dinner is spoiled.'

She had disappeared into her house, however, by the time Tom and Dryden came back when it was late and dark. Vinia offered them food and tea. Tom ate heartily but Dryden refused with a shake of the head. He stood by the front-room fire, but Tom followed her into the kitchen.

'Do you think she's lost her mind, Tom?' Vinia asked, looking anxiously up into his face.

'I think it's possible.'

'Why didn't the doctor know that?'

'I don't think doctors know anywhere near as much as they think they do. I'd better go round and make it up to my mother.'

'Don't be long.'

'Don't worry, I won't be.'

Even so she clutched at his coat lapel.

'You don't think something awful's happened?'

Tom hesitated.

'She's done herself in? Maybe.'

'Oh, God—'

'Look, we've got no reason to think that yet so don't go thinking it, and she's hardly likely to perish in this. It's warm,' Tom said flatly, and off he went.

When he had gone she went into the front room. Dryden hadn't moved. He hadn't even sat down, though he must have been tired after the kind of day he had had.

'Shall I make you some tea, Dryden?' she offered for perhaps the third time.

'No, thanks.'

Vinia looked at him, and she thought it was no wonder that people wouldn't have anything to do with him. Even standing there in the front room of a pitman's cottage he looked like the kind of traveller people turned away from their doors in fear and loathing, and yet in Durham she had seen them, dressed in bright colours, wearing gold, selling goods on Framwellgate Bridge. How strange, how different. The unknown. Yet Dryden was not like that at all when she looked at him the second time. Wearing dark clothes, his face hidden from her, turned towards the fire, he was just like any other pitlad except for that unruly hair, a black tangle, and something else, she wasn't quite sure what, as though he might cast a spell, make a curse, have some power that ordinary people did not possess. If he had, she thought sensibly, surely he would have used it in the search for Esther Margaret. He had no vision of the future, only his memories of the past, and from what she could judge they were not worth recalling.

Tom was a long time. She sat over the kitchen fire since Dryden was not inclined towards company. When Tom came back she gave him more tea.

'What do you want to do?' she said.

There's nothing we can do before it gets light, and we covered a lot of ground today. I don't know where else to look. We'll have to tell the authorities tomorrow that she's missing. Why don't you go home? I'll stay here with him. She might come back here or to our house.'

Vinia went home. Tom was right, the weather was unseasonally warm. There were a lot of men in the pubs judging by the noise and light coming from them, but many of the houses were in darkness, women and children having gone to bed early after such an important day. She had a faint hope that Esther Margaret would be waiting at the door, but she was not, or that at some time during the evening she would come back, but although after every sound she leaped up from her chair by the kitchen fire in false hope, nothing happened.

It was very late when Tom came home. He had to come back, he was at work the next day, but she could tell by his face that it had not been easy. Tom was sensible. Vinia was so glad to hear the voice of reason that she clung to it as if it were a person.

'I think she's left him. I think she's lost her mind and gone off. I don't think she's dead.'

'But where would she go, and the winter's all to come?'

'I'm going to go and talk to Mr Hunter tomorrow when I get back from work.'

'He wasn't much help today.'

'We've got to do summat and I can't think of owt else,' Tom said, and they went to bed.

Vinia didn't sleep. She lay there all night imagining what had happened, thinking of Esther Margaret lost up on the fell, perhaps not even remembering that she had a home, a husband, a place to be. She imagined her dying and shuddered and turned over and breathed against Tom's warm back. She thought about Dryden lying in bed by himself and probably thinking all the same things and possibly even more, and how he was responsible and what he had done. Maybe he didn't feel like that — there were an awful lot of men in the village who would not have thought it was their fault no matter what happened, that Esther Margaret had nobody but herself to blame.

Sometimes Esther Margaret thought she could hear her baby crying. She would search and search but she could not find it. Sometimes she thought she could feel the child still inside her, as though it were alive and she could feel it moving, and there was a great emptiness where the child had been. She could not bear it. It was as though she had been enclosed in her own secret world where nothing could get to her, nothing could happen. There was herself and the child and the pain, but she would rather have that than anything else. Nobody's voice must get inside, nobody much touch her, and they were fussing, their voices floated past her at the window when all she wanted to do was look outside at where the road went away beyond the village. Somewhere past it she would see her baby.

Vinia fussed. She was always there, talking and doing things and wanting Esther Margaret to do things, and she did not understand that the baby had absorbed and needed all her attention. She grew tired of Vinia and her fussing and of the tall dark man who said nothing much but who would sleep beside her, taking up a great deal of room. All she wanted was to sing to her baby, and they would not leave her alone to do so. The doctor who came was a fool who talked about things that she did not understand, which had nothing to do with her, and Esther Margaret became very tired of them all and she watched the road and then she understood. She did not have to stay there.

The road beckoned to her, leading away somewhere else. It occurred to her that they would try to stop her, she was not quite sure why, and the more she thought about it the more she convinced herself that they must think she had died. She spent a long time trying to compose a note but in the end all it said was 'I can't stand any more. I must end it. Forgive me. Esther Margaret'. After she was satisfied that it conveyed her meaning despite its brevity, she could not think where to put it. If she left it somewhere obvious they might find it too quickly and then they would do everything they could to bring her back. She wandered about the house trying to think of somewhere to leave it, and in the end she opted for the little box on the kitchen mantelshelf where the money was kept. That would give her some time to make her escape.

She took few clothes and little money so that it would not look as though she hoped for anything beyond death, and she hid this under the bed and in the very early winter's morning when he was still asleep beside her she crept from the house in the quiet darkness and walked away from the village, following the road that she had watched in the days after her baby had left her alone there.

CHAPTER ELEVEN

Dryden went to the pit office that first day to report that his wife was missing and he was surprised to find Joe's face pale and by the fact that he immediately offered to help. Several times during the meeting Joe began to say something, his face darkening with anger, and then he stopped himself and instead of that he organised men to help with the search. The weather became worse after that first day. It wasn't snow, it was sleet, hard and wet, which went on day and night, finally freezing hard on the third night so that when Dryden came back in after searching all day he stood by the kitchen fire and wanted to cry.

Vinia was there so he couldn't. She had been coming and going from his wretched house for so long now that she was like part of the furniture. The bare house shone from her labours. There was always hot water and hot food. Dryden was happy to have the hot water but he couldn't eat.

'You haven't eaten in four days,' she pointed out. 'You can't go on like this.'

'It isn't that I don't want to, it's just that I can't. It won't go down.' He glanced at the window. 'Nobody could survive in this.'

'She probably isn't out in this,' Vinia said stoutly. 'She'll have got away somewhere and be safe, I'm sure she will. I hate to ask this but I need some money for things for the house—'

'I told you, take it. It's in there.'

She took the little box down from the mantelshelf and opened it and after that there was nothing but the crackling and moving of the fire.

'Dryden . . .' There was something funny about her voice, it wobbled and was much quieter than usual, and it made him turn away from the fire towards her and the piece of paper in her hands which she was staring at in horrified fascination. She seemed to read it several times before holding it out to him, and he took it from her and read it again and again, and he kept on hoping that it would disappear or that it could be those few moments before she had found it. He had thought that nothing could get any worse, but now he discovered that it could. Hope was gone. In the back of his mind there had existed a small picture of them finding her and of there being a reasonable explanation for what she had done, even that she would get her mind back and that in some way they would manage to do better. He had kept clutched to him this idea, that she would come home to him and that he would have learned from it all and would become a much better husband, that they could make a real home together, live as married people, gather around them precious things. He would not drink or mistreat her any more and she would be kind to him and they would have some sort of future that he could bear to think about and it would get better.

The note did away with any of those ideas. Esther Margaret was dead. She had killed herself and it was his doing. Somehow he felt as though the world had stopped, as though nobody had got any older since Vinia had picked the note out of the box. He couldn't move. Esther Margaret was seventeen years old and she was dead. Vinia was looking anxiously at him as though he might drop down dead too. Tom came in; he had been seeing his mother, who was barely speaking to him because he had not been there for his dinner on Christmas Day and Tom kept going over every evening to mollify her. He looked from one to the other and Dryden handed him the note.

'Well, that means we can call off the search, then, doesn't it?'
Over the last few days Dryden had come to love Tom's sensible
tones. 'I'll go and see Mr Forster first thing in the morning and
tell the police.' He wished that Tom would tell him that it was
not all his fault; he might try to believe him. Anything was better
than this dreadful guilt which he could not get away from. It was
like carrying a boulder on his back. He went to work day after
day and was glad of it; working was so much easier than being at
home. Tom tried to persuade him to the pub but Dryden
wouldn't go, and Vinia was busy looking after Tom so Dryden
spent his free time sitting over the kitchen fire, wondering what
his young wife had done to end her life, waiting for news of any
kind, trying to get used to the idea that he would never see her
again and reliving over and over the wrongs that he had done.

There was no news of any kind; the winter days pushed past
one another and the weather worsened. Vinia came every day to
look after him but there really was little to do. In his mind
Dryden painted a picture of Esther Margaret not dead, en-
tertained a faint hope that she would come back and relieve him
of these dreadful feelings of responsibility, but nothing happened. On his free days he walked the fell, and when he was at
home he took to sleeping a great deal, which distanced him from
the problems. It seemed to him that Vinia was always coming in
and finding him nodding over the fire, and he would hear the
door and pretend that he had been awake all the time. She had
taken to making food at her house and bringing it to him
between two plates and then putting it into the oven to reheat,
and he tried to eat it because she had gone to such a lot of
trouble but it was always difficult.

He avoided Joe. Again and again he remembered Esther
Margaret's voice telling him that she loved Joe, had always loved
Joe. Dryden even tried blaming Joe for what had happened as he
was sure Joe blamed him. Nothing was said. Joe cast long looks
at him sometimes but they didn't speak. January went on its
bitter way and it was only when it was coming to its end that

Dryden was called into the office. There he found Joe, not looking at him much, with something to say.

'I'm sorry about this, Cameron, but you can't go on living in that house. You'll have to find somewhere to lodge. I have married men with children living in cramped quarters and that's a big house. You'll have to find somewhere else.'

Joe spoke flatly as though he didn't care. The only comfort that Dryden had fell away from him.

'Give up the house?' he said. Visions of Mrs Clancy's gritty beds and dried-out food flashed through Dryden's mind. When he had been there he had known nothing better, had been glad of the way that nobody and nothing mattered, but he had grown accustomed to Vinia's cooking and cleaning, the space and the fire. At Mrs Clancy's he had never got near a fire, never had a bed to himself or clean clothes or a kind word. He looked miserably at Joe.

'What if she comes back?' he said. It was the first time that he had spoken hopefully of the situation, and it caused Joe to shift in embarrassment.

'She's not going to come back, is she? She's dead.'

'It was only a piece of paper. It was only . . .' Dryden could hear his voice, desperate, guilty.

'What was it only?' Joe was looking at him and Dryden didn't like the look. 'You got her pregnant, married her and made her so miserable that she killed herself. You're worthless and useless and . . . oh, get out of the office. You've got until the end of the week.'

Dryden didn't move. He couldn't. He had told himself a thousand times that it was all his fault, but nobody else had said it to him. He knew very well that Joe didn't like him, that Joe held him responsible, but he had not until that moment known that Joe loved Esther Margaret.

'Get out!' Joe said again, so he went.

CHAPTER TWELVE

At first Esther Margaret didn't know where she was going. All she had in mind was to walk up the road she had looked at so many days from her window since the baby had died. She was happy there, she felt that she was doing something useful, something she had long wanted to do, but it was cold and she was soon tired, so she was very glad when a horse and cart came along.

'Want a lift, missy?' the man offered, and she was glad, even though he was inclined to talk and ask questions. She said as little as possible to him, and as the horse trudged along Esther Margaret realised where she was going. She would make her way to her mother's cousin, who lived in Northumberland. Her mother had come from a little fishing village there and had not been back, as far as Esther Margaret knew, so it was likely that they couldn't stand one another. Her mother's cousin might take her in for a day or two until she found a place to stay and a job. She would be like her mother in that she would never go back and they could mourn her and wish they had done differently and they would never know.

The man with the cart was only going as far as Esh Winning, which was a little pit town about halfway to Durham, but when they reached the middle, stopping outside the co-op in the street, he shouted across to another man.

'Blakey. A young lady here wants to get to Durham today. You going there?'

'I'm off now.'

'There you are, missy. Get you down.'

Esther Margaret got down, thanked him and hurried across to the other, slightly better equipage, and they set off at a smart pace on the road that led out towards the city. This man was not the kind who asked questions and she was glad of that because it took all the rest of the light to cover the miles and the weather began to worsen. Only when they were on the outskirts did he say, 'Going to family, are you?' and Esther Margaret confessed that she was. She wished that she had not done so, she did not want to give information to anybody, but she was glad after that because he said that it being Christmas Day she might have difficulty finding somewhere to stay and that his wife would be glad to put her up for the night. Esther Margaret thanked him gratefully, making up a story about travelling to her aunt because her mother had died and she had nowhere else to go. His sympathy won her somewhere to stay and hopefully food and a bed – the weather was freezing and it was beginning to sleet.

She spent the night in the shadows beneath the great cathedral in a room from where she could hear the river. The house was not quiet because the carrier had children, but she was glad of shelter and the food they gave her, and the conviction stayed with her that she was doing what she was meant to be doing, getting away from that place and her husband and all the dreadful memories. She had accepted that the child was dead but the pain of that realisation made her want to keep on going, as though if she went fast enough she could leave it behind.

The following day she sold her wedding ring and the gold cross from around her neck which she had been given as a little girl and had learned to hate. That gave her sufficient money to catch a train to Newcastle and then on to Alnwick. She sat by the window in the train after it left Newcastle and

watched the sea, and she began to feel better for the first
time since the baby had been born. She had made her escape,
had not given her real name to anyone. The snow flew past
the window but she was safe inside, listening to the chatter of
the other passengers and glad that she was putting miles
between herself and her past.

She found a hotel for the night in Alnwick and set out the
following day to walk the few miles to the coast. The weather
was bad and she had not gone far when the snow came down so
fast that she could hardly see in front of her. She could not tell
how long it took or how much distance she had travelled but she
was beginning to feel as if she could go no farther when she
finally came in sight of the little village which she knew from the
correspondence her mother had once held with her cousin was
the right place. She stopped, afraid. The correspondence had
been a long time ago. The woman could have moved. She knew
little about her other than the address, which was not difficult to
remember, being Cormorant Cottage, and her name, which was
Daisy Selwood.

The road split into two halves and most of the houses were
dotted about on the right-hand side, but Esther Margaret chose
to go left, which was just as well, because there were two cottages
joined there by a yard and there was a sign on the stone wall
which said 'Cormorant Cottage'. Esther Margaret was so relieved
that she forgot to be apprehensive. She walked as quickly as her
last energy would let her and banged boldly on the door. A short
time passed and just as she was about to knock again the door
opened and a stout woman, looking much older than her mother,
stood there.

'Well?' she said.

Covered in snow, Esther Margaret knew she did not present
much of a picture.

'I'm Esther Margaret Hunter, your cousin's daughter. I've
come to stay with you.'

The woman stared.

'Have you indeed?' she said finally. 'You'd better come in then, hadn't you?'

Joe had thought he could put Esther Margaret from his mind, that he could learn to think of her as Dryden's wife. If the child had been safely born and healthy he knew that everything would have altered. A woman who was a wife was still of interest but a woman who had another man's child was something quite different. Esther Margaret had no child and she had lain in her bed looking not much more than a child herself, and it was all he could do not to pick her up in his arms and run away with her. There was, however, nothing to be done but endure, and he managed that. He managed until Esther Margaret went missing, and after that he felt he could not stand any more. By day he organised other people searching and did so himself from dawn to dusk on the short days in the freezing wet, and by night he sat over a meagre fire which he lit and tended himself in his bedroom and began to wish that he could, like his father, stave off the hurts with alcohol. He could not sleep; he pictured her dead, dying, badly injured and freezing to death up on the fell. He tried to think of her returning but that didn't happen. Each day that it didn't happen was a new horror, so by the time Joe discovered that Esther Margaret had left a note which indicated that she had killed herself he thought he could manage no more. After that he found that he didn't care what happened to Dryden so long as it was nothing good. He wished he could have manufactured an excuse to get rid of him. Short of that the loss of his house, which was inevitable, would do.

He was surprised, however, the day after he had told Dryden that he must get out, to have Mary Cameron pay him a visit. Joe had always hoped that he would like Tom's mother simply because she had suffered so much, but there was something about her which always reminded him of his own situation, so it was not easy. Mary Cameron had given Dryden up. His mother had left him. There was a similarity which always made him feel as though he did not want the woman's acquaintance. She smiled at him from across the street because he was the pit-owner's son and that was all. Joe was distantly polite. This time, however, he had to ask Mary Cameron into his office, the clerks in the bigger office being curious and looking. He closed the door.

There was not an ounce of her which looked anything like Dryden, Joe observed; Dryden must be all his father. He took savage satisfaction in deciding that this was the case. He asked her to sit down and she did so and Joe did not and she smiled and he decided that he did not like her smile.

'The news about Esther Margaret Hunter is very nasty,' she said.

'Yes,' Joe said.

'I never thought much of her. I never thought much of her parents, for all they go to church every week. Not nice people. The thing is, Mr Forster, that I was wondering, and if I have this right that man can't stay in that house on his own, can he? It isn't the way of things, is it?'

'It isn't the way of things, no, Mrs Cameron.'

'And I was thinking. My Tommy is a good worker and he has never had a pit house. I know, I know . . .' She held up both hands even though Joe hadn't said a word. 'He does have a house but it's a very small house and it was his wife's before she was married and it is tiny and it isn't a pit house so you've been spared that all this while and I know that we have a house but then my Alf is a good worker too and I was thinking that after that man leaves Tommy and his wife could maybe have the house. It's only two doors away from us and they'll be . . . well, you know, they've been married a while and when the bairns come along which they will be any minute it would be ever so handy for us to be close. I know that you've got plenty of deserving cases and I wouldn't want you thinking that I was trying to change your mind when you might have made it up but it would be very nice for us, it really would.'

Joe had not realised until that moment that Mary Cameron

hated Dryden. Only a really vindictive person would have come to him like this. The man had lost his wife and now the pit-owner and his mother were about to put him out of his home. So far Dryden had not said a word. Joe was almost ashamed. Mrs Cameron was right, Tom was a good worker, though he was no better than his brother, but he had a wife and would undoubtedly have children and he was as entitled to a house as any other man.

'I can't promise anything, Mrs Cameron, but I'll do my best.'

'I'm sure you will, Mr Forster,' she said, giving him her imitation of a sweet smile.

Joe was glad when she had gone. If that was what mothers were like, he thought he was better without one. He felt sorry for Tom as well as for Dryden. At least Tom was married to a sensible woman. Joe liked Vinia. If every man in the village had a wife like that his life would be much easier.

That evening, when Vinia was about to go up to Dryden's house with his dinner, Dryden called in. She was pleased about that. He had not set foot in their house since before the baby had died. She was worried about him. The talk in the village was that Dryden had killed his wife and child. People would believe what they wanted to believe, in spite of the evidence.

'I didn't want you going all the way up there when I'm not in,' he said as she encouraged him to sit down with them and eat. 'I'm being put out of my house by the end of the week. Did you want any of the furniture? I know it isn't much but—'

'The bastards can't do that!' Tom declared, banging on the table and making everything on it jump.

'Mr Forster had me in when I came off shift. It's his house, he can do what he likes with it.'

'He could at least have waited a week or two. You can move in here with us.'

Dryden shook his head.

'I can't do that.'

'We've got two bedrooms.'

'You've got one room downstairs. There's only just enough room for two of you.'

'What else will you do?'

'Go back to Mrs Clancy's.'

There was silence after that. Vinia didn't want Dryden there but the idea of letting him go back to a dirty boarding house was more than she could stomach.

'You can't do that.'

'I must.'

Tom went off to the pub after tea, trying to get Dryden to go with him as usual but finally giving in when Dryden declared that he must go home.

'Why don't you sit here a while? There's been nobody in your house all day, it won't be very warm. You could even stay—'

'No.'

The way he said it made her look at him.

'You've done too much already. Mrs Clancy says she has room for me—'

'She'd say that to anybody, just for the money, you know she would, the miserable old . . .'

Vinia cleared the table, hasty in her anger. Dryden came to the pantry door when she washed up, as he had done the first time he had ever been there. She had been surprised and then had realised why he was so grateful – it was because of his mother and Mrs Harmer and Mrs Clancy. Dryden must think women were connected to the Devil, she decided.

'I'd better go. Thanks for the tea.'

Vinia stopped washing up and dried her hands swiftly on her pinny. She said, 'You can have the spare bedroom and welcome.'

'No, thanks.'

'You didn't eat your tea again. Wasting good food like that. It isn't right. Anyroad' – she swept past him back to the table – 'it would be a lot easier for me looking after one house than looking after two.'

'And one man instead of two.'

'I didn't say that!' Vinia found herself flustered, wanting to cry because everything had gone wrong and more was following, as if nobody had any control over anything that happened in their lives. 'You can't go back to that mucky woman's house, not after . . .'

'Not after what? The joy of being married, the benefits of living two doors away from my mother, the happiness of being a father? Believe me, I'll be glad to go.'

'So you can pretend that none of it happened? Sweep it away like Mrs Clancy does with muck under the carpets, if she has any carpets, which I doubt.'

'She hasn't,' Dryden affirmed, 'but it doesn't matter because she doesn't sweep up,' and he left the house and banged the door.

Vinia hadn't cried all the way through the death of the baby, Esther Margaret's moods and disappearance and the note, but she did now. She sat down at the table and howled. She did not want Dryden in her house, God knew what more trouble he would cause before he was through, but neither did she want to send him back to that awful boarding house. There were better boarding houses, of course, but none of them would have had him even before all this had happened, and certainly not since. She had heard talk in the shops that day, that Dryden had driven his wife to her death, he had caused it; some said that he had even killed the child and disposed of Esther Margaret himself. If she took him in she believed that the talk would stop. If she didn't Dryden might end up farther in the earth than the wife who had killed herself, though how she had done it no one had any idea since there was no evidence.

People have died before, she told herself, sitting down at the kitchen table and finding a handkerchief in the pocket of her skirt, but it didn't feel like that. Esther Margaret's death had made such a huge difference to everything. If the baby had lived things would have been so much better. It would have been the making of their marriage.

She heard footsteps through the passage and knew them only too well for Tom's mother, so she hastily dried her eyes and got on with her clearing up. Mary Cameron was smiling when she came in. She accepted a cup of tea from Vinia and seemed happier than usual, sitting by the fire and looking around the room and talking about the people she had seen that day.

'You've always lived in this house, haven't you?'

'I was born here,' Vinia said.

'And you like it?'

'It's the only home we ever had.' Her dad had worked at the local foundry.

'You're entitled to a pit house, you know, you always were. Mr Forster's like that, trying to get everybody cheap. He's owed our Tommy a house ever since you were married. You'll need a bigger house soon, I went up and told him. This place won't be big enough once the bairns come along.'

Vinia's face burned like good coal. Nowadays Mary was always going on about when the bairns came along. She was unconvinced that anything like that would ever happen. At first she had thought she would be pregnant soon. Tom liked taking her to him in bed, but she saw other women who had been married at around the same time and they were expecting and she was not. Mary Cameron could not know how much it grieved her, or perhaps Mary was desperate for a grandchild because as far as she was concerned all she had was Tom and it was not enough. All women had were their husbands, their children and their homes, and she was lonely because Tom was always at work, in his bed or in the pub. She felt as though she had so little. The idea of a business was nothing but a dream. It seemed that she was condemned to nothing more than what she had, and she wished that his mother would stop going on about it.

'We have a spare room,' she said.

'Yes, but you have to say that the downstairs is cramped.'

Vinia supposed it was. She looked around the room. There was a curtain that came across under the stairs to hide the things she did not need and had pushed in there, and on the far wall was a dresser. In the middle was a square table and four chairs, most of which were usually pushed in as far as they could be, and on the other side, under the window, was the settee and an armchair. It had never before seemed cramped to her, even with two big men in the room, and she had not envied Esther Margaret the space she had had in her house because there was very little furniture and too much misery. It was not the house which mattered, she decided, it was the people.

'I think people should take what they're entitled to and our Tommy works hard at that pit and you should have a pit house. Mr Forster must know that.'

Vinia wondered what Mary would think if she knew that Tom had invited Dryden to move in with them. It made her want to laugh. Mary would have been hurt and horrified and would probably never darken their doors again. On the other hand to upset his mother like that was unthinkable. Tom obviously hadn't thought about it, just about Dryden. Dryden was the only person in the world that Tom really loved.

CHAPTER THIRTEEN

The house on the seashore swiftly became Esther Margaret's delight. She had not seen anything like it before. It was a cottage not as pitmen's houses were so termed, but a cottage in its small neatness, in its cosiness with its fires and hugged-to rooms and its wonderful view of the North Sea. Each day as she looked out of the windows at the back beyond the tiny garden there was nothing but the beach and the waves and the seabirds which came and sat above the bobbing waves when the tide was full. Did they come to feed, she wondered? It was like a party, the gulls and the ducks and the curlews with their long bills and the tiny little birds whose names she did not know who swept gracefully low above the sea and came to run along the sand as though each day were a new delight to them.

She soon discovered why her mother did not see her cousin. No two people, she thought, could have been less alike. Daisy lived alone in her house by the sea; there was no husband or children to care for and it did not seem to bother her. She was a very fat woman and ate a great deal and she cooked better than anyone Esther Margaret had ever met. She appeared to make her living from writing articles and books about the seashore, the creatures and the birds. There were few visitors, but those there were were taken into the back room where the sea rolled in and out beyond the window and the fire burned merrily. Daisy would produce tea and cake for them and there would be long intricate discussions about things that Esther Margaret knew nothing about. Daisy had no religion that she could see and appeared completely content.

On fine days she went for walks along the beach and along the road towards the ruined castle in the distance which stood out on the very edge of the headland. It was a very long way so she never got that far, but the cold air and the idea of going back to the house made her feel much better and she began to remember what she had given her mind to forget – that the baby had died, that she had not, that she could have done better, that she had possibly been wrong to pretend to have killed herself. This conviction grew on her as Daisy continued to ask no questions. Esther Margaret had never come across anybody less curious. She had always thought that a person living alone must be lonely and crave company, but Daisy spent her days with pen and paper sketching and writing or in the kitchen, or reading or taking walks when it was fine or watching the birds beyond the window, and each morning she would go outside and give the birds great pieces of cake or hang a whole loaf on the washing line at the back, and the birds flocked into the garden.

The more Esther Margaret thought about it the more she realised that she had been wrong in pretending to have died. At the time she thought it was no more than Dryden deserved. Away from him and beyond the situation she saw that it was not so, and that however bad things got she had no right to expect him to take on such a burden. But she did not want to go back. Each day she told herself that she must do something about it and each day was so comfortable and interesting at the little house that she refused to face the problems. In her mind the idea of going back soon became so big that she could no longer face it. This was another world. It occurred to her that Daisy did not live in the real world, that her comfort and her work were in a way as much of a hideaway as Esther Margaret's own escape. She lived inside her head, and the day that Esther Margaret saw pictures through the open door of Daisy's bedroom and ventured inside, she began to understand. Sunlight fell upon the rug by the bed and on the bedside table was a likeness of a young man in soldier's uniform and a beautiful young woman. As she stood there, the sunlight warm through the window, she heard Daisy behind her and turned around, apologising.

'No need to worry,' Daisy said in her bluff way. 'I haven't any secrets. That's Chester. It wasn't his real name. Major John Chesterfield. He was a soldier, he was killed. His parents thought I wasn't good enough for him. 'We were married for ten years.' She laughed her hearty laugh.

'But you aren't called Chesterfield,' was all Esther Margaret could think of to say.

'I don't use it but it is my name. After John died all I wanted to do was run away so I came here. He left me comfortable and I have my work.'

Esther Margaret didn't think the situation very comfortable at all; it was as bad as her own problems. She sat down on the bed and proceeded to tell Daisy everything that had happened, stumbling over the parts of the story which were making her ashamed. The sun had gone from the room by the time she finished and Daisy, never one to stand when she could sit down, was propped up against the pillows, saying nothing and frowning from time to time, not in a way that made Esther Margaret want to stop but just as though she were mulling over in her mind the tale she was being told. When it was over Esther Margaret looked at her, waiting for wisdom. Daisy pressed her lips together for a second and then she said, 'I had no idea that your mother was such an incredible fool. No, that's not true, I did and that's why we never visit. It seems to me that you have two choices. You can either stay here, which you're quite welcome to, or you can go back to your husband and make the best of it.'

'I don't think I can go back to him.'

'Well, then, it isn't a problem,' and Daisy got up and

wandered back to the kitchen and was soon heard singing and making tea. Esther Margaret listened to the waves breaking on the beach and shivered. She could never go back.

Joe kept himself busy so he wouldn't think too much about Esther Margaret. His father was never sober now and Joe had got him to sign the appropriate papers so that they became partners in Thaddeus's business and he did in theirs. Joe started to go about the country with Thaddeus to gain orders for the foundry. They undercut other people in the selling of the coal and things began to get better. Joe tried to make some changes at home but his father became so upset about it that it was too difficult. More and more often he went back to Thaddeus's house for dinner, and at weekends and when the weather was bad he stayed. If his father noticed he was not there he did not say so. Joe found the state of the house and his father's worsening drunkenness and Jacob's presence harder to bear since he had seen the way that other people lived.

Thaddeus introduced Joe to his friends and the friends had daughters but he could find little of interest in any of them, even though some were beautiful and some were interesting and charming. They came to Thaddeus's house for parties. Luisa, married, came back with her husband sometimes, but Joe liked her less and less. She ignored her mother, and Joe had become fond of the woman who had been his mother's best friend.

As for the house in Prince Row that Mrs Cameron had asked him to give Tom and Vinia, Joe was less inclined to do so. But somehow, just at that time, he had several free houses and was able to accommodate all the families he needed, so other than for sheer vindictiveness there was no reason why he should not give Tom and Vinia the house. Their place was tiny, she was his favourite woman in the village, and Tom was one of his best hewers. Joe had some conscience about Dryden but he could not let Dryden stay there or other single men would be coming to him thinking they had the right to a house. He therefore called Tom into the office after his shift one late afternoon during the first week in March and told him that he could have the house two doors down from his mother's if he should want it. Tom listened in silence. He took up a lot of room in the office. His dark eyes looking out of his blacker face were almost as disconcerting in their cold inscrutability as Dryden's own, and Joe was not feeling very comfortable as he told him. He knew that the brothers went drinking together but he had not expected that Tom's stare would turn into a glare.

'I see,' he said finally. 'So you're turning our Dryden out to make room for us when we already have a house. Doesn't that strike you as just a little bit daft, Mr Forster?'

'I can't let him have the house, you know that.'

'Why me?'

'Well, your house isn't a pit house, it's smaller so I believe, and . . .'

'You seem to know a lot about it.'

'I don't need the house.'

'Our Dryden needs it. He's going to have to go back to Ma Clancy's. A nice state of affairs, Mr Forster.'

'I can't help that.'

'Can't you? Well, I can. Thanks for the offer but no.'

'Cameron, if you don't take the house I still have to turn Dryden out. It can stand empty but I still have to do it. That's the way it works. Single men have to lodge with other people. There aren't enough houses to go round usually.'

Tom looked carefully at him.

'So that means that if I take the house our Dryden can stay there.'

Joe was more than surprised; he hadn't realised Dryden and Tom were such good friends.

'He could lodge with you, certainly, if that was what you wanted.'

'It's the only way I would take it,' Tom said roughly, and he left the office.

Vinia wondered whether she was at fault. Usually when Tom came home in a bad mood he had been brooding about something for days and it would all come out in a rush and she was careful not to argue or get too close. He ate his tea in silence, washed and changed, and she waited.

'I saw Mr Forster tonight. He's offered us our Dryden's house.'

'Offered it to us?' Warning bells rang in Vinia's head, and her mind showed her Mary Cameron saying that they were entitled to a pit house and she realised what Mary had done. She hoped that Tom would not find out; only a little bit of her wished that he would, but he would not hear tales or half-tales from her.

'That's what I thought,' Tom said, having interpreted her astonished reaction.

Vinia wanted to stay exactly where she was but she could not say that to Tom, she could not tell him that the little house was dearer than anything in the world to her, that it had been her parents' and that sometimes she thought she could still smell her father's pipe tobacco and the cloth his best blue suit had been made of.

'What did you say to him?'

'I said that the only way we would take it would be if our Dryden could live there too,' Tom said triumphantly, and Vinia's heart beat hard and painfully. She did not want to live two doors down from Mary and Alf, she did not want Dryden in their house, and she certainly did not want the house where so many awful things had happened. She had nothing but hurtful memories of it. She knew that given the chance she could grow to hate it.

'It would be nice for my mam to have us there. She's always going on about it and she would be company for you.'

It was the very last thing in the world Vinia wanted but she held her tongue because she knew that Tom would never understand.

'It's a nice house,' Tom said. 'It has a view of the fell.'

A view of the fell where Vinia was convinced Esther Margaret lay dead, a view that she had sat and stared at day after day when she was poorly after the baby died.

'It would look nice with our furniture in it,' Tom said, and she realised that possibly for the first time in their marriage he was asking her for her consent to something. He would undoubtedly, if she disagreed, go ahead anyway, for Dryden's sake and for his mother's. She had only one place to fight him from.

'Do you think your mother would accept Dryden living with us?'

If this had occurred to Tom he gave no sign of it. He considered.

'Our Dryden's not going back to Ma Clancy's,' he said.

A little song of praise started up in Vinia's head because that was the first time she thought Tom loved Dryden better than he loved his mother. And then she thought no, she had always known that. Tom tolerated his mother from a sense of duty and because things had been hard for her, but he didn't love her and he would sacrifice his peace of mind and his closeness to her for Dryden's sake. She could not help being glad that Tom would stand up for the person he most cared for, because Dryden was not easy. It was also laughable that Mary Cameron's plans should misfire quite so successfully. Vinia only hoped she was privileged enough to be there when Tom told his mother that they were going to take the house in Prince Row and that Dryden would be staying. His mother would never visit them again. It would be wonderful – no waiting for her footsteps in the passage, no examining of the food or the ironing or the dust, no nasty remarks about Vinia's childlessness. Vinia thought she would be glad to put up with Dryden for the sake of that. She had half forgiven him for what he had done, though if she had had the choice she would never have let him past the door again. She didn't really think that he was evil, but she thought that he carried evil with him. There was no safety where he was, but he did not deserve what Mary Cameron was trying to do to him. She thought he never had. She went over and kissed Tom, to his surprise.

'What was that for?' he asked.

'You're lovely, Tom,' she said.

CHAPTER FOURTEEN

During the second week in March, the weather, which had been hard and frosty, began to thaw. Joe preferred the hard weather to the wet mud that followed, though it didn't affect him too badly. He had acquired a horse so he no longer had to trudge to work. His father became ill and took to his bed. Joe couldn't feel sorry for him; he was only relieved that he no longer had to come home every day to the sight of his father drunk over the study fire. He had been doing it so long he would have thought he would have become used to it, but he hadn't. With his father banished to bed but well enough to shout against having the doctor, Joe felt that the house became more his own. Jacob was not good in health either and had gone back to his little tumbledown cottage, which was the only other building in sight. Joe felt obliged to visit him there but Jacob wouldn't let him in. Joe hired a widow from the village to come and clean the house, and though she was not allowed into his father's room he was satisfied that things had improved and went off to work happy with the progress.

On the Sunday of that week, however, Joe was astonished to receive a visit from the police, two of them with faces on them like tombstones. Joe took them into the study, which was nicely free of his father and the smell of brandy – at least he hoped it was – but then they probably knew. Policemen knew everything, including how people lived, and it was common knowledge in the area that his father was a wretched drunk.

'There's been a body found, sir, up on the fell. A woman.'

Joe had been dreading the words for weeks. Inside him there had remained a small hope that Esther Margaret's letter was some kind of mistake, some dreadful joke, that it could be misinterpreted. He thought, having loved her for so long, that he would know if she were dead. His second reaction was anger. Perhaps that was some sort of defence. He was angry with Esther Margaret, that she would prefer killing herself when she could have come to him . . . The thought faded. He knew that Esther Margaret had lost at least part of her mind, and even when she had known her mind she had not wanted him.

'Is it . . . is it Mrs Cameron?'

'It's hard to say, sir. She's been . . . she's been in the water.'

Joe felt sick.

'It seems likely,' the policeman said. 'Golden hair, blue eyes. A member of her family would know, I dare say.'

Joe thought about Dryden being put out of his house today. What wonderful timing. On the other hand there was always Mr and Mrs Hunter. They deserved to have to do this.

He rode to the pit and left his horse there and walked slowly down the row to the house where the last time he had visited Esther Margaret had been lying in bed ill after the death of the baby. The front door stood open and from inside he could hear the sounds of a row. Joe hesitated. The disagreements of his workers were not his business. He could hear the umistakable sound of Mary Cameron's voice. Joe was inclined to take a step backwards.

'I will never set foot in this house again and you needn't think I want you in my house! You scheming, deceitful lad, our Tommy!'

'You couldn't just accept it, could you? You've never given him the time of day in almost twenty years. What did he ever do to you?'

'You are the only son that I have.' Her voice was lower and steady.

'That's not true and your saying it won't make it true!' Tom said. 'He's not going back to Ma Clancy's because I won't let him. He's my brother and I care about him!'

Well done, Tom, Joe thought, wanting to applaud. There were more sounds from inside, and then Mrs Cameron careered down the hall. Joe stepped back. She looked darkly at him.

'This is your doing!' she declared, and stormed past him. Joe hesitated on the doorstep and then knocked tentatively and went inside.

It looked so different. There was good furniture but it was in disarray for all their possessions were boxed and not yet organised. Tom was standing by the fire and Vinia was beside him, as though she were about to offer comfort, and then she sensed Joe's presence and turned.

'I would have knocked,' Joe said.

Tom turned as well, wiping the vestiges of temper from his face before his employer. Joe had never felt such a boy. He had dealt with a great many problems during the last few years when he had had no help from anyone, but this was new.

'Is Dryden here?' Joe said.

'No, he isn't bloody here. You put him out,' Tom accused him.

'I thought—'

'He wouldn't stay,' Vinia interrupted. 'He knew what would happen.'

'Where is he?'

'He went to Ma Clancy's,' Tom said, bitterly. 'Who the hell else would have him? He's not staying there. I'll go and bring him back.'

'I think I'm about to make things worse,' Joe offered.

They both looked at him.

'I've had the police. They've found a woman's body up on the fell. They think it could be Esther Margaret.' Joe never knew afterwards how he got the words out. Vinia's face registered shock and sorrow – also pity, he thought.

'Oh God,' Tom said, and he turned back towards the fire.

Joe had never been to Mrs Clancy's establishment and he didn't particularly want to go now. Tom did offer but he felt that he ought to go himself since he had subjected Dryden to this place. It had probably been a decent building at one time but neglect and dirt had won the day. In the windows were frayed yellow nets and the windows themselves were rotted and so was the front door. Joe banged hard on it several times and then it was flung back and Mrs Clancy in all her glory, fat and red-faced, filling the doorway, stood there amid the smell of burned cooking and grease. She looked him over as she might have looked at a pig at market.

'Well, bonny lad,' she said, grinning happily.

'I'm Joe Forster—'

'Aye, I did know.'

'I'm looking for Dryden Cameron.'

'You've come to the right place,' she said, and flung back the door triumphantly and let Joe inside. The floor was sticky and the walls were dark. 'They're nearly all abed but I think the lad's in the lounge. Dryden, you've got a visitor.'

She opened the door. It was another dark room at the back of the house and overlooking a yard. A tiny fire burned there against the cold but made little impression. Joe could see his breath. Dryden was standing up by the fire as any sensible person would, and it struck Joe for the first time how much alike he and Tom were. The room had various bits of furniture, but none that Joe would have trusted with his weight, and it looked ill used, as though for countless years things had been spilled and thrown and leaked out upon the surfaces. The window was dirty, and beyond it were the last signs of winter, the gleam of dirty slush.

Dryden barely acknowledged him and Joe was ashamed, too ashamed to fulfil his errand, until Dryden finally turned around.

'Have I got summat else you want?' he said.

'Why don't you just leave?' Joe said. He hadn't intended to say it, he couldn't think how the words had got past his lips without any recognition from his mind.

'Are you taking my job off me?'

'No. No. I didn't mean that. I meant . . .' Joe cursed his clumsiness. 'I don't understand why you stay.'

'I've got a brother,' Dryden said.

'I thought he'd offered you lodging.'

Dryden looked at Joe as though he were a complete fool.

'With his mother in the middle of it? Did you think I would?'

His mother. Joe wished himself back a day or two when things had been easier.

'Dryden . . .' The word came hard; he hadn't addressed Dryden by his first name before and he hadn't realised that just two syllables could be so difficult to say. Dryden watched him, knowing worse was to come, Joe thought.

'Well?' he prompted.

'I had the police to see me. They've found . . . they've found a woman's body up on the fell.'

'She's dead, then,' Dryden said, as though he had always doubted it.

Joe wanted to shout at him, you never loved her, you didn't want her, now look what's happened, but he didn't.

'Mr Hunter is . . . is taking care of things.'

'That'll be a first,' Dryden said.

Joe didn't know what to say after that. He had seen few places that were more cheerless than his own home but this was definitely one of them. He didn't like to think how the bedrooms would be. All he wanted was to get out of there, to be anywhere else. There was nothing more that he could do and he had to try to grow used to the idea that Esther Margaret was dead. She had not gone away, she would not come back, and somewhere between the day he had asked her to run away with him and now everything had gone wrong. He wanted to sort it out in his head. He excused himself and left, taking deep breaths of cold air once he got outside. He didn't linger at the pit but rode home, and was glad to stable the horse and go inside. The woman who helped, Thelma Ferguson, was a childless widow, and although Joe told her that she didn't have to come on Sundays she came every day.

'If you don't mind me saying so, sir, this place wants a good clean,' she had said to begin with. Joe had no quarrel with that.

She was there now. His home had changed. He thought as he walked in that it was such a contrast to Mrs Clancy's. A big fire burned in the hall and it was all bright and shiny, as much as it could be in its dilapidated state. Thelma came out of the kitchen, drying her hands.

'I went up to see to your dad, Mr Forster, and it's my opinion that he's very poorly.'

'He won't have the doctor.'

'He said, but if it was up to me I'd get him anyroad. Do you want me to call in on my way home?'

'That would be kind of you,' Joe said.

He trudged upstairs, and at first he thought his father had died. There was no movement coming from him. For the first time in his life he didn't stink of alcohol, but he was pale and his breathing was uneven.

'Father?'

Randolph Forster opened his eyes; they were watery and narrow and had lost their colour and light. He didn't speak.

'Mrs Ferguson is leaving soon and she'll ask the doctor to come.'

'No.' He clutched at Joe's coat.

'I think we should. You don't want to die sober, do you?'

Randolph closed his eyes.

'Do you think I am dying?'

'No. I think with help you'll be fine.'

'I can look forward to a long, happy life, in fact.'

'Oh, I think that would be going too far,' Joe said.

He watched until his father went back to sleep and then he trudged downstairs. Mrs Ferguson put a perfectly good dinner in front of him with great ceremony in the dining room, but too much had already happened that day and Joe couldn't eat it. She left. It was almost dark when the doctor arrived. He was upstairs for what seemed to Joe like a long time, and when he came down had little to say.

'The drink's killing him.'

'If he stopped would it help?'

'It's too late for that. Only his will has kept him alive this long.'

When the doctor had gone Joe went back upstairs. His father was sleeping but he awoke when Joe approached the bed.

'The doctor says you'll be fine.'

'I'll be fine when I'm dead. There's something I want to say to you.'

'Wouldn't you rather wait until tomorrow?' Joe suggested.

Randolph Forster shook his head.

'I have to say this. You couldn't dislike me any more than you already do so the only difference it will make is to me. I'm not a religious man, I don't care what you do with me after I'm gone.'

'I assumed you'd want to be buried near Mother,' Joe said with a touch of irony.

'She isn't there.'

Joe thought he had misheard.

'Isn't what?'

'She's not under that stone in the churchyard. She never came back.'

Joe tried to take this in. The alternative was to assume that this full day had been a kind of gigantic nightmare.

'She never came back?'

'There's nothing in there but stones. She didn't run off. She would have done, if I'd given her enough time, but I didn't. She wanted to take you and I wouldn't let her. You were all I had to carry on the name and the house and the business so I wasn't going to have her running off with you. She was weak and stupid. She wanted to go so I put her out. It was a very bad day, it was snowing. I don't know what happened to her after that. I didn't go after her and I didn't let her back in. I never saw her again.'

There was a huge mountain trying to get past Joe's throat to his eyes and an enormous sickness rolling up from his stomach. His ears had given up on him and the whole world shook. His father, after the huge effort of speaking, closed his eyes again and seemed to go to sleep, and Joe's first instinct was to strangle him. Only the knowledge that he would then be no better than this man stopped him from doing so.

'Then why did you pretend?' he managed softly.

'Because I didn't want people to think that harlot could get away from me,' Randolph said, and with that he fell asleep.

Vinia saw Joe leave and she hesitated, wondering whether Dryden had had enough for one day, and then she made up her mind and banged hard on the door until Mrs Clancy opened it. She wore the dirtiest dress that Vinia had ever seen. There was some kind of print on it but she could not tell whether or not it was flowers. Mrs Clancy's hair had never seen a wash; it hung in great iron-grey hanks down past her shoulders.

'And what can we do for you, miss?' she said.

The smell from the house made Vinia want to put her fingers over her nose. She had to stop herself. It was of unwashed, sweaty bodies, stale tobacco and old beer, boiled cabbage, greasy meat and the unmistakable gritty dust that made her long to reach for mop, bucket, scrubbing brush and soap.

'I've come to see Dryden Cameron.'

'My, my, he is having a busy day,' and Mrs Clancy ushered her in through the dank flagged passage and opened a door beyond. Vinia went inside. Dryden looked completely out of place, she was glad to see, like a butterfly in a cobweb, all neat and clean and shiny from her washing and ironing and looking after. It was the dirtiest room imaginable and he was standing by a fire that was almost out, as though he had been standing there for hours.

'Dryden, you can't stay here, it's awful,' she said.

He moved, glanced around as though he were seeing the room for the first time.

'Come back. Tom and me, we'll look after you.'

Dryden turned and looked at her.

'Haven't you had enough yet?' he said.

'You can't stay!'

'I lived here for eight years and what I had before and after it was much worse. This is the best that things have ever been,' he said, sweeping a hand around as if it were a theatre, all gilt and velvet. Vinia could not imagine such an existence.

'Mr Forster came and told us about Esther Margaret,' she said, moving towards him. 'Come back with me, please. Tom's already rowed with his mother about it and it would all be wasted. I'll make your bed up, clean and soft, and I'm going to make a dinner later. Tom's got the front-room fire going.'

'You don't understand, do you?' Dryden said flatly.

'Understand what?' She drew closer and stared into the impenetrable depths of his eyes.

'I killed her. It was because of me. You can't possibly want me there, not after what I've done. Leave it.'

Vinia began to cry. She had no idea that she was going to, and he was right, she didn't want him in her house and she did blame him for what had happened, but she couldn't leave him there. It was like putting a small child or an animal out into a snowstorm. She could see quite clearly that the only love Dryden had ever experienced was his affection for Tom, and if he stayed here he would lose it.

Even worse she had the impression that if she didn't get Dryden out of here he would go completely to the bad, because there was nothing left to hold him, she could see that. All she could do was appeal to what better instinct she thought he had.

'You have to come back with me, for Tom's sake, please.'

In the end that was what did it, though he took more persuading, but she just kept on in the same vein about how Tom had not wanted to come because he was so upset and how much Tom wanted him there and in the end Dryden gave in, though she could see it was not what he had intended at all.

Much to her relief, Tom managed to talk Dryden into the pub, got him drunk and brought him back to eat a huge dinner. When they had eaten Dryden collapsed on to the settee in the front room and fell asleep there. When he came round at teatime she had built up an enormous fire

'You coming back to the Lion?'

'No thanks.'

'See you later, then.'

The back room was as comfortable as Vinia could make it, and she hoped that he didn't associate it with Esther Margaret. It looked different because before it had had no furniture in it. There was a big bed, clean and warm with blankets, plenty of pillows, a rug beside the bed, thick curtains to keep out the draughts, a dresser with drawers and a wardrobe, all of which had been her mother's, and a complete set of bedroom furniture, which she was very proud of and had polished to a high shine. She showed Dryden into it just as he was about to fall asleep on the settee. She had even put a hot brick in the bed.

No more was heard from Dryden that night. She had to waken him to go to work and that morning she marched up to Mrs Clancy's and collected his things and brought them back and installed them in the drawers and wardrobe so that he should have no more excuse to leave. She smothered him with good food, warm fires, a soft bed and all the comforts that she could devise. She knew also that Dryden was tired, exhausted with everything that had happened. Every time he sat down he went to sleep. Tom couldn't persuade him to the pub again after that first time, and she was glad. Tom came rolling home every night, unable to bear himself, for having upset his mother so much. She could do without Dryden drunk as well.

'You're a disgrace!' Alf shouted down the row at him as Tom came home from work.

Tom said nothing. He was breathing heavily by the time he got into the house but all he said was, 'Well, at least my father's speaking to me.'

Vinia had no intention of saying anything to him. Tom had made the biggest sacrifice of his life for his half-brother and she knew that he longed to make peace with his mother. He only slept well because he drank and he drank to destroy his thoughts. He went to work every day and that, she thought, was as much as anybody could ask.

Dryden, on the other hand, was completely and rather frighteningly sober. He was not the world's easiest lodger. He made no conversation other than civilities. He ate what he was given without comment, he slept long (she always had to wake him), but she knew that he was aware all the time of what Tom suffered for him.

Mr and Mrs Hunter had arranged the funeral. Vinia didn't want them to be left to do it but Dryden had nothing to say. He went to work every day that week just as usual. Tom tried to talk to him but in the end she stopped him because Dryden didn't take any notice of anybody.

Mr Hunter, having seen his daughter dead, buried her with all the ceremony he could manage, as though it would make up for his having ignored her after she went wrong. Vinia thought she had never seen such hypocrisy. She went to the ceremony out of love for Esther Margaret and found Mrs Hunter wearing black and crying as though she had stood by her daughter and Mr Hunter pale and tight-lipped, and half the village there from curiosity.

Alf turned Tom from their door three times that week until Vinia went wearily there on his behalf when all the men were at work.

'Tom's heartbroken about this,' she said.

'Then he should have behaved better to his mother. I'm due respect from him.'

'We've lost Esther Margaret this week.'

'That dreadful girl,' Mary said, 'causing her parents grief like that. She's better off dead than married to him, and while he stays in your house I'll not be back.'

She would not listen, so Vinia went two doors away to what was now home and tried not to rejoice that she was being spared Mary's constant presence in her house.

Joe had not slept after the conversation with his father. He got up early and went back to his father's bedroom to find that Randolph had died during the night. Joe sat down and cried, but it wasn't for his father – it was for the confusion and deception and the loss of his mother so long ago. It was the second funeral in a week, and Joe was only sorry that the off-duty pitmen had so little respect for his father that they stayed away. He wished in a way that they had cared for him, it would have meant he was a better man, but at least they weren't afraid to stay away. He wished he could have done so. Even Jacob didn't turn up. When Joe went round by the house later in the day it was empty and the door stood open.

Thaddeus and his wife came to the funeral and they tried to persuade Joe to go home with them, but he knew that the longer he stayed away from the house the less he would want to be there. He had thought he was used to the loneliness but it was strange how much movement and noise were lost.

While prowling the attics later he found a portrait of his mother hidden away in a corner and covered by dustsheets. There was also a great deal of furniture, some of it useful, much of it elegant, so he thought it must be her taste – good wood, nothing so dainty that it looked silly, but well made with clean lines. A big sofa had been eaten by mice or rats but much of it was untouched. He paid a couple of men to help him out of the attic and into the house with it all, and after that he decided the house looked better. He had builders in to do repairs and he started to make plans about what he might do with the house. It stopped him thinking about his father and more especially about his mother and what had become of her. He walked the grounds looking and thinking, and he found small flowers in the grass, which must once have flourished before the fell took over what had previously been a garden. There were snowdrops by the back wall of the house and around the front crocus leaves and what might be the small beginnings of daffodils. Had his mother planted these? He hung her portrait above the drawing-room fire. She looked exactly like him except for her blue eyes. He could not bear to think of how she had been turned away. How could his father have hated her so much?

Once the house was furnished there was nothing more to be done and Joe spent more and more time at work, in the office and underground and making sure that everything was done as it should be, and he would go to the foundry and be there long hours. He felt as though there were nothing else left for him.

He awoke in the middle of the night with the growing conviction that the body found up on the fell was his mother. He knew that it was ridiculous, but once awake he could not explain to himself satisfactorily that such a notion was impossible. He got up at first light, and because that day he was going to the foundry in Wolsingham he called in to see one of the local policeman whom he had seen before at the house. Having been ushered into a small back room, he sounded foolish to his own ears and obviously the other man's when he spoke of his mother and her disappearance.

'How long ago do you say this was, sir?'

'Twenty years.'

'Twenty years.' The man evidently had a lot of fools to deal with. He tried to hide the sigh that followed but didn't quite manage it. 'A body deteriorates a lot in twenty years, sir.'

'But you said . . . you said it had been in the water. If . . . I don't know, if there had been ice . . .'

'The ice age, sir?'

'No! I meant . . . I just meant could there have been any mistake?'

'There is always room for error and it is possible that the woman Mr Hunter identified as his daughter was someone else. People go missing all the time. She could have been anybody.'

'But you're satisfied that it was her.'

'In this job you learn to be satisfied with very little. If you have a body it makes the family feel better when they have something to bury. The woman had fair hair and blue eyes and Mr Hunter seemed to think that it was his daughter. That's good enough for me. It is unlikely that it was another woman unless they were from somewhere else – that is always possible.'

'If there was another woman dead up on the fell, could she have been there for twenty years and not have been found?'

'Very possibly. There's a lot of land up there, sir. It does happen.'

It was not much comfort, Joe thought, and he pushed away from him the idea that Esther Margaret might still be alive. It could be somebody else, yes, but the possibility was slight, it seemed, and he resolved to think of it no more.

CHAPTER FIFTEEN

That spring Vinia received a letter from a solicitor's office in Durham to say that her father's aunt, who had lived abroad for many years, had recently died and left her a hundred pounds. She did not often get letters, and when the thick white envelope dropped on to the floor she assumed that it was bad news, so to open it and find that it was not, indeed was such good news that she had to sit down, made her tremble with excitement. The only money she had ever had of her own was money she had made herself. To be actually given some without any reason was strange and wonderful. At first she wanted to tell Tom, who was asleep upstairs, and her second thought was not to tell anybody, and then she was suddenly aware that she was not alone. When she twisted around on the chair Dryden was in the room. She hadn't heard him come downstairs. She clutched the letter to her but all he said was, 'Any tea going?'

'Yes. Yes.' She stuffed the letter into her pocket and got up.

'I'll get it,' he said, but she poured out the tea and all the time her mind ran round in circles. The shop in the main street that had been empty for so long was still there. She often walked past it, and sometimes she stopped and looked in at the window and wished and wished . . . A hundred pounds would do a great deal, it would get her started. Suddenly she was filled with excitement. She wanted to leap up and down, run around the yard and maybe even down the back lane. Surely Tom could not object when it would be with her own money and she could start something that would belong entirely to her, something which, once it was set up, would make money. She would be a businesswoman, she would draw designs and make clothes and wear the black dress that she had perfected in her head, and there would be one woman or even two at the back of the shop with sewing machines and they would make up the clothes and all the best ladies in the district would come to her shop and she would be known far and wide. She could see her name above the door.

She gave Dryden his tea. He didn't say anything, didn't ask about the letter she had so hastily concealed, and she was bursting to tell somebody but she didn't. She went into the pantry on the pretext of getting something for the table and there she took the letter from her pocket and read it again, just to make sure that there was no mistake, that she had not imagined it, she really was going to get a hundred pounds. It was a fortune. She went back into the kitchen. Dryden had gone back upstairs. They had not been long off shift. He was going to bed.

She put on her hat and coat and left the house and walked as slowly as she could manage up the main street, and she stopped and looked in the windows of the shop, one on either side of the door. Everything was neat and clean inside. The shop belonged to Mr Samson, who lived upstairs on the premises. He had been a boot and shoemaker, the best in the district, but he was very old and his wife had died. She walked up the street until she came to the first opening, and then down the back lane until she came to the gate that led into the yard at the back of the shop. She took a big breath and let herself into the yard. She banged on the back door and after a while Mr Samson came to the door and she explained to him that she would like to look around with the intention of renting the shop from him. He looked surprised but he let her inside and a magic descended on her the moment she went in.

It was as though the shop had been built for her, or that the moment had been fashioned with her in mind. The room behind was very big and had windows overlooking the yard, and the room at the front had two big windows which she had known looked out across the street, and it was hers as nothing had ever been before. There was a big wooden counter to one side. The room had been cleared but she could see it — fashionable clothes on show in the windows, elegant chairs for the ladies to sit in, rooms so that they could try the various dresses, designs for them to look at and magazines from London.

Mr Samson said she could take as much time as she wanted looking around. He went back upstairs and left her there and she lingered, not wanting to go back to a life that was nothing to do with this because reality had crept up on her here as it had not done when she got the letter. Tom would not be pleased, it was no good pretending to herself. On the other hand — she sat down on a small chair at the back of the shop and gazed out across the street where the spring sunshine made everything look better — she must do something. She was not apparently going to have a child, at least it didn't look as though she was, and if she had nothing to do but the housework and the shopping and looking after two men the years were empty of anything she wanted and it was not enough, it was not nearly enough. She had yearned for a chance to do something like this for as long as she could remember. Perhaps if there had been a child it would have been different, though she was not sure that anything could dispel this need and feeling.

She thanked Mr Samson, who did not press her but said she could come back and look any time before making up her mind. He didn't even ask her what she wanted it for, though whatever it was he could hardly mind — there was nobody in it and he must be glad of the money. She walked slowly back down the street and began her daily work. When she had to go shopping she managed to walk past Mr Samson's empty shop four times.

Tom had his tea and went to the pub. Dryden sat at the table with a half-full teacup, staring into the kitchen fire and saying nothing. She subsided into a chair with her teacup and saucer and looked at him.

'Dryden, do you think that shop of Mr Samson's is a good one?'

He turned his gaze from the fire.

'What, the empty one? Aye, it was a good shop. He was the best bootmaker in the area for a long time. Pity he had to stop.'

'But do you think it's in a good position?'

'For what?'

'For a ladies' clothing shop. Do you think there's room for another?'

'I don't know. How can you tell?'

'There's only the Store and Miss Applegate and neither of them is any good. If it was a good one it might bring people in, don't you think?'

'I don't see why not. The nearest would be Crook. Why? I thought you made your own stuff.'

'I do and I could make things for other people.'

'I suppose you could.'

'I could open a shop.'

Dryden considered.

'You always look nice,' he said, 'but don't things like that take money?'

She could feel the letter in her pocket. She fished it out and handed it to him and when he stared at it she said, 'Go on, open it.'

'You got it this morning?'

'Yes.'

He turned the envelope over twice and then took out the letter and perused it for what felt to her like a very long time and then he said, 'A hundred pounds?'

'Do you think that would be sufficient to start up a shop?'

He handed the letter back to her.

'It's a lot of money,' he said.

Vinia waited for him to say something else, and when he

didn't she began to describe the inside of Mr Samson's shop. She even thought it might be good for him to distract his mind from Esther Margaret, because he said so little that she knew he must be thinking about her all the time. Talking about the shop was almost as good as walking around it had been. She left out no detail, and she told him too about the designs she had made and the ideas and ambitions she had.

'Have you got them?'

'What, the designs? No.'

'You didn't throw them away?'

'Tom . . . Tom put them on the fire.'

'Why?'

Vinia didn't want to tell him about it; it made her feel sick.

'He wants a baby,' she said. 'When we got married I thought I would go on working at Miss Applegate's but Tom wouldn't hear of it. He thinks I should be here, looking after him. He doesn't like . . . he doesn't want me to do anything else.'

Dryden didn't say anything to that and eventually she prompted him.

'Would you feel like that?'

'I don't know. I would give anything for my wife and bairn now that it's too late.'

Vinia got up.

'There's no point in worrying about it,' she said. 'Nothing's happened yet.'

They were brave words but when she went to bed that night she felt sick again and as the days went by she couldn't put from her mind the hundred pounds that might alter her life, and she wished that she had never got the letter because then the shop would have been nothing but a safe dream, something that would never happen. Dreams that came true had a nasty edge to them; this one was particularly uncomfortable.

The weeks went past and nothing happened. The weather warmed and sometimes Dryden went to the pub with Tom but apart from that they carried on just the same. Then she had another letter from the solicitors. She knew it was them because it was the same thick white envelope and when she opened it she discovered that the money was hers.

That day Tom and Dryden were on the day shift and were coming in at teatime. Her hands shook all day but she went to see Mr Samson again and talked to him about how much he wanted for the shop and what he would allow her to do, and she could not contain her feeling of exhilaration. It lasted all afternoon until the two men came home, and then it died. She thought, with a sinking heart, that she would have to fight Tom for this and she had not won one of their fights yet, but then nothing had been this important.

She gave them their tea, and before Tom was about to go out to the pub she said, 'I want to talk to you.'

He looked surprised, as well he might, she thought. It was a good moment to catch him because Dryden had gone upstairs and she wanted to say this to him in private.

'I've had a letter from some solicitors. My Great-Auntie Cissy has left me some money.'

Tom looked merrily at her. She thought he had been happy of late; he had sorted out the dispute with his mother, though she still didn't come to the house, and he had got his way, having Dryden there. If only she was pregnant Tom's cup would be full.

'I didn't know you had a Great-Auntie Cissy,' he said.

'I've never seen her. I suppose if my father had still been here he would have got the money.'

'Is it much?' Tom said.

'A hundred pounds.'

'Nice. What are you going to do with it?'

Astonished that he should say something like that, Vinia was struck dumb.

'You've never had any money of your own before and . . . I don't always manage to make good money. You should do something you want.'

Vinia couldn't believe it was going to be this easy.

'Yes, I . . . I thought I might.'

'That would be lovely,' Tom said and, assuming that the discussion was over, pushed his cap on over his dark hair and would have made for the door.

'I have actually done something about it.'

'Really? But it'll be some time, won't it, before the money comes to you. Isn't that how it works?'

'Yes.'

'Well, then.' He went to the foot of the stairs and shouted up, 'Are you coming, our kid?'

'No,' Dryden shouted back.

'Oh, howay, man. You'll be taking up knitting next. Have you heard this about my wife? She's rich!'

Tom, I went to see Mr Samson. I went to look round the shop.'

Tom came back into the room.

'The bootmaker's?'

'Yes. A hundred pounds would start me up.'

The good humour left Tom's face.

'Do we have to go through this again?' he said.

'I want to do it. I want to have a shop. It's what I want more than anything in the whole world. Please, Tom, let me try. Mr Samson says I can have it very reasonably and it would make money, once I got it going, I know it would. We could have somebody in to help and you wouldn't be made uncomfortable and—'

'No,' Tom said. 'I'm not going through all this again with you. We've been through it again and again and I'm sick of it! We are not having anybody in the house and you are not going to have anything to do with shops. It's a stupid, ridiculous idea. I don't want to hear any more about it.'

From somewhere Vinia found anger.

'You are going to hear more about it because it won't do. I don't seem to be able to have a child and I've got nothing to do all day but clean and shop and I hate it—'

'You should have thought about that before you married me,' Tom said.

'I didn't know it was going to be like this.'

'Like what?' Tom said. He sounded dangerous and she recognised the signs – the lack of light in his eyes, the way that he seemed big enough to fill the room.

'That I wouldn't be able to do anything I wanted, that there would be no child.'

'Is that supposed to be down to me?'

'I just want to try to do something myself. I know I could do it if I tried.'

'You're my wife,' Tom said.

'I want to be other things besides your wife!'

'Maybe you should try getting good at that first. Nobody is coming in here to do anything and you are not going anywhere. That's my last word on the subject, do you hear?'

Vinia knew him very well by now. To push any further would be madness.

'I can't give it up,' she managed.

'Can't you?' Tom said, and he got hold of her by the hair and slapped her face. He did it twice before she heard Dryden clatter down the stairs.

'Tom—'

'You keep out of this,' Tom advised him flatly. 'Either go back upstairs or go out.'

The grip on her hair and the smarting of her face had brought so much water into her eyes that Vinia could see neither of them, but she could hear Dryden move nearer.

'Tom . . .' he said again, and the hand on her hair gripped tighter and brought her hands up in protest.

'I told you,' Tom said.

'You won't mend it like that. Let go,' Dryden said.

'Don't interfere.'

'Just let go.'

Tom did. He got Dryden up against the nearest wall, both hands at his throat.

'This is my house. You are the lodger. You are not my brother. You are just some bastard's leavings. Do you understand?'

He pulled Dryden away from the wall and banged him up against it again and tightened the grip on his throat when Dryden didn't answer.

'Do you understand?'

'Yes.'

Dryden slid down the wall when Tom let go of him. Tom turned back to Vinia and got hold of her and he hit her so hard that she fell and it was as if the whole world had exploded. The impact of his hand was savage and the room going past was terrifying and she screamed and then fell and everything was dulled. From far off she could hear the sounds of them fighting and she knew that she must get up and stop them. This was nothing to do with Dryden, he shouldn't have interfered, he shouldn't have got in the way. If she had known what was going to happen she would have waited until he went out to tell Tom, though Tom was hardly ever there whereas Dryden was there a lot so she didn't know when that would have happened. She tried to get up but the room was far off and even though she badly wanted to stop them because she could hear what was happening she couldn't.

She heard the sound of breaking furniture and vaguely wondered what it was – the table, the chairs? They had belonged to her mother, she valued them. Tom was swearing, he always swore when he was angry, and she had never seen him more angry than this. She tried to shout at him to stop but the words wouldn't come out, and the noise went on and on until she thought they must have demolished the whole house and by now somebody must be hurt. The din in her ears was horrible. And then Tom came over to her and he didn't look as if he was hurt and he got hold of her and pulled her up and he said, 'I'm going out now and when I come back I want this whole place tidied up and put right and I want you in bed and I want that scum off my floor.'

She could stand when he was holding her but he didn't go on holding her so that when he let go she slid back on to the rug. Things were clearer. Tom slammed the door when he went out and the room stilled after the shuddering had stopped.

There was very little left of the kitchen. Broken crockery was all over the floor because she had not cleared the table and the teapot had spilled its brown contents down the side of the table. The chairs were in pieces and there was glass out of the kitchen dresser, broken and littered everywhere, and the ornaments from the sideboard which stood along the back wall were all gone. But the worst thing was the way that Dryden was lying in the middle of the room, not moving. She was too afraid to go to him. She kept willing him to get up, she kept waiting for the clock to turn back because this was not his fight, it was nothing to do with him and he shouldn't have interfered, but it didn't matter how long she went on looking at him, he didn't move, until she was afraid that he was dead, face down, all angles and torn clothes.

It took her a long time to get to her feet and cover the short distance to him, and then she got down beside him and said his name quietly for some reason.

'Dryden?'

He didn't respond.

'Dryden, you can't lie there. He's coming back. If you're still there when he comes in he'll kill you. You've got to get up, you've just got to. Oh God, Dryden, I'm sorry.' She started to cry from frustration. 'Please get up. Please.' She began to stroke his hair, and as she did so he started to come round. Vinia had never been as grateful for anything in her life as she was to discover that Tom had not murdered his brother.

'Don't cry over me,' he said, 'I'm not dead yet,' and he sat up and shook himself like a dog.

It was too much for Vinia. She burst into fresh tears.

'I don't see why you had to interfere! You're hurt.'

He was, bleeding profusely from his hands and face and looking accusingly at her from narrowed eyes.

'You knew that was going to happen.'

'I didn't know it was going to happen to you. You could have stayed out of it.'

'Hits you a lot, does he? Oh, Jesus.' This because he had got to his feet.

'He doesn't,' she said.

'It's happened before. Hasn't it?'

'No.'

'Yes it has.' Dryden pulled her up and her head went dizzy. 'At least once. More than that? How many more times?'

'It's happened twice,' she said, trying to get away from him and failing because she was weak. 'As long as I do exactly what he wants it doesn't happen.'

Dryden looked hard at her.

'Getting tired of doing what he wants, eh?'

'It's nothing to do with you!' She pulled away. The tears seemingly were endless. 'I love Tom.'

'Oh yes? What do you love best about him, his bloody fists?'

Dryden started to move towards the stairs and stopped and stood, leaning against the dresser.

'Do you need a doctor?'

'I've had hidings before. I'm all right.'

He went very slowly up the stairs. Vinia began to pick up the broken crockery, the smashed ornaments. She didn't cry over any of it because she had no more tears. She put the surviving crockery in the sink in the pantry and then she took a bowl of warm water and a soft cloth and followed him upstairs into his bedroom. He was lying sideways on the bed and he didn't object to her attempts to clean the blood from the broken skin on his hands. The bruises were beginning to darken on his face.

The window was open in the room; it was a mild early

summer evening and soundless for some reason except for some bird twittering somewhere near.

'I wish you hadn't done anything,' she said.

'Right. He wouldn't have knocked you around any more.'

'I don't know. All I know is that I can't let him treat me like . . .' She couldn't think like what – something she didn't want to be, that was the only way to explain it.

'Are you going to give up?'

'I can't.'

Dryden lay back down again as though he couldn't face that. She put the bowl of water down beside the bed and lay down too and stared at the ceiling. Neither of them said anything for so long that she thought he had gone to sleep, and she was aching so much that she would have quite liked the idea of going to sleep herself, except that Tom was coming back. And then Dryden said out of nowhere, 'I don't think you're going to be able to have Tom and the shop.'

It was the one thing she could not accept.

'He'll get used to it,' she said, and then, exhausted, she turned over and went to sleep.

She woke up suddenly when she heard the front door. Night had fallen; she had no idea what time it was. As she was about to get off the bed an arm came over and stopped her.

'Wait a minute,' he said.

Tom crashed about down below.

'He won't hurt me. He's drunk.'

'Just wait.'

She waited, heart beating, and the crashing about stopped.

'He's not coming upstairs,' she said. 'He doesn't when he gets really drunk. He sleeps on the settee.'

Her words proved correct. Nobody attempted to climb the stairs. She got off the bed. Dryden sat up.

'You're not going down there, are you?'

'No, I'm going to bed.'

She went, but it was miserable. The full impact of what had

happened hit her just as hard as Tom had done. She couldn't bear to think what might happen next; she was only glad that Tom had drunk so much that he couldn't do anything. She wished she hadn't left Dryden, it was better with him there, she wasn't quite sure how. It took her a very long time to get to sleep and she had to get up early because they were on shift in the morning. She tiptoed into Dryden's room. Both his eyes had darkened and closed and his face was covered in bruises so she didn't disturb him. She went downstairs and found Tom getting up off the settee.

'Are you going to work?' she said.

'Of course I'm going. Where's that bastard?'

'He's hurt.'

Neither of them said anything else. She put up his bait, made him a meal and saw him off from the door. Tom even kissed her. She couldn't believe it. Before she had time to think about it any further she went up the street to Mr Samson's and told him that she would take the shop. He stared at the marks on her face.

'Are you sure, Mrs Cameron?' he said.

'Quite sure,' she said.

CHAPTER SIXTEEN

On one of her infrequent trips away Daisy came back with an old *Durham Advertiser*. She showed it to Esther Margaret.

'They think you're dead,' she said.

Esther Margaret said nothing but read the article about her body being found on the fell beyond Deerness Law. She had disappeared so successfully that she no longer existed.

'Is this what you wanted them to think?' Daisy said in her forthright way.

'I left a note, certainly, but . . .' She began to think about Dryden being told that her body had been discovered and how he would feel. Would he be glad that she was dead? Would he think that he was better off without her? It made her uncomfortable, thinking of those last days after the baby had died. She thought he had been as unhappy as she was, and he would feel responsible that she was apparently no more. She read the article several times and then went through into the kitchen where Daisy was making tea.

'Do you think you should go back?' Daisy said.

'I don't know. I don't want to. He treated me badly but . . . I haven't behaved very well either, and right from the beginning . . .' Right from the beginning of their marriage she had been unfair to him, she thought. She had known that what Vinia said often was not true, that Dryden had not gone with other women during their marriage, though people might have thought him entitled to if they had known that she would not let him near her, and he had not got drunk or kept her short of money. He had tried to make his marriage work even though he had not wanted it, but she would not allow it to work and in the end, having pushed him far enough, he had done the wrong thing at exactly the right time for her to condemn him. She could see it so much more clearly at a distance.

Daisy was fussing over the teacups. Esther Margaret watched her and suddenly saw her own situation too.

'You don't want me to go back, do you?'

'I think you should,' Daisy said stoutly, 'but how could I want you to? I was lonely here until you came and I'll be lonely after you've gone, but it doesn't stop me from knowing what the right thing to do is. You've got a young husband grieving over you while you're still alive. How can it be right?'

'He's not very nice.'

'No, but he's a man for all that and he's yours. It's a strange thing, is a marriage – you can run away from it but it's still there.'

'And you don't think I'm right to let him think I'm dead?'

'No, I don't,' Daisy said, and she poured out the tea.

After that Esther Margaret spent a great deal of time thinking while she went for walks to the ruined castle. She had started walking farther. It was easier to think while you were out here. The warm weather had arrived and in the mornings the gulls were silver-winged above the sea. She was forever finding things to do, working hard at the cottage and it was so tidy that Daisy complained, always washing and ironing, and making cakes and cooking and leaving Daisy nothing to do. They had little society, and Esther Margaret was beginning to miss the company of men and the sound of their voices. Her brief romance had not lasted, it had not matured into love as she now knew some relationships did, like Daisy's with her major. Daisy had nobody, but she had known what it was like to have a man love her, to have someone to herself, not somebody pushed into a marriage that he did not want. Dryden had never loved her, she knew, and there was no guarantee things would be any better if she went back. She had never loved him either, nor would she in the future, she could see that too, so perhaps it was just as well to stay away.

The trouble was that she remembered him more and more clearly, the way that his body felt close to hers, and many was the time she awoke in the night and thought of the day that Joe Forster had asked her to run away with him. She could not understand why she had not done so.

On the beach that summer she saw couples walking hand in hand and young married couples with small children, and she became restless. This life that Daisy had made for herself was an old person's life, it had nothing to do with her. The days were suddenly too long and there was little to do which was interesting. Daisy could cut herself off for hours with her reading and writing and she was content, or had made herself content.

'Haven't you ever thought of marrying again?' she asked one day when they were sitting out on the grass together in front of the house and the waves were hardly breaking upon the shore, so warm and still was the day.

Daisy laughed.

'Who would have a fat, lazy old woman like me?'

'He's been dead a long time, though, the major.'

Daisy hesitated, and then she looked at Esther Margaret.

'Not to me,' she said.

Esther Margaret went for a walk after they had drunk their tea but she was bored, and when she thought she might make a cake on her return she came back to find Daisy in the kitchen undertaking that very task, and she had to admit when they ate it that Daisy's cakes were much better than her own. That evening she prowled the house, which had suddenly become too small and nothing to do with her, finally going into the little sitting room, which was her favourite room in the house. Daisy was sitting in her usual armchair by the window, sipping sherry and looking out across a full tide.

'I think I ought to go back, Daisy,' she said.

Daisy smiled, struggled out of her armchair and came across to give Esther Margaret a kiss.

'I knew you would. It's the right thing,' she said.

As the summer evening shadows lengthened, Esther Margaret stood in the garden watching the fat black-and-white ducks bobbing up and down on the water. In a way she didn't want to leave the peace, the ease and the comfort, but it was no longer the right time in her life to be here. She was beginning to feel left out, as though the world were rushing past and she was standing behind a window not taking part. In a way Daisy had died when the major had and was not in the world any longer, but Esther Margaret could feel herself getting ready to return; she could feel the strength that would enable her to do difficult things.

CHAPTER SEVENTEEN

When Luisa Morgan had first been married she had not come home at all, but that summer she came back for a long stay. Her parents organised a party for her, and Joe was invited to attend and to spend the night. He had forgotten how beautiful she was. She looked to him rather like Esther Margaret, fair haired and blue eyed, but her eyes were not innocent and young – she was self-assured and went around talking to everybody, her silk dress rustling as she moved.

It was a perfect summer evening and the windows were open, so that the noise of the music streamed into the garden like a flood. People sat about outside, drinking champagne and talking, the men in dark suits and the women in pretty dresses, the young ones showing off their creamy shoulders. The garden was thick with flowers and trees in full green leaf.

Joe felt obliged to ask Luisa to dance. He hadn't seen her much since she had been married, he had always managed to keep out of the way when she visited, and he didn't know what to say to her. Luisa reminded him that he had not wanted to dance with her the first time they met.

'You hated me,' she said.

'I did not.'

'Yes, you did. You declined to dance with me a second time. I was mortified.'

'You told me your mother was boring.'

'She is. She's also my mother. I didn't realise that being boring was not confined to my mother.'

Luisa said she was hot and they walked out into the garden, and when they were well away from the house she stopped and put a white-gloved hand up to his cheek and kissed him. It was a sweet kiss and Joe was not pleased with himself when he liked it.

'You're supposed to join in,' she said.

'You're married.'

'Oh, don't be so stuffy. It's just a kiss. Lord, I wish I had you in Edinburgh – my friends would go wild for you. They all have old husbands, you see. Old men have money. You don't know anything about this, do you?'

'No.'

'You're so refreshing,' she said. 'Who else would admit it?'

Joe found himself kissing her, pulling her into his arms, ashamed of himself because he didn't care about her. He realised the difference between wanting someone and caring for them but he couldn't help it. He wanted to go on kissing her for ever and feeling the curves of her body beneath the rustling of her dress. He kissed her until she stopped him. She did it gently enough, putting a restraining hand to his shoulder and smiling at him, but Joe couldn't look at her and when they went back inside he felt wretched, thinking of how much he had loved Esther Margaret and had had not even a kind word from her, whereas this woman, whom he didn't even like, had given him her mouth until he was shaking with want. He went back outside without her, and in the cool of the evening Thaddeus found him.

'I saw you dancing with Luisa.'

Joe hoped that was all he had seen. What a way to behave in the house of the only man who had ever been kind to him. No, more than that, Thaddeus was generous. Joe couldn't speak he was so mortified.

'She isn't happy,' Thaddeus said. 'McAndrew is too old for

her. I thought so at the time but she wouldn't be told. Money and power are strange things, they take a hold of people.'

Joe knew that he should have gone home but he couldn't. He wanted to hold Luisa again. People danced until late, and although he didn't want to dance with anybody else he made himself be polite and talk about things that did not interest him. But even when the music stopped, the party was over and he went to bed he was unhappy. He called himself weak and stupid, he stood by the window and wished himself at home where there were no temptations, and then he heard the door and when he turned around Luisa slid into the room. There was no light but the dawn, which was breaking in spectacular gold and pink beyond the windows, but even from across the room Joe could see that she was wearing something very thin and clinging. She stood back against the door after she closed it and then she came to him.

Joe didn't look at her any more; he regarded the view from the window – all trees and lawns with the River Wear below it – as though the rest of his life depended upon it.

'Where is Mr McAndrew that he doesn't come with you?'

'He's at some boring meeting in Glasgow.'

'Is everything boring to you?'

'You aren't – at least not yet.'

That made Joe smile, and as he did so she reached up an almost bare arm and kissed him and already he remembered how wonderful her kisses were.

'I don't love you,' he said.

'I don't love you either. Does it matter? You're not going to go all puritanical on me, are you? You cannot imagine how appalling it is being bedded by an old man. Really, you just cannot think.'

'I don't understand why you married him if you don't like him.'

She laughed.

'He is a very rich and powerful man. He is one of the most powerful industrialists in Scotland, whereas you are . . .'

'I'm what?'

'You own a pit, or rather half a pit since my father owns the other half, and part of a small foundry in a backwater. When my father tried to persuade me to marry you I have to say that I couldn't take him seriously. Dear me, how old are you – twenty? I didn't want to marry a boy. Don't look at me like that. You wouldn't have married me for the world. Be honest, you thought I was a nasty little wretch.'

'I still think you're a nasty little wretch.'

'Do you, darling?' She kissed him again and put her slender white arms up to his neck. Joe couldn't resist her. She encouraged him to do all the things he had wanted to do and tried not to think about with Esther Margaret. He hadn't known how bitter he was until then, or that he could want a woman so much without having a regard for her, but when he had pulled the clothes off her and kissed her and caressed her and and had her he discovered that this was not true either, that nothing was that simple, because he did have some regard for her. He liked her laughter and her enthusiasm and her body, he liked the way that she didn't care about anything, he liked the champagne she had brought with her and insisted on sprinkling all over the bed and over him and drinking out of the bottle. He liked her reckless-ness, the way that all she cared for was now – and her husband's money and power, of course, she said.

'Does he love you?' Joe asked.

She laughed.

'Of course he doesn't. He says that he does. Just think if you were very old, say forty and you could buy and possess a girl who looks like me and have her when you wanted her and own what other men desire and dress her up like a doll and have her pretend that she wants you in bed, wouldn't you want that?'

'I don't think so, no. I can't imagine being that advanced in years but I rather hoped that I could marry and be happy and have children and grow old with somebody I loved.'

She laughed again and squirted champagne at him.

'What a romantic you are, Joe, and how young!'

He took the champagne from her and fought with her, since she wanted him to, and rolled her over and made love to her and afterwards she looked up into his eyes and said earnestly, 'No one loves anyone, you know, darling, not really.'

And he thought it was true. Esther Margaret had not loved or she would not have killed herself. His father had despised his mother and been the cause of her death, just as Dryden had with Esther Margaret, and Thaddeus and Alice tolerated one another. Perhaps it was all you could hope for, that and to have a beautiful woman in your bed. And then he thought of his house, of the emptiness, the silence. If the future was to be like that there was nothing worth having. But in the morning, when she had to leave him, there were tears in her eyes.

'You will stay tonight, won't you?'

'I can't. I have to go to work.'

'Then come back.'

'It will look obvious to your parents and I wouldn't hurt them.'

She looked patiently at him.

'You're never going to get what you want that way,' she said, and left.

Joe felt as though he had betrayed Thaddeus and Alice, but Luisa's father in particular. If she was not happy with George McAndrew he was not making things any better by complicating it and he owed Thaddeus more than that, but it wasn't easy. During the day he managed because he had work to distract him, but that night and the one that followed and all the other nights that week he couldn't sleep for thinking about her and wanting her, and it made him bad tempered during the day so that the office workers and the men he came into contact with looked at him in surprise. He had to stop himself from going to her. He wished that she would go back to Scotland and he could have some peace.

On the Saturday evening he came back from work angry and

tired and wishing he could make up some excuse and go to the house when he had already told Thaddeus that he was too busy to attend a dinner party. He thought of her wearing one of those exquisite dresses which McAndrew was rich enough to buy for her, the kind that showed off her shoulders and the tops of her breasts to advantage. He thought of her smiling and making conversation and drinking champagne, and he wondered whether she would make up to some other man if he were not there. It made him want to groan aloud or follow his father's example and hit the bottle.

The following morning, having not gone to church or the office, he was surprised to hear a banging on the front door. When he opened it she stood there, wearing a blue riding dress. A white pony grazed the lawn behind her.

'Wretch!' she declared. 'Why didn't you come to the dinner party? I devised it especially for you. How dare you refuse?'

'How dare I what?' Joe said. 'Do you think I'm a puppy to come to heel? You chose what you wanted.'

'I want you!'

'No, you don't. You're just bored. You want laying. I'm told some men do it for money.'

She went for him. Joe was astonished at how easily he stopped her. That brought her into his arms and then she raised swimming eyes. Joe couldn't help but laugh and when he released her she said, 'You're horrible.'

'I am, yes. Aren't you glad you didn't marry me?'

'I'm going back tomorrow.'

'Give my regards to George.'

CHAPTER EIGHTEEN

Dryden had thought that he would wake up and it would be the morning before or the week before or almost any other time but the time that it was. He had told himself when Esther Margaret said she was pregnant and Tom told him he would have to marry her that things couldn't get any worse. After all, he had been through quite a lot for somebody his age. And then he married her and she kept from him and he thought again it couldn't get any worse. And then the one night that he had gone to bed with another woman she had gone into labour and the baby had died, and he thought once more it couldn't get any worse. And then she had disappeared and then there was the suicide note and then they found her body and then . . . He didn't want to think any further because he had reached the conclusion that for some people things just went on getting worse all the time. He wished that he had gone back to Mrs Clancy's to live. It might be dirty and uncomfortable and have awful food but there were much harder things in life.

Vinia was ambitious, she was difficult, she had even maybe planned to start on at Tom about the shop when he was in the house. She knew that she could push Tom too far. Had she not already done it at least once? Afraid and almost crying, she had looked like a different person, and Dryden had changed his mind and decided that if he could do nothing else at least he could draw Tom away. Beyond that he had not thought. He didn't want Tom to be a person who would hit his wife; however provoking she might be there was nothing seriously wrong with what she wanted. He did not understand why Tom had become so upset about it. She had not run off with another man, she had not had a dead child, left a suicide note, done away with herself. Vinia had done nothing that really mattered, as far as he could see.

So he drew Tom away and then he wished that he hadn't. He loved Tom too much. There had been too many good times, too many evenings in the Golden Lion and the Black Horse, too many games, too many pints, too much warm conversation, too much laughter, and all those late nights, full of stars, when they had left the pub and walked down the main street and everybody else was in bed and they were fairly drunk and their footsteps resounded on the opposite pavement and the whole world had been empty except for them. Dryden knew with the simplicity of the unloved that there was nothing in the world to better that.

When there was no more fight left in Vinia or in him, Tom still had to prove something and he chased her and even when she screamed, and she was so slight, Tom drew back his fist and hit her. If Dryden could have closed his eyes over it he would have but he couldn't, it would have been the coward's way, and he thought that it was in that moment that all the love between himself and Tom ceased. It was a nasty short death for something that had been so important, and Dryden knew in those moments that he would never have anything like it again, that Tom would hate him. Even then Tom didn't stop. Dryden thought that when she was hurt and on the floor it might be enough but it was not. He didn't know what Tom planned to do after that, and he had no intention of waiting long enough to find out. He pulled Tom away from her and after that he wished he hadn't. No love or compassion deterred Tom, he could see nothing but his quarry, and although Dryden told himself that there had been that time at the pub when he had put Tom on to the floor with three punches he could see that it was not going to happen here. Tom had not been angry then like he was now. Tom had even laughed after it had happened, but now laughter was the farthest thing imaginable. Tom liked hitting him, who he was didn't matter, and Dryden knew as the blows followed one another and his strength left him that the feeling that Tom had for him was dying. It was the only thing in his life which mattered, and so the more Tom hit him the less will he had to do anything about it. He got to the point where he didn't mind if Tom killed him because the regard between them was stone dead and his insides were weeping and grieving over it and there was no repair to be made; beyond it there was nothing.

Tom became misty after a while, his well-loved face became a blur beyond the pain and the blood, and Dryden didn't care what happened. He was not there, he was in the street with his brother when it was late, when the pavements were empty and the air was keen and the wind blew in from the fell with snow behind it like a cold caress and there was nobody else. It was like a painting to him. He would have hung it on the wall, the images of himself and Tom and the shadowed houses and that peculiarly wild fresh stillness which only the fells had, all heather and sheep and wood smoke and the view that went on for ever. It was the best. When you have had the best then it doesn't really matter, he thought; when you had heard Tom singing in the dead of night you knew that even the angels listened. They did not hear now when Tom beat him to the floor and everything became slow and then slower. Mary Cameron would have been proud of Tom, Dryden thought; she would have been pleased with him.

And then there was peace. When he came to Vinia was crying and she was all over him, begging him to come round, as though he wouldn't, and accusing him of things, as though it had anything to do with him, which it hadn't, and going on about how much she loved Tom, which was too much for his stomach. He resented her. He wished he had never got involved. And for what? For some bloody stupid shop! And after he had managed to climb the stairs, and it had been a very long way, she came up and started sponging his face, which was bliss, he wished she would never stop. A bird was singing outside as though everything were normal, and then she had gone on and on about the bloody shop and how she couldn't have it. Didn't she know what was happening here? Didn't she realise that Tom would not let her do it? He tried to tell her but she wouldn't listen. She was like somebody from another age, another place.

She had finally shut up and gone to sleep and let him rest, and he needed to, everything hurt so much, and then he awoke. The door had slammed. The enemy was in the house and she nearly got up and went downstairs; he had to stop her. But she was right in what she said. Tom was drunk. He did not attempt the narrow steepness of the stairs, which Dryden thought very sensible of him. Soon there was peace again and Dryden breathed more easily. Nobody was going to kill him that night, and it was all he cared about. Vinia went to her own room. He was glad when she had gone because he had all the space to himself to ease the hurts. He stretched out and went to sleep.

Mr Samson had said she could have the sign repainted. Vinia thought she would have it plain in black with her name in white and it would read 'Vinia Cameron, Ladies' Fashions'. That very first day she went into Bishop Auckland and bought two sewing machines, and she bought chairs and tables from the auction rooms and ordered everything to be delivered, and then she went back to the shop and dusted and swept it out; it didn't need much. She and Mr Samson signed an agreement for the rent; she paid in advance and spent all her time during the day at the shop. With thick paper and pencils and pens her fingers could not move fast enough to suit her brain – it was as though all the ideas had backed up and were now being let out in a hurry. She took materials and fashioned a hat without even thinking about it, and then another, creating from nowhere beautiful things.

She asked Mrs Perry, two doors down, who had nobody

except her husband to look after, if she would come in and see to the house and the cooking during the day, so Tom came home on the Friday afternoon to one of Mrs Perry's lovely meat pies. Dryden had gone back to work after two days. He didn't look very good and he was very tired when he got home, and he washed and ate and went straight back to bed. Tom said nothing; he went on as though everything were the same. All that weekend Tom kept to the pub, turned away from her in bed, but on the Monday when he came home he threw down his bait tin and said, 'So, you went ahead and did it.'

'I told you I was going to.'

Dryden hadn't gone to bed; he was sitting in a chair to one side of the fire.

'I suppose you think he's going to save you.' Tom jerked his chin in Dryden's direction.

'I don't suppose anybody will need to save me,' she said, looking straight at him.

Tom didn't look at her. It was Dryden he turned to.

'I want you out of my house.'

'Tom, you can't.' Vinia took a step towards him but Tom stopped her.

'I don't want to hear another word,' he said.

'Tom, please. It's nothing to do with him.'

'I'm going to the Lion and I want you out by the time I come back. If you're still here then I'll break your neck.'

'Tom —' she said again, but Tom walked out.

Dryden watched the door for a few seconds as though it might reopen and Tom would come in and say that it was only a joke, he hadn't really meant it. Then he walked out of the room and up the stairs and after a few seconds she ran after him. He had already begun putting his things together.

'He didn't mean it,' she said from the doorway. He didn't reply. 'You can't just go. Dryden. Dryden! Don't go. This is your house.'

'It doesn't feel like my house any more and I can't say I cared much for it when it did. I'm going to leave you and Tom to fight this out. Don't blame me if you get hurt.'

'I'm sorry. I didn't mean to involve you.'

'It's all right. Maybe just once you needed somebody on your side,' he said softly, and then he left.

Vinia sat down and cried over it and over him and over the friendship with Tom which had meant so much to him. She had not been alone for long when the back door opened and Tom's mother came in. She never came in except during the day when she knew Dryden was not there. Perhaps she had seen him leave.

'What's this I hear about you setting up shop?' she demanded. 'I had it from Mrs Everton. I told her it couldn't be right, that our Tom would never let you do such a thing, but she says it is, that you've rented Willie Samson's shop. Whatever would you do with such a place?'

'I would sell things in it,' Vinia said, putting up her chin.

'Sell things?' Mary Cameron stared at her. 'What on earth are you talking about?'

Vinia stood up from the chair she had sat down in when Dryden went.

'I'm going to design and make and sell ladies' clothing, hats and dresses, and repairs and mending too. I'm going to have my name above the door and employ people to help and Mrs Perry to come in to see to things and I'm going to pay her.'

Mary stared.

'You impudent little baggage!' she said. 'How dare you? You couldn't do such a thing. How could you ever afford to do anything like that?'

'I can. I've got some money and that's what I'm going to do with it.'

'We'll see what our Tommy has to say about this.'

'Tom already knows and he's had his say. Can't you see the state of my face? Your precious son knocked me across this floor.'

'Our Tommy wouldn't do such a thing. You little liar!'

'Use your eyes. How else do you think I ended up like this?'

'That man did it. He would do anything to women. Look at what happened to his wife. Our Tommy should never have had him here. I said no good would come of it.'

'You'll be glad to hear, then, that he's left.'

'I am indeed,' Mary said, 'I'm very glad. That's the best piece of news I've ever heard. We'll soon have you sorted out. Shops indeed. You've got enough to do here—'

'I've got nothing to do here, nor am I likely to have. There's no bairn to see to and Tom's always at the pub. What am I expected to do?'

'If there is no bairn it's because of you, never at home, always gadding about, interfering where you shouldn't be and giving homes to people who don't deserve it. Our Tommy deserved better than you. Any lass in this village would have given him a bairn by now. You with your funny ideas!'

After she had left Vinia was exhausted. She fell asleep on the settee and awoke only when Tom came back from the pub. She wasn't sure what to expect; she only hoped he was so drunk that she could get past him and up to bed before he started anything else.

'Has that bastard gone?' Tom said.

'Of course he has. You told him to.'

'Right. You get up those bloody stairs to bed. I don't want to hear any more tonight!'

Vinia went. She was quick, but she was only half undressed by the time Tom got there, and afterwards she thought he had done it on purpose because he got hold of her as he had before, by the hair, and turned her over on to the bed, and she was more afraid than she had been the night of the fight.

'No, Tom, don't. We don't have to quarrel about this. I love you.'

'Who's quarrelling?' Tom said.

'You're hurting me.'

'Am I? Well, fancy that. I wonder why you think so? I wonder what I would be doing such a thing for when you are such a good and obedient wife.'

It was not far to Mrs Clancy's and yet it was a whole world away, a world without Tom's regard, that chilly place which Dryden had inhabited for all those years before his brother had spoken to him. Mrs Clancy seemed to be expecting him, but then the whole village knew that they had fought.

'Come in, bonny lad,' she said, offering him her gummy grin. 'You look like you've been in the wars. Your Tom likes to keep his wife to himself, I hear.'

Dryden didn't respond. He hadn't realised that people were talking or that they were saying such things, but they could only guess at the reason he and Tom had had a fight and that was the obvious conclusion they would come to. It wasn't so very far from the truth, though he hoped he would have tried to help any woman in a similar situation. Maybe he wouldn't. Maybe it was just that she was the only woman he had ever had any positive feelings towards. It had cost him Tom so he wasn't feeling very charitable any longer.

He dumped his belongings and then he walked across to the Station Hotel, one of the pubs that Tom didn't go to. Nobody spoke to him and he stood there all evening until he was very, very drunk, and then he walked the dark streets. Dora Sims was coming out of the Black Horse by the time he reached it. He wasn't sure whether he had arranged it on purpose.

'Hello, Dryden,' she said. 'I've been hearing things about you.'

'It's not true,' Dryden said.

'You don't know what they are yet.'

'I do.'

'Your face is a picture,' she said. 'You should keep your hands off other men's wives, you know,' and she drew very close and then she kissed him.

It hurt to kiss her but it was a lot better than not kissing her.

'How would you like to come home with me?'

'Last time I went home with you my life fell apart.'

'As bad as that?' she said. 'Look at it this way, petal, you've got nowt much left to lose by all accounts.'

Dryden had got to the door of her house, and it was then that he remembered the day the baby had been born and died and he couldn't go in.

'Are you all right, lover?' Dora said.

'I'm drunk.'

'I'm used to drunks. Hart's always drunk when he's here. You could sleep. It's got to be better than the other place you have to go to.'

'I don't think so, thanks.'

He wandered away and was at the end of the street by the time she closed the door. He didn't want to go back to the boarding house. He didn't know where he wanted to be. He walked down the street and past the Golden Lion and over the railway crossings and then down Church Lane with the fields on either side until finally he reached the churchyard. It was dark so he had to search for Esther Margaret's headstone. He hadn't seen it before, but being new it stood out in its position not far from the gates that opened on to the path towards the heavy church door. He couldn't believe that she was actually in there, that anybody could be. Her stone read 'Esther Margaret Cameron. Sleeping'. Sleeping? If she was sleeping then he wished to God she would wake up and end this nightmare. He felt as if he had come full circle. Could it be that he was about to die? Could it be that when you lost everything it was the end? He felt as though there were nothing more to be done, nothing to be tried for. He was suddenly very tired. He sat down and then lay down and it was surprisingly comfortable. The churchyard, Dryden thought, was a lot better than Ma Clancy's beds.

✳　　✳　　✳

Tom tore the clothes off Vinia and laid heavy hands on her until any goodwill that she had tried to salvage was gone. They had not before this fought in bed, she believed him incapable of such a thing, but then in the beginning she had thought Tom wanted her for who she was and not a woman made in his mother's image, not somebody to hold beneath his will. He subdued her, had her until he was tired, and then in the morning he told her that while he was at work that day she would go back to Mr Samson and tell him that she no longer wanted the shop. She would send everything back and by the time he came home that afternoon she would be there with the tea ready.

'I won't do anything of the kind,' Vinia said. 'If I have to I'll move out.'

'You can't. If I have to come to the shop for you I'll thrash you all the bloody road home. Do you understand me?'

Even after he had gone out and slammed the door she shouted after him, 'I will never forgive you for this, Tom, never!'

CHAPTER NINETEEN

The following day Dryden and Tom were on the back shift, which was normally Dryden's favourite, being during the day, but then he would have given anything not to be there. Tom was still ignoring him and he had nothing to look forward to. He thought that maybe if he went to one of the more respectable boarding houses somebody might have the grace to take him in. He didn't fancy another night in the churchyard, even though it was warm, and he needed somewhere with a few comforts if he was to take any pleasure at all from his life.

They worked. He could hear Tom's voice in the distance now and then as Tom spoke to other people. Dryden didn't think about the work, he just did it, got paid for it, and was always aching and tired at the end of it. He made good money and often other men couldn't keep up, but he was glad of it when times were difficult, you knew where you were with it. If Tom hadn't been there Dryden would have been much happier. As it was he tried to make the best of it, which wasn't saying much. He thought about Vinia and hoped Tom had been kind to her, but he doubted it. Tom wasn't the man to give in over anything, but if she gave in now over this she would never again be able to do anything she wanted which Tom didn't want, and he knew how badly she wanted it by the fight she had put up so far. He just wished he had been out of the way when it happened, though it was always possible that Tom might have hurt her badly or killed her when he was in a temper like that.

They stopped to have something to eat and Dryden reconstructed the last few days in his mind so that none of this had happened and he was living with them and there was nothing beyond the nice day-to-day monotony that seemed to be as much as he could hope for. He would have liked that, sleeping in a soft bed and having meals prepared and not having to fight with anybody.

After a short time they went back to work, but they had not been started up again for very long when Dryden thought he heard something that sounded like distant thunder, a rumble and then another rumble and then something louder. He stopped and the men around him, after a few more seconds, stopped too. They weren't confused, it wasn't thunder, it was the ground moving, shaking, altering. You didn't know necessarily where it was coming from or going to and everybody stopped because you had to know which way to run if there was going to be a problem. There was no more noise. Dryden listened hard but it was silent. He relaxed. And then there was a huge noise, ear-splitting; it hurt and suddenly everybody was running everywhere and some of them were getting tangled up in other people. He could hear Tom cursing and somebody else shouting.

The ground shook, everything shook, and then it was like when you were tossing the die in a game, it all got mixed up round and round and the whole area started coming apart with a huge noise and then it began to cave in. That was the most frightening part of it. It didn't matter where you went, it seemed to him, though people pushed and shoved, it was like a game with everybody going crazy, and then there was the biggest noise of all, so big that his ears wouldn't take it, and he could hear Tom's voice and he began to run in that direction and everybody else was going the other way, as they did in crowded streets. Tom's was a voice in pain, a cry of distress. The air was full of dust, thick so that he couldn't see, until there was nothing in front of him but the sound of his brother shouting for help.

Joe was sitting at the desk in his office trying not to think about the taste and feel of Luisa McAndrew's body. Thaddeus was sitting in the office with him, puffing at one of his blessed cigars, filling the place with smoke. Having done the right thing did not make Joe want to go on doing the right thing; he wanted to go up to Scotland and grab her and run away with her like some stupid man in a poem, dashing off with her on a horse.

Luisa, Joe thought, was like a party, and his life had been particularly bereft of parties. Thaddeus was going on about markets and demands for coal and steel and the problems of pricing and all the things that usually were of great interest to Joe, but today he couldn't bring then closer than the edge of his mind. The rest of his mind was full of Luisa's eyes and mouth and the way that he missed her carelessness, her levity, the fun that she had brought with her. She had no plans to return, Thaddeus had said. Joe knew this was sensible but he was tired of being sensible.

One of the clerks burst into his office just as the pit siren screamed.

'Mr Forster!'

Men were brought to the surface almost immediately. Thaddeus insisted on going down with Joe to see how extensive the fall had been. The men were collected by their families as they came to the surface. Joe found Vinia at his shirtsleeve.

'Tom and Dryden are both down,' she said. 'What are you doing?'

'When you let go of my coat I'm going down to have a look.'

'How bad is the fall?'

'I don't know yet,' Joe said patiently as he disentangled her. 'I haven't seen it. Just wait.'

Joe felt reassured as more men were brought up. It was like

being a magician at a fair, magicking them before people's eyes, but when the flow of men stopped and he and Thaddeus went below ground and saw the fall Joe felt sick.

'How far back do you think it goes?' Thaddeus said, and his voice sounded ghostly, unearthly, as though people might already be dead. Joe tried to push the thought away.

'No idea. We need to get working. We need to organise.'

Thaddeus went up to deal with this. Joe refused to go, staying there to help. Thaddeus ascertained that fourteen men were missing. Joe felt even more sick then – all those people trapped.

They worked for several hours before they broke through, and even before that Joe could hear the sounds, the men's voices, and he was so glad he prayed and thanked God and hoped they were all there; there was a good chance they would all be saved and he could go home and sleep soundly in his bed. He helped bring the first men through the narrow opening they had sweated for, and as he did so he looked each time for Tom and Dryden but twelve men were counted out and Tom and Dryden were missing. When they were all out Joe went back himself, and he could see that beyond there was another fall.

The men were taken to the surface. It was a slow process because some of them were hurt though nobody was too bad and no one was dead, and he started the rescuers digging again farther back but the tunnel was blocked completely and by the end of that first day Joe wanted to sit down and cry.

After Tom had gone to work that morning Vinia tidied up and then she walked slowly to the shop. She couldn't give up no matter what Tom did because it had cost too much to get this far, but she was afraid of the immediate future, of Tom and his mother, but most of all of herself. She had not realised that she would fight so hard for something she had wanted for so long. She thought that she had probably always wanted this more than anything in the world except her husband. That morning was the first time ever that Tom had left without kissing her, and the significance did not escape her. He must be very upset indeed to break the code like that but she didn't care, she wanted him never to touch her again. This was going to be a long, hard battle of wills between them, and she did not know where it would end.

The sign-painter had finished. She walked up the other side of the street and stood for a few moments admiring her name, and various people stopped and remarked on it and several women said to her how nice it would be when there was a proper ladies' clothing shop in the village, and did she think they could bring in various pieces of cloth to be made up, and when she walked across the street one woman stopped her and said that her daughter was getting married before Christmas and was she really going to think up the ideas herself and put them on paper for people to see?

The news had certainly travelled fast, Vinia thought. She assured Mrs Jamieson that this was so and thought that if people were going to treat her as well as that she might have a good chance of making this work. It cheered her considerably to think that it had not necessarily been nothing other than the best dream of her life, that other people might see it as reality.

She unlocked the door and walked into the shop. Sunlight was spilling in through the windows and across the bareness of the big room, and suddenly a huge excitement filled her and ousted the awful thoughts about herself and Tom.

It would get better; it had to. She would tell him all about this when he came home, how keen people were, how admired the shopfront had been. It was hers. She had had a house of her own before but not a business, not an enterprise. She wanted to hug it to her. She walked round and round and after a while she sat down and began sketching, her favourite occupation. She had arranged to see a woman who would help with the sewing, Miss Little, who lived in the village and made her own clothes. She hoped she would need more than one person after a while, but she thought that to begin with if she took care of the front shop and there was somebody to do the sewing and alterations in the back that would do very well. She showed Em Little the sketches she had made.

'I thought if we could make some of these up and a variety of hats and put them into the window it would give people some idea of what we could do. A lot of them mustn't be too expensive. I don't want to frighten folk away.'

Miss Little was enthusiastic and ready to start, so they sat down in the back to begin together, and Vinia began to think about the fabrics she would need and other materials. They talked about it and decided to go to Bishop Auckland that afternoon to find what they needed and to speak further about this great new venture.

Vinia had almost forgotten about Tom when she heard the pit siren blow. It was the most frightening sound on God's earth when it went off like that at the wrong time because it meant only one thing.

When Dryden came back to consciousness it was the biggest nightmare of his life come true. He had no idea how long he had been there but he remembered what had happened. He was not hurt. He sat up carefully. There was no light, he couldn't even see the fingers in front of him, but there was space around him and at least there was water, he could feel the damp beneath him. He listened in the silence for somebody else's breathing and thought he could hear the shallow sounds of pain.

He moved carefully with his hands in front, and after a few feet of crawling he came across something solid and heavy and warm to the touch, and he knew with the finality that has no illusion that it was Tom.

'Tom, can you hear me? Tom?'

There was no response; nobody spoke. Dryden would have given anything to have heard Tom speak. He moved his hands over Tom's body and found the faint beating of his brother's heart. He moved away as far as he could, which was not far, but there seemed to be nobody else, nor could he hear anything at all. He went back and lay down beside Tom and listened to the reassuring sound of Tom's heart. He didn't sleep. He had never been so wide awake. It was strange. The only way that you knew your eyes were open was by blinking. The darkness was so thick, he imagined that being dead was like this. Or perhaps they were dead and the blackness was a tomb. He couldn't think about that, it made him panic, but he thought that Tom was not obviously hurt.

He got as close as he could and put an arm around Tom, closed his eyes and buried his face against Tom's warm body. They would be rescued; Mr Forster wouldn't let them stay down here. Something would be done. He listened carefully for the sounds of people trying to reach them but there was nothing, which worried him. After a long time he could feel himself drifting into sleep and he was grateful. Maybe when he woke up someone would be there, or it would all have been one of those particularly nasty dreams that you were pleased to come back out of.

He didn't quite sleep, he was aware all the time of where he was; he would almost get there and then come back to consciousness again, as though he could not quite let go of the circumstances, alert when he needed to conserve his energy. From time to time he thought that he and Tom were back in the house in Prince Row and Vinia was there and sometimes Esther Margaret was there too, it all got mixed up, but there was a space in his mind that was fully aware of where he was and of Tom's breathing, which seemed to him to get shallower, with more time in between each breath. Dryden stopped breathing himself quite a lot so that he could make sure that Tom was still with him.

'Don't die, Tom. Don't die and leave me here, please. I don't care if you never speak to me again, just don't die. Are you listening to me?'

His own voice was quickly lost in the thick blackness. Tom lay there beside him and didn't move.

Mary Cameron fainted at the pithead when told that Tom was trapped underground but she would not go home and when the other twelve men were brought to the surface she screamed and screamed and tried to get into the cage with the rescue workers so that Alf had to force her to go home. When Vinia went to see her Mary was huddled over the fire like an old woman in a thick shawl.

'You let that lad into your house,' she said. 'And now look at you. Messing about with shops when my Tom could be dead. You're unnatural. I never wanted him to marry you. Where are the grandbairns I wanted, eh?'

'Don't take on, Mary,' Alf said.

Vinia had not been to the shop again after that first day; it was as though the place itself were some kind of judgment against her. She had gone against Tom and was to be robbed of him because she had done so. Mary's face was red and lined with crying but she couldn't cry; all she could think was that she had let Tom go without making up the fight over the shop. And Mary blamed her, just as she blamed her for everything. Dryden's name was not mentioned by anyone. It was strange, almost as though Tom were there alone. There was nobody to come to the pithead for Dryden. If he came out of there alive there was nobody to claim him for theirs as other families had done.

Rumours began to get about, that Mr Forster was thinking of giving up, that he could close that part of the pit, that the possibility was the fall went back so far that it was not sensible to go on. Alf had to stop Mary from going back to the pithead. Even the weather was against them. The rain had gone on and on until the land around the pit was thick with mud.

*　　*　　*

They dug for four days. The men came and went in shifts and Thaddeus eventually came down and told Joe that he ought to go back to the surface. In the office with the rain coming down beyond the windows, Thaddeus gave Joe tea and tried to make him eat a sandwich and then he sat Joe down. The grave look on his face took away the very small appetite that Joe had attempted to summon.

'I don't want to hear this,' he said, throwing down the sandwich so that the egg fell out of it. Egg was disgusting, he thought, as the yolk parted grey and yellow from the white.

'Drink your tea,' Thaddeus urged him.

'I don't want it.'

Thaddeus's face was sagging with fatigue.

'That roof fall could go back and back. You know that. There's no saying how far and . . . Sometimes,' he went on, his voice very steady, 'being a good pit manager is making a decision you don't want for the sake of the rest of your men. You can't go on digging for ever. Sooner or later you have to stop. Only the pit manager makes that decision. Are you going to make it?'

Joe felt sick, dizzy.

'Dryden saved my life. I can't give up on him now. He and Tom are two of my best hewers and Tom's married and . . .' Joe got up as though being on his feet would help. 'And he has that dreadful mother. How would I explain myself to Mary Cameron? She would run me through with her knitting needles.'

Thaddeus smiled in acknowledgment of Joe's attempt at lightness and then shook his head.

'Dryden's a pitman, Joe. He understands death just as well as the next man. So does Tom. We're risking other men's lives all the time. Do you think they would want that? Let it go.'

Vinia burst into the office then, rather like the clerk had on the first day, and Joe jumped and spilled tea all over his fingers, which weren't in any wonderful shape, anyhow, from helping underground.

'They say you're going to stop,' she said, glaring at him and slamming the door.

'What?'

'That the roof fall is too bad and you're going to give up.'

'Who said so?'

'My Tom is still down there, and his brother.'

'I do know that,' Joe said, short of sleep, food and temper.

'Joe –' Thaddeus offered and Joe glared at him.

'You said we were going to give up?'

'No, I haven't said so.'

'But you think I should?'

Thaddeus didn't reply and looked away. Vinia searched Joe's face and then Thaddeus's for clues.

'You aren't going to leave them down there?' she said accusingly.

'They're probably dead,' Thaddeus pointed out, meeting her eyes.

'Dead?'

'There's no air getting in or out,' Joe said.

'Tom's not dead! He's not dead. You get down there and you get him out!'

She had reached Joe's desk and was leaning over it in a threatening manner, both hands on the top.

'Men are risking their lives all the time,' Thaddeus said.

'You get down there and get them out!' she told Joe.

'Mrs Cameron, you're going to have to leave this to the experts,' Thaddeus said.

Vinia turned to him. Her teeth were set and her eyes glittered.

'I don't see any experts,' she said. 'You shut up!' She turned on Joe. 'You get them out of there.'

Thaddeus left the office. Joe wasn't surprised that he couldn't stand any more. As soon as he had gone she began to weep, not politely and softly into a handkerchief as Joe knew ladies did, but all wet and noisy and without retreating a single step or caring what her face looked like, and all the time she glared at him as though the tears had nothing to do with her.

'We quarrelled so badly and I let him go,' she said.

Joe didn't feel like a magician any more, he felt like an undertaker – Dryden and Tom buried under all that rock, or on the other side of it, he didn't know, just that they had dug for four days and found nothing. He had stopped wishing he could produce a miracle and felt that he would be grateful even for a body so that at least he would not have to make such an awful decision. He didn't care very much about Tom beyond the bounds of humanity, but he found that he did care about Dryden. Sometimes he hated him because of Esther Margaret and often he was reminded that but for Dryden he could have been dead, but he didn't ever feel indifferent when it came to Dryden.

'One more day,' he told Vinia, 'but after that, if we don't find anything, I'm going to give it up.'

They worked all that night and most of the next day and Joe got past exhaustion, he got to the stage where he couldn't see what he was doing or remember why he was doing it. His whole being was focused on that fall of rock and he was determined to beat it, to find the end of it, to reach a satisfactory conclusion, if it killed him. He did not think he could cope with having to call off the rescue and leave two good miners to die, though he, like Thaddeus, was half convinced that they were dead already. He felt that if he did not get Dryden out of there he would never sleep easily in his bed again. He also knew that this stubbornness or unwillingness to take responsibility was costly. The men helping him were worn out, disheartened, ready to give up.

All that day Joe fought with himself over it, and then finally, when he was just about to call the whole thing off, there was a shout from one of the men and Joe believed for the first time that he might win. There was what looked like the end of the fall, the beginning of space, the chance of finding . . . what? Joe went cold with the image in his mind of Dryden and Tom dead. It was no longer enough to find them. He wanted this to be a total victory, just for once to beat the earth at this game. If he could bring them out he swore to God he would never again ask for anything. His heart beat hard like a rock because there was no sound coming from the other side, and though the men shouted as the hole got bigger no reply came from beyond. When it was big enough for a man to crawl through Joe took a lamp and wriggled and pushed and shoved his way in.

It was the hardest thing he had ever done and he regretted every negative thought that he had had about Dryden. He was cut and bruised and sore by the time he got there and more tired than ever before, and his dread of finding no one alive almost consumed him, and then he managed to scramble through, and when he got there and lifted the lamp his heart stopped. The two brothers were lying close together, perfectly still, Tom on his back and Dryden on his side with one arm around him. Joe had seen dead men before but he hadn't got used to it and he didn't want to. He made himself crawl up to them. Dryden was warm and Joe's fear was that he had not been dead long.

'Dryden?'

Joe put down the lamp and reached for his water bottle, and he moved Dryden away from Tom and turned him over and supported him and pressed the bottle to his lips.

'Come on, Dryden, don't give up on me now,' he urged. He managed to get water between Dryden's lips and then Dryden opened his eyes.

The only light in them was the reflection of the lamp, and his voice was a cracked whisper.

'Tom's dead,' he said.

There had been the question of who was to tell Tom's mother. It was late at night when they brought his body to the surface, and by then, as on each day since the beginning, Alf had finally managed to persuade her to go home. The rain was pouring down, giving everything a sheen. Dryden leaned against Joe in the pit yard and let the rain hit his face, and Joe didn't know what to do.

Vinia was there, bending over Tom's body and letting little sobs escape to reach Joe's hearing from time to time. Joe was worried that Dryden would collapse. He wouldn't see the doctor. The man had pronounced Tom dead and retreated gratefully into the night and most of the rescuers, exhausted, had gone home. Those who remained accompanied Vinia and Tom's body back to her house, where Tom would be laid out in the front room until the funeral.

'I'd better go and tell Tom's mother,' Joe said as he and Dryden and Vinia stood about awkwardly in the kitchen.

'I think I should do that.' Dryden's voice was hoarse with lack of use.

'Is that a good idea?'

'Probably not, but I think I should.' Dryden glanced around as Vinia went into the pantry for something and added softly, 'I can tell them he died straight away.'

It was what he had told Vinia when they brought Tom to the surface. Joe thought of Carrington's death and wanted to hope that it had been the same, but he knew by the way Dryden spoke that he had listened to his brother die slowly.

Joe offered to go with him to see Mary and Alf but Dryden shook his head. Vinia made tea. It was the only comfort any of them had – the ritual of the tea-making and drinking. Joe was glad of it. The house and the tea seemed so normal after the horror of the last six days underground. He had been lucky to lose only one man, but that was not how it felt. It always felt like his fault because it was his responsibility, his pit, his loss. Tom had been one of his best hewers, but even if he had been the worst miner ever to go underground Joe would have been sorry at the loss. As it was he was glad to find Dryden alive, glad of the thirteen out of fourteen men, sad, sorry, bereft over Tom.

Vinia suddenly stopped drinking her tea and set down her teacup and saucer and then she got up. She had spent six days waiting at the pithead in the hope that Tom and Dryden were still alive. Every time Joe had come back to the surface she was there. It had only been when they finally brought up Dryden alive and his brother's body that Joe realised she had nobody, no parents, no family, and Joe knew that Tom was the kind of man who would not have tolerated other people in his house, so it was unlikely that she had any friends. He had the feeling that her life with Tom had not been easy. There were bruises on her face and a bleakness in her eyes. He knew that Tom was a hard-drinking, hard-working, hard-fighting, opinionated man. When she had seen his body any hope in her face died. She had ignored Dryden. Joe wasn't sure that she had even seen him.

Now she ran out of the back door and into the lane as though she would follow Dryden, as though she had suddenly realised that he had been in the house and gone and about his mission and how impossible it was. When Joe went after her she was standing in the street, the rain plastering her hair and clothes. She gazed towards the Cameron house and said, 'He can't go there.'

She began to weep hopelessly and Joe did the only thing he could think of other than urging her inside, which she resisted. He put an arm around her, and she turned to him as though she had had no one to turn to in her life, surprised, hurt, unable to bear any more. She put both arms around his neck and hid her face against him.

Joe had had a great many people need him during his life as the pit-owner's son and lately as the pit-owner. He prided himself on doing everything he could for the pitmen and their families after twenty years or more of neglect by his father, but he had never before comforted a woman. He would have liked to have been Esther Margaret's husband and to have looked after her and had children with her and come home to her in the evenings, but somehow it had taken until this moment for him truly to know the difference between affection and the kind of feeling he had for Luisa McAndrew. At that moment he would have given anything to shield Vinia from what was hurting her, and the regard that he had for her was a very small part of what he felt. He cared about the very air upon the moor, each piece of ground where the houses stood, the wind and the rain that were the chief source of weather here, the heather above the village, the gorse bushes, the distant farms and each person who lived there. They were his responsibility. He enclosed her in his embrace and after a while he heard her give a sigh of ease. He didn't think she was even aware of the relentless rain.

When Dryden had been a little boy he had often dreamed of being allowed into this house, and in his mind it was full of colour and warm cake and quickening fires, but when he had forced his legs to the back door and Alf had opened it and had admitted him inside without a word it was nothing like he had thought it would be.

You could smell unhappiness, and it was not just the unhappiness of the past week, it was something of long standing. It was not a house where children had played together while growing up with loving parents. It was swept clean and bare, as though Mary Cameron wanted to deny to herself that she had ever had a moment's levity.

It was the first time Dryden had come face to face with his mother. To him she had always been Tom's mother, and she would cross the street before she would tolerate Dryden's presence. He had never before looked into her eyes. They were Tom's eyes. She backed away.

'No,' she said. 'No, no!'

'Tom died,' Dryden said.

She put her hands over her ears.

'My Tommy's not dead,' she said, 'he can't be! You're a liar! You get out!'

Dryden looked at Alf, who lowered his eyes but didn't move.

'He died straight away.'

As a pitman Alf would doubt the truth of this. As a father Dryden knew that he needed to hear it as he was being told it.

'The fall killed him.'

Dryden had no idea how long Tom had lived, how many hours had gone past before he took his last small breath. Underground in the black silence time was different, magnified, something to be feared and respected. He felt as though he had spent one lifetime there before Tom died and another since. Mary Cameron looked at him and there was true hatred in her eyes.

'How can you be here and my Tommy be dead? How can God be so cruel?'

Alf went to her and Dryden was amazed. They comforted one another. They touched other than for sex or violence. How strange, how apparently civilised, and yet he remembered those long church services, those endless Sunday afternoons at the Harmers'. Jesus had said that even the publicans and sinners should love one another. You were supposed to love your enemies, weren't you? All those self-proclaimed Christians – Alf and Mary Cameron had given away a tiny child, Mr and Mrs Harmer had mistreated that child, and Tom had professed love for his half-brother and had none. This would have been his home, these people could have given him a childhood. He was being punished by them all for something another man had done. It made Dryden angry, and suddenly he didn't care about Tom's death or their grief; their loss meant nothing to him. All the old ideas about what it could be like to have a family and belong to people died right there. He didn't long for it any more. He turned around and walked out.

CHAPTER TWENTY

Thaddeus and Alice had a party to celebrate their thirtieth wedding anniversary and Luisa and George came to Durham for the celebrations. Thaddeus had told George of the accident. George looked bored.

'Really,' he said, 'how very trying for you,' and he changed the subject.

Joe wasn't in the mood for parties. Thaddeus had had to talk him into it. He went out and walked in the gardens and through the orchard beside the house where the fruit was ripening on the trees. He wondered how many dead men George McAndrew had ever seen that he cared about, how many sleepless nights he had spent worrying about his workforce, how many widows had gone crying in rain-sodden back lanes for men who had treated them badly. Joe had wept for his own shortcomings and for the sight of a good pitman dead and for Vinia and Dryden. Suddenly he heard a noise behind him. It was Luisa.

'I'm so sorry, Joe,' she said.

For days Joe had tried to put Tom's funeral out of his mind — the way Mary Cameron had wept throughout and had to be supported from the church, the way Vinia would have been sitting alone if Joe hadn't gone with her. Dryden wasn't there at all. Joe had braved the Black Horse later and had had to practically carry him out. He had taken Dryden back and let him fall on to Vinia's settee in her front room, where the late evening sunshine fell so unsympathetically on to her shabby furniture.

'I've nowhere else to take him,' he said apologetically.

'He's the only pitman left in the house. Where else would he go?' she said tiredly.

Mary Cameron had had a get-together after the funeral at her house but Vinia and Joe had refused to go. Dryden had not been asked.

'Vinia, look.' Joe had stopped calling her Mrs Cameron. It changed things when a woman put her arms around your neck, he had discovered. 'I want to help. If there's anything at all, because it shouldn't have happened—'

He stopped because she came to him, and in the delightful understanding way she had she said, 'It wasn't your fault.' Until then Joe had not realised that he blamed himself entirely.

'It was my pit. There will be full compensation, of course. There will be—'

She put her fingers to his mouth.

'Shh!' she said. 'It was an accident. It isn't always somebody's fault.'

'My father could have done such a lot that he didn't, but I will put it right—'

'You can't put everything right. There is God,' she said.

Joe hadn't thought of God like that before. It seemed such a useful view.

Now, in the orchard, with the most beautiful woman on earth, Joe couldn't speak.

'Was he married, the man who died?' Luisa asked softly.

'Yes. She's a fine woman is Vinia. If all the pitmen were married to women like that the world would be an easier place. She's starting a shop in the main street.'

'What sort of shop?'

'Fashions, hats and things. You should go. She'll probably carry on with it.'

Luisa smiled.

'I buy my clothes in Paris,' she said.

'London, Paris, Deerness Law.'

Luisa laughed.

'I will call in,' she promised, and then she came to him and kissed him.

'You shouldn't do that,' Joe said.

'I think I should.'

After that Luisa would make any excuse she could to see him. She told lies. Her father and mother started to worry about her staying away from Edinburgh, and Joe took time off as he never had before. She would not let him go to Edinburgh because too many people knew her there, but they spent nights in Berwick, Alnwick and Newcastle. He tried to stay away from her, it was madness to want another man's wife so badly, and at first was convinced that she thought it a game. She was merry, reckless, and the accident had made Joe feel the same. He accepted invitations to be where she was, even though he was certain people were beginning to notice her partiality for his company and to talk. When she did not see him she would turn up at his house, which she had claimed was ugly and poor, crying and beseeching him to make love to her.

For the first time in his life Joe found himself unable to resist a woman. His nights were tortured with dreams of discovery, his work interrupted by thoughts of her. Every day without her was endless, every hour with her like a second. He remembered her saying that he had no conversation. Now he needed none beyond endearments. No matter how much he had of her, it was not enough; he began to think it never would be.

One particular morning he awoke in the Golden Crown Hotel in Newcastle and thanked God to be alive. Since the accident he had been filled with wonder at the simplest of things, and this to him was perfect.

Luisa was sleeping, one bare arm flung across the pillow, the sun streaming in where the curtains were not quite closed. There was an empty champagne bottle on the bedside table and glasses on the floor. She was so precious to him, and after that dark week at the pit he thought that he deserved as much of her as he could get.

Luisa stirred and then realised where she was and who with, and she smiled and opened her eyes.

'Joe,' she said.

He kissed her in reassurance. They had to leave that morning – she was going back to Edinburgh and he to his pit. He didn't want to face it, not after what had happened. Her train left before lunch. It seemed so final. He wouldn't be seeing her again for weeks; she was going on holiday with George to Paris.

'And perhaps Milan,' she had said.

'Oh, Milan, very nice.'

'Don't pretend you care,' she had said, hitting him with a pillow.

They had to go. They dressed in silence though it would be the last chance for privacy since there would be nothing between them beyond public small talk after that. They wouldn't take breakfast; they didn't take meals in hotel dining rooms – somebody might see. Putting on her hat before the big mirror over the dressing table, Luisa turned around.

'Do you ever think that we might have been married?'

'Often. Do you?'

'I would have been poor.'

'You certainly wouldn't have been going to Paris on holiday, wearing diamonds and spending nights in hotels with other men.'

'Would you have beaten me?'

'I would have killed you.'

Joe expected her to come back with some light retort but she didn't. She pulled the hat off her head and sat there with it in her hands, turning it round and round.

'I don't suppose George will,' Joe said, getting down beside her chair. She pulled away from him.

'I was so stupid!'

'I couldn't have given you anything you wanted. You would have hated it.'

'I could have had you every night, and possibly children. We could have had a child by now, maybe two. George doesn't make love to me. He tried several times when we were first married but he doesn't really want to.'

'That's what you have me for.'

'Is that what you think?' She looked at him with stricken eyes so that Joe laughed.

'Oh, sweetheart, I'm sorry, I didn't mean it.'

'I love you.'

She began to cry, so hard and so desperately that Joe got up and would have gone to her except that she turned away, shaking her head.

'He's an old man,' she said, shakily. 'He's boring and . . . opinionated and he says the same things all the time. He does everything out of habit and his friends are all old and so are mine and . . .'

'Leave him. Come and live with me.'

'I can't. We couldn't stay here and you can't leave the pit and the people. I know you would never do that. It would be a terrible disgrace.'

'Then we'll stay lovers. There isn't much wrong with that.'

'I want to do normal things with you. We can't go to the theatre or eat in a restaurant or even go for a walk. We have to pretend all the time. I'm tired of pretending. I want to show you off to my friends, I want them to envy me. Why didn't I understand what this was going to be like? I can't have you to myself.'

'You do have me to yourself. It's me that's sharing.'

'It's not real sharing. I don't love him as I love you and I never will. I never, never will.'

She kissed him all over his face. If they had had enough time Joe would have taken her back to bed. As it was they had to leave the room when her tears were dry and go downstairs and carry on as if nothing was the matter, smile, leave without fuss and part before the railway station because in such a public place they might be seen. They separated without another kiss and Joe went home and she went back to Edinburgh to prepare for going abroad.

CHAPTER TWENTY-ONE

Esther Margaret put off going back to Deerness Law. She kept telling herself that she would do it the next week and then the next. She did the shopping for Daisy, taking the train into Alnwick, and it was there one Friday morning in the local butcher's that she heard the familiar sounds of a Deerness Law accent, that soft, broad and to her somehow warm sound, and it made her feel homesick. Suddenly Esther Margaret stopped thinking about the sounds and began to listen to what was being said, and as she listened she grew cold, as though she had been standing outside on the beach in a bitter wind.

'Poor soul,' the woman was saying, 'poor Mary Cameron. Six days it took to get them out of the pit and then the younger lad dead. I remember her when everything went wrong. There wasn't a nicer woman in Deerness and she's never been the same since.'

Esther Margaret went out and bought a newspaper, and there it was – the two brothers had been trapped by a pitfall and the younger one had died. She read the article several times before she took it in, and then she had to do the shopping. She didn't know how she got through the next two hours; she couldn't see or hear anything but that Dryden had died down the Black Prince Pit and she was widowed. She managed to buy everything on her list though the day had an unreal quality about it, and then she got the train home and trudged with her groceries to the village, and when she saw Daisy she burst into tears. The words tumbled all over the place so that she had to keep on re-explaining because she couldn't manage to get them right. She showed Daisy the newspaper.

'He's dead, Daisy. I ran away from him and let him think something had happened to me and now something's happened to him. He's dead.'

She couldn't sleep that night, couldn't get used to the idea that they would never meet again, and she blamed herself freely for what had happened. She thought of all the weeks when she had been happy she would not see him again, when she had thought that she would never go back, and now everything had changed.

Her thoughts became clearer the next day. She didn't have to go back because Dryden was no longer there, so what was the point? She could go anywhere. Being able to go anywhere meant that she sat about, watching the tide go in and out and doing nothing. By the following day her thoughts had taken a completely new turn and it was the evil in her that took over. She could not believe that in three days she had gone through shock to believing that Dryden was dead, to thinking she need not go back, to wanting to because the image of Joe Forster grew in her mind and flowered there.

Sometimes, she thought, it was possible for things to work out for the best. Joe was not a boy any longer. Her dreams were filled with images of him just out of sight and reach but he might not be if she went back. Joe was a good prospect. It was true that she would have to return and play the widow and that would not be too difficult because nobody in the village had ever liked Dryden, nor would they mourn his passing, but she would be free to marry again, and after a decent interval, if Joe was still of the same mind as he had once been – and she smiled, thinking of how he had come to the house after the baby died, his arms full of fruit and flowers and his face so concerned for her – if he still cared, and she believed that he would always care for her, then she might win Joe Forster and the whole world would be put right.

She thought more and more about Joe and became better and better convinced that for once God was looking after her. There had been all kinds of obstacles put in their way, not least her stubborn stupidity. Looking back on it, she would have given anything to have run away with him. Perhaps it was best like this because Joe was doing well, he didn't need to go anywhere. He had made the village and the pit and the fell his own, and she would be his wife, and her parents . . . She thought that they would be pleased that she had at least made a respectable alliance.

The idea took such a hold on her that she got her belongings together and said a tearful goodbye to Daisy. Daisy pressed paper money into her hand. Esther Margaret stared at it.

'I can't take this,' she said.

'Esther Margaret, I have nobody to give anything to. I'm very fond of you and this is the only thing I can give you to take back. Spend it the way you choose, and if you ever need help again you can always come to me.'

Daisy kissed her and Esther Margaret left. Leaving was difficult, but once she was on the train bound for Newcastle she felt excitement at the idea of going back. She was a different person and she would look different to them. She was no longer afraid of the future.

She was going to get another train straight away, she had not intended to linger in Newcastle, but the streets were inviting. She found herself walking up where the big shops were and looking in the windows of the department stores. Miss Applegate's was never like this, and neither was her father's precious Store. She remembered how her parents had not let her take a job. How different things might have been if they had given her a small amount of liberty. It seemed to her that, having never been let out, it was not surprising that she should have gone wrong when she had, but she was mature enough to understand that she couldn't blame her parents for everything, even though it was a nice idea.

She began to walk back down the streets towards the station, and was passing one of Newcastle's finest hotels when a man and a woman came down the steps. There was something about the man which made her stop. She recognised him — not immediately, but there was something. He was wearing a very good suit. His fair hair glinted in the sunlight and he was smiling and talking intimately to the woman who was with him. It was Joe Forster.

There could have been a dozen explanations for their presence in the hotel, and although several flitted through her mind Esther Margaret's instincts told her that the couple were close. She drew well back, but she doubted whether they would have noticed anybody. He looked even better than she remembered, and the woman was so beautiful that Esther Margaret's heart did nasty things and so did the pit of her stomach.

The woman was young and slender and golden haired. She wore a navy blue and white costume and a blue-and-white hat, frivolous and obviously expensive, and her upturned face looked into his with love. Esther Margaret did not fail to notice the rings on her left hand, one diamond and the other a wedding ring. Joe had fallen in love after she had left, had married this beautiful creature, was happy and probably never gave a thought to Esther Margaret Cameron.

They made a perfect couple, faces close as they spoke softly, coming down the steps of the hotel. She put her hand through his arm, they walked slowly down the street together, their footsteps matched, and they were still talking and she was smiling at him and he was looking down at her and there was no mistake. They were in love.

Esther Margaret was shaking by then. She had gone from paradise to hell in a few moments and it was too much. All the rest of that day she walked the streets, trying to compose her thoughts. If Dryden was dead and Joe was married there was no reason for her to go back, but where else was she to go, and what could she possibly do that would be of any use or any satisfaction to her? Her life was completely empty. She could hardly go back to Daisy; she was too young, she realised, to accept the slow existence by the sea. She could not envisage anything in the future. When it grew late and she became tired she found herself outside a modest hotel. At least she could afford to stay here until she worked out what she was going to do next. She climbed the steps, responded wearily to the woman's enquiries and fell into bed, caring nothing for yesterday or tomorrow. The world had collapsed. Nothing else mattered.

CHAPTER TWENTY-TWO

When he slept Dryden dreamed of Tom dying over and over again. Even when he was awake his mind carried the black images and heard the last breaths in the deep silence, but when he was asleep the nightmare began again and continued. It was worse when he was working during the day because he kept on waking up in the darkness and thinking he was back there. It was summer so the windows were open and all the small night sounds and the warm wind came in from the fell. Often he would get up and go to the window and take in great breaths and see the night sky and be glad, but he shuddered to think that Tom had not come back out of the pit alive. What a hard way to die. But Tom had not known it – at least he didn't think so. Even the slightest doubt about Tom's knowing would send Dryden downstairs to where the reassurance of the kitchen was all around him. He wished that the house was farther away from the pit. Tom's death could not be set at a distance even after Dryden knew that his body was underground in an even more final way. He dreaded every minute of his own existence. Tom had died down there and a part of Dryden would always be there.

Joe had tried to stop him coming to work at first, called him into the office and told him that he didn't have to.

'What else am I supposed to do?' Dryden said. 'Besides, I have to do it some time. Do you think a week or two weeks will make any difference? I'd just as soon keep working if it's all the same to you.'

Even the window of Dryden's bedroom overlooked the pithead. He came to hate the sight of it. He gave Vinia six weeks and then he said to her, 'When are you going to the shop?'

She wasn't eating, any more than he was. She looked down at her plate.

'Soon,' she said.

Another week went by. Dryden didn't like to interfere. In a way he supposed that even being on their feet was good. She was seeing to the house and he was going to work and in a lot of ways it was as much as many people did, but every time he saw the empty shop with her name above the door he wished things otherwise.

The following Sunday, therefore, when she had come back from chapel and started fussing with the Sunday dinner, he said to her, 'Do you fancy taking a look up the shop after dinner?'

She didn't answer. The vegetables were all pretty with butter and the beef was neat and brown and moist and there was onion in salt, pepper and vinegar; the Yorkshire puddings were large golden clouds and the gravy was thick and dark and the potatoes were creamy. He couldn't get the taste. Since being stuck down the pit everything was coal, thick and gritty. He hid the meat in the mashed potato, put carrots into a small heap to hide, and when they had both pretended to eat for long enough she got up from the table and began to clear away.

'When are you going to the shop?' Dryden persisted.

She ignored him.

'When, Vinny?'

He stopped her as she tried to go past him between pantry and table. All those memories of himself and Tom on Sundays, the talk and the beer and the jokes, came back, and they were to him now as bitter as vinegar. She stayed because he made her stay.

'Never,' she said.

He waited. The summer was soon over and the nights began to draw in and in the house there was the kind of silence that seemed to deepen with each day that passed. Tom's presence in the house was heavy. Dryden went to work and in a way it was as though Tom had never been – it became a gap which closed. Nobody spoke of him.

The other men were not inclined to be friendly as they had when Tom was there. The people he had drunk with, played darts and dominoes with night after night when Tom was alive, did not talk to him except for a perfunctory greeting when they met. He began to think that he might leave. The woman of his dreams had always been Tom's and he was beginning to think that she always would be, that in spite of Tom's opposition to everything she wanted that did not suit him, in spite of his violence, Vinia loved Tom and would go on loving him. Only Dryden's regard for her kept him there. If he left where would she go? She would not be able to stay in a pit house and she could not live in any of the boarding houses which were full of workmen. He felt also that he was not entitled to any of her affection, having wanted her so much when he had loved Tom. Perhaps this was a kind of retribution, to be living in Tom's house with Tom's widow without even conversation to brighten the days.

She cried when he was at work and did not look at him for fear he might notice her red eyes. Finally, one Sunday afternoon, he suggested they should go for a walk, and when she agreed he walked her past the shop. He was certain that she had avoided going anywhere near it when she did the grocery shopping. He could see her footsteps slowing, though she looked determinedly ahead.

He thought it was a sorry sight, the empty windows and her name so neat above the door.

On the way back, after a couple of miles of trudging through the country when nobody spoke, he thought that if there had been another way she would have taken it. She might have crossed the road, but Dryden kept on striding out. As they reached the shop for the second time she hurried so much that he thought she was going to run past, and then, opposite the door, she came to a halt. Dryden stopped too and turned around, pleased that his idea had borne results.

She stood there for so long that he became impatient, but he didn't say anything. One awkward word or movement and they would be on their way down the street towards home. She went to the door and then the window and pressed face and hands up against it, the better to see inside beyond the sunshine. Dryden did the same. There wasn't much to see, just the empty counter.

They stood for so long that Mr Samson came downstairs and into the shop and opened the door. Dryden could have hugged him. She was unable to resist the open door. He followed her inside. She lingered. The shop was clean and tidy.

'I swept and polished only this morning,' Mr Samson said. 'I hoped that some day soon you would call by.'

In the back room Dryden could see the preparations she had made, the tables and chairs, the sewing machines, the material, and he realised then that until Tom had died, right from the beginning when she had received the letter about the inherited money, she had intended going through with this, and short of death nothing and nobody would have stopped her.

On one table was a pile of paper and pencils, and when he got closer he could see that they were sketches. She examined the room carefully until finally she came to where he was standing. She picked up the sketches one by one and looked at them. Then she said, 'I think I'll go home now. Thank you, Mr Samson.'

That evening Dryden made himself go out. He thought that if she was left alone she might think about what had happened that afternoon. He went for a long walk, even though they had had a walk already that day and he was not inclined, and then he went to the pub. He could see Wes and Ed and most of Tom's friends, but he merely nodded at them. He hadn't had a drink in weeks, and the beer tasted good. Before he was halfway down the first pint Wes had sidled over.

'Fancy a game of darts?' he said.

Dryden had not thought to be accepted there without Tom but he agreed and played, and although he didn't contribute much either to the conversation or to the darts they were not excluding him any longer. He had another two pints before he went home.

The lamps were burning in the kitchen, and when he let himself quietly into the house he could see her sitting at the kitchen table, sketching. She was so absorbed that it occurred to him that if there had been half a dozen people coming in screaming and shouting she wouldn't have noticed. She didn't stop or look up for several moments, and then suddenly she realised that he was in the room and, pencil raised, she turned her head. Guilt rushed into her face.

'I was just . . .' He could see that she was remembering what Tom thought about the shop and everything to do with it.

'Can I have a look?'

She hadn't been expecting that, he could see. Surprise registered. Dryden went over to the table before she had a chance to refuse and began asking questions. She smiled shyly and started to explain. Most of it was incomprehensible to him but he went on trying to ask what seemed to him sensible questions and she talked, rapidly and enthusiastically.

Then she seemed to realise what she was doing. She looked down at the sketches and she gathered them into a rough pile and got up from the table. At first he didn't realise what she was going to do, and then in one movement she threw the whole lot on to the fire. Dryden stared in horrified fascination. She began to cry, hard, choking sobs, and then she ran out of the room and clattered her way up the stairs. He listened to the heaviness of her feet. It was not her body which weighed her down, it was her heart, he thought.

Up to now his mind had been filled with the past, but it had seemed to him that afternoon that suddenly he had grabbed something from the ruins and run with it so that they were going forward again. Now he was not so sure. She had tried to do something that Tom had not wanted her to do, she was breaking some rule, hitting out at her dead husband, but she couldn't do it. He heard her reach the top of the stairs and slam the bedroom door after her. He could hear her crying faintly through the floorboards.

In the end there was nothing for Esther Margaret to do but go back to Deerness Law. The money ran out in the late autumn, she had no reason to stay in Newcastle, she didn't know anybody, had made no friends and had no references to gain any kind of work. Suddenly the world seemed against her, alien, nothing to do with her, so she took the train home. She did not know what to do when she got there. As she stepped down from the train the town looked so small and bleak. A cold wind blew in from the fell and everything was grey.

It was dark so she didn't have to face anyone. She went automatically to Prince Row. Lights burned in the house so somebody was there, and Esther Margaret was not altogether surprised when moments later the door opened and Vinia stood there. She looked blankly at her and then recognition followed disbelief and finally she said her name.

'Esther Margaret?'

'Yes.'

Vinia let her inside. It was quite a different place from the house that Esther Margaret had left. All Vinia's furniture was there, and she thought it looked lovingly polished. The whole house was welcoming with a big fire in the kitchen. Esther Margaret held her hands out to the blaze. Vinia hovered behind her, saying nothing.

'I should have let you know, shouldn't I? Written or . . . I wasn't myself for a long time.'

'We thought you were dead.'

'I wished I was, I wanted you . . . Dryden to think so, I wanted him paid out for what had happened. I wasn't thinking properly.'

'Where did you go?'

'My mother has a cousin who lives on the coast in Northumberland. She looked after me, was kind. Do my parents think I'm dead?'

'Everybody.'

'I'm sorry. I couldn't think about anything but the baby for so long.'

Vinia didn't ask any more. Esther Margaret was tired. She sat down by the fire while Vinia made tea. They drank it, and all the time Vinia watched her as though she was some kind of ghost and could disappear at any moment. Esther Margaret didn't know what to say, whether to talk about Dryden and the accident.

'I read . . . in the newspaper . . . about the accident,' she said.

'Was that why you came back?'

'No, not exactly. I was thinking that I must come back. I couldn't stay there for ever and . . . in the end there was nowhere else. It must have been very difficult for you. Tom and Dryden had become close.'

'For a while, yes. Tom and I moved in here after you . . . after you left. Dryden couldn't stay here by himself.'

'No, of course. It looks so nice with all your things in.'

Vinia said she must put the tea on and Esther Margaret thought of Tom coming off shift and wondered whether he would mind if she asked to stay. Vinia hadn't said that she could, and since Tom was the pitman it was their house. She was glad in a way because she liked how different it looked, but she felt so homeless, so aimless, quite lost. Time went by.

'He didn't say he was going to the pub,' Vinia said when Tom was late.

'Doesn't he always?'

'No, not since . . . no. Hardly ever.'

'That's good, isn't it?'

'I suppose, but it would have been nice. He keeps out of my way.'

'Why?'

'It's just so difficult.'

Vinia fussed with the vegetables as though she was glad of something to do. Esther Margaret would have liked to have done something but it didn't seem right so she sat by the fire. It was about an hour or so after the time he should have come back that she heard him come down the yard and in by the back door. She was surprised. Tom had always been a big drinker and would not usually have been so prompt. He wasn't the kind of man who could down two pints and go home to his dinner. He clashed the back door and came into the room, with a 'Now, Vinny', and then he saw Esther Margaret sitting by the fire and she stared at him.

Even through the coal dust she could see it was Dryden. He was more sparely built than Tom, not as tall. Esther Margaret felt very strange, as though the world had altered. She felt sick; she got to her feet and wobbled and her breath was doing odd things. She had only just grown used to the idea that her husband was dead. To see him there, and also to realise in that instant that it was Tom who was dead, made her think how dreadful and how funny it was. What must Vinia think of her that she had not said a word about him? There had been some horrible mistake. She wanted to burst out laughing, she wanted to run out of the door. She had been so wrong, firstly thinking that this man was dead and secondly thinking that she was free and that Joe would want her. Joe neither wanted her nor could marry her. She was married; her husband was standing in the kitchen of his own house. He had been there all along, thinking that she was dead. She had been the one who was dead and yet not, and it was Tom, it was poor Vinia's husband, who was the one underground. She felt trapped, she felt that nothing had happened, nothing had altered in her life. All the running away, all the heart-searching, the deliberating what to do next, the time spent in Newcastle, none of it mattered, none of it meant anything. Her situation was just as it had been before she ran away, and she realised, looking at him, why she had gone. There was no love in his face, there was no relief, no happiness; he was no more glad to see her than she was to see him. She wished she could faint, pass into blessed unconsciousness, but there was no release. They stood there, gazing at each other, until Esther Margaret wished she was unborn.

'Dryden,' she said.

He looked at Vinia and then at her and Esther Margaret thought of how she had remembered him when they were first lovers, and she could not imagine being in the arms of this man. He had the coldest eyes in the world. How could she have wanted somebody without humour or forgiveness, somebody who stood there and condemned her without opening his mouth? And then after a lifetime or two he said in a very low voice, 'And just where in the bloody hell have you been?'

Esther Margaret stood trembling. Vinia looked as though she might be about to say something to him but he silenced her with narrowed eyes, and that was when Esther Margaret realised she had been wrong. He had changed. He was older and, more than that, he filled the room just as though he had been Tom. She hadn't been near men in a long time and she had forgotten that they could make the world seem small and unfriendly. If there had been anywhere else to go she would have gone. If she could have imagined her parents welcoming her she would have left, but there was nowhere except this room, and she was tied to it and to him just as surely as ever. The life that she had tried so hard to cast off had been here all that time, waiting for her.

Vinia squared up to him as she would not have done to Tom.

'Give her a chance,' she said. 'Here, Esther Margaret.' She came across and took Esther Margaret by the hand. 'Sit yourself down again and don't take any notice of him. It's just shock.' She stroked the back of Esther Margaret's hands with her thumbs. It was oddly reassuring.

Esther Margaret tried to think of something normal.

'I could take my things upstairs.'

'You could, yes. Would you like a hand?'

'No. No, thank you.' Something occurred to her. 'Where am I going?'

'It's the back room,' Vinia said calmly.

Esther Margaret picked up her bag and went slowly upstairs. She opened the bedroom door and all the unwelcome feelings piled on top of one another in their rush to assault her brain. In the semi-darkness there was the pithead from the window, the view that she had looked at day after day when the baby had died. She had watched the road out of here as though she could go somewhere, and now it felt as though she could not, had not, that nothing made any difference. She lit the lamp. Clearly somehow it was Dryden's bedroom though there was little evidence of him there. The room next to where they had lain clear of one another in the darkness, where her baby had been born and died, where she had felt the hope leave her just as the baby had. This was the house where he had breathed drunken breath in her direction, and where she had denied him her body, where they had never yet been man and wife, where she had cried herself to sleep more times than she wanted to think about, and where she had grown bigger and bigger with his child.

Vinia listened to Esther Margaret's feet as she trod reluctantly, slowly up the stairs, and then she looked at him. He looked more like Tom at that moment than she thought he ever had before, as though if he didn't smash something he would die of frustrated temper.

'It's hardly her fault,' she said. 'When you lose your mind—'

'I know.' He cut in swiftly but said nothing more, so Vinia left him to get washed and changed while she attended to the dinner. It was always the same when he came in – a routine, and routine was sometimes all you had left. It took care of the great big spaces where other things should have been. She had not realised that. When the dinner was on the table she called up the stairs to Esther Margaret to come down and have something to eat, and they sat around the table. Vinia was always concerned when Dryden didn't eat. He had lost a lot of weight since Tom had died. So had she. To have a third person at the table playing the same game was even worse. Esther Margaret sat with downcast eyes, silent. Vinia couldn't think of a thing to say.

When the meal was over Dryden pushed back his chair and looked at his wife. She was his wife, Vinia thought, having to remind herself.

'So,' he said, 'you were sane enough to pretend to kill yourself but not to let us know that you were alive and well.'

'I wasn't alive and well,' she retorted.

'What were you, then?'

'I don't know!' Esther Margaret almost shouted.

Vinia looked doubtfully at him.

'All I could think about was the baby.' Esther Margaret had lowered her voice but the impact of the words was bigger than their sound. 'I wanted my baby.'

'And in all this time you didn't think it would have been kind to let us know you were still alive, or was it just that I didn't deserve to know?' Dryden said.

'I thought you were dead!'

The words came from her almost strangled. Vinia stared. Esther Margaret's hands twisted.

'You thought I was dead?' Dryden said.

'I read the report about the accident in the newspaper. They got it wrong. It said you were dead and Tom . . .'

'You came back here thinking I was dead?'

'Yes.'

'Well, what a dreadful disappointment for you.'

'Dryden!' Vinia had not known that she was going to shout at him.

'What were you going to do back here without me?' he said to Esther Margaret.

'I don't know.'

'Maybe you thought some other lad would marry you, keep you?'

'Why not?' she shot back at him.

'Well, I'm sorry, but I'm still here and we're still married.' He got up and walked out. Vinia braced herself for the sound of the door and closed her eyes over the impact when he slammed it. Esther Margaret began to cry when the noise of it was over.

'I didn't know Tom was dead. I'm so sorry.'

'Oh, Esther Margaret, why didn't you tell me? It must've been awful for you.'

'The newspaper got it wrong. It's funny, isn't it?'

Vinia didn't see the humour in it. All she knew was that there hadn't been a slammed door in the house since Tom had died, and the echo of it went on inside her head long after the sound had died away and he had almost taken the yard gate off its hinges too and then disappeared into the back lane and the night. If Esther Margaret hadn't been so upset Vinia would have gone after him. She had visions of him coming back drunk. He hadn't done that since the day of Tom's funeral, and she had got out of the habit of expecting it. It was a part of Tom, along with the violence, that she didn't miss. Dryden worked hard, made good money and the faults that he had displayed appeared to have been buried with Tom. She wasn't looking forward to the rest of the evening.

It was only now that she realised they had been on the brink of breaking past the grieving, so that maybe in time there would have been some kind of contentment, if not happiness, but it was now lost under the weight of Esther Margaret's arrival. She was an unwelcome intrusion, and Vinia was ashamed of herself for thinking it.

Esther Margaret ran upstairs. Vinia cleared up and then she sat by the fire and waited for him to come back, dreading it. It was late and dark and cold by then, but her vast experience of such matters told her even before he got as far as the back door that he hadn't been to the pub. Where else he would have been – she dismissed the idea of another woman even as it formed in her mind – she couldn't think. He came in and to the fire, not acknowledging her. It was only then that Vinia realised that in a way she had lost him as well as Tom. She had somehow counted on him.

'You should be in bed,' she advised him. 'You have to get up early.'

'Hell, yes,' he said. 'My wife's in my bed. I should be there.'

Vinia was about to suggest that she might sleep with Esther Margaret for tonight and he could have her bed but she didn't. It wasn't a good idea. Or that he might sleep downstairs, but that wasn't either, she thought.

'Surely you don't resent her being alive?'

Dryden looked at her.

'Do you know what it was?' he said. 'It was twice. Once in her bed and one Sunday afternoon in a hay shed. Do you think people should forfeit their whole lives for that? I never cared about her and she never cared about me, and it's a lot to have to pay for like this, over and over with a dead bairn in the middle. It was wrong but it wasn't that wrong,' and he went to bed and left her to bank down the fire.

Esther Margaret was not asleep. She had been waiting for him to come back. She could not believe that she had to sleep in the same bed as him. He didn't even need a candle, he knew the room so well. He shed his clothes and got into bed and it was as though she had not been away. He didn't touch her. The bed could have been as big as an ocean for all the contact. Esther Margaret listened to his breathing. She was not used to anyone else in the room. She thought longingly of her room at the cottage with the window open to the breeze and the sound of the waves as they slid up the beach. She wished she had not left; there was nothing for her here, but she could not go back. She would have to stay and make do as best she could, although she could not imagine that it would be any better than it had ever been.

She did not wake up until halfway through the morning, and then for a while did not know where she was, and when she did she wished again that she had not come back. She wandered downstairs. Vinia was just coming in with shopping bags in her hands, and she made Esther Margaret some tea and tried to persuade her to eat something. After that she said, 'Don't you think you should go and see your parents? The minute you step out of the house people will know you're back, and whatever you think of them they ought to know.'

She went immediately to her home, not meeting the stares of people in the street. Peggy answered the door, stared, stuttered. Esther Margaret made her way past her and was astonished at the appearance of the house. Not even a chair had been moved, nothing had changed. Her mother was sitting at her writing desk in the sitting room with a pen in her hand as though she had important correspondence to deal with. It made Esther Margaret want to laugh. The pen dropped as she walked in and her mother looked up. She got to her feet and there was no gladness in her face to find that her daughter was alive. She started, the tears came into her eyes, and she said, 'Wherever have you been?'

'I went to see Daisy.'

Her mother stared.

'You were there all this time and she didn't let us know? You wicked, wicked girl, How could you do such a thing as to let us think that you were dead?'

'My baby had died. My mind wasn't working properly,' Esther Margaret said, but she could see that her mother was unaffected by this.

'Does your father know that you have come back?'

'I haven't seen him yet.'

'I suppose you will have to go back to that dreadful man?'

'He is my husband.'

'His brother died in that accident. It's a pity it wasn't the other way round,' her mother said.

She didn't even offer tea. Esther Margaret's father came in while she was there and he was equally unforgiving, as though her appearance was going to cause them more bother than it was worth. They talked about how much the funeral and the headstone had cost, they questioned her closely about where she had been and what she had done, and her mother talked at length about Daisy's betrayal, as though it had been Daisy's fault. There was no word of thanks that her cousin had taken in her daughter and looked after her all this time.

'She wanted to contact you but I wouldn't let her. For a long time I wasn't like me,' was all the explanation Esther Margaret could offer.

'You cared nothing for us, for how we felt — that's how you have been right from the day you met that dreadful boy,' her mother accused her. 'Letting us believe all that time that you were dead. We grieved over you.'

'You hadn't seen me since my marriage.'

'You were still our daughter. I wish you hadn't married that dreadful man. You could have had anybody. Billy has married, of course — a very nice girl. Do you remember Mary Patterson? She has made him such a good wife. Her house is very clean and she cooks a proper dinner every night when he gets in from work.'

Her mother went on about Vinia too.

'It's disgusting, living with a man she isn't married to. It won't do her reputation any good, I can tell you. It's as well you've come home. Did you know that she started up a shop? As though she could possibly be any competition for the drapery department of the Store. She's supposed to be mourning her husband, that no-good Tom Cameron. All he ever did was drink. He'll be no loss to the pit. She should stay at home, but I suppose she's out there bold as you like, caring nothing.'

Esther Margaret hadn't seen the shop, so she walked up the

main street to have a look. She liked what she saw but it was shut. She walked back to the house. Vinia was busy cleaning brasses on the kitchen table. Esther Margaret helped her.

'I saw the shop. Are you going to open it?'

'I don't know what I'm going to do. Tom hated the very idea, but I wanted it so badly I thought I was prepared to do anything for it. I made us unhappy because of it and I can't forgive myself. It doesn't feel right to go on when Tom's dead.'

'What did he think was wrong with it?'

'I don't know. Just that I was a pitman's wife and they should be at home.'

'You're not a pitman's wife any more, though, are you?' Esther Margaret pointed out. 'You didn't tell me that Mr Forster was married.'

Vinia stared at her.

'Joe? He hasn't married. Who told you such a thing?'

Esther Margaret's heart turned a somersault. She resented Vinia's use of his first name, as though she knew him better than Esther Margaret did.

Had her mind been more organised than the rest of her, she would have kept quiet or invented something quickly, but she couldn't and didn't.

'What made you think Joe was married?' Vinia said.

'I saw him with a woman in Newcastle, walking down the steps of the Golden Crown Hotel.'

'Walking down the . . .?'

'She was very beautiful. She was wearing a wedding ring and a diamond and she took hold of his arm when they got to the pavement and they walked off down the street together.'

'There must have been a good reason for it,' Vinia said. 'What did she look like?'

'Tall and slender with golden hair, and she was wearing the most beautiful outfit. It must have cost a fortune – navy blue and white with a big hat.'

Somehow, finding out that Joe was not married made it

worse. If there was an innocent reason for his presence there with
a woman he wasn't married to, then it was her own marriage
which prevented their happiness. If there was not, then he was in
love with another man's wife. It undermined all her ideas about
him. Joe wasn't like that, he was kind and loyal and caring. She
had carried in her mind a picture of him unchanged, so when he
walked down the steps of the hotel looking well off, confident
and with a beautiful woman on his arm, it had brought her ideas
crashing down.

Vinia was frowning.

'Her husband could have been right behind them. They could
have been having a meal—'

'It was the middle of the morning and there was nobody with
them. I watched them walk away down the street.'

'Esther Margaret, if he was sleeping with another man's wife
he would hardly do it in Newcastle, would he? Everybody knows
him.'

'Loving people makes you careless.' Esther Margaret felt sick.

'He wouldn't do such a thing,' Vinia said.

The problem remained the same. Joe Forster was in love with
another woman whether he was married to her or someone else
was. He did not love Esther Margaret; he had doubtless
forgotten her.

It was almost as though talking about Joe brought him to her.
Esther Margaret saw him later that day, riding a fine black horse
away from the pit and he stopped the horse abruptly so that it
threw up its head and then he walked it across to her as she
stared.

Seeing him so closely Esther Margaret was reminded of
Daisy's husband. How could her parents ever have seen Joe as
anything other than well-bred and eligible? He must be the best
catch for miles around and yet they thought he had not been
good enough for her.

He got down from the horse and, still holding the reins, took both her hands and kissed her on the cheek and she was glad that somebody in the village was pleased to see her.

'I never believed that you had died,' he said.

Esther Margaret thought bitterly that if her parents had ever imagined Joe would turn out so well, if they ever saw him, which they must, how regretful they would feel that they denied him her company and spoiled all their lives.

He loved her no longer, she thought sadly, she could tell by his polite relief and jealousy cut her like a knife. She had forfeited Joe's love with her innocent stupidity. It made her wretched and she brought to mind once again the images of him with the beautiful woman he could not marry.

She managed a smile.

'I ran away,' she admitted.

'But you came back.'

Esther Margaret said nothing to that. Deerness Law was like a prison to which she had gained a lifetime's sentence.

Vinia was in the yard that afternoon when Tom's mother was in the back lane. Mary Cameron saw her and screamed down the lane, 'You're a whore! Living with another man under my Tommy's roof. It's disgusting. You ought not to be in my Tommy's house. You have no right there. And him, the dirty gypsy!'

Vinia regarded her with indulgence. Mary's mind had been lost with Tom's death. She didn't say anything. She swept the yard and then went into the house. Mary didn't follow her but Vinia could hear her screaming and shouting until she closed the back door.

When Dryden came home Esther Margaret was conveniently upstairs. Dryden came to the pantry door.

'Did you go to the shop today?'

'What on earth made you ask that?'

'I just wondered.' He paused and then looked at her and said, 'You should be there.'

'No, I shouldn't.'

'You've got no excuse now. Esther Margaret can do this.' He went to the foot of the stairs and yelled, and when she didn't reply he went upstairs. He had come home in an awful mood, Vinia decided. No doubt Esther Margaret's reappearance story was all over the village by now. He had probably put up with a good many cynical remarks. She could hear clearly through the open door.

'What are you doing?'

'Nothing.'

'So get downstairs and find something to do.'

It was perfect Tom, Vinia thought. He clattered back down the stairs.

'Do you know what you sound like?' she told him. 'Like Tom Cameron.'

'Is that why you aren't at the shop? Maybe if I slapped you round the kitchen you would go to the shop, eh?'

A wet plate slipped out of her fingers and crashed on to the stone floor.

'Don't talk about Tom like that!'

'It was a pit accident,' he said. 'It happens all the time.'

'You shut up!' Vinia said.

'So the whole point of it was to annoy Tom?'

'Of course it wasn't.' Vinia couldn't think how they had got to here. He was making her lose her temper, something he never did.

'He half killed both of us over it.'

'Don't talk about it! Don't! Don't!' She came out of the pantry and pushed him up against the wall. Tom would have knocked her off her feet for it. She slammed a fist into his chest. All he said was, 'I wish that you would go. Just once. I wish you would.'

She could hear Esther Margaret coming down the stairs and

she moved away, and after that the evening took on a strange quality, as though she were viewing it from somewhere else. Esther Margaret helped though she wasn't needed, and after that Vinia felt worse because there was not enough work for two women in the house. She would be the one who was not needed soon. For that and for other reasons, she must find somewhere else to live.

The next morning she made herself go to the shop, but it took all the courage she had to walk up the main street with the keys heavy in her coat pocket and unlock the door and go in. Dryden was right. She needed Tom there to kick against in a way, and without him there seemed to be no point in anything. She felt guilty too that she might actually enjoy something when he was dead.

The counter was bare; the windows cried out for the clothes in which she had envisaged dressing them. She remembered having worked out her window displays, excited, keen. There were still a few sketches about. She sat down and gazed at them for a while, flicking through, and then she heard a tapping on the shop door. When she went through Em Little was standing there, looking embarrassed and not quite smiling.

'I heard you were here. You don't mind?'

Shortly afterwards, while they were talking at the front of the shop, a woman walked in, asking if they were open for business and saying that she had a dress she needed altering – would they do it? Em looked at Vinia and when she nodded said they would do it straight away. Shortly afterwards another woman called in, Mrs Jamieson, who had been before. Her daughter was getting married and they didn't know what kind of dress she wanted but would like some ideas.

'I didn't know what was happening. So sorry to hear about your husband, Mrs Cameron. It's best to keep busy is what I always say.'

Em began with the dress alteration and Vinia found herself making sketches of what the bride might like as her mother discussed her height and colouring. They agreed that she should bring her daughter in the very next day. At teatime Em went home and Vinia locked up and walked slowly down the street. There were lights on at the house, and when she went in Esther Margaret had the tea table laid and she had baked and everything was on the table. It gave Vinia a strange jolt – she had not experienced anything like it since she had been a little girl when her parents were alive. Tom's mother had not made her welcome like this. When Dryden came home they sat down in a civilised fashion and ate. This time they did actually eat something.

The following morning Esther Margaret said she would like to see the shop, so Vinia took her there and showed her around. Halfway through the morning a carriage pulled up outside and Mrs Morgan, whom Vinia knew by sight, and a young woman got out of the carriage and came into the shop.

'That's her,' Esther Margaret whispered as the young woman got down, 'that's the woman Joe came out of the hotel with.'

Mrs Morgan came in, all politeness, and introduced her daughter. Vinia didn't know what to say. She knew that Luisa Morgan had married a rich man and gone to live away, and from the look of her dress she didn't usually buy her clothes in little shops in pit villages. She couldn't imagine Joe with such a woman. Luisa was bright and hard like a shiny penny. Vinia brought out various hats she had made and then stored in boxes when the accident occurred. Luisa Morgan, being fair and beautiful, suited all of them and actually bought two. Vinia was inclined to be sceptical. They were hardly smart enough for such a person and she doubted whether the woman would ever wear them, but she had become shopkeeper enough to be glad of the sale and to have some money to put into the till.

After they left Em made tea and they sat about in the back room talking about what they would produce for Christmas. Mid-afternoon Esther Margaret went back to see to the house. It was a heady feeling – somebody else was going to do the domestic things and Vinia could stay and take pleasure in her new project. It held her with its possibilities, with its magic.

Mid-evening there was a knock on the door. When she opened it Dryden stood there, washed and changed and ready to go to the pub. He came in and wandered about the shop and asked about the customers. She related the incident of Mrs Morgan and her daughter to his willing ears, and heard herself laughing.

'Don't stop,' he told her.

'Shouldn't you be at home with Esther Margaret?'

'I'm going for a drink.'

'She's just come home.'

'So?'

Only a very narrow-minded person would have said that Dryden was drunk when he got home. In fact he timed it nicely because he walked into the bedroom while his wife was undressing. He was well aware that Vinia's room was dark and silent and that every sound could be heard through the wall, but there was no help for it – his wife was there and they belonged to each other with a kind of life sentence than he could not bear to think about. However, the sight of her almost naked body was pleasant, especially in candlelight. She grabbed the skirt she had taken off and held it up in front of her.

'You don't need to bother,' he said. 'I have seen you before.'

She got into bed and turned her back. Dryden finished his undressing and got in beside her. The room was uncomfortably cool but nothing compared to her back. He didn't mean to touch her but the bed had suddenly got smaller. They brushed up against each other twice before he got back out of bed.

She was the wrong woman. She had always been the wrong woman, and even sheer animal instinct wouldn't have got him to her. He heard Vinia turn over.

'Where are you going?' Esther Margaret said into the darkness.

'Nowhere.' Dryden began to dress, got into shirt and trousers and felt his way down the stairs. He put on his boots, which were near the door, and went outside. It was freezing. The buildings were iced like big cakes and the pithead loomed in the blackness and brought back Tom's death, so close that Dryden thought he could hear him breathing.

All those weeks he had thought of Tom as the person who had beaten him, as the awful husband who had hit his wife, but his memory allowed him the wonderful evenings in the pub with Tom's smile and silly remarks and the way he would clap an arm around him. It had been the way he wanted to remember him, only he hadn't been able to because of the horror of the accident and what had happened before, and also because of Vinia. What kind of man lusted after his dead brother's wife?

He heard footsteps down the yard.

'Dryden, what on earth are you doing out here? You'll catch your death.' She was wearing her outdoor coat over her night-dress, so she was nobody to talk, he thought. He was, Dryden realised then, crying. How awful. He turned away.

'Come inside. Come on. You could at least have put on a coat.'

The woman he adored was at her most practical, dragging him up the yard by his arm, closing the back door and sliding in the bolt. She started going on at him in the usual kind of way about drinking too much. Dryden listened to her gentle nagging and looked at her. Her hair was in one thick plait and she was wearing a long nightdress. There wasn't an inch of her on show that didn't have to be. He thought she was the most beautiful thing on God's earth, completely out of reach and yet near enough to touch. He wasn't allowed to touch her; it would have to be enough to see her, hear her voice, breathe in the scent of her.

'You're not listening to me, are you?' she said severely. 'People die through getting drunk and going to sleep in back lanes. For goodness' sake, go to bed.'

He pretended he was going so that she would leave and in the end she went upstairs and left him there. Dryden lay down on the old settee in the kitchen. It was much warmer here than upstairs. He pulled a cushion to him against the draught and closed his eyes.

CHAPTER TWENTY-THREE

Luisa and George came to Durham just before Christmas, and Joe was invited to a party at the house. He didn't want to go. He hadn't seen Luisa all that autumn and was determined not to. Out of her sight he could think of other things. In her presence he was obsessed with her. She was his drug. He understood when he saw her how his father had felt about whisky. She looked like an ice queen, wearing the palest blue, and Joe thought she was more beautiful than anyone he had ever seen. Her eyes were blue flame, her skin was like pearl. She glowed.

'Milan suits you.'

She laughed.

'We went to Florence and Rome after that. The churches and the buildings were so beautiful, Joe. You would have hated it.'

'But George liked it.'

'George likes to humour his wife. It's so good to see you again, though I have to say that you are very skinny. Have you pined for me?'

'Certainly not.'

She danced. Joe watched her smile, her graceful movement. Alice came to him.

'Doesn't she look well? There is a world out there beyond the moors. I told your mother so. People can do better, try for other things – they don't have to put up with this place. There's

nothing here. I wanted for her all the things I didn't have –
culture, society, riches. George has those.' She looked at him
beyond Joe's shoulder, smiling.

'And my mother thought so too?'

'Why, yes. I think women all do. Your father was a nice
enough man in his way. You're very like him. He didn't drink in
those days. He thought he could hold her in this forsaken place.
She deserved better. She was beautiful like my Luisa. All he
wanted was the pit and the people and to look after things, but I
always thought she wanted a lot more than he could give her.'

'They were never happy?'

'I wouldn't say never. Unlike Luisa she didn't realise until
after they were married how dull it would be. It was easier for me
with Thaddeus. He always tried so hard with the right people.
Your father was not one for society. Luisa is so like your mother.
She always hankered after cities and travel and . . .'

'Money?'

'She was a very beautiful girl. She could have had anybody, I
knew that.'

'You didn't want her to throw herself away.'

'Oh, I knew she wouldn't. All George needed was a little
encouragement.'

'You thought she could be happy?'

'Happiness is elusive. We did the best we could for her.'

Luisa danced and danced. Joe longed to have her to himself
even for just a few seconds, but she was always surrounded by
other people, and George McAndrew watched her every moment.

'Will I see you?' he couldn't help but ask before he left.

'Why yes, of course. You're invited to Christmas dinner, so
my mother tells me,' she said.

Joe had not been long in the office on Monday morning when he
had a visitor. He had not quite yet, by his own estimates, turned

into his father, but he was beginning to understand how women drove men mad. He wanted Luisa in his arms. He couldn't think, eat, sleep, work. The time without her was a torment. Therefore when her husband was announced in the outer office he could not think what George might want and he could not be easy.

He tried affability, smiling. McAndrew was a big smiler. It was the worst kind of smile. It meant nothing, least of all civility. He offered a seat. It was a good seat, a big armchair with a tall back, and made George look like a gnome.

'I had to see you. There is something I particularly wish to discuss with you.'

'Really?' Joe said, sitting back in his chair across the desk. He was glad of the desk between them.

'I don't know how to put this delicately, Mr Forster, but it seemed polite to tell you. My wife is . . . *enceinte.*'

Joe had to hold himself in the chair and maintain the indifferent look on his face.

'That's nice for you,' he said.

'Yes. It's what we hoped for, dreamed of. You see, I have long wanted an heir. I doubt you would understand but a man in my position needs a son.'

'Yes?' Joe said politely.

'You think I'm foolish.'

'I would never think that.'

'I think you have.' George McAndrew looked at Joe in such a way that it turned his stomach. 'You seemed to think that you could – what is the polite term for this? – bed my wife without my noticing. You bedded her in Berwick, Alnwick, even New-castle. How very dangerous. I'm told the danger adds a certain piquancy to these things, that and the fact that you did it under my very nose.'

'Who told you this?'

George McAndrew laughed.

'Nobody told me. I knew all the time. You have supplied me with an heir. I am in your debt.'

Joe couldn't think of a thing to say. He just looked.

'There is no point in protesting your love. I'm quite sure that you love Luisa very much, I saw the devoted way in which you looked at her on Saturday evening, but she is my wife. She cares too much for wealth and position to leave me and you will have no claim on the child. She chose to marry me and I must ask you to leave her alone now. If you fail me in this matter I will take steps to ensure that you follow my wishes.'

He left. Joe didn't get up or see him out.

That night, when Dryden was playing dominoes in the Golden Lion, Joe walked in. The men fell silent immediately. It was an unwritten rule that the pit-owner did not frequent the same pubs as the men, and Dryden was sure that Joe knew that. He believed that Joe had hardly ever been in a pub anyway because of his father being a drunk. He hadn't seen Joe take a drink at all. Maybe if he had Joe would have had sufficient sense to know that he could go into the Station Hotel, where the farmers drank, or one or two other places, most especially the Brown Horse just beyond the village where the local professional people went to drink, the doctors and the solicitors. Joe had rescued Dryden from pubs in the village more than once, so he should have known, but he walked straight up to the bar without acknowledging anybody. The men who were in were all foundry workers or pitmen so they were all employed by him and he knew every one of them by name. It was a bad sign all round, Dryden thought.

He watched Joe approach the bar. He ordered brandy, you could hear it. Another unwritten rule was that you drank beer. Real men drank nothing else. Brandy was for visitors, people who were ill and drunks. Joe downed the first one and coughed and ordered another, and then he got that down in a very short time. Dryden finished his game and got up and wandered across. There was a big space around Joe, purely from politeness; the men couldn't drink with him.

'Mr Forster,' Dryden greeted him.

'Dryden!' Joe said cheerfully.

'You on the road home, then?'

'Not exactly.' Joe finished the second brandy and ordered a third. The landlord didn't say a word. 'Would you like a drink?'

'No, thanks, I've got one. You want to go easy with that stuff,' he advised quietly.

'My father used to get through a lot of it.'

'Yes, well, it didn't do him any good. Maybe that should be the last,' Dryden said.

Joe eyed it.

'Yes, but it was years and years, you know, not just . . . not just the odd one.'

'It gets hold of people.'

'Something should, don't you think?' Joe said.

'What?'

'Get hold of people. Things should matter. They should.'

Joe downed the third. The landlord hadn't even had a chance to move away. Joe pointed at the glass.

'Shall I just leave the bottle, Mr Forster?'

'No!' Dryden said.

'Yes,' Joe said, reaching for it.

'Look, why don't I see you home?'

'I don't want to go home. It's quiet. It's very quiet, you know. My parents are both dead.'

'Why don't you come home with me? My house is anything but quiet.'

Joe looked at him.

'Your wife,' he said.

'Yes. My wife.'

'And Vinia. Vinia is . . . she's lovely.'

Dryden thought by the silence in the rest of the pub that it was definitely time to leave. Joe wouldn't go without the bottle, so Dryden paid for it and manoeuvred him outside. It was freezing. Joe wavered slightly. They began to walk up the bank towards the corner that led to Dryden's house, Joe stopping from time to time and taking large swigs from the bottle.

'Your wife is lovely. Do you know that I once asked her to run away with me?'

'She was a bloody fool not to.'

Joe eyed him.

'Do you think she was?'

'Definitely.'

'I thought I loved her. Do you love her?'

'No.'

'Didn't think so,' Joe said. He stopped. 'I have done something very stupid.'

'Everybody does eventually.'

'No, really stupid.'

Joe slid down the wall. Luckily there was a wall to slide down. It belonged to the bank, banks being the kind of institution that can afford walls. It was a good wall, well built, and had a tree behind it, the kind of tree that looks good even naked in winter and jagged with frost. Joe took the bottle in both hands.

'This is nice,' he said. 'I didn't realise it was so nice or I would have started sooner.'

'No, you wouldn't,' Dryden said, getting down beside him. 'Remember your dad.'

'Did you know that my mother wanted more?'

'Did she? That's women all over.'

'She drove him to drink.'

Dryden took the bottle from him and sat down and took a swig, more for the cold than anything else. At least there would be less for Joe to drink, though there was a surprising amount left. He hadn't ever had much brandy. It was expensive stuff but it was nice. It had about it a sweetness that defied its effect. It caught nicely at your throat as it made its way down and then it went all warm and encouraged you to have some more, rather like Joe's mother.

'What more did she want?'

Joe waved a hand.

'Everything,' he said. 'McAndrew gave Luisa everything except . . .'

'Except what?'

'Except what mattered. He didn't give her anything that mattered.'

'Maybe she didn't want it.'

'Do you think not? Maybe you're right.' Joe took the bottle from him. 'Do you think there's really more than this?' He swept a hand at the clear black sky and the bright silver stars.

'Aye, I do. A warm fire at my house. Howay.' Dryden got up and pulled him to his feet.

Joe hesitated, and then he looked clearly at Dryden.

'She's having a baby,' he said. 'Mine.'

'Why don't you run away with her?'

'I've tried that before — with your wife.'

'Howay,' Dryden said again.

By the time they got up to the top of the hill towards Prince Row and the pit, Joe couldn't have got anywhere without Dryden. Dryden managed to get him as far as the house and then inside. Esther Margaret and Vinia were both in the kitchen. Esther Margaret put down the sewing she was doing and Vinia stopped sketching. They ran across.

'What's happened?' Vinia said.

'Nothing. He's drunk.'

'But he doesn't drink,' Esther Margaret said as Dryden let Joe down gently on to the sofa.

'He's forgotten.' Dryden put the bottle on the table.

'I'll light the fire in the front room. He'll be more comfortable there when it warms up,' Vinia said.

Esther Margaret looked disapprovingly at Joe.

'Did you have to bring him here?'

'What else was I supposed to do? Let him pass out in the pub with all his workmen there?'

Esther Margaret stared at Joe, and then she went stamping up to bed and left Vinia to put a pillow at Joe's head and a thick rug around him. Dryden took off his boots.

'There's more to it, isn't there?' Vinia said.

'Mrs McAndrew is having his bairn.'

'Oh God.' Vinia tucked the blanket in tenderly at Joe's neck. 'She came to the shop and bought two hats. She's so . . . what my mother used to call brazen.'

When Joe came round it was light and he felt as if somebody was sitting on his head and his stomach was going round and round. Vinia came into view.

'How are you?'

Joe buried his face in the pillow.

'I've put clean sheets on the bed in the front room. You can stay there if you want to.'

'I have to go to work.'

He sat up slowly and then wished he hadn't.

'I don't think you're going anywhere,' Vinia advised. 'There's a jug of water and a glass.'

Joe tried to get up and realised that she was talking sense, but he struggled against it.

'I have to go.'

'I'm sure it'll survive a few hours without you.'

He decided she was right and practically crawled up the stairs. The bed was soft and smelled of soap and was quiet. Joe shed his clothes and climbed in gratefully. From time to time after that he awoke and took a few sips of water and then went in and out of dreams about Luisa, running, hiding, him pleading with her, seeing George McAndrew's face behind every tree. His head spun at first but gradually slowed down and the sick feeling left him, until after a long time, by what he considered to be early afternoon, he fell into natural sleep, and it was like a cool bath, peaceful and dreamless. He became aware of somebody in the room, and when he opened his eyes Vinia was standing by the bed.

'I've got Mrs McAndrew at the shop. She wants to see you.'

Joe turned over away from her.

'I can find you a clean shirt,' she offered.

Esther Margaret had insisted on being at the shop. She said she didn't want to be left alone with Joe and anyway Vinia liked the way she dealt with the customers, so she left Esther Margaret and went into the back with Em. They had been asked to do several alterations and the doctor's wife had ordered a dress that morning. Vinia was happy. She had spent some time working out what the woman wanted, making suggestions and sketches, and when the doctor's wife had left she was pleased with her ideas. She was planning to go into Bishop Auckland that afternoon and find material, and then a carriage pulled up in front of the shop and Luisa McAndrew got out. Everybody in the whole village would know within an hour, Vinia thought. Couldn't she have left it somewhere and walked up the back road or something, because although she pretended interest in the shop, Vinia knew instantly that Luisa was not there to buy clothes. She walked about nervously and, ignoring Esther Margaret, went with Vinia into the back and said in a furious whisper, 'I must see Mr Forster.'

'The pit's the place for that,' Vinia said, thinking of Joe asleep in her bed.

'I can't go to the pit. He'll come to the house otherwise, I know he will, and George is there and my parents. Please help me. If he could come here . . .'

'What on earth would you want with Mr Forster?' Vinia said.

Luisa didn't answer. She stuck her hands into her muff and her head came down so far that Vinia could see the top of a very well-made blue hat, all done with velvet. It was very pretty.

*   *   *

Joe, left alone with clean clothes, washed and dressed and made his way slowly out of the house. It was almost teatime. The men had not come off shift and most of the women, having done their shopping, were at home preparing the tea, so there were not many people about, nobody to wonder what the pit-owner was doing not in his office. He took the back street to the shop and opened the gate and came up the yard. He opened the back door and let himself in. Luisa was alone in the back room. He thought Vinia very organised to have managed such a thing.

Luisa had never looked more beautiful or less his, so richly dressed, with a diamond on her finger and her eyes like blue jewels. He thought of the hotels where they had stayed, of her body naked and in his arms, of her laughter and the way that she looked when she slept, of how he had adored her carelessness. She came across eagerly and kissed him and told him that she loved him, and Joe forgot the things he had just realised and begged her to leave George.

'Come to me.' She was so lovely and sweet and he could not let go of her. How had he stayed away from her? How had he not gone running to the house the day before and snatched her up in front of George's eyes and proclaimed his love and claimed the child she was carrying as his in front of George and her parents?

'You know I can't. You can't afford disgrace, not here. I want you to promise me that you won't come to the house and cause a scene. George would have you murdered.'

'You have my child in you,' Joe reminded her.

She moved away.

'As far as the law is concerned you have no rights, and George has told me that he would never let me take the child. If it is a boy . . .' She looked straight at him.

'If it is a boy it will inherit everything. Do you know what that means? Everything that George has. I want that for my son. All those things . . . high position, society, amusement, enter-tainment, education. Everywhere we go everything is of the best.'

She stopped there, slightly shamefaced, not quite meeting his eyes, moving her feet, laughing shortly.

'I suppose you think that's poor-spirited of me, the results of a shallow mind – it's what my father has said. I find it strange. Most men are happy with women who don't think too deeply. They presume their feelings match.'

Joe didn't say anything.

'I know that it seems incomprehensible but I do enjoy the life I lead. I'm used to the best, you see, the wittiest people, the cleverest men, the most beautiful women. I take great enjoyment from it. You couldn't provide any of that for me. I have come to love that awful shabby house of yours, but I could never live there. I don't think any woman could in all honesty enjoy living there, even with you. Let's face it, Joe, it isn't much of a life. Your mother couldn't stand it and my mother hates it here. Look around you. There's nothing. That's why my mother wanted better for me. She wanted me to be able to leave. I could have chosen to come back but I didn't, and neither would anyone who had the chance to get away. Haven't you ever wanted to?'

'Lots of times,' Joe said, glad to be able to contribute something sensible to the conversation.

'Then why haven't you gone? I dare say my father would have bought your share of the business and then you could have gone.'

She said it so lightly, he thought. He almost suggested to her that if she came with him then he would leave, but when he tried to imagine such a thing he couldn't. He had wanted to leave, it was true, but in fact in all the time that had elapsed since Esther Margaret had said to him that he could not run from things he had found it to be true. She was the one who had run in the end, not him. When he had been growing up, and his father had turned into a drunk, he had itched to improve things at the pit and the house and in the village, and that was what he was doing, it was what he was supposed to be doing. He couldn't leave it. Thaddeus, no doubt, would do his best, but it was too difficult for one person. The image of Dryden Cameron saving his life also came into his mind. You couldn't have that happen, nor the accident to Tom and Dryden, and then leave. That was not how things were meant to work. To leave Thaddeus and Dryden and Vinia would be an act of cowardice. Thaddeus would soon become old doing the work of two men. He would lose heart when there was no one to follow him. What would become of the pit and the village then? There was no point in saying any of this to Luisa, she would not understand, just as he did not understand the kind of life she led, but to give up his child when he had always sworn to himself that he would do better than his father made him want to weep. At least his father had kept him. Strange how you thought you were going to do better than your parents until you knew how difficult it was. All he wanted was to have a wife and a child. It was what his father had wanted, and in that respect he was failing just as surely.

'I can't leave,' he said.

Luisa smiled pityingly at him.

'Then we must part. Goodbye, Joe.'

Joe didn't watch her leave, but he heard her.

Esther Margaret had said very little since the previous evening, other than that she did not want to stay at home if Joe was going to be asleep upstairs, though Vinia couldn't see what difference it made. When Luisa arrived at the shop Esther Margaret slipped out the front so that she didn't have to meet her, but when Joe came and Luisa went into the back room to talk to him Vinia could see Esther Margaret across the street, taking a strangely interested view in the ironmonger's window. Vinia called to Em to mind the shop and stepped outside. It was a cold December afternoon, near enough to Christmas for her to hope that business would keep them going from their modest start, close enough so that many of the shops had pretty things for sale. She could not think what Esther Margaret was doing there, standing motionless before the window, alone.

She crossed the street. There was nobody about that she knew, nobody to stop her with enquiries about her health or the shop. She joined Esther Margaret in front of the dull shopfront, which had nothing in it to interest any woman who wanted anything more exciting than pots and pans.

'Esther Margaret?'

She was not crying. You couldn't cry in the street; it would draw attention to you.

'She's so beautiful, Vinia.'

'She's a whore.'

'Vinia!' Esther Margaret looked around to see if anyone had heard. 'I have never heard you say such a thing before.'

'Well, she is. Not content with having married the richest man in the whole blessed world, she had to take the nicest.'

Esther Margaret didn't look at her.

'Joe is very nice,' she said. 'I'd forgotten. And he's very handsome.' She sighed. 'I hate her. How can she be having a baby? It's not fair.'

She still didn't cry. Vinia had the feeling that if they had been anywhere else she would have.

'You could have a baby.'

'Huh.' A tear ran. Vinia looked around but there was nobody close.

'Come inside.'

Esther Margaret shook her head, and they both studied the window for what felt to Vinia like a very long time as the odd tear ran down Esther Margaret's face. Eventually Luisa came out of the shop and got into her carriage and drove away.

'Come in now.'

'He might still be there.'

Vinia walked back across the road, through the shop and into the back room. Joe was still there, silent, head down. He looked up as he heard her, a new hard look in his eyes, the same kind of look that Dryden had always had. Vinia was sorry for it.

'I should get to work. Thanks.' He went out, shutting the back door with a neat little click. She cursed Luisa McAndrew.

Mrs Morgan came to the shop just before teatime.

'Did you know that my daughter is having a baby?' she said. 'I want you to make me a summer dress for the christening. Such wonderful parties we will have.'

Esther Margaret went out into the back yard, and when Mrs Morgan had gone Vinia went to her there and hugged her.

'I don't mean to cry over the idea of someone else's baby. After all, Joe's nothing to do with me.'

'She wouldn't mean anything,' Vinia comforted her 'She wouldn't know anything about your baby.'

'I miss my baby. I keep on thinking how old it would have been and the things it would have done and . . . I'll never have a baby. He doesn't forgive me for what I've done and he's awful. We don't touch each other. He doesn't want me. What am I going to do?'

Thaddeus was at the office when Joe walked in. He had just got there, was taking off his overcoat and was all smiles.

'I'm to be a grandfather at last,' he confided when the office door was shut. 'I didn't know old George had it in him. If it's a boy, won't it be wonderful?'

It would be, Joe thought, his son inheriting everything that McAndrew had and half of everything Thaddeus had. How very odd. When he was forty he could be working alongside his son. He sat down. He could have laughed at himself for this vision. It wouldn't be like that. He would have turned into his father by then and would probably have to be picked up off the floor every morning and the boy . . . the boy would be called McAndrew and would be brought up in that society which knew all about power and . . . He listened to Thaddeus going on about what a Christmas present this was, and as if the outside world had heard him it began to snow. All Joe wanted to do was crawl back into the bed he had got out of a couple of hours since.

He worked until mid-evening, glad when Thaddeus went home. He didn't want to go, there seemed even less to go home to, and his mind was filled with Luisa and the child. It began to snow heavily and he was obliged to go home or he would not have reached it. Nobody was in the house but his dinner was just to one side of the stove to be heated and the fire was blazing in the study. Joe almost expected his father to shout from the empty room. When he had eaten he sat by the fire and watched the snow fall beyond the windows and thought of the evenings spent in hotels with Luisa. It was past, it was over, it was finished.

CHAPTER TWENTY-FOUR

Four days before Christmas Dryden came back from work to find that there was nobody at home. Some welcome, he thought. The fire was banked down and the house was cold. There were no signs of festivity or of food, and he was hungry and tired and very dirty. It had been a long, hard shift. Esther Margaret came hurrying in after him. He knew they had been extra busy at the shop that week and he was pleased that things were going well. He just wished it didn't preclude warm houses, hot water and meals being on the table when you got in.

'I'm sorry,' she said.

'It's all right. I know you can't be in two places at once.'

Dryden was a happier man when he was clean and fed and by a big fire, and it was then that his wife hovered in front of him.

'I've got something to say to you.'

'Let's hear it, then.'

'I want a baby.'

It sounded so stark Dryden was astonished.

'That's going to be a bit difficult. You don't like me and I don't like you. It's the right time of year for an immaculate conception, of course—'

'It's not funny!' She was trembling. 'We're married. We may not like it but we are. We're stuck with each other until we die and since we're quite young that could be an awfully long time. Vinia may be happy in a shop but I'm not.'

Dryden considered escape – the pub, the warm place where the beer went down and women were not about. He wished he had gone earlier.

'As far as I can see . . .'

She started up again. He couldn't stand it.

'As far as I can see you don't go with other women and you don't drink too much any more and since things are getting better—'

'Better? You think this is better?' He got up. If he could just make it as far as the door . . .

'It is better.' She placed herself in front of him. 'I am not going to lie in that bed with you with your back turned for the next fifteen or twenty years and pretend to people that everything is all right when it isn't.'

'So you want me to go to bed with you when we don't like each other?'

'Plenty of women do it every night.'

'Do they? Like prostitution.'

Esther Margaret looked straight at him.

'If you're honest and haven't really slept with anybody in so long you must be desperate enough to do it with anybody, never mind that I'm your wife. I'm sure you can manage it. You used to go to bed with just about everybody.'

Dryden could see his coat hanging up beside the door. Wes and his friends would all be in the Golden Lion by now. The air would be thick with tobacco smoke and beer fumes and the smell from the coal fire. He imagined the thick hoppy taste of the beer. This was real marriage, women wanting things that you didn't want to give them – money, time, your body, your thoughts. He felt as if he were suffocating. He imagined what it would be like when there was a child. It would cost more and babies screamed a lot and did disgusting things and small boys . . . small boys were evil and . . .

'You used to like me.'

'No.'

'Yes, you did.'

'No, I didn't, it was just something to do on Sundays, that's all.'

'But you fancied me?'

'You were pretty.'

She was silenced. Dryden cursed himself. It had been a low blow and he had not intended to say anything like that. If he pushed now he would get out of here. He couldn't do it. She had been unhappy since she came back. At first he defended himself with the knowledge that she had returned thinking and perhaps even pleased that he was dead, but she had not left again and her unhappiness had deepened.

'Why don't you go and see Joe Forster? You like him and he seems to be able to do it.' Dryden had no idea where that came from, knew only that it completely humiliated his wife. She stood there for a moment and then she ran from the room, up the stairs, and after that there was no more sound. He could get out. He eyed the door, considered it and then listened. There were carol singers some way off, inappropriately singing 'Away in a Manger'.

Very slowly he made his way upstairs and opened the bedroom door in the darkness. It was freezing up here and black. He found the lamp through the shadows and lit it, and then he closed the door. He put a match to the fire, which was always laid and never lit. It caught immediately. It was ridiculous, but in his mind he owed her a child because he had always blamed himself for the death of the other one. What a wonderful place the world was when you felt responsible for everything that went wrong. It must have been early religious teaching – all that sin, all that supposed wrongdoing. It was all right for the Catholics, they could confess and get let off, but the Protestant Church was just miserable, he thought, and when you were born in sin and of it there wasn't a lot of hope for you.

She was sitting on the side of the bed like a visitor. He sat down beside her.

'I'm sorry. I didn't mean any of that. I just . . . you know, it was . . . self-defence.'

'It's true, though,' she said. 'I'm not very pretty any more and I do care about Joe. Only I have to live with you and I can't see you being pleased with another man's child.'

'Aye, I'm just like Alf that road,' Dryden said.

It made her laugh.

'And you are bonny,' he said. 'You always were bonnier than everybody else. C'm'ere.' He put a hand to her cheek and kissed her, and the moment he did he remembered how sweet she had been, how sweet women always were. It was no hardship taking her to bed, it was just that he didn't love her, but then he had never loved any of the others. He had never touched the only woman he had ever loved. She was probably busy counting the day's takings at the shop.

Thaddeus insisted that Joe should be at his house for dinner on Christmas Day. He looked offended when he reminded Joe of the occasion and Joe tried to get out of it. The last thing Joe wanted was to see Luisa and George together. Alice would go on and on about the baby and he didn't think he could bear it, but Thaddeus frowned when he said he didn't think he would come.

'But you must. Alice has arranged everything. Especially now when we have such good news about the baby. It's what we've longed for, prayed for.' He threw Joe a searching look. 'You can't be going to sit in that draughty old house of yours all on your own.' He looked harder at Joe. 'Why don't you bring her with you?'

'Who?'

Thaddeus smiled.

'The woman you're intending to spend Christmas Day with instead of us.'

'Thaddeus—'

'No, really. Alice would be pleased. She's always saying we must find a wife for you, though God knows you aren't very old. You've had to be older, that's the trouble. She must be a nice lass if you like her. Bring her with you. I'll tell Alice. She'll be very pleased.'

Joe couldn't think of anything appropriate to say. He didn't want to go; he didn't want to go by himself, and he certainly didn't want to take anybody with him. Neither did he want to spend Christmas Day at home. The arrangement with Thaddeus and Alice had been made so long ago that he didn't see how he could not go.

He finished work late. It was Christmas week and he hated it, looking in the houses for signs of festivities. The miners bought good food for their families and presents and hung their houses with holly and mistletoe. The churches were lit as people practised carol services and there were good smells from the houses in the row as cakes and puddings were made and left to mature. This year there would be extra for everyone – the wages were good and Joe had put more on top for the holiday – but to look into the lit windows and not be able to go inside was hard for him.

Instead of going directly home he wandered up the street. The sounds of laughter coming from the pubs made him feel worse. His status in the village ensured that he had no friends and he had had none from boyhood, not having gone to school and his father being a drunk. He should have been grateful for Thaddeus and Alice, instead of which . . . He didn't want to think about that.

The lights were on in Vinia's shop and she saw him and waved and unlocked the door, smiling. Joe did not feel that he deserved the smile.

'Come in.'

'I shouldn't.'

'I'll make you a cup of tea.'

He went reluctantly into the shop and the memory of the meeting with Luisa came up into his mouth like bile. Vinia either didn't notice or chose not to. She went off into the back and he followed, and he remembered each detail, each word. He felt he was breathing the same air again.

'What are you doing for Christmas?' Vinia asked, as she busied herself making tea. Joe could suddenly see the point of these ceremonies. They were so useful to hide in.

'I'm supposed to be spending the day with Thaddeus and Alice.'

'Won't that be difficult?'

'It'll be wonderful,' Joe said. 'Luisa and George will be there.'

'You could come to us.'

'I can't get out of it, but thanks. What are you doing?'

'Nothing.' She hesitated for a second and then said, 'At least this year I won't have to put up with Mary. That's about all there is to be said for it.'

Joe had an idea. He almost dismissed it but his mouth got in the way.

'You could come with me,' he said.

Vinia looked at him.

'I could?'

'You wouldn't want to, of course. I shouldn't have asked.'

She looked at him and frowned, and then the frown cleared.

'Can you take somebody?'

'Yes, but if you did . . .'

'If I did what?'

'They'll think that we're . . .'

'Luisa and George won't think it.'

'True. Don't give it another thought. It was a stupid idea and I didn't mean to insult you. You must think I'm . . .' Joe couldn't face her. He walked around the room as though it were a pleasure garden.

Vinia poured out the tea, and then she put the teapot down and watched him as he went on meandering and said, 'Look, Joe, you're the pit-owner so I shouldn't say things to you but we know each other quite well and . . . everybody's allowed to make one big mistake, you know.'

Joe stopped.

'Where is that written?'

'I don't know where it's written but it's true.'

'It was one hell of a mistake,' Joe said.

'Not really. Think of what some people do. Some men send hundreds of men into battle and get them killed.'

'I got Tom killed.'

'No, you didn't!' She went to him. 'I won't have that. You can't be everything, save everybody. You can't do it. You provide jobs for all these people—'

'They risk their lives every day.'

'It's what they do. All you did was to fall in love with the wrong woman. Haven't most men done that?'

'I don't know. And there'll be a child.'

'These things never work out. I would have given anything for a bairn. Things might have been different. And Esther Margaret . . . Is it going to be a big party?'

'I should think so. Thaddeus has a lot of friends.'

'And they have a nice house?'

'Lovely.'

'And there'll be lots of food and drink and the women will wear pretty dresses?'

'Sure to.'

'I would love to go.'

'What? Really?'

'Yes. Why not?'

It was bitterly cold. She locked the shop and they walked down the street together. Vinia was glad it was before the pubs came out. She and Joe could not be seen together, people would talk, but she could not regret having said she would go to the party. She had never been to an elegant party and might never go to one again, and she had a dress than she had not been able to resist, dark red like plums. It was not quite finished. It had been not quite finished for some time, but she determined that it would be and she would wear it. She deserved to go to an elegant party, just once. She imagined what it was like walking into a room with somebody like Joe, in a nice dark suit, all tall and handsome. She thought she should have cared that what he really needed her there for was for camouflage, but she didn't. She and Joe liked each other and other things didn't get in the way. It was not romantic but it might be fun, and she hadn't had much of that in her life, and she didn't think Joe had either.

When she reached home there was a lamp burning in the kitchen and the fire had gone almost to nothing, as though nobody had thought about banking it down for the night, or perhaps they had not gone to bed. She locked the back door and took off her coat and was rather glad of the fire because the room kept its heat well. It looked so pretty with holly along the mantelshelf, and Esther Margaret had mischievously put mistletoe at the foot of the stairs, though nobody had taken any notice of it and they were too busy to have visitors. They weren't planning anything for Christmas Day and she didn't think Esther Margaret or Dryden would mind her not being there.

Esther Margaret had left some supper in the pantry. She came back into the kitchen to find Dryden at the bottom of the stairs.

'Oh, I thought you'd gone to bed.'

'You're late. If you're going to be that late I would come and walk you, you know.'

'Thanks. Joe was there.' It made her self-conscious to say it and it sounded daft.

'Joe? What was he doing there?'

'He came to the shop.' She busied herself rather as she had when she was making tea earlier and she had felt awkward with Joe. It was annoying to have to feel so guilty when you hadn't done anything. 'He asked me to go to a party on Christmas Day. You wouldn't mind?'

There was the tiniest hesitation before he said lightly, 'Who am I to mind?'

'No, but . . .' Her appetite had gone. She stopped trying to arrange something to eat and looked at him. He was standing under the mistletoe. He didn't know it. 'He has to go to Mr and Mrs Morgan's and you know what that will be like and . . . I just thought . . .'

'Their house is really big,' Dryden said, moving into the room. 'I think it would be nice, don't you?'

Vinia couldn't understand why she had lost her appetite. He was not Tom, he was not menacing, anything but, and she had worked hard that day and it was late and she should have been happy, what with the invitation and the shop doing so well. She wasn't even thinking quite so much about the accident and Tom. But her instincts told her that there was something wrong.

'Is Esther Margaret all right?'

'Yes, she's asleep. Aren't you going to have anything to eat?'

Vinia gazed down at the dinner that had been left for her to heat up.

'I don't fancy it,' she confessed.

'Here, I'll put it in the oven for you.'

'You've let the fire down.'

'It's still warm.'

She turned her attention to the fire so that it began to burn with flame. He said suddenly, 'I'm going to bed. Goodnight.'

He got to the bottom of the stairs and there he stopped again, quite unconscious of the mistletoe, as though afraid the darkness beyond would swallow him up. Vinia never knew afterwards why she went to him but she did, and she kissed him, reaching up into his thick dark hair. Dryden looked at her in surprise. Vinia indicated above his head. She had always hated and avoided such customs, she couldn't understand herself, or that she had invited him to do the same. She had kissed nobody but Tom in her life. Dryden took a very light hold of her and brushed his mouth against hers. It was nothing, but it was the kind of nothing that was almost something, that could have been too much, as though he were in fear of it and of the consequences. Vinia wished she hadn't done it. Tom's kisses had always been uncomplicated and fierce. He had no idea about affection or caresses and she wondered where Dryden had learned such things, for although he didn't exercise them he was certainly capable of them. He had not had a happy home life. Could the women that he had known have taught him? He said goodnight again and went to bed, and she stared after him.

CHAPTER TWENTY-FIVE

It seemed to Vinia that Luisa McAndrew's hot gaze followed Joe all that Christmas Day. If he was aware of it he gave no sign, and she was amazed at his coolness. He behaved as though there were nothing wrong. He kissed Luisa's cheek and that of her mother, he spoke civilly to George McAndrew, and Vinia came to the conclusion that it was Thaddeus Morgan he did it for. It was obvious to her that the Morgans knew nothing about any liaison between Joe and their daughter.

The party was heaven to her. She wore the dress and was pleased with it, even though it was obvious that some of the other women wore dresses made of more expensive material by experienced dressmakers, and she liked being with Joe simply because she was not used to being with anybody any more, and he kept her close for his own defence's sake. The house was like nothing she had seen before and seemed rich to her. The food was good and there were sufficient people so that she did not feel conspicuous or out of place. Thaddeus Morgan was kind and kissed her and welcomed her to his house, and so did his wife after her initial surprise. Vinia thought that people who did not know her looked askance, but she didn't care.

Free to wander after the meal in the early afternoon, she found Luisa alone in a small book-lined room with a fire. When she looked up, Vinia could not help saying, 'You love Joe, don't you?'

Luisa laughed.

'Of course not. How could I possibly love him?'

'It isn't something people can help. Whoever would have wanted to love Tom, but I did. Doesn't Joe love you?'

'He was a child in a chocolate shop, that was all.'

'I don't think Joe's like that.'

'How do you know?'

'He could have anybody, I dare say, but he hasn't.'

Luisa stood by the window. It was a bleak day, cold and turning grey with evening.

'My husband is a difficult man.'

'So you've made a bargain?'

Luisa looked respectfully at her.

'You're very quick. There was nothing to be done.'

Alice came in then, saying briskly, 'What about a turn about the garden before it gets dark?'

'Don't be silly, Mother. Winter is the world's best reason for not going outside,' Luisa said, smiling.

Alice came across and pressed her hand.

'My dear, you're right,' she said. 'We must look after you.'

'You have a beautiful house here, Mrs Morgan,' Vinia said.

'Do you know, I've never liked it. Thaddeus's father built it for his mother and I don't think she ever liked it either. It's too near the river, so damp.'

Vinia looked beyond to where the little fields made up a quilt and the river ran through them in silver. Across the other side of the valley the hills rose in a bare jagged outline that hinted at the fell beyond, and there were long grey farmhouses with stone walls and the sky was grey and white like sheep's fleece. Inside, the lamps were being lit and the smell of good cooking permeated the hall. Mrs Morgan collected her daughter and walked her away to where George McAndrew was holding forth on some political issue in a bigger room across the hall.

Vinia went in search of Joe and found him leaning against the desk in Thaddeus's study, with Thaddeus sitting at the desk. They were talking in low voices as though they were at work. She paused apologetically in the doorway.

'It's getting dark,' she said. 'We ought to go.'

They had been asked to stay the night but Vinia didn't think she could be polite for two days running, and besides, she had turned into the kind of person who didn't like to leave her shop for too long. The men would be going back to work the following day.

Thaddeus's carriage took them home.

'Do you love Luisa?' she asked him when they were well away from the house.

Joe started at the question.

'I don't know. I wanted to, but maybe that was just . . . because nobody's ever cared for me.'

He said it without a trace of self-pity and the flatness gave the words impact. Vinia squeezed his arm.

'I had a lovely day,' she said.

Joe smiled at her.

'Good,' he said.

Esther Margaret had thought that if she could get Dryden to go to bed with her everything would be vastly improved, but she was not very surprised when it was not. He treated her as she was sure he had treated every woman he had ever bedded. He was happy enough to have her but it was something apart from the rest of his life and it demonstrated clearly to her how little he thought of her. She had nothing to complain of – he made love to her often with imagination and expertise. Esther Margaret hated it. She hated the way he didn't talk to her either before or after – or during – and how soon he put her from his mind. There was no sweetness, no touching except in bed. Finally, mid-morning on Christmas Day when Vinia was long gone to the Morgan house and they had stayed in bed, she pushed him away, turned aside.

'Enough,' she said, into the pillows. 'Enough, enough!'

He lay in silence for a few moments and then said tersely, 'Am I doing it wrong?'

'Wrong? You wouldn't know how to do it wrong! My God, how many times have you done this with other people?'

'I don't remember. You don't want me to do it?'

'No, I don't want you to do it!' Esther Margaret shouted, and she reached for her nightdress and threw it on and went downstairs.

He followed her down a few minutes later, roughly dressed, hair all over the place, looking impossibly romantic, as though she were another man's wife and he were about to go home.

'Since I met you I only ever did it once. I know it wasn't right because it was the night the baby died. I haven't touched anybody other than that, I swear it to you.'

'You don't need to swear it to me, I know it. I know.'

'So what do you want me to do?'

'Nothing! I just wish . . .'

'That I was Joe?'

'No, no, that you cared even for a second. Even when you do that you don't care!'

'It's just a . . . just nature,' Dryden said, 'tisn't love.'

'How in the name of God would you know?'

'Because you can love people without touching them. In fact sometimes it's better that way. Then you don't . . . fall down anywhere and they don't hate you. I would rather be like a photograph in a frame to somebody. Shall I go out?'

'I don't mind what you do,' Esther Margaret said, and didn't look at him even then.

So he went. He didn't come back all that Christmas Day. She sat over the fire, and when the back door finally banged shut she got up swiftly and was disappointed to see Vinia in her festive finery.

'I thought you were Dryden.'

'Why, where has he been?'

'I don't know. He went out mid-morning and hasn't come back.'

'Did you have a fight?'

'Something like that. He couldn't be in the pub all this time, surely.'

He was soaking wet when he came back some time later, and the rain and wind showered the floor as he walked in. Vinia had gone to bed. He didn't say anything, but came to the fire and took off his coat.

'I'm sorry,' she said.

Dryden sat down by the fire.

'I can't please you,' he said, 'except when you thought I was dead.'

'That's not true!'

'If I was dead you could marry Joe and be happy. Isn't that why you came back?'

She was surprised at his intuition.

'I thought Joe was married when I came back.'

'So what did you hope for?'

'Nothing.'

'Just as well, eh?'

He made as if to leave the room and she said, 'Dryden, please—'

'You weren't happy when I didn't touch you and you still aren't happy when I lay you. I don't know what you want.'

'I suppose I wanted you to fall in love with me.'

'I don't do that.'

'What, never?'

'No.' He looked past her to the stairs. 'I did love a woman once but it was nothing to do with bedding her, it was enough to know that she was alive.'

'Was it your mother?'

He looked at her and started to laugh.

'Hell, no. Who could love that old witch?'

'And none of the women you went to bed with?'

The laughter was still in his eyes.

'I had a sort of thing for Porky Morley's missus once.'

Mrs Morley was the fattest woman in the village and twice as old as Dryden with five children. Esther Margaret began to laugh.

'You terrible fibber, Dryden Cameron! You did not.' She went to him and she kissed him or he kissed her or it all happened at the same time and strangely the laughter had altered something between them. The kiss was magical. If the house had dropped down around them Esther Margaret couldn't have stopped. Dryden put her down on to the rug in front of the fire and it was, Esther Margaret thought afterwards, guiltily, nothing but a lay, the kind of thing men did to their wives when they were short of time or they did to other men's wives for the same reason, but it was not like him. He had never put her down and taken her simply like that, but it was somehow all the better for that simplicity. There was not another kiss or a caress but Esther Margaret was entranced, pleasured just as she had been so long ago in her bedroom at home and in the barn. She liked it so much she was embarrassed afterwards and said nothing on the way to bed. It did not occur to her until the next morning that he had not offered to tell her who the woman was and she would not have asked him for the world.

CHAPTER TWENTY-SIX

That winter Mary Cameron took to standing in the back lane at the end of each shift, waiting for Tom to come home. Sometimes she got confused and thought Dryden was Tom until she came hurrying down the lane towards him, and then she would realise and spit curses at him. Alf had to come out and collect her. She didn't seem to notice the bitter weather and would not rest until she had seen the pitmen all into their houses, and often she would break down and cry and Alf could not persuade her into the house. More and more often she was there, and sometimes she would walk down into the pit yard and wait at the pithead, her eyes full of hope and expectation.

One day that March when she thought Dryden was Tom she held him and kissed him and put her fingers into his hair and cried.

'They told me you were dead and I knew it wasn't so. You would never leave me. Tell me you'll never leave me.'

Alf tried to take her away but she clung to Dryden's arm. 'Tommy, Tommy!' she cried.

Esther Margaret had seen all this in the back lane, and when Dryden finally got into the house she had no idea what to say to him. She was spending much less time at the shop. She liked being at home for him and she had something special to tell him that day, but since she was unsure of his reaction and after what his mother had done she didn't say anything. They had the house practically to themselves. Vinia came home from the shop late to eat and go to bed. She had talked of moving out but Esther Margaret had dissuaded her. Where could she go and what was the point anyhow? So she didn't. It wasn't until very late, when they were lying quietly in each other's arms, that she whispered, 'Are you all right, Dryden?'

'Why shouldn't I be?'

'I thought you might be bothered about your mother.'

'She's not my mother. She's Tom's.' He would have turned away but Esther Margaret held him there.

'Dryden . . .' she said. 'I'm going to have a baby.'

She thought he wasn't going to say anything at all, he didn't react for so long, and then all he said was, 'At least we won't have to get married this time.'

'Couldn't you be pleased?'

'Be content that you're pleased,' he said. 'It'll have Alf's name and you can have my wage for it and that's all. You'll have to do the rest. I don't want children where I am,' and he pulled out of her arms and turned away.

Esther Margaret moved close in against his back and kissed him.

'It won't be like that,' she said. 'I'm not going to give up my child or ill-treat him.'

'I don't want to hear about it,' Dryden said.

One Monday that spring Thaddeus came to the pit office in the middle of the morning. He was grey-faced. He hadn't looked well for some time, Joe thought.

'Luisa is coming home to have the baby. George says she's not ill but I'm worried about her. I think he's tried to keep her there, which undoubtedly is the best thing, but she won't stay. She shouldn't be travelling in her condition. She always was strong-willed, as you know. She wouldn't let me tell her anything, otherwise I would not have let her marry that . . . that man.'

'She wanted to marry him,' Joe reminded him gently.

'She always wanted to get away from here. I don't blame her for that but to be honest, Joe, I don't like him. I know he's very successful and prominent, but there's something about him I find chilling. I think I'm just envious that I couldn't be that kind of man.'

'You wouldn't want to be.'

'I wish I had wanted to be. Power must be a heady thing.'

'You've been a good employer.'

Thaddeus laughed.

'I shall have to be thankful for that.'

The following day a man arrived with a note in Luisa's hand. All it said was 'Come to me' signed with her name.

Joe went. Thaddeus was at the foundry. Alice, though she fluttered like a caged bird in the hall, did not stop him, and when Joe got upstairs he scarcely recognised the young woman in the bed. The hand she reached out to him was so thin that it had no grip, and her face was pale and her eyes were dull and the golden hair which had been one of her claims to beauty hung about her like weeds.

'You certainly know how to get a man's attention, travelling all that way.'

The nurse hovered behind him. Joe turned to her.

'Could you leave us, please.'

'Mrs Morgan said—'

'Leave us,' Joe said again.

'I lied to you,' Luisa said when the nurse had gone.

'Never in this world.' Joe sat down on the bed and kissed her hand and then the inside of her wrist.

'I wanted to say it to you. I love you. I want so badly that horrid old house you have and the past that should have been ours. I'm sorry. I should have left George. All those hotels.'

'They were wonderful hotels,' he said.

'I knew you would come to me. I'm so glad. I didn't want you to think I didn't love you though in the circumstances it would have been easier. I wish I had married you. Kiss me.'

Joe touched her forehead with his lips.

'No, properly.'

Joe kissed her very gently on the mouth. There was a commotion outside, a carriage arriving swiftly.

'It's George. You must leave. He mustn't see you. Quickly!'

Joe tried to calm her but she was too alarmed, and the only way she would be quiet was if he left her. He walked slowly down the stairs in time to see George McAndrew stride into the hall.

'What the Devil are you doing here?' he said running upstairs. Alice was there too.

'Luisa asked for him.' Alice began to cry. 'She is so poorly.'

'Nothing of the kind. She's having a child is all.'

Alice looked at Joe through her tears.

'She's not coherent, she doesn't really want you, she doesn't know what she's saying, you must understand that. Whatever she says it isn't true.' She came to him and clutched at the lapel on his coat. 'Thaddeus should not have let you come here at all. George wouldn't have allowed it had he been here, but Thaddeus won't listen to me. You shouldn't be here, it's nothing to do with you.'

Thaddeus came in for his midday meal.

'You read my mind,' he said. 'I want you at the foundry this afternoon.'

'He came to see Luisa,' Alice said.

Thaddeus looked hard at him but said nothing. Joe sat down to eat with them, but all the time his thoughts were of Luisa. Thaddeus talked brightly about work. George did not appear. While Thaddeus dragged him around the works talking about this problem and that order, neither of them concentrated. Finally, at five o'clock, they sat in the office beside the pattern shop and Thaddeus looked at him across the desk and said, 'Have you been in love with my daughter long?'

Joe couldn't meet his eyes.

'It's worse than that, Thaddeus.'

'Yes, I rather thought it was. I had a feeling this was going to happen. George may be turning the world upside down but he's a bore and a bully. No woman likes that, no matter how many diamonds she has been given. Do you see her much?'

'Hardly at all.'

Thaddeus gave him enough time to say more and Joe tried but the words wouldn't be said. Thaddeus meant a great deal to him and something told Joe that after this things would never be the same.

'You fathered Luisa's child, didn't you?' It was softly spoken, as though it didn't matter.

'Yes.'

'And was it intentional?'

Joe caught his gaze. 'No.'

'Was it deliberate on her part, to use you to give her a child?'

'I don't know. Perhaps. It seems George can't.'

Thaddeus stood up.

'If I was a younger man I would break your neck. How could you do such a thing? Clandestine meetings in nasty little places—'

'It wasn't.'

'Wasn't it? You're just like your mother.'

Joe caught his breath.

'Thaddeus, please.'

'I was in love with her. They wouldn't let me marry her but she was more accommodating after she married your father.'

'No,' Joe said.

'She was a greedy, ambitious, lying whore.'

'No.'

'She would go with anybody. She had no idea who fathered you, did you know that? It could have been the stable lad. Anybody could have her! No, you're not mine. Do you think I would have let you anywhere near Luisa? But you got there anyway, didn't you? If anything happens to her I'll kill you.'

He got up, and when Joe got up too he said, 'Don't come to the house.'

'Please . . .'

Thaddeus left the office.

Darkness had fallen long since. Joe waited outside. He stood there for hours and hours until the day turned into evening and evening into night. The wind was bitter beside the river. The doors were locked, he had tried them all, and the curtains were pulled along the windows. The lights burned upstairs all through the long night and then, just as it was beginning to come light again, the outside door opened and the doctor emerged. As he did so Joe hurried inside. George was standing in the hall.

'I have a son,' he said, and his eyes glowed with satisfaction.

'And Luisa?'

'I'm afraid not.'

Joe ran up the stairs and burst in on the nurse and Alice.

'Mr Forster!'

Down on his knees beside the bed he gazed at her but she saw nothing.

'Luisa. Luisa.' He kissed her, all over her face and neck. 'I love you. I love you.' Kissing her, kissing her, her breath warm, her lips alive, her golden hair sticky with sweat. 'Luisa.'

'Mr Forster.' The nurse close beside his ear. 'Mrs McAndrew is dead.'

'No. No, she isn't. She isn't. She isn't. No. No.' Placing kisses everywhere, and in a moment her eyes would take him and she would say his name and he would run away with her as he had threatened and promised to do so many times, like that stupid man on the horse. She had always laughed and said how silly it would look, but he would. He would pick her up in his arms and run away with her, down the stairs and out of the door and past all the dark flowers in the garden and down to the river, and there, if she did not open her eyes and speak his name, he would drown them both.

'Mr Forster.' Firm hands descended to his shoulders. 'Mrs McAndrew is dead.'

'It was because of you,' Alice said. 'My husband told me. You did this.'

He heard Thaddeus's voice behind him.

'Leave. Leave before George sets the dogs on you.'

Hands pulled him up, shoved him out of the room and down the stairs and finally beyond the front door.

Joe walked slowly down the drive and then the road and began to take the bank that would lead him up towards the little pit town and the fell. He stopped when he got to the top of the first bank. The sun was beginning to come up, turning the river silver and lightening the tops of the hills and the windows of the little houses into golden squares.

By the time he reached the streets of Deerness Law the shops were beginning to open. He walked down the main street. He could see Vinia moving about at the front of her shop. She looked up as he was about to pass the door and opened it.

'Why, Joe,' she said, 'whatever's the matter?'

Joe came inside the shop and stood back against the closed door and regarded the gloom.

'I did it worse than my father. Can you imagine that? I actually did it worse. Luisa's dead and the child is a boy and I have no claim on him at all. George McAndrew has my son.' He closed his eyes.

'Come and sit down.'

'I can't. I have to go to work.'

'Won't it wait?'

'I daren't. God knows what Thaddeus will do. I have to see to the pit.'

'She loved you.'

'It doesn't matter. They wanted so much for her and she wanted it too, so that the boy . . . the boy will have everything.'

That afternoon Thaddeus came to Joe and stood in the office.

'George is taking the child to Scotland. You have no legal claim, of course, and as far as I can determine no moral rights. As for our partnership you can consider that finished. I will have my solicitor attend to it as soon as it can be arranged. I wish you well of your pit, Joe. It was your father's and now it's all yours.'

It was late when Joe got home. The lights were burning. He didn't expect his housekeeper to have waited for him; she usually left in the early evening and went back to the village before dark. He didn't bother going into the kitchen, but went straight into the study and poured himself a stiff whisky.

'And you can put that down as well,' said a stern voice behind him.

Joe nearly dropped the glass. When he turned around Vinia was standing there. She came across and took the glass and the bottle out of his hands.

'You aren't your father or your mother and you aren't going the same way.'

'What on earth are you doing here?'

'Men always do it. Tom did, Dryden did, and now you think you're doing it. Well, you're not. You can come and sit in the kitchen like ordinary people do and have your dinner. Come on.'

Joe followed her.

'It's a beautiful stew,' she said. 'Get it eaten.'

'If it's so nice you eat it,' Joe said, and he took the bottle and the glass from her and downed what was in the glass and poured some more and sat down with her at the kitchen table with his legs up on another chair. 'I'm not going to drink a lot, honestly. Why did you come here?'

'Because I don't want you ending up like your father. You're too nice for that. I won't have it. I'm sorry about Luisa, Joe, I really am, and about the baby. You can do a lot. You don't need Thaddeus.'

'Would you like a drink?'

'What, that stuff?'

'I think there's some wine in the cellar. Shall I look?'

'I don't drink.'

'I'll look.'

Joe came back with something so pale that it looked like water, but when he opened it and she tasted it Vinia approved.

'It's really nice,' she said. 'You mustn't tell anybody that I did, mind. I should go home.'

'It's almost midnight.'

'It can't be. I can't stay. People will talk. She did love you.'

'You keep saying that.'

'I can't forget how when we were coming back on Christmas night you said nobody had ever cared about you.'

Joe winced.

'I think she just wanted a child.'

'Is that so very bad?'

'No, it isn't bad. It's the most important thing in the world, surely. She got what she wanted. Luisa was very good at getting what she wanted.'

They went back to the study fire with a bottle of wine and a bottle of whisky and sat there on a big sofa that Joe had found a good long time ago in the attic. It was a great big soft piece of furniture which was made for nothing but comfort, and Joe found that he needed all the comfort he could get. Luisa was lost to him and so was the child, and the world was suddenly a much older, much more difficult place, and there were echoes of his father and mother in the room and of his failure. He didn't drink the whole bottle or even half the bottle, so it was a relief to realise that he had not turned into his father. Vinia fell asleep eventually and so did he, but somewhere in the depths of the night he found himself in her arms. There was no more to it than that, but if there had been he was not sure he would have been able to say no or wanted to. The night was suddenly too dark and too limitless and too frightening, because you just didn't know what it was going to do next and in the end you needed another person there as close as you could get them. As it was he went back to sleep in the knowledge that he was not alone and the night would end and he would be able to begin again tomorrow.

CHAPTER TWENTY-SEVEN

When she got back the following evening Dryden looked darkly at her. He didn't say anything but Esther Margaret did from where she was ironing in the kitchen.

'Where on earth have you been?'

'I went to stay with Joe. Luisa Morgan died yesterday.'

Esther Margaret stared.

'You stayed?'

'He needed somebody.'

'You could have said.'

Dryden left the room at this point. It was Saturday night and the fire was on in the other room. When he had gone Esther Margaret said in a low voice, 'He spent half the evening looking for you.'

Vinia followed him into the sitting room and sat down on the rug before the fire and looked at him, twisting around and leaning her arms on his knees.

'I'm sorry.'

'You don't have to excuse yourself to me.'

'But you went looking for me?'

'When the shop was all shut up and dark I thought you must have gone somewhere. If you want to spend the night with Joe Forster that's your business.'

Vinia's face burned.

'I didn't spend the night with him!' she objected, and then realised that she had. Dryden looked at her sceptically.

'Like I said, it's nothing to do with me.'

Vinia didn't understand why she cared what he thought or why she had been sitting on the floor at his feet with her arms on his knees.

'Joe was upset and on his own and—'

'I don't want to hear about it!'

He shouted as Tom would have done. Vinia got hastily to her feet, trembling, and he got up too and took hold of her by the arms.

'I didn't mean to yell at you.'

'Nothing happened. Joe doesn't think of me like that.'

'Doesn't he? He must be nuts.'

Vinia smiled, and then she suddenly realised that she wanted to get nearer and she broke free of his light hold. She panicked and ran back into the kitchen, where Esther Margaret was busy and everything seemed normal. All night she had lain against Joe and felt nothing, but every time she went near Dryden she began to think about how he had kissed her under the mistletoe and how she wished he would do it again. The baby was already showing under Esther Margaret's clothes. Vinia left the house and went outside and took great breaths of air, and then she began to walk away from the house. In the end she went to the shop and worked, bringing the books up to date and trying to think of sketches for new clothes, but nothing worked. She couldn't concentrate.

Saturday night was noisy, and the later it got the noisier it became – drunks singing and a fight some way down the street with swearing and various crashes. There was a knock on the door and she ventured out slowly, fearing it might be somebody undesirable. It was Dryden. Vinia opened the door.

'You needn't have bothered,' she told him as they went into the back room. 'I'm perfectly capable of walking home by myself.'

'It's rowdy,' he said. 'Vinny, look . . .' He stopped, not meeting her eyes. 'You don't have to worry. You didn't have to run from me. I'm not the stupid lad I used to be. I'm not going to touch you.'

Vinia stared at him, standing there with his hands in his pockets like he wished he was somewhere else. He went on, and his voice was hoarse.

'I know which side my bread's buttered. I've got a wife and a bairn on the way and I'm not going to make a mess of it this time, I swear it to you before God. You don't have to be afraid of being by yourself with me. I wouldn't dream of it.'

Suddenly all she could see was him lying in the middle of the floor unconscious, having stopped Tom from hurting her. She understood why she had gone to him at the bottom of the stairs and kissed him, why she had run from the sitting room earlier on.

'Oh no,' she said. 'No.'

'I said it's all right—'

'No.'

'Vinny—'

'You don't understand. I want you like I've never wanted anything in my whole life. I feel like I can't breathe without you. I want to run home to you all the time. I didn't want you to think that I'd . . . that I would . . . with Joe.'

'I wish you would.'

'Do you?'

'Yes. No. You really love me?' He looked as if he couldn't believe it.

'Yes.'

He smiled at her idiotically. His eyes shone like black stars for a few moments and then dimmed.

'I've loved you since the day Tom took me back to your house for Sunday dinner. I remember you standing in the pantry, wearing that black dress with the little collar. I wanted to scoop you up and dash down the back lane with you and keep you somewhere very close and secret. Isn't it awful, considering how I felt about Tom?'

'You didn't do anything.'

'I tried not to even think about you.'

'And do you now?'

'I try not to betray my wife even with a thought. She doesn't deserve that I should do that.'

'She's unhappy.'

'I didn't want the child and I didn't want her but I will do the best I can.'

'I think I should move out.'

'I think so,' Dryden said.

Mary Cameron had gone mad with grief. As the weeks went on she not only waited for Dryden coming home but watched for him going out, called after him down the back lane and came to their house constantly 'with something for Tommy's tea'. She appeared perfectly normal but she began to time her visits for when Dryden came home, most especially if he was coming in at teatime. If Alf was on the same shift as Dryden he would take her back to their house, but often he was not. She began to come inside. Her eyes shone over Dryden, just as they had for Tom all his life – hungry, desperate. She came to him, touched him as though she feared his loss, feathering her hands over his hair and smoothing her fingertips across his face. She almost crooned. He didn't stop her and neither did he say anything, even when she kissed him on the mouth. It seemed such a proprietorial thing to do. Vinia had to stop herself grasping hold of Mary and marching her to the outside door.

Vinia had tried absenting herself but she found Esther Margaret crying upstairs one evening when Mary had been there.

'I wish I'd never wanted this baby. He doesn't touch me. He doesn't even kiss me when he goes out and she's making it worse. He hates me pregnant.'

'It's her he hates, and it's difficult hating people who have lost their minds. Give him time.'

As she spoke Dryden walked into the bedroom, his face full of concern.

'Summat the matter with you?' he said to his wife.

'That woman . . .'

Dryden sat down on the bed. Vinia got up as he did so.

'Don't upset yourself, sweetheart. Think about the baby.'

Vinia went downstairs and left them. They didn't come back down and she didn't want to think of them so she went to the shop. She was avoiding Joe. She was avoiding Dryden. She spent so much time at the shop that she was in danger of becoming tired of the place and the business. She couldn't find anywhere to live but Dryden had been true to his word. They had not so much as brushed past one another on the stairs and she was becoming used to it, though she thought she would never grow used to living with him as another woman's husband – it was too hard, too much to ask, and she was tired.

She had been there for only a few minutes when she saw Joe stop outside. She opened the door.

'Are you busy?' he said, not coming inside.

'No.'

'Would you like to come home and have a drink and a meal with me? I'm not trying to get you to stay. It's light enough so that I could see you back.'

Vinia nearly fell over herself accepting. Having been to Joe's house only once she found herself overwhelmingly glad to go back there, to go anywhere that wasn't the house or the shop. His housekeeper had left good food and she liked the wine and she liked the way that the last rays of light seemed to linger in the garden. She had only once been in another big house, Thaddeus's home, but she preferred this one for some reason. Maybe because there was nobody in it but herself and Joe, so there was no intrusion and no whining woman like Alice who was discontented and had made her daughter reach out too far and fall.

Joe had a gardener who was making plants grow around the house, but she thought it would not take much for the fell to encroach once again. A week or two left to itself and there would be little trace of such civilisation. That was what she liked about it, she thought – there was nothing to stop the howling winds, the hard rain and now the still eventide as it fell soundlessly across the open land. You could see for miles and miles. It looked as though it went on for ever, easy on the eye and with that rarity of air – like champagne, Joe said.

'I haven't had champagne.'

'Would you like some?'

'You have champagne?' she asked, astonished.

'There could be some in the cellar. My father didn't drink stuff like that. He specialised in spirits.'

She followed Joe into the house and down the cellar steps. He dusted off various bottles until he found what he thought they wanted and then, carefully by candlelight, they made their way back to the kitchen. He opened the bottle and found some wonderful glasses with long stems and wide mouths in a back cupboard. The pop of the cork made her laugh. The way the bubbles foamed and danced as he poured mesmerised her, and the taste was beyond anything that she had ever imagined. Sweet like honey and dry upon the tongue and unlike anything she had experienced before. One glass made her happy but she was unable to refuse a second.

Joe produced chicken from the larder and bread and cheese and they sat at the kitchen table and talked about the shop and the pit and business in general, so when it was late and he offered to take her home, made brave by half a bottle of champagne, she ventured, 'I would like to stay, if you don't mind.'

Joe showed her upstairs into a clean neat bedroom which smelled of polish and lavender and beyond which a moon hung gracefully in a cloudless night sky. She opened the window and said as he was about to leave the room, 'Stay here with me.'

Joe stopped by the open door.

'Am I forward?' she said. 'I'm so tired of being alone.'

'Me too.'

Joe closed the door and came back to her, and then it was just a question of not knowing one another and of the surprise that he was not Tom, nothing like Tom, and she was glad of that. He was not like Dryden either, but there was no use in grieving over it because she could not and would not be able to have Dryden. Esther Margaret's baby was due in the late summer and Esther Margaret should be happy. She did not have the right to intrude upon the chance of that happiness. There was nothing to be gained from wishing.

Luisa McAndrew had taught Joe how to make love, or he had known and she had given him confidence, and something else new. He was a gentleman, and although he was not rich it was all rich compared to anything she had known before. The bed was huge and the house was far enough away from the village so that there were no noises from either it or the pit. There were no interruptions, nobody to overhear, such as there might be in a pit row. Nobody needed looking after and, best of all – and she felt guilty over it – Joe pleased her. Tom had never done anything to make her want him, he just assumed she did. In the beginning she had, when he was kind, which was not often, but he had not made her want to take part, had not made her laugh, had not made her feel safe. That was the best of it. That was what money and a little power and independence did. It gave you a house apart up on the fell and cold champagne and a man clever enough to know what you needed. For the first time then in bed with Joe, Vinia understood a little of why Luisa had married George. Cold beds and rough men played their part, but luxury gave an edge to pleasure like nothing else.

Also, Joe had class in a way George McAndrew never could. Vinia could see why Luisa would want the one as well as the other. You could tell it was Joe's house just by this bedroom, which was not his personally. There were lots of books. There was a writing table over by the window with pens and paper and a silver inkwell. The furniture was old and stout and well polished and there were big rugs on either side of the bed. The bed was thick and wide and the sheets had not been slept in before now. As for Joe himself, he was the way that men ought to be. When the day began to dawn again the light fell upon his pale golden hair and smooth shoulders. She didn't love him, she thought, while he slept, but she liked him very much and she enjoyed the way he made her feel.

They left the house and went to work before his housekeeper arrived to find them, but he lingered at the shop, kissing her in the back room when he should have been at the pit.

'I have to open the shop,' she objected, laughing.

'Not yet.'

'Now.'

He went. She didn't want him to go but she didn't want anybody to see him there either, and he had made promises to come back at the day's end. Em arrived and later the customers and she was caught up in the work and the day, but at the back of her mind were images of the night before and she kept smiling, thinking of him.

In the early evening, when Em had gone, she heard the doorbell and called out from the back, 'We're closed,' and then went through and Dryden was standing with his back to the door as though to hold off intruders.

'You went to Joe.'

She looked deep into the dark eyes and said flatly, 'Yes, I did. Would you have me not?'

Dryden seemed to have difficulty in breathing.

'No. No. Of course I wouldn't. If I didn't want your happiness what would I be?'

'Human?'

He smiled.

'Nobody ever accused me of that before. But you are all right?'

She took a deep breath.

'I'm all right, yes.'

'And expecting him?'

'I'm hoping.'

'I'm going.'

He went. And shortly after that Joe arrived.

'Was that Dryden?' he asked, looking down the street.

'Yes.'

That was the love of her life, not given expression nor room nor time nor space nor any hope. In heaven she would be Tom's and on earth she might be Joe's, but there was nowhere and no way that she would ever look across a room and think that she might be going home to bed with Dryden Cameron legitimately, bound in church, fêted by friends, allowed by God. It was a clawing in the darkness at empty air. It was not meant to be in the great grand scheme, it held no substance and had no time. It was a cry unanswered in the night, it was the disappearing around the corner, it was the empty main street in the early evening.

She walked slowly through into the back.

'I could come by later,' Joe said.

He was not insensitive, she thought, smiling.

'No, no, I want you here.'

'Are you certain?'

'Quite sure.'

'I wouldn't want you to think that . . .'

'I wouldn't think it. Tell me, Joe, do you still consider Esther Margaret?'

'Consider her what?'

'Just consider her.'

'Sometimes. Yes. It wasn't meant to be.'

'But you love her?'

'She was my first love. Luisa was my second.'

'And am I to be the third?'

'You could be the last if you wished,' he said.

CHAPTER TWENTY-EIGHT

Esther Margaret's baby was a boy, born upon the hottest August day, and it was as unlike the last time as possible. For one thing its father was at home since her labour started on the Saturday evening and went on all through Sunday.

Dryden hardly moved from the house and kept on coming upstairs. It was sweltering and all the windows were open to catch even the slightest breeze coming in from the fells. He had insisted on having the doctor there at the beginning and nobody objected. The doctor didn't seem to mind Dryden intruding all the time, anxious and fretting and sitting down on the bed and generally getting in the way, though he did calm Esther Margaret by holding her hand quite a lot of the time in the early stages.

By the time the baby was born he had retreated to the front room. It was late on Sunday evening and long shadows fell across the houses. Vinia found him asleep on the settee.

'Long day?' she said sarcastically as he opened his eyes.

Dryden sat up abruptly.

'Is it all right?'

'Everything's fine. You can go up now.'

Dryden ran. Vinia felt left out but she didn't want to intrude on what should be a private moment for them. Esther Margaret was so happy she almost shone, Vinia thought, and she determined to leave the shop for Em to look after during the first few days when Esther Margaret would need rest and perhaps some reassurance.

That first morning, unable to shut the doors because of the heat, Vinia was treated to a visit from Mary, who crept into the house wide-eyed and stopped when Vinia barred the stairs.

'I've come to see the baby,' she announced.

Vinia was reluctant but Esther Margaret shouted down the stairs.

'Let her come up.'

Mary took the stairs nimbly, Vinia following. She stopped when she reached the doorway, gazed at the child asleep in Esther Margaret's arms and then tiptoed into the room. She stood looking down at him and her eyes filled with tears.

'They took him from me,' she said. 'Alf wouldn't have him there. Those awful people, they took him away.'

'Would you like to hold him?' Esther Margaret offered.

Vinia frowned but Esther Margaret gave the baby to Mary.

'He's just like his father was,' Mary said.

'Dryden says he looks like Tom.'

'He does have a look of Tommy,' Mary said, beginning to smile.

'We're going to call him Tom.'

Vinia was not worried that Mary would drop the baby or try to run from the house with him. Suddenly the air in the room was no longer oppressive; from beyond the open window a cool breeze fluttered upon the curtains.

We'll never get rid of her, Vinia thought, watching Mary trundle happily up the yard some time later. She turned at the gate and waved.

In the afternoon Joe arrived, bearing champagne and smiling, but when he went upstairs to see the baby Vinia realised that it was an act of bravado. After he was born Joe had not seen his son, nor, she thought sadly, would he.

'Poor little beggar. He looks too much like Dryden to call him handsome,' he said.

'My husband is very handsome,' Esther Margaret declared, laughing, and it made Vinia feel hollow to hear her say it. She watched Joe with Esther Margaret. She could see that to him the woman in the bed was another man's wife with his child in her arms, and although she was beautiful motherhood had changed the way she appeared to Joe. When he left the room Esther Margaret no longer looked wistfully at the doorway; she was too busy watching her son sleeping in her arms.

Joe walked slowly downstairs.

'I should go.'

'Should you? Why?'

'You're busy with the baby and everything.'

'The baby's father will be due home soon and I don't see why I shouldn't have a little free time.'

Joe said nothing.

'If you're busy . . .' Vinia said.

'No.' Joe looked at her. 'Vinia, have you ever thought about getting married again?'

She stared at him.

'What sort of a question is that?'

'I know you weren't very happy with Tom and you have the shop and . . .'

'I certainly couldn't consider getting married again if it meant giving up the shop.'

'And if it didn't mean giving up the shop?'

'I don't know. I know what's brought this on,' she said frankly, 'but I don't think I can bear a child.'

'Why not?'

Under his cool look Vinia blushed.

'Because I haven't, and in the light of what's happened in your life I think it could become very important to you. I've been through one bad marriage. I'd rather stay single than be blamed for you not having a son.'

'I'm very fond of you,' Joe said.

It made her want to laugh. It was such a middle-of-the-day

kind of declaration, whereas on Saturday nights in his bed he wasn't happy until she was exhausted, bruised and completely satisfied.

'Why is that funny?' he said, looking offended.

'We could go on as we are until I'm pregnant.'

'Oh, I see. I'm just some village lad who might have to get married. I'm tired of just Saturday nights. I want you to be my wife. I'm proud of you. I want you to myself.'

Vinia was suddenly aware of Dryden filling the doorway. Sometimes when he came in he was nothing but Esther Margaret's husband, black and weary from the day. Sometimes he was Tom, irritable and hungry, and other times he was the traveller from the moor with eyes a hundred years old.

'Now then,' he said, as though he hadn't heard anything.

'Dryden,' Joe acknowledged him.

'Joe brought champagne for the baby.'

'Really? Did he drink it all?'

'If you tidy yourself up we could open it and toast the baby's health.'

'Is he all right? Is Esther Margaret all right?'

Vinia was beginning to think he would never lose the anxious note in his voice, or the question in his eyes.

'They're fine.'

Dryden's ill temper did not dissipate, though she believed she was the only one to realise that he was angry. To anyone else he would have seemed perfectly friendly. They drank the baby's health, and though Joe found the champagne too warm nobody else was complaining.

When Joe had gone she began to make the tea. Dryden hovered in the kitchen, saying finally, 'So, are you going to marry him?'

Vinia turned from where she was busy slicing cold boiled eggs on to plates. She was not altogether surprised at the question.

'And if I did, would you take me to church?'

Only she would have detected his split-second hesitancy and known it for reluctance.

'I'd be proud to.'

'But in fact you would rather I had a little house somewhere tucked away discreetly so that you could come over when you had time and take me to bed, yes?'

'It's an alternative,' Dryden said, making her laugh. And when she had stopped laughing he said, 'I've had women like that before and I don't think it's ever the answer.'

'Whatever makes you think I would?'

'Because you want me.'

Vinia had to stop chopping; she feared for her fingers.

'But you won't mind if I marry Joe.'

'I couldn't bring myself to stop you from having a bigger house and a richer husband than any other woman in the area.'

'I should think not!'

She stopped there, pulled a hand across her eyes and went out the back into the yard and farther into the lane to where the road reached out beyond the pit and beyond the village. Dryden followed her and looked uneasily about him.

'Here, don't cry. People will think I've smacked you one.'

'I never wanted you like that and you . . . you shouldn't . . .'

'Never?'

'Only once.'

'I've always wanted you,' he said.

Vinia kept her eyes on the road. It was such a warm evening that a haze obscured the horizon.

'Joe says that he would be happy for me to keep the shop on.'

'That's nice.'

In the quiet of the early evening, from inside the house, Vinia could hear his son begin to cry.

'Mary says the baby looks just like you.'

'She didn't want to give him away, then?'

'Esther Margaret says you might call him Tom.'

'It seemed fair. Will you come in now? I'm starving,' and he walked back inside.

Later that evening Vinia took some flowers to the churchyard to put on Tom's grave. The stone had been removed from what was supposed to be Esther Margaret's grave, and the headstone where Joe's mother was buried had fallen over some time since and been propped up against the outside wall of the church. Tom's gravestone stood out all fresh and newly carved. Usually when she came to the churchyard she would feel a rush of guilt because of all the times they had quarrelled and the fact that she had taken up the shop again and was going to make a success of it. Tom would have hated that. She didn't feel guilty this time, even about her love for Dryden. She thought of what it would be like being married to Joe, what fun it might be and how she would have a lovely big house and be wed to the pit-owner and be Missus Forster. It sounded good. Perhaps they would even have a child. Joe would like that.

She looked briefly at the grave that had been Esther Margaret's and stood for a few seconds, wondering who was in there. Somebody lost and lonely or some poor soul, as Esther Margaret had been, running away. She shivered in the warm air and decided that she would walk over to Joe's house and surprise him. It was a still night, and as she walked a great big bright round orange harvest moon rose in majesty before her, so perfect that it seemed unreal.

The lights were on in Joe's house, suffusing the area in pale yellow. When he answered the door she hugged him. Joe kissed her. She imagined herself standing in the church porch on a bright sunny day, wearing a pale-coloured wedding costume and with her hand through Dryden's arm before they went inside. It was not an easy picture.

Joe led her through into the drawing room, where the portrait of his mother hung on the wall. She was wearing a pale blue dress and a deep blue cloak and seemed to cast a glow over the whole room. There was a secret expression in her eyes. Vinia knew how she felt.

'So,' he said, sounding doubtful, 'did you decide whether you want to marry me?'

Vinia took a deep breath and turned around. She looked him straight in the eyes.

'I would like to but I'm not sure how much I care about you.'

Joe looked down and said after a few moments, 'He's married and has a child.'

Vinia went on looking at him.

'How did you know?'

'It's exactly how I felt about Esther Margaret for a very long time. I think he thought, when Tom was killed and Esther Margaret didn't come home, that you would be married.'

'Tom is still in the way,' Vinia said, not realising until she said it that it was true. 'I see him in Dryden so many times. You're quite different.'

'Can I consider that a "yes," then?'

'I want us to come home to one another in the evenings.'

'I could come to the shop and collect you.'

'I could come to the pit and collect you.'

'And when we get home there will be a big fire burning in here and a lovely dinner ready in the kitchen. I've never belonged to anybody before and I really would like to, properly.'

She came to him and kissed him and then she said, 'Have you got any more of that champagne in the cellar?'

'Why don't we go down and have a look?' Joe said. And they did.